CADDYWAMPUS

MURDER AT WOEBEGONE DUNES RESORT

ERIK & JUDY MARTIN

A LIEUTENANT BARON DUNNING NOVEL

Caddywampus: Murder at Woebegone Dunes Resort

Published by Wheatmark®
2030 East Speedway Boulevard, Suite 106
Tucson, Arizona 85719 USA
www.wheatmark.com

ISBN: 978-1-62787-945-3 (paperback)
ISBN: 978-1-62787-946-0 (hardcover)
ISBN: 978-1-62787-947-7 (ebook)
LCCN: 2022900470

Bulk ordering discounts are available through Wheatmark, Inc. For more information, email orders@wheatmark.com or call 1-888-934-0888.

What is the definition of Caddywampus?

Caddy: In golf, a caddy is a person who carries a player's bag and clubs and gives the player advice and moral support.

Wampus: A strange, objectionable, monstrous person with an attitude and a lifestyle exhibiting extreme self-fulfillment despite adversity. An uncouth and aggressive lout that acts entirely out of self-interest in the pursuit of extraordinarily murderous or perverse affairs spoken of in hushed tones to the severe detriment or inconvenience of others.

Caddywampus: In disarray and disorder, out of kilter, lopsided, crooked, confused, diagonally off-center, and not lined up correctly, like a crooked bicycle wheel. Everything has gone badly, awkwardly, and in the wrong direction with too many loose ends. Nothing is normal. Everything is screwed up, cockeyed and unlevel, fishy and suspicious, out of alignment, and skewed off-center. Everything that has happened is whacky, off-kilter, and out of balance.

To Cadbury—always calm, relaxed, and self-amused

1

NIGERIA

Boko Haram militants wielding military-grade weapons stopped Lieutenant Baron Dunning's vehicle at a temporary roadblock made of burning barrels of oil. They confiscated his passport and identification papers; stole his cash, credit cards, and personal belongings; and torched his rental car. He was threatened, harassed, and terrorized. Finally, they threw his clothes in one of the burning oil barrels and left him standing naked on the side of the road.

A dozen wealthy tourists riding in a bright-green jungle van with "Yankari Game Reserve Safari Tours" written in bold letters on the door panels approached cautiously.

"Sorry about your predicament, mate," the African driver with traditional Igbo facial tribal markings shouted from inside the van. "There have been intermittent assassinations, suicide bombings, and clashes between the government and Boko Haram terrorists in northern Nigeria for more than fifty years. Nigeria has suffered the highest number of kidnappings and terrorist killings in Africa. Militants are a hostile Islamic faction in northeastern Nigeria, Chad, Niger, and Cameroon known for exceptional brutality. Tens of thousands have been killed, including three hundred thousand children. More than 2.3 million people have had to flee the country. They usually kill tourists after robbing them and discard their corpses in the jungle for wild animals. Still, if you are an important person of substance, they demand a ransom. Are you a person of substance?"

"I'm a modest American tourist hoping to photograph elephants in the wild," the naked lieutenant falsely understated.

Passengers flocked to the passenger side of the van to gawk at the naked American man. Many of them leaned out the windows, indiscreetly taking multiple pictures.

The driver removed a pressed pair of khaki shorts, a new safari shirt with epaulets, and a lightweight pith helmet from a duffel bag behind the driver's seat. He tossed the welcome bundle of clothes at the feet of the self-conscious American standing forlornly on the side of the road.

The lieutenant paused briefly to notice the lapel pin: Atlas's Royal Enouement Society logo holding up the world. The driver and several other individuals were wearing similar pins.

"Thank you. You are very generous."

"Would you like a ride to the American Embassy?"

"Yes, that would be helpful."

The lieutenant slipped on the khaki shorts and shirt before entering the van. He suspiciously analyzed the audience, checking facial expressions, body language, and energy. One empty seat remained beside an adorable blond bombshell sitting in the back row. She had the classic look of an all-American cheerleader. She was athletically fit with narrow hips and long legs, accentuated by tight ivory-colored shorts. Her skin was lightly tanned. She had a charismatic presence; a seductive, captivating smile; and a friendly, adventuresome, outgoing spirit. Her fingernails were the same red color as the silky Wisconsin Bucky Badger jersey she was wearing.

"I see that you have lost your wallet and identification papers, as well as your shorts. You are welcome to share my hotel room in Lagos until you recover your identity," she offered with a hauntingly alluring and prophetic smile.

"Is that a Wisconsin accent I detect?" The lieutenant quizzed as he finished buttoning his shirt.

2

THE KILLING

Pop, pop, pop! Three bullets fired in rapid succession exploded the driver's side window of the van, breaking the glass and making a loud crashing sound. After being shot twice in the heart and once in the head, the driver slumped over. Tiny bits of broken glass and blood dripped from his hands and face.

A beautiful busty Frenchwoman wearing a provocative balcony bra to create rounded cleavage without fully covering her breasts was sitting directly behind the driver. Militants emerging from the jungle caused uncontrollable shaking and hysterical screaming. The passengers watched in horror as they waved machetes over their heads while shouting 'Allahu Akbar.'

"They are going to rape and kill us," the Frenchwoman screamed.

Lieutenant Dunning raced to the front of the van, dragged the driver out of his seat, and respectfully laid the body on the floor. He leaped into the driver's seat and slammed the accelerator pedal to the floor. The rear tires squealed loudly, spraying the terrorists with hundreds of pebbles. Several shots penetrated the bus through the back window, exploding a red water bottle held by the Frenchwoman. The water soaked her blouse, allowing her skin-tone undergarments to be seen through the fabric, giving the illusion of exposed flesh.

The lieutenant reached for the cell phone on the dashboard and handed it to the Frenchwoman. "Dial 112, ask for Kingsley at the British Embassy, and put it on speakerphone."

"Hello, Kingsley," the lieutenant shouted frantically. "Code Red. I'm in immediate danger. I'm driving a green safari van carrying a dozen passengers. Terrorists stole my money, passport, and identity papers before lighting my rental car on fire. They roughed me up and left me bloodied and standing naked on the side of the road. A safari tourist van stopped to offer help. Still, the militants killed the driver, and two of them are following us on motorcycles. What do you advise?"

"Drive south as fast as you can. There's a temporary roadblock several miles down the road, and you may have to smash through the barriers. Let me know if you get past that point."

The lieutenant flinched as a bullet shattered the right rearview mirror. Sharp turns, drop-offs, blind curves, and improperly graded shoulders created hazardous driving conditions. The asphalt surface was bumpy and potholed, without markings or guard rails. The road was narrow with treacherous ditches. When one of the motorcyclists pulled beside the van, the lieutenant veered to the left, forcing him off the road. The motorcycle slammed into the ditch, dramatically sending the rider high in the air with arms flailing. He twirled around three times in slow motion before slamming into a tree, breaking all the bones in his face and chest.

Directly ahead, deadly black toxic smoke from burning barrels of oil was rising into the mid-afternoon sky. The lieutenant warned of a severe immediate risk of death or serious physical harm. "Bend over, stay down, and stay seated to avoid head and neck trauma."

He gripped the steering wheel tightly, aimed for the center barrel of burning oil, and accelerated. The crash produced a spectacular fiery explosion. The barrel of hot boiling oil expanded violently on impact, explosively splashing a dozen militants sitting in the shade of a tree with the flammable liquid. The momentum of the van allowed it to continue speeding forward through the illegal checkpoint. The lieutenant temporarily lost control. The bus accidentally slid off the side of the road.

The front right fender demolished a small chicken coop, smashing it into dozens of small fragments and bent wire. The dispersed flock of distressed chickens startled the trailing motorcyclist, causing him to slide sideways on the slippery oil. He slammed into a second burning barrel of oil, accidentally tipping the flaming liquid onto himself, producing horrifying screams.

Feelings of shock and awe overcame the passengers as the lieutenant sprang into action, removing the fire extinguisher from under the driver's seat before stepping outside to prevent the tires from burning up. A monkey screamed rudely at the intrusion. He picked up a handful of elephant dung and flung it at the lieutenant, hitting him in the back of the pith helmet as he rushed to get back on the van.

Kinsley hollered into the phone. "When you see the abandoned building on the right side of the road three miles ahead, pull over. I have a security detail with me."

3

BRITISH AGENT KINGSLEY

British Agent Kingsley flagged the green van with oversized jungle tires and broken windows at the prearranged checkpoint.

"Thanks for coming to our rescue. That was quite a harrowing experience. How's my favorite MI6 foreign intelligence officer?" Lieutenant Dunning asked wholeheartedly with a broad grin followed by a friendly handshake, downplaying the severity of the life-threatening experience.

"I'm fine, but you need to leave Nigeria immediately. Why is it that every time I see you, the enemy is lurking close behind?" Kingsley asked in amazement, astonished at the sight of so many bullet holes, broken windows, and burned paint. And the tires smelled of burned rubber.

Kinsley turned his attention to the passengers, pointing to a new white luxury bus with chrome wheels and light-blue velour seats. The British security team moved with precision and haste, transferring the luggage from the green jungle van into the storage compartment of the new bus.

Kingsley warned, "I hope you weren't involved with the Seal Team Six rescue mission? Our embassy has picked up chatter indicating that you are investigating the embezzlement of millions of dollars of crude oil and rare-earth minerals. Rare-earth elements are a geopolitical issue affecting the shifting global order. China and the United States are engaged in an escalating high-stakes trade war. Everyone in power turns a blind eye because corrupt people looking to impose their will through violence and intimidation will harm anyone who tries to stop them. Exposing profits from the theft of natural resources creates overt anger that will lead you directly into a dangerous state of affairs, a cauldron of instability."

"Do you know the driver?" the lieutenant asked curiously.

"His name is Noah," Kingsley informed. "Noah is a celebrity in Nigeria as one of the greatest advocates of tourism in the country. He publishes a tourist magazine and promotes wild animal theme parks, scenic byways, and tourist businesses. The Royal Enouement Society sponsors him."

"Who shot him?"

"The shooter is likely a faithful follower and unscrupulous henchman of Bo-Bo Bigelow acting on behalf of his powerful corrupt master. Bo-Bo is the largest exporter of natural resources in Nigeria, a true super-villain, mastermind, and most certainly the antagonist in this story."

Kingsley was distracted as a woman with an exceptional figure made her way into the new luxury bus. "What's the name of the high-class buxom woman with the wet blouse in the flowery red pants?"

"Chloe Crouton. She's French," Dunning told him, having spoken to her briefly on the bus.

"She's very stylish with a classic feminine nature that I find exceptionally seductive," Kingsley confessed, having always been attracted to full-figured European women.

Kingsley saluted the lieutenant out of respect as a larger-than-life legend; a heroic icon regaled in incredible stories and folktales. The blond girl sitting in the back of the bus with an enigmatic smile watched and listened carefully. She overheard Kingsley referring to the lieutenant as a highly famous and notorious person in international espionage circles, especially in Africa. She learned that he was a key contact for essential people in many countries, respected and cherished for his unique skills. He was generous and helpful, touching many around him with his storytelling prowess. Military leaders and analysts highly respected his advice and opinions. His exalted military virtues and ideals, and aggressive defense of national interests were exemplary.

"Rumor has it you were in Equatorial Guinea recently?" Kingsley said with a rhetorical flair, uncertain if he would receive a response.

"China is aggressively outmaneuvering the United States militarily and economically. Beijing is actively pursuing military bases and footholds all over the African continent. The Chinese deep-water navy port on the Atlantic coast in Guinea has significant strategic military advantages. It will be large enough for nuclear submarines, warships, armored combat vehicles, and aircraft carriers. The threat to national security, economic prosperity, and fair trade is worrisome," the lieutenant warned.

Kinsley had the last word. "You must leave on the first flight out of Nigeria tonight," he commanded.

4

MOONSTRUCK

The lieutenant confidently strolled to the back of the air-conditioned bus and selected a vacant seat next to the blonde girl from Wisconsin. She was beautiful, with large eyes, white teeth, glowing skin, and a genuine smile. Dunning casually leaned closer and tipped his new safari helmet as if nothing had happened. With a sheepish grin, he whispered, "Thank you for offering to help me earlier. What's your name?"

"My name is Crystal Glass. I was listening to the men speaking outside. British Agent Kingsley referred to you as Lieutenant Baron Dunning, a US marshal, a military strategist, and a legend. The embassy guards referred to you as a man of substance with much power, money, and influence.

"US Special Operations, led by Seal Team Six, launched a hostage rescue operation during the early morning hours. I offered support as they successfully recovered an American citizen held hostage by armed militants in northern Nigeria. The insurgents that attacked me knew I was indirectly involved."

"Tell me about your job—or isn't that allowed?"

"I was a US marshal, a criminal investigator, and intelligence analyst with broad arrest authority. I cooperated with international law enforcement agencies to apprehend fugitives. The agency plays a critical role in disrupting and dismantling illicit enterprises, depriving criminals of the proceeds of illegal activities, deterring crime, and restoring stolen property to victims. Marshals are the primary custodian of seized property, including real estate, commercial businesses, cash, financial instruments, vehicles, jewelry, art, antiques, collectibles, vessels, and aircraft. We evaluate, manage, and dispose of the assets seized and forfeited by criminals."

"I thought the US Marshals Service was responsible for operating the federal Witness Protection Program, providing new identities and protection to entire families? You have the appearance of a self-reliant, creative, intelligent, and brave individual. You seem more like the type of authority the president would assign to assess the enormous strategic risks of Chinese military investments in African seaports," she probed inquisitively.

The lieutenant was stone-faced, completely caught off-guard. He pretended he never heard the comment. "Where are you staying?" he queried.

"I have a reservation at the Federal Palace Hotel and Casino, Victoria Island, Lagos."

"So, do I. Let's meet for dinner this evening at six o'clock."

The attractive young woman from Wisconsin approached the dining room with the flowing grace of a fashion model. She wore a silky black dress with her side-swept wavy blond hair in a classic bridesmaid wedding style. She warmly and openly extended both arms, embraced the lieutenant, and kissed him lightly on the cheek.

"You resemble the desert waiting for rain—a beautiful flower about to bloom. The dress you're wearing is both relaxed and elegant. It's a very inspiring design that looks splendid on you," the dashing lieutenant remarked.

"I enjoy the outward appearance and comfort the Sicilian Seduction collection of alluring little black dresses provides." Pausing suggestively for effect with a coy smile, she then added, "If you think it looks good on me now, you should see what it looks like crumpled in a ball and lying on the floor."

Visions of Crystal without her silky dress danced in his head as the hostess politely escorted them to a romantic corner table. Her words and the alluring mystique created by her choice of scent infused his imagination with an allusion that was subliminally lovely, glamorous, and haunting.

"Mother Nature couldn't have said it better. What brings you to Africa?" he inquired after pausing briefly to stifle his emerging sense of desire.

Crystal smiled and looked into his eyes without constraint to show she was not afraid. He appeared healthy, strong, and full of vigor, speaking the truth using sweet, loving, soft words. "*National Geographic Magazine* sent me to Africa to photograph families of the Nigerian schoolgirls abducted by Islamic terrorists to tell the tragic story to the world. I took a few extra days to go on safari to film elephants in the wild."

A waiter with brilliant white teeth shattered the romantic atmosphere. The interruption temporarily torpedoed the lieutenant's attention to the enigmatic woman from Wisconsin.

"Have you decided what you would like for dinner?" the waiter inquired with a deep *basso profundo* voice like a truckload of gravel falling on the ground.

"What do you recommend?"

"Jollof rice is well-liked and regarded with much affection by many of our customers. It's popular in West Africa. It's a simple, spicy, one-pot dish comprised of rice, tomatoes, onions, and pepper, served at parties and other festive gatherings. Jollof rice is the origin of jambalaya."

"Thank you. We'll follow your recommendation—two jollof rice dinners," Dunning stated before the waiter walked away.

The flickering candlelight stimulated the lieutenant to raise his wine glass and toast his new friend. "Here's to Eve, the mother of all races, who wore a fig leaf in all the right places."

"Here's to Adam, the father of us all, who was Johnny-on-the-spot when the leaves began to fall," she countered. Her cheeks were flush, and she was feeling excited and nervous. The lieutenant's hypnotic eye contact and warm, seductive smile gave her a feeling of not being in control. She liked the way he oozed swagger and the immediate and profoundly positive spell he had placed on her. He was mysterious and endlessly intriguing—someone to be pampered and cherished.

Crystal was intrigued to learn more. "Are you a specially trained and highly disciplined agent working for a tactical unit within the US Department of State responsible for protecting national assets?"

The lieutenant was evasively modest. "Never be bamboozled by appearances, past job descriptions, or circumstances," he attested. "You seem unpretentious and free, natural and open. You're an inspiration to me, everything I ever dreamed of, just you and me. One sip of wine, and I've got this feeling that I can't explain."

When she leaned forward, she gained his interest. When she leaned back, it seemed to create a vacuum that sucked her back into the original intense, warm, welcoming sensation. She found herself staring at him with starry eyes, drinking in his features, trying to figure out his every move, thought, and action.

The lieutenant smiled and raised his glass of sparkling water with increased confidence, hoping to impress. "Here's to this water, wishing it were wine. Here's to you, my darling, wishing you were mine."

Crystal lit up like a firefly, flirtatiously responding with a come-hither toast of her own. "Here's to trigger-fingered Cupid—the blind gunner."

The lieutenant was smitten. The evening was a highly memorable, romantic encounter with a beautiful girl he had only fantasized about in passionate youthful dreams.

Crystal was moonstruck, unable to think or act normally. She smiled courteously and reached for his hand. "The way you express your sentiments is so lyrically imaginative and delightful."

Later, as they walked out of the restaurant, he whispered in her ear,

"I very much enjoyed your companionship this unforgettable evening. I look forward to seeing you again."

She playfully wrapped both arms around the lieutenant's neck. Then she smiled coquettishly, tickled his wazoo, and kissed him passionately on the lips. She gracefully pivoted on her Italian stiletto heels and headed for the exit. The slack-jawed lieutenant was left in a state of shock and awe, unable to speak or articulate a coherent thought.

"Call me soon if you want me to be the mother of your children," she called to him.

His head was tilted back with clenched hands atop it. As he lowered his head, his pupils dilated. His eyes were wide open in a fixed gaze, mesmerized by the motion of her skirt seductively swishing back and forth from side to side. Striking a cowboy pose with his thumbs in his belt, he resisted the urge to pump his fist in the air. Her enchanting words and actions distracted him. So much so that he completely missed an obvious warning sign. Peering through the window directly behind him was the scar-faced Nigerian who shot and killed Noah.

5

FLIGHT TO SPAIN

Lieutenant Dunning waited patiently in the shadows of the hotel lobby. British Agent Kingsley arrived precisely on time. He discretely presented the American with a first-class airline ticket to Spain on a Boeing 737 and a British passport using the false name Christian Churchill. A new wallet contained an international driver's license and two thousand British pounds. A suitcase held a new pair of Oxford dress shoes, aviator sunglasses, and British business attire. "I booked a seat for you on the first flight out of the country leaving for Barcelona."

"I'm not looking forward to flying over the Sahara Desert in the middle of the night," the lieutenant casually mentioned. "Do you know anyone from Wisconsin with connections here in Nigeria?"

"Father Feely is the founder of a religious hermitage at Gravestone Castle in Wisconsin. Three years he served in Nigeria; he set multiple fundraising, charitable-giving, and church-building records. Bo-Bo Bigelow is Nigeria's most notorious embezzler. Bo-Bo is the bank robber, and Father Feely is his accomplice waiting outside in the getaway car to steal natural resources from the African continent. I'll send you a full report."

The lieutenant squeaked past the final airport checkpoint thanks to a false British passport, altered hairstyle, and dark aviator sunglasses. He deceived the security guards with exaggerated stuffiness and a posh English accent associated with aristocracy and educational institutions.

Forty minutes from Barcelona's El Prat airport, Dunning was awakened by a loud explosion under the airplane's wing. The noise and vibration of the aircraft quickened the collective heartbeats of everyone onboard. A putrid oily black smoke with droplets of hydraulic fluid floating in the air began pouring out of air-conditioning ducts into the passenger cabin.

A panicky woman with a French accent screamed hysterically, "Merde, we're all going to die."

The lieutenant recognized her as the same nervous full-figured woman from the safari tour with the curvy hips and large breasts that had attracted the admiration of British Agent Kingsley. A portly, plump man sitting beside her tossed his double gin martini cocktail in her face. "Shut up and drink your wine, Chloe. You're scaring everyone."

The lieutenant pulled a white linen handkerchief out of his vest pocket, holding it over his nose, eyes, and mouth to avoid breathing the polluted air in the cabin. The black droplets of hydraulic fluid floating in the air left black smudge marks on everything they touched. Passengers sitting next to the windows recoiled, shying away in fear of the endless sand hills comprising the Sahara Desert thousands of feet below, the largest, hottest desert in the world.

"One of the engines has exploded, resulting in damage to the hydraulic systems and cabin air-conditioning," the pilot stated as the official explanation for the explosion. "We have been cleared for an emergency landing at El Prat airport and should not have any problem landing with one engine. For your safety, do what the flight attendants tell you."

Panicky passengers suffering from uncontrollable fear and anxiety were left breathless when they observed numerous fire trucks lining up on both sides of the runway. It was a hard landing, and the cabin shook as the wheels squealed loudly in contact with the ground. The brakes were misaligned and unbalanced, and a tire exploded when it hit a pothole.

The panicky Frenchwoman was the first to remove her seatbelt and run toward the exit. Her joints were highly flexible. Her hips and shoulders swung back and forth in animated large sweeping circles. Her breasts moved in surprising ways, bouncing up and down in an intriguing figure eight, the way that belly dancers entertain.

The flight attendant wore luxurious long black eyelashes and metallic dark eye shadow from a romantic smoky eye palette. "Please excuse the hard landing," she apologized. "It wasn't the pilot's fault; it was the asphalt," she feigned insincerely in defense of the pilot with whom she had been enjoying a salacious romantic tryst.

Lieutenant Dunning hailed a taxi and checked into his hotel. He took advantage of the twenty-four-hour layover time between flights by visiting La Sagrada Familia Cathedral and taking a stroll through Barrio Gotico. Out of the corner of his eye, he noticed a stranger with an exceptionally dark face wearing military-type camouflage clothing and a black beret spying on him from behind a gray utility vehicle.

The lieutenant evaded detection when the stranger paused for a smoke by darting into a narrow alley and crouching behind an ancient Roman rock wall. Puzzled by his sudden disappearance, the stalker nervously scanned the alleyway, looking in all directions before rushing off toward the Jewish Quarter.

Seeing no other suspicious individuals before reappearing from behind the wall, Dunning followed the stalker into the heart of the historic center, angling on a diagonal toward the Aquarium Barcelona in Port Vell. He mingled briefly with a group of noisy beer-drinking tourists from Trysil, Norway, to avoid detection and observed from a distance as the stalker crossed the swing bridge heading toward the marina. The lieutenant picked up a newspaper, slipped behind a steel pillar, and positioned himself on a park bench where he could keep the marina under surveillance without being seen.

The African stalker glanced in his direction before boarding a large private yacht. The boat *Ebony* was flying a white Nigerian ensign flag. The name was displayed on a black shield with a white skull and crossbones logo as a warning symbol of death—a luxury yacht belonging to Bo-Bo Bigelow, the notorious Nigerian playboy millionaire. The shadowy figure silhouetted against the white backdrop of the yacht cabin. The setting sun glinting on the stalker's face exposed a ragged knife scar on his left cheekbone. It was distinctly familiar in appearance to the gun-toting militant who had shot Noah. The stalker cussed and angrily tossed his black beret on the deck before entering one of the luxurious staterooms.

A bright light inside the cabin illuminated the faces of two wealthy Chinese investors in dark suits suspiciously pointing to a map of Africa. The high-stakes discussion they were having was seriously concentrated and emotionally intense.

The Nigerian luxury power yacht departed the harbor at twilight, shimmering on the placid combers of the briny deep. The powerful diesel-burning engines produced deep cavitation sounds that vibrated the heart and energized the imagination. Frightening thoughts raged through the lieutenant's mind as he watched, portending profoundly wicked characters and sinister plots.

"Prestige and celebrity are the nefarious shadows of power and money," he mused as the yacht vanished into darkness on the edge of the horizon.

6

NATURAL RESOURCES EXPLOITATION

Lieutenant Baron Dunning was a legend, a spy, and a chameleon. He had a reputation as one of the most popular, smartest US marshals in his profession, a classic alpha male at the top of the social status hierarchy with tremendous access to power, money, and friends gained through physical prowess, intimidation, and domination. Nobody was ever sure about what he was doing, his background, or the validity of his credentials. Very few details escaped his analytical, intellectual, and scholarly mind. He did his best to solve highly complex analytical problems using logic and intuition.

The flight back to Washington Dulles International Airport was smooth as glass. Lieutenant Dunning stayed up all night in a state of nervous excitement, finalizing his report. He was confident about his mission, but everything about this case was *caddywampus*, in disarray and disorder, askew. Everything had gone badly, awkwardly, and in the wrong direction. There were too many loose ends. Nigerian Bo-Bo Bigelow was the alleged kingpin and a hostile antagonist. Still, framing a case against him was like building a barn without tape, level, or plumb-bob. The case was not airtight. It was as if crooked studs caused the door to jam and the roof to leak. He had discovered many things of interest to share with the US State Department. Nevertheless, the script seemed spoiled by a lack of consistency and plausibility.

Dunning carefully laid the report on the desk of Colonel James Roberts at the Pentagon and waited for his response. The colonel was wide-eyed, quoting directly from the lieutenant's report.

"'There is massive theft of Nigerian crude oil worth 1.5 billion dollars being stolen every month and sold on international markets on an industrial scale. Piracy has become so prolific that there are advertisements for stolen oil on the Nigerian version of Craigslist for giant tankers full of oil. The forging of bills of lading and other corporate documents disguises the nefarious acts of thieves illegally tapping into pipelines and diverting oil onto waiting barges in return for money, guns, and narcotics. The oil is then pumped into coastal tankers at night to export the product globally. Proceeds are laundered through world financial centers and used to buy assets outside Nigeria. Shell companies, tax havens, bribery of bank officials, cash smuggling, cycling cash through legitimate businesses, and cash purchases of luxury goods disguise the source of the funds. No one knows or cares how much of the oil that comes out of the ground gets diverted en route because oil theft finances politics and election campaigns.'"

The colonel finally looked up. "Your report is quite revealing," Colonel James Roberts explained at the Pentagon in Arlington, Virginia. A cast of multiagency security representatives from the National Security Administration, American International Development, Defense Intelligence Agency, CIA, NGA, NRO; intelligence elements of the five Department of Defense services; and multiple accredited diplomats concurred.

The lieutenant respectfully engaged the audience. "Ebony wood, illegally smuggled out of the country at an alarming rate, is used to build wooden crates, palettes, and shipping containers. The value of the wooden crates far exceeds the value of the products shipped. Ebony is one of the most expensive woods globally, and it is so coveted by artists and craft makers that it sells by the gram. The amount of money generated from the selling of ebony, ivory, and other valuable natural resources is staggering—much larger than anyone could have imagined."

Attendees were captivated by Lieutenant Dunning's findings and way of communicating. "All of the issues mentioned previously pale in comparison to the value and importance of rare-earth minerals mined by China in sub-Saharan Africa. China has a worldwide monopoly over rare-earth minerals and control of the most extensive uranium deposits globally. The rare-earth mineral tantalum is more valuable than gold. Aerospace engineers claim that the metal is critical to the future of the US Armed Forces, the electronics industry, and the space force. There is a very dark side to the Congo mineral rush, where nearly sixty percent of the world's cobalt reserves exist. China is a significant player. Tesla uses cobalt to produce lithium batteries to fuel their cars. Tantalum alloys are known for high-temperature strength, and cobalt alloys are resistant to oxidation. A much more assertive China has aggressively gained control of over half of the world's manganese, an essential ingredient for steel production.

"China's direct foreign investment in African countries yields significant financial, political, and military gains. The changes are unlike anything the world has seen before, the final frontier of the fourth industrial revolution. China is building and engineering every building over three stories in Africa. Railroads, highways, and airports are piercing the heart of the continent. China's colossal investments in the Belt and Road Initiative, sometimes referred to as the New Silk Road, fuel one of the most ambitious infrastructure projects ever conceived. Analysts predict the 'string of pearls' geo-economic strategy to create unsustainable debt burdens will allow Beijing to seize control of strategic regional military choke points. The future status of these countries will eventually be equivalent to subordinate vassal states in the feudal system in medieval Europe."

Colonel Roberts reacted with a high level of aggressive energy. He forcefully pushed his chair back from the table before summarizing his suppositions with a dire warning. "The future seems perfectly orchestrated for a catastrophic disruption of the critical supply chain of crucial rare-earth minerals essential for national defense. The Chinese have monopolistic control of production and tremendous international political leverage. The swiftness of the changes in the world order is driven by a Chinese commitment to world domination, leaving panicky, unsettled political policymakers with an urgent need for answers. Chinese control of rare-earth mineral deposits on the African continent is highly unsettling and disproportionate to the rest of the world. Moreover, China is using political payoffs and bribery at an alarming rate."

The lieutenant summarized the problem. "The dilemma: there are limited rare-earth processing facilities in the United States. Currently, China controls the vast majority of the global rare-earth production. China's world market dominance puts it in a powerful bargaining position in US-China relations. It also raises broad questions about supply chain security in the interconnected global economy."

7

BIOLOGICAL WARFARE

The lieutenant paused to make eye contact with the audience to ensure he had everyone's attention before addressing the second part of his report.

"Hard evidence of biological and entomological weapons used against Boko Haram militants in northern Nigeria is difficult to find. When entire villages have died of mysterious causes, the government blames it on gas from a volcano. Panicky insurgents subjected to repeated attacks by swarms of killer bees are always on edge. According to eyewitness reports, the ongoing stings and lethal poisons are unbearable and often fatal. Victims become disoriented and mysteriously disappear into the jungle. There has also been a significant increase in snake bites, fleas, and parasitic ticks, delivering biological agents that infect people they bite or sting. Some individuals and animals are sickened or killed by exposure to biological toxins, including yellow rain, infectious agents, bacteria, viruses, COVID germs, and fungi. These incidents appear to have international implications for biological and entomological warfare."

Dunning interjected a personal observation. "Assigning Americans to work in such extremely challenging geographies and social contexts makes for a highly volatile situation. Militants targeted me for assassination during my visit to Nigeria. I was obviously in the wrong place at the wrong time. Rangers and paramilitary forces tasked with protecting natural resources and political boundaries are facing increasingly violent, vigorously active, and aggressive, heavily armed criminals engaged in mineral exploration and poaching."

Pausing for effect, he soon continued speaking with a high degree of self-assuredness. "Fear permeates the air in northern Nigeria, where Boko Haram, an Islamic militant group, is spreading its terror across mountainous borders into Niger, Chad, and Cameroon. Violent Muslim extremists brutally impose a religious ideology on local populations and persecute innocent civilians, using torture, sexual assault, and extra-judicial killings to intimidate. Over five thousand people are dead, and thousands more abandoned their homes to escape the violence—that is, until recently, when the number of acres of territory under the control of the jihadists unexpectedly decreased thanks to the efforts of one man: Bo-Bo Bigelow."

Holding a scale model of a beehive above his head for everyone to see, the lieutenant explained, "Every beehive in the possession of Bo-Bo Bigelow's servile underlings and followers was modified to accommodate a sliding glass window to install an Apple iPad as a way of graphically communicating with the bees, directing them to specific individuals. I traced the source of the beehives to a former government research center at Gravestone Castle in northern Wisconsin."

Colonel Roberts offered a cautionary warning. "Condemnation of America by Muslims worldwide will be swift and harsh if anyone leaks rumors about biological warfare to the press. Further investigation is warranted to define our end goal, prioritize tasks, list steps to be followed, set milestones, and establish an action plan."

8

ACTION PLAN

Later that afternoon, representatives from multiple federal agencies gathered around a conference table in the A-ring of the Pentagon. Colonel James Roberts tapped his knuckles on the whiteboard to alert everyone in attendance that the meeting was about to begin.

"Our goal is to prepare an action plan in response to recent observations and findings disclosed in Lieutenant Baron Dunning's report. The major topics of concern are a continuing supply of critical rare-earth minerals, pilfered crude oil sold on an industrial scale, major new Chinese naval ports on the African continent, and possible scientific breakthroughs in entomological warfare."

The colonel began with the section of the lieutenant's report dealing with aggressive Chinese military intervention on the African continent and the implications of a deepening relationship.

"'Chinese practices are poorly understood and often misquoted in the press. Their role defies conventional stereotypes and punchy news headlines. China represents modern infrastructure improvements, friendship, and economic prosperity to developing African countries. The powerplants, telecommunications, fiber-optic cables, and smart coastal cities they are building pose a significant challenge to US global security and investment. It's the most ambitious foreign policy undertaking in modern times, drawing countries into tighter economic and political relationships with Beijing.'"

Colonel Roberts shrugged his shoulders, deliberately concealing his personal opinions. He was unhurried, and his verbal response was intentionally vague, brief, constrained, and mysterious.

"'Americans are viewed as neocolonialists arrogantly espousing cultural imperialism. American financial aid is viewed negatively because it is always conditional, forcing African countries to comply with political acceptance of social justice programs, green new deals, humane working conditions, religious freedom, political correctness, and climate controls. US policymakers have paid little attention to the strategic and political implications of the Chinese Belt and Road Initiative. There has been no official US response to the twenty-seven seaports China is building to support the military, industrial, and commercial development programs.'"

Breaking from the report, Colonel Roberts continued, "I have asked Lieutenant Baron Dunning to lead this investigation. The lieutenant is a graduate of West Point, a Rhodes scholar, and a descendant of English boxing champion Robert Gregson. He has recently returned from a fact-finding mission in Nigeria, Africa. Our task is to choose an appropriate goal and clearly define the objectives with action steps that are concrete, measurable, and attainable. Please welcome Lieutenant Baron Dunning, a former US marshal, a global investigator, military analyst, and world-renowned detective."

Lieutenant Dunning stood up and pointed to a map of Nigeria with authority. He was an imposing figure, tall, broad-shouldered, and muscular with long dark-brown hair and the countenance of a general, the ideal combination of masculinity, civility, intelligence, and brawn. He was critically informed, entertaining, educated, and persuasive. The clarity of his voice was the most powerful element in his leadership arsenal.

"The matters at hand are outside the normal range of military etiquette, and they are a treasure trove of curiosities. They lead me to believe a unique set of interpretive skills will be needed to accurately determine the risk to national security and appropriate future courses of action. There are multiple topics on the clipboard needing robust interactive discussion and substantial workarounds to determine which threads to follow."

Scientists from the Agricultural Research Service (ARS), headquartered at the George Washington Carver Center, and representatives from the Internal Revenue Service (IRS), National Security Agency (NSA), American International Development (USAID), and other organizations were in agreement.

"We know that billions of dollars of Nigerian oil assets are flagrantly stolen each year from the African continent on an industrial scale. Illegally diverted pipelines fill mammoth oil tankers with stolen crude oil every month. The United States was energy-independent in 2019 for the first time since 1957, when we exported more barrels of oil than we imported. Energy is critical for economic development. It is critically important that we remain energy independent because energy drives productivity and industrial growth. Lower energy prices reduce costs for nearly all goods and services in the economy, thus making them more affordable. Stealing oil is a criminal offense in an international court of law. Still, the consequences of calling attention to this illegal activity in foreign countries are entirely negative. Corrupt political leaders benefiting from the theft of natural resources violently oppose any actions that impede or constrain their primary source of income. Ultimately, only one antagonist is a true adversary hostile to anyone who confronts him. His name is Bo-Bo Bigelow. He is a wealthy playboy, influencer, intimidator, and dealmaker."

The lieutenant was genuinely impacting the audience. He was an upbeat leader with a positive vision and a can-do attitude. His opening statements left them speechless, stimulating a curious desire to learn more. Taking a few steps away from the podium with solid eye contact and meaningful hand gestures gave the impression he was comfortable onstage. He had swagger, and he looked confident. He knew what to say and how to say it, stating accurate facts that allowed the audience to form a firm idea of what he was saying.

An inquisitive NSA agent stated the obvious. "Most of us are well aware of the importance of rare-earth minerals and the billion-dollar theft of oil taking place in Nigeria. A possible scientific breakthrough in how Africanized killer bees control Muslim insurgencies and political violence intrigues our agency the most. Killer bees trained to assassinate military officers and political opponents? How is that possible? Is this breakthrough technology connected in any way to research previously paid for by USAID and performed by American entomologists at the University of Nsukka, Nigeria, and Indonesia Jakarta?"

Colonel Roberts performed the cutthroat gesture. Drawing his hand and fingers across the larynx represented someone metaphorically having their throat slit as a theatrical threat to drop this line of questioning. "That information is classified—there is no proof that any research of that type ever existed. Stick to the information in the report," he demanded. "We don't want any incidents of this sort blamed on Americans. Suppose the value of the entomological scientific breakthrough is as significant as Lieutenant Dunning believes it to be and the value for covert operations is as positive as predicted. In that case, the research will be veiled and kept behind a shroud of secrecy indefinitely due to international laws restricting chemical and biological warfare."

The representative from NSA concurred. "This country is constantly seeking new strategies, equipment, and advantages to counter opponents conducting suicidal missions. Guerrilla warfare and unconventional asymmetrical military strategies are better than direct military encounters. Belligerent global jihadist terrorists covertly conducting sneaky back-alley attacks are highly motivated, resilient opponents, despite being less equipped and understaffed against our vastly superior armed forces."

"It's true," the lieutenant reminded them. "Medieval scholars and idealists intent on preemptive attacks commissioned by political authorities, promoted by a theological struggle between Islam and the non-Muslim world, are constantly seeking nuclear, biological, and chemical agents to sabotage, subvert, and destabilize devilish Western governments disrespectful of their religion."

Colonel Roberts summarized the lieutenant's findings, noted the key takeaways, and outlined the vision, mission, objectives, and strategies in the action plan. "Entomological warfare is the most pressing topic needing to be dealt with immediately, a military matter of national importance. I trust everyone to explicitly maintain secrecy when it comes to the importance of this investigation," he explained, pointing to everyone in attendance.

"There is one other person on the agenda for today," Colonel Roberts stated, pointing to an isolated stranger with a devilish look.

9

WARFARE RESEARCH

An older man seated in the back of the room flashed a supercilious grin. Every labored breath he took had a static charge. His steely eyes seemed to conceal the truth within, leaving the audience wondering if the shadows across the window were birds in the wind, or was the stranger hiding something sinister? His voice rattled like the sound of debris in a tin can, making their skin crawl, with every muscle tense to the extreme, trying to comprehend his implausible dreams.

"My name is Dr. Whet Faartz. Gravestone Castle is a private estate in Wisconsin formerly leased by the federal government to support war efforts during World War Two, the Korean Conflict, and the Cold War. I worked as a lead scientist conducting biological and entomological warfare studies at the castle under the lead scientist, Professor Adam Baum, for over thirty years. Research conducted by trial and error often produced unreliable results. The isolated, secluded location and prevailing west winds blowing east toward Lake Michigan provided a secure setting and a relatively safe environment for secret biological experiments. Experiments involving chemical and biological agents took place on barges towed offshore. Trained suicidal monkeys from Nigeria were used to pull levers and open containers in exchange for food. If the barges became contaminated, the US Army and Air Force used them for target practice. Missiles launched from nearby Camp Haven and submarines from Manitowoc firing torpedoes sunk most of them. No private or commercial boats or airplanes were allowed offshore."

The older man left them wondering if he was living in extremes, willing to accept the risk and dangerously go the distance. His stories seemed driven by an imagination that spins out scream-producing nightmares. He seemed to hold the promise of a mind-blowing adventure with a hair-raising beginning and a heart-stopping end as he summed up the briefing with a startling revelation.

"Many of the funds used for military research were disguised as USAID grants to universities. A two-hundred-thousand-dollar grant covertly paid five times in the same year could result in over one million dollars. With this cryptic method of accounting, Gravestone Castle was able to continue operating as a federal science research laboratory until about the same time Whistling Straits golf club opened."

Dr. Whet Faartz spoke quietly and assuredly about the need for confidentiality to protect national security. "USAID plays a critical role in our nation's effort to stabilize foreign governments and build responsive local governance. They work on the same problems as our military and CIA to protect American interests worldwide but with a different set of tools. Moving a few million dollars from one country to another to obsequious foreign legislators supporting American political, business, and economic interests is a routine practice. In addition, USAID protects American international assets abroad, including strategic military facilities, natural resources, rare-earth minerals, and cooperating states. Unfortunately, Americans are generally unaware and incredibly naïve." The old man gasped as he labored painfully to suck in another shallow breath.

"Professor Baum is very clever and intelligent. He is a leading scientist in entomological research who loves bees. Unfortunately, the professor has the mentality of a serial killer. He's a curmudgeon who causes people of ordinary sensibilities to run away for fear of injury or harm. He is acutely aware of the body's reaction to pain and various forms of torture. His insight was always based on firsthand personal experience, learned from direct hands-on involvement in the field rather than academics. He is a brilliant scientist but highly unpredictable, moody, and volatile—quite scary and sinister."

The older man's mind was going a million miles a minute as if trying to solve nonexistent problems.

"Professor Baum reeked of surliness. He pioneered ethnic bioweapons, genetic bombs designed to target specific ethnicities with similar genotypes, the same type of research Japanese scientists did in Manchuria during World War Two. Chinese scientists have been actively researching deadly viruses for many years—who knows how far they have progressed since then? Rumors have them working on viruses that will only attack Europeans with blue eyes. The plan is to extinguish the entire population of multiple African countries by introducing viruses specific to the mitochondrial genomes encoded in the DNA of the natives in regional locations known to contain uranium, rare-earth minerals, and other priceless natural resources. Nobody will ever know who developed the viruses and stop the mass extermination. Baum created long-range sonic grenades to create mental confusion and psychogenic illness in crowds. This technique was highly effective at dissuading Dakota Access Pipeline protestors. Russian agents attacked the American Embassy in Cuba using the same technology. Inaudible sound waves make breathing erratic and cause heart attacks. Infrasonic sounds cause nausea, headaches, annoyance, dizziness, and heart palpitations."

Dr. Faartz pulled up his shirt sleeve to expose a massive amount of lumpy scar tissue on his arm. "Professor Adam Baum did experiments with giant hogweed plants and poisonous honey. His hobbies include controlling and manipulating killer bees and making large animal taxidermy and fiberglass sculptures of deceased human figures."

"Did Professor Baum imply that seeds escaping from plants grown by government scientists at Gravestone Castle caused the sudden outbreak of giant hogweed in Wisconsin?" the lieutenant asked, looking the shriveled scientist directly in the eyes.

"I formed my conclusions without prejudice," the old man

confidently said, dispelling any doubts. "The science laboratory at Gravestone Castle under the direction of Adam Baum resembled a storm-threatened ship manned by a drunken crew experiencing a mid-life crisis or two. Don't let the fluffy white flowers fool you. I can attest from firsthand experience that giant hogweed is a plant from hell that causes burning, incredible pain, lifelong scarring, and even death. It's especially excruciating if it gets in your lungs," the old man uttered with a whistling, rattling sound in the chest.

Lieutenant Baron Dunning was distracted by the man's physical appearance, his messy white hair and severe scarring on his hands and neck. The audience reacted disquietly with an intense unease at the wheezing sound of his breathing as he sucked in as much air as his lungs would allow. Still, he was self-assured with a credible presence and a persuasive message, and his body language signaled a treasure trove of undisclosed cloak-and-dagger exploits. His hand gestures with thumbs pointing upward showed that he had something powerful to say. His comments were believable based on a perception of the communicator as an experienced biological warfare scientist.

"How does the professor spell his last name?" Dunning inquired imaginatively.

"B-A-U-M!"

10

OPERATION PROCOL HARUM

Lieutenant Dunning stroked an imaginary beard, thinking about Professor Adam Baum and Dr. Whet Faartz's dangerous research, concerned about where the investigation might lead. He then addressed the audience. "Colonel Roberts has assigned me the task of determining the reasons for multiple transfers of funds originating from embezzled oil and stolen rare-earth minerals on the African continent in exchange for biological weapons. Public exposure of these transactions to subdue Muslim extremism is a dilemma that has a high potential to create social and political havoc."

"This operation will take place with discretion and confidentiality," Colonel Roberts conveyed. "The name of this operation, *Procol Harum*, will instill confusion because nobody knows how to interpret the lyrics from the 1960s British band. They were 'skipping to the light fandango' and 'a whiter shade of pale' and all that nonsense."

Lieutenant Dunning deliberately scrutinized each participant in the audience with a chilling thousand-yard stare. "Honeybees have known for thousands of years that honeycomb made with six-sided hexagon-shaped cells is a masterpiece of engineering that economizes labor and material. So, imagine the cheeky insolence of the architectural committee that chose a five-sided building for the Pentagon."

The audience reaction was spontaneously warm, with respect and enthusiasm for the highly popular lieutenant. The representatives were leaning forward, grinning, and taking notes.

One of the participants from NSA demanded to know, "Does your inquiry have anything to do with Professor Baum, who, as we heard, is the retired lead scientist at the former ultrasecret laboratory at Gravestone Castle in Wisconsin? How is it possible that a monster like the professor is still living at Gravestone Castle? The research center was closed, decommissioned, and disputed by the federal government over ten years ago."

"Lurking in hallways, backrooms, and hidden laboratories, confidential research using infectious bacteria continues to unfold amid the highest levels of secrecy. Never underestimate the financial resources of universities or exclude the profit motive of private companies, the greed and wealth of corporate money lenders, or the evil intentions of corrupt nations. Science in the shadows with deadly high-risk supercharged pathogens will continue regardless of the amount of passionate debate that opposes it," Dunning concluded.

Colonel Roberts raised one eyebrow as a sign of disbelief. "There is no evidence in the public record proving that a federal research laboratory ever existed in northern Wisconsin," he explained gravely. "There is also no statute of limitations on the disclosure of chemical, biological, and entomological weapons research. The world has no idea how far research has progressed since World War Two because record-keeping and experimentation have remained classified and hidden from public view for over fifty years."

Penny Pincher, an employee of the IRS, escalated the discussion. "Every aspect of the international financial trail we are following begins and ends with Bo-Bo Bigelow. He is the world's largest exporter of stolen Nigerian crude oil and rare-earth minerals from Chinese mines on the African continent. He is a large, menacing man accustomed to using strong-arm tactics, frequently threatening injury and bodily harm to others. He is the owner of Ebony LLC and the largest financial benefactor of the Hermitage at Gravestone Castle. He also provided Jack Daniels with the financing of Woebegone Dunes Resort."

The group paused to absorb the weightiness of the disclosure. Colonel Roberts forcefully reminded the group of the need to maintain the confidentiality of all phases of the investigation. "What everyone needs to know is that cash is the preferred medium of exchange in the African shadow economy. Money laundering using cash transactions leaves no footprint, and there is no need to pay income taxes. The financial trail leads us to believe that collaboration occurs routinely between Bo-Bo Bigelow from Nigeria and Father Feely, the founder of the Hermitage at Gravestone Castle in Wisconsin."

The audience showed a tremendous amount of respect and admiration for Colonel Roberts to the point of feeling nervous and fearful around him. "The IRS issued a fraud and forensic accounting advisory as a red-flag warning. However, let me warn you: don't focus excessively on prospective future outcomes without paying adequate attention to national priorities. From a security and defense standpoint, the nation's highest priority is a continuing supply of rare-earth minerals. The military-industrial complex would fail without it."

The shock from the colonel's comments paralyzed the team's perception of the problem. It obliterated preconceived notions of the multilayered task at hand. The colonel assured them, "The only person I know with the skills and the imagination needed to decipher and disentangle a Gordian knot is Lieutenant Baron Dunning, the man you see standing before you. The lieutenant is a highly effective communicator. He is persuasive and assertive, sweeping everyone along with his enthusiasm and intelligence. His optimistic, charismatic nature makes him a natural leader. He has an abundance of confidence and common sense. He possesses the quality of attracting, charming, and influencing others around him. That is why I have asked former US Marshal and international investigator Dunning to lead this investigation with tact and diplomacy."

The highly atypical accounting investigation and the intriguing possibility of working closely with alpha males Lieutenant Baron Dunning and Colonel James Roberts roused several IRS agents to volunteer to assist in the assignment. Their collective display of animated enthusiasm was an entirely unpredictable reaction outside the traditional range of emotions for typically somber, low-energy federal employees in gray business suits.

All eyes focused on the lieutenant. "I hope that you will find me to be as authoritative and provocative as Colonel Roberts suggests. A Gordian knot is a metaphor for an intractably complex problem that is impossible to unravel. When you are not able to locate both ends of the rope or discover the cipher code, the obvious solution is the brutal cutting of the knot," he explained.

Hearing no objections, Colonel Roberts exerted his leadership. "Disclosure of any of these topics outside this conference room is forbidden. We will not be sharing any of this information with biased news media guaranteed to politicize and distort the facts. From this day forth, all correspondence related to this investigation is to be labeled by the code name Procol Harum."

11

PRIORITIES

Colonel James Roberts cleared his throat before clarifying the mission. "The Procol Harum investigation is a four-prong inquiry—a four-ring circus—ranging from income tax evasion and international subterfuge to biological warfare, rare-earth mineral exploitation, and Muslim insurgencies. The IRS is taking the lead in tracing wire transfers of cash and identifying tax cheats. Confirming whether or not Professor Adam Baum is the source of entomological and biological weapons to subdue the Muslim insurgency in northern Nigeria is a far more complex issue. Deception by artifice or stratagem to conceal, evade a rule, escape a consequence, hide something, or evade the law is tricky. I have the experience that financial fraud encompasses scams meant to profit an individual financially. Attorneys who secretly commit white-collar crimes are generally at the core of money-laundering schemes, internet crimes, computer fraud, and bribery."

"Yes," the lieutenant responded. "I also see this as a multiprong investigation. What we need to know first is what the priorities are. Priorities are difficult to decide when your house and barn are both on fire. Do you save your dog or your horse? In either case, an ethically right decision may produce undesirable outcomes from a national security standpoint."

Colonel Roberts was a man of action with a clear purpose in mind. He was openly genial. His complexion was florid, his cheeks bright red like a flower at the end of bloom, in response to a unique set of circumstances and state of affairs that were admittedly complicated. "The current state of affairs raises grave moral concerns between the tools of tyranny to safeguard our national interest versus the health, safety, and welfare of innocent civilians. A highly complex set of circumstances rests on the horns of an ethical dilemma, a double proposition with no satisfactory solution. Some parts of the world are a cauldron of political, social, and economic instability."

"There is no magic wand or witchcraft that can resolve the problems, and the solution rests with our work and discipline. Psychologists have consistently shown that a detective's ability to detect lies is no more accurate than flipping a coin," the lieutenant conveyed with a marginal belief in a quick outcome.

"Never forget that a continuous and adequate supply of rare-earth minerals is a national priority for this country and the entire free world," the colonel emphasized. "The demand for critical natural resources is increasing exponentially. A disruption in the flow of availability would be catastrophic for our military and the space force. Bankers in multiple countries have concerns about tax evasion, illegal money transfers, and illicit profits gained from the theft of natural resources. The loss of millions of dollars in tax revenue from stolen oil and other national resources is tremendous for the Nigerian government. Disclosure of egregious entomological and biological warfare taking place in Africa could have lasting moral and ethical consequences, leading to political embarrassment and a severe social backlash."

The lieutenant expressed a concern. "My authority to investigate is broad, but it is not unlimited. Any investigation of the secret Royal Enouement Society in Wisconsin must consider the common law of torts and discrete privacy rights. Common law affords members of any organization the right to sue when their seclusion and solitude have been intruded upon in any unreasonable or highly offensive manner. I recommend a safe, light-handed approach until we know more about the structure, mission, and membership of this organization."

His words hung in the air while the audience members played with them in their minds, creating the feeling that something ominous was on the horizon. "I continually ask myself if it is nobler to bemoan the pain and unfairness of life or acknowledge that the alternatives may be worse. Should we expose a sea of troubles to end them? Or is it nobler to suffer the outrageous fortune of unpleasant things that are likely to happen if we don't intercede?'"

The colonel ended the meeting on an optimistic note. "I'm sending you, Lieutenant Baron Dunning, on a luxury vacation. You're going to enjoy the 'Cape Cod of the Midwest' with its picturesque coastal towns, specialty shops, fish boils, cherry and apple orchards, and hundreds of miles of spectacular waterfront views."

"You may be telling the truth, but I have my doubts," the lieutenant expressed. "Are you sure this is going to be a blissful vacation in the land of milk and honey? Door County, Wisconsin, is referred to as Death's Door (an entryway to hell) because many people have died and disappeared there over the centuries. Scores of deaths have occurred on the rocky shoals in the surrounding waters. Over thirty thousand people have perished on Lake Michigan over the years. The souls of Native Americans, French explorers, British soldiers, fishermen, boaters, and recreationists haunt the peninsula. Many historical sites and ghost stories are shrouded in mystery. Death's Door Gin produced by Dancing Goat Distillery sold in liquor stores across the United States, United Kingdom, and the European Union underscores the validity of the legends."

12

LUXURY VACATION

Colonel James Roberts set the stage affirmatively. "Ignore the folklore and supernatural drama. This assignment is a rare hands-on opportunity to enjoy a 'luxury vacation' at Wisconsin's lavish five-star Woebegone Dunes Resort to hobnob with celebrities and scrutinize their operations. You will need to wear complementary clothing and accessories on the golf links, formal dining vestments and accessories around the lodge. A black tuxedo is required to blend in with the evening crowd."

"I'm looking forward to the new assignment," Lieutenant Dunning acknowledged attentively. "I want this to be a thorough investigation from a detective's standpoint, not a dramatic theatrical production achieved from a distance using remote techniques."

"The Hermitage at Gravestone Castle where Professor Baum resides is adjacent to Woebegone Dunes Resort. I expect you to investigate the Hermitage's structure, purpose, and operation to determine its authenticity and legitimacy. The lifestyle of the four priests and four nuns living there is unique. The Hermitage is exempt from federal income tax and receives favorable treatment under current tax laws. Massive donations to the Hermitage are tax-deductible. The IRS is particularly interested in knowing more about the head priest, Father Feely, and any irregular financial arrangements unique to his situation and this property."

"I have mixed emotions and conflicted feelings about attaining a valued outcome. The IRS appears to be leading us into a simmering cauldron of international instability, conspiracy, and unpredictable political dynamics with the potential to evolve into something very intense, lethal, and brutal. Gaining a basic understanding of the inner workings and hierarchy of the Hermitage will be difficult. I assume that most Episcopalians are ex-Catholics who failed to learn Latin," the lieutenant responded with forthrightness, unexpectedly catching the colonel off-guard.

"The Hermitage isn't the only group that concerns me. Members of the Royal Enouement Society headquartered at Woebegone Dunes Resort are subscribers to an organization whose activities, events, inner functioning, and membership are unfamiliar to others. The purpose and goals of the organization are unknown to uninitiated outsiders. Whatever the reasons for the club's existence, whether it's a religious cult or a politically motivated organization exercising positions of governance, it's impenetrable and suspicious to strangers. The organization has numerous lucrative investments in highly successful startup companies. So, learn everything you can about the Royal Enouement Society during your investigation."

Dunning downplayed expectations. "I suspect that the club acts as a brain trust of realistic, down-to-earth, practical-minded strategy advisers guaranteeing the financial success of entrepreneurs by underwriting startup businesses. An organization where businessmen and -women get answers to how things work out in the real world, understanding risk and knowing where your choices will lead you."

"Jay Walker, a college professor at the University of Wisconsin, is the best source of historical information," Roberts said. "Jay is a caddy at Woebegone Dunes Resort during the summer. His father, Benedict Walker, leased Gravestone Castle to the federal government for over four decades. Benedict died several years ago under mysterious conditions due to a severe peanut allergy. Ownership of the castle was nefariously transferred to Father Feely immediately after Benedict passed."

The lieutenant calmly blew a heavy smoke ring in the air, believing that pipe smoking contributes to calm and objective deliberations in all human affairs. "Secrets comprise over two-thirds of the value of most successful firms' information portfolios—proprietary, confidential information that increases revenue and profit. The formula for Coca-Cola, WD-40, KFC, and Google Algorithms is priceless intel, and it is not accessible to outsiders. The greater the value of the information, the more desire there is for isolation, security, and confidentiality. Stealth and seclusion fog the lens of discovery, and silence adds a dim haze of mystery. To break through the most sophisticated layers of security, one must blend with the background the way whispering children with bare feet sneak through dark shadows."

The colonel countered with authority. "There are two types of investigators—the silent and the belligerent. Desperation is the enemy of stealth. Vikings wearing metal helmets, carrying large wooden shields and axes, never sneaked into battle. They banged the sides of their boats and bellowed loudly before bashing the enemy. Most scientists, soldiers, federal investigators, and IRS agents act the same way, behaving like heartless marauders, tearing everything apart to analyze the details. They use dissection, calculated analysis, conjectures, and hypothesis to assess logical consequences coldly."

Dunning doubled down on his way of conducting surveillance. "The sweetest smiles and nervous laughter often hide the darkest mysteries— the way some women conceal their deepest thoughts and suppress their feelings. Passionate suspicion is what whets the appetite of a detective. I prefer to imitate cats and wolves that live by instinct and patience, hunting by night, knowing that the moon will eventually expose the deepest desires and habits of the antagonists."

"What else concerns you?" the colonel inquired curiously.

"The IRS may be overreacting when it comes to the function and finances of Royal Enouement Society. *Énouement* means intelligent foretelling, predicting, forecasting, and revealing future success based on wisdom, imagination, and experience using modern scientific methods. Predicting the future is difficult without a comprehensive understanding of the consequences of your actions. The organization appears to be good at predicting future business cycles better than others, the same way that meteorologists forecast rain and astronomers predict eclipses. They seem to possess priceless intel that you instinctively want to learn to reduce unnecessary financial risks. Énouement is the bittersweetness of having arrived in the future, seeing how events unfolded and wishing that you could tell your past self."

There was a pregnant pause of contemplative silence. The colonel was rendered speechless by the lieutenant's grasp of the esoteric meaning of the word *énouement*.

Lieutenant Dunning incredulously raised one eyebrow as a sign of vexation before speaking. "Excuse my incertitude," he responded with a contorted facial expression, signaling uncertainty and apparent lack of assurances. "Covert operations and undercover surveillance to secretly collect inside information is not a one-person job. I'll need an assistant familiar with the state of Wisconsin; not one of your typical agents in a gray suit from the IRS or NSA, preferably a female."

"I've already made arrangements. One of our top female agents will be accompanying you. She is an excellent marksperson and collegiate shooting champion. She has degrees in law and accounting, language fluency, police experience, computer skills, and a highly analytical investigative mind. She is an honor graduate of Dominican High School, a highly rated private Catholic school in Whitefish Bay, Wisconsin."

"What's her name?"

"Emily. The two of you will be staying in an elegant two-bedroom guest suite at Woebegone Dunes Resort as the personal guests of Wayne and Kate Kennedy, owners of Shadow Structures Inc. and potential buyers of Woebegone Dunes Resort. They will be there to formally greet you and act as your hosts when you arrive."

"Is there anything else I should know about Emily?"

"Be sensitive to her emotional outbursts. There are times when you may have to walk on eggshells because she is prone to wheezing and feelings of being overwhelmed when things become unraveled."

Appropriately framing the assignment weighed heavily on the lieutenant's mind. He quietly, soberly, and deeply reflected on the events of the day, pondering the ramifications of the task. "I have one more question. Is the Procol Harum investigation attributable to the National Security Administration, or is it a covert black operation, hidden from public view and congressional oversight?"

"NSA is tasked with global monitoring and analysis of information for counterintelligence purposes to protect the nation from tampering by both domestic and foreign enemies. Permission to allow surreptitious cloak-and-dagger entries into structures for intelligence purposes automatically qualifies this exercise as black op. We never admit incidents involving illegal spying, forced entry, and undercover information gathering. We'll blame the Linguine Brothers Trucking, Excavation, and Storage Company if there is trouble."

Knowing that everything would be kept secret and conducted undercover prompted the lieutenant to remark, "Beware of exposing your secrets to Mother Nature and Father Time. The sea is boundless. If you expose your intimate thoughts to the ocean, don't blame the waves for revealing them to the rocky shoal."

13

BLACK OPERATIONS

Colonel Roberts explained, "Hundreds of black operations are conducted daily by military units, paramilitary organizations, private companies, and special groups. Key features of a black operation are that it is secret and is not attributable to the organization carrying it out. Black ops involve a significant degree of deception to conceal who is behind them and make it appear that some other entity is responsible. It'd be nice if all reporters were objective, but we know that is not the case. We're living in an era of opinion journalism. Be on the lookout for Renée Malarky, an aggressive local reporter seeking to sensationalize the news. The primary scapegoat will be the Linguine Brothers. If anything goes wrong, blame them."

"Sometimes, when answers are difficult to find, you need to change the question. As a starting point, I need a thorough briefing on the history of Gravestone Castle. Tell me more about the research the government conducted there, especially this guy Baum."

"Unfortunately, that information is classified—the public is unaware that a federal science research center existed. Nobody has ever heard of Gravestone Castle. The focus was on biological and entomological methods of warfare targeting the ruination of food crops and animal production. The destruction of human populations was not the main objective," Colonel Roberts explained vigilantly.

"Agents Orange, Blue, and White and some of the other rainbow herbicides and defoliants may have been used during the Vietnam War to destroy rice crops. Today, most of this type of research occurs in foreign countries lacking government restrictions and environmental laws—particularly in Africa.

"Gravestone Castle has thick stone walls, a multibuilding complex designed as a military fort. It is located in a mature forest to conceal the structures and hide the auspicious research activity. The lease extended during the Korean and Vietnam Wars, the Cold War, and again during the modern Middle East conflicts," the colonel added with the confidence of a federal prosecutor extracting a confession.

"I'm hoping you can learn firsthand the source of the beehives you discovered in Nigeria and any advances in entomological warfare, allegedly perpetrated by Professor Adam Baum."

"How was this research funded?"

"Like Faartz said, funding for covert scientific warfare research is often disguised as USAID university research grants or international aid intentionally unlinked from military budgets. University professors and scientists using this method of grant funding have operated clandestine science research laboratories for multiple decades," Roberts reconfirmed.

"Is there anything else you can tell me about Professor Baum?" the lieutenant asked. "I'm eager to read his biography."

Colonel Roberts paused to reflect before choosing his words carefully. "His identity and life story are confidential for obvious reasons. According to the public record, the company he created never officially existed. Officially, the activities he was involved with never happened. In reality, he led a secret paramilitary group specializing in covert black operations. The government paid for his military and intelligence activities in black budgets hidden from congressional leaders. He was the acclaimed leader of the wet operations branch specializing in assassinations. Black operations are secret, involving a significant degree of deception to appear that some other entity is responsible for fabricating plausible denials. Public disclosure of a dossier on Baum's military career would lead to a plethora of disastrous complaints, a toxic, politicized media vilifying, debasing, and destroying national leaders, and acts of retribution from world leaders."

Gaze cues exposed the lieutenant's moral compass, religious views, intuitive understanding, and ability to perceive the underlying truth. "To see the truth and discover reality, we need to avoid false conceptual images and misperceptions put forth by political elites that are perpetually misleading, biased, and inaccurate."

The colonel continued unabated. "Father Adam Baum is a taciturn loner and a recluse with an odd personality. He never married or was interested in anything other than his experiments with killer bees, herbicides, and poisonous plants. He has experience as a taxidermist and sculptor specializing in fiberglass resin statues. When the research center at Gravestone Castle closed, he accepted a modest government buyout and retired."

"To live at the Hermitage, wouldn't he have to be qualified as a priest?"

"The federal government forged a new social security card, birth certificate, and driver's license and falsified his biography to make him appear qualified as a priest. He was a military analyst and researcher, frequently engaged in undercover back-alley covert operations disguised as a priest. Acquaintances referred to him as the Padre. He gloated over his new secret identity and relished the idea of remaining anonymous within the confines of the Hermitage for the rest of his life. He gives the sign of the cross whenever he detects blasphemy, which happens pretty regularly at the Hermitage."

"Churches have always provided a safe harbor for felons, fugitives, runaways, illegal immigrants, and criminals hoping to avoid custody, jail, and arrest. Providing sanctuary has been one of their primary missions for over two thousand years," Dunning interjected.

"The Padre has pathological emotional incontinence. He has more fun chanting the Dominican rosary in the dark with multiple 'Hail Marys' than playing golf. What everyone needs to realize is once the fruit is rotten, it can never ripen again."

14

THE LEASE

"How did Father Feely gain control of Gravestone Castle?" the lieutenant asked.

"Feely started the Hermitage, somewhat by accident, with money donated by Bo-Bo Bigelow from Nigeria. According to the IRS, Bo-Bo uses the Hermitage to conceal the source of significant financial transactions and wash dirty money generated from the theft of natural resources."

The rest of the colonel's story went like this: Four years previously, Benedict Walker's spirits took a turn for the worse when the long-term lease to the federal government expired. Feeling sad and embarrassed, he gazed at the polished terrazzo floor with downcast eyes. His crestfallen expression was reminiscent of someone who had lost a beloved pet. He was downhearted and demoralized. He was upset with the loan officer for rejecting his application for a bridge loan to cover his short-term cash flow needs.

"The bank can't give you a loan because you have no credible experience managing a luxury hotel and restaurant. You haven't prepared a reasonable cost estimate, and you have no cash flow to pay off the loan. I suggest you temporarily lease the property to carry you over until you are financially prepared to open your hotel. Otherwise, your best bet is to secure a loan from a private lender," the loan officer candidly rebuffed.

Benedict Walker desperately needed to devise a new way to raise cash to keep creditors at bay. He pleaded in vain. "My son attended Lycée Jaccard, a private boys' school in Switzerland famous for its multilingual programs and cosmopolitan aura. They teach social graces, upper-class cultural rites, sports, and academics. When he graduates from the University of Lausanne, I plan to convert Gravestone Castle into a luxury hotel and restaurant specializing in resort living, weddings, honeymoons, and conventions. Gravestone Castle is a fabulous complex of buildings in an ideal location."

His pleas had fallen on deaf ears. Visibly disappointed and long-faced, Benedict Walker furrowed his brow, turned his back, and humbly walked out of the bank with his hat in his hands.

The loan officer immediately telephoned her boyfriend, Johnny Linguine. "I found the perfect opportunity for you. Gravestone Castle is exactly the type of property that your friend Father Feely is hoping to find—but it's much better."

Johnny hastily called Father Feely to arrange a meeting. "Are you still looking for a property suitable for a *hermitage*, a religious retreat where you can live in seclusion? I found the perfect place for you. I'm hoping we can work out a deal to rent part of the storage space."

Father Feely had already accumulated several million dollars in private investment accounts and a growing list of international business contacts. He owned a sizable number of valuable antiques. He had amassed a fortune by fraudulently selling over three million dollars in church real estate properties by converting them into a tavern, an abortion clinic, a liquor store, and an embryonic stem cell research laboratory.

"Gravestone Castle sounds perfect, and it's exactly the type of facility I was hoping to find. It's much more luxurious, secluded, and secure than I ever anticipated," Father Feely gushed excitedly.

Benedict Walker had wholly fallen for the cunning ruse, hook, line, and sinker. Converting Gravestone Castle into a religious hermitage was an appealing short-term solution. It would provide the cash flow he needed and save thousands of dollars in annual property and income taxes. The arrangement eliminated the need for a short-term bank loan and an excuse to discourage predatory real estate buyers. It was a win-win situation for all concerned parties.

Father Cellophane quickly became the public face of the organization. He was Clintonesque in stature and mannerisms, a dishonorable womanizer. "You never can tell what you're going to get when you troll through a trailer park with a hundred-dollar bill," he professed with an Arkansas accent and a sheepish grin.

Father Marcello impetuously filled out the forms seeking an unofficial ordination just one day before Father Feely and Benedict Walker signed the lease agreement. He was relaxed and easygoing, an Italian Casanova-style playboy, a former celebrity race car driver, and a world traveler. Alluring and charming in the presence of women of all ages, he refused to abstain from sexual relations and ignored a solemn set of promises committing to a vow of poverty and celibacy. His routine of gently massaging the nuns' legs to relieve tension and stiffness and soothe sore muscles and bruised egos became a cherished daily routine during afternoon naps. The nuns passively acquiesced to his demands based on the notion that "joy is the infallible sign of the presence of the Holy Spirit, and Father Marcello brings us great joy."

His skills as an art forger and a certified appraiser were highly lucrative. Deliberate fakes, misattributions, and poor restorations frequently introduced into the realm of the authentic brought some of the highest amounts paid. The monstrous sums of money at stake for a single expertly executed Old Master knockoff had the potential to finance a long, comfortable retirement. Forgeries were a tremendous incentive for a life of luxury and a comfortable lifestyle. If the authenticity of a painting was in doubt, it was valued the same as the genuine original.

Father Adam Baum referred to himself as the Padre, a sordid character of destiny. He was an extremely intelligent, high-functioning schizophrenic, a bingeing alcoholic with a seriously unsettling mental illness that occasionally frighteningly interfered with his ability to relate to others. The Padre clandestinely sold experimental agricultural chemicals and biological weapons, poison honey, and fiberglass sculptures on the black market. He was an unshriven survivor of a former life of unconfessed sins, deaths, and lawlessness that were unlikely to be absolved. His little blue "pain pills" were in high demand because they were far more effective than standard over-the-counter remedies for ED and other cold and flu symptoms.

Sister Olivia Seno Grande, an erotic young Italian woman, and Sister Mary Pompino, with the beautiful auburn hair, were huckleberry friends, small-town wanderers with a sun-drenched youth.

Sisters Lova and Lola Kurvig, recently arrived from a religious convent in Sweden, were polyandrous identical twins. They were attractive, seductive, and flirtatious, living a comfortable life of entitled ease without problems or worries.

"This is your apartment," Father Feely pointed out.

"I love the small balcony with the French glass doors and the view of the courtyard. The shower is very spacious—big enough for all three of us," Lova teased.

Her words and her ideas seduced Father Feely. The thought of two beautiful, youthful, naked women standing in a hot steamy shower triggered imaginative possibilities. Fantasizing about the twin sisters disrobing and soaping each other was a highly seductive flight of fancy. The pleasure he was experiencing in his imagination lit a bonfire of wondrous fantasies. The thought of kissing their soapy pendulous pear-shaped breasts, kneading and squeezing them how a pizza maker prepares dough, was intoxicating. What if Lola jumped excitedly into his arms and wrapped her legs around his waist cowgirl style? Hormonal tension released in a series of mind-blowing muscle spasms and vibrations at the crescendo peak, terminating in blissful happiness, stimulated his passions. Father Feely imagined himself stumbling out of the shower with shampoo bubbles on his head the way an exhausted marathon runner crosses the finish line.

"Welcome to the Hermitage at Gravestone Castle—the place where exotic dreams come true," he exclaimed feverishly with high expectations.

The motley crew of undisciplined men and women, commonly found in fantasy and science fiction novels, experienced all of the growing pains, struggles, and old-fashioned challenges of horny children coming of age. The odd, mismatched assortment of bunkmates didn't seem like they would work well together, but somehow they did. Combining multiple conflicting personalities into a cohesive and unified team was a daily challenge for Father Feely. He kept the group intact through grit and perseverance by providing leadership, direction, and stability. A modicum of peace was created by exchanging sordid bribes and unique favors involving shameful actions and motives, arousing moral distaste and disgrace.

Excessive surplus energy triggered systemic arousal with too much time on their hands. Horny men and women, wandering the hallways in the midafternoon seeking casual hookups, frequently engaged in flirty banter. Horniness triggered fantasies that ran wildly through their heads, causing spontaneous excitement that was seldom left unsatisfied. Searching for new positions became the latest rave in the spirit of inquiry and curiosity. Cravings for the thrill of an afternoon drunken dalliance and compulsive instant sexual gratification became the cultural norm. Romantic relationships with shifting boundaries were exceptionally bold and adventurous, creating a bubbling cauldron of spiritual feelings and emotions.

15

AVARICE

"*Multiple competing parties* covet the ownership of Gravestone Castle. All of the potential new owners are highly conflicted with strongly divergent views about the best use of the property. Competition and overbidding will be fierce if Gravestone Castle ever becomes available on the open market," Colonel Roberts predicted.

The lieutenant agreed. "A desire for money and possessions is prideful arrogance. Avarice is extreme greed for wealth and material gain, a wild longing for acquisition, status, and power, and an excessive covetous wish to be rich. An insatiable, voracious appetite for money plunges a person deep into the mire of this world with stinginess and a miserly, sinful desire to gain and hoard possessions. Is this what the Hermitage is all about?"

The lieutenant waxed philosophical with an uncanny understanding of human nature. "There are many facets to an investigation of this type. Detective work is about understanding the influences of player behavior, a complex, reflective, and impulsive process. Gamesmanship becomes all about gaining a resource, eliminating another player, or moving up on a victory point rack. The higher the value, the more an individual is willing to risk. The stronger the motive, the greater the reason for doing something hidden and not obvious. The higher the stakes, the more likely competitors are to engage in deceitfulness, cheating, and immoral behavior."

"There are other players you need to know about," the colonel continued. "Jack Daniels has his eyes on Gravestone as the ideal location for the Royal Enouement Society headquarters. Regrettably, Father Feely is preventing him from acquiring the property. Wayne and Kate Kennedy are equally excited about the possibility of turning the castle into their private manor and developing a luxury motor coach RV resort on the remaining property. Bo-Bo Bigelow is the greatest threat of all. He wants to convert Gravestone Castle into a playboy mansion and develop a casino on the remaining property. When he makes up his mind, he is tough to mollify."

The colonel was damn certain about a future collapse of the Hermitage. "No organization can remain financially solvent without a reliably consistent source of income. Selling indulgences, receiving charitable donations, and holding art auctions aren't enough. Someone will eventually cut their tent strings. Even if they do have enough money, religious institutions of this type eventually collapse due to bitter internal feuds, struggles marked by mutually destructive behavior. Father Adam Baum is a good example. He is known to be an awkward loner and social outcast. He is certain to flounder helplessly and cause conflict. His poor interpersonal, social, and communication skills and annoying sarcasm are certain to irritate others and increase stress and anxiety. These are the things I intend for you to find out as the focus of the Procol Harum investigation."

Dunning's imagination painted vivid images of colorful people, unconventional behavior, and unpredictable events.

"Bo-Bo Bigelow is an intimidating figure with an assertive, booming voice that leaves Father Feely feeling frightened into submission. Bo-Bo's hostile physical posturing, ridiculing, malicious bullying, threats of bodily harm, and verbal insults make it very difficult for Feely. There is little he can do other than comply. Father Feely has remained loyal to Bo-Bo for many years, and Bo-Bo has made him a millionaire as a result. If Bo-Bo gave the order, Father Feely would probably set a church on fire and commit other criminal acts. Bo-Bo never follows the rules. His glowering countenance, a sullen, brooding look of annoyance, and emotional manipulation constitute legal harassment on the judicial level of fraud and perjury. His personality is like a menacing hurricane posing a significant threat to entire communities."

But there were things that Roberts didn't know, such as how Bigelow's request to acquire Gravestone Castle caused considerable angst. Father Feely raised sufficient nerve with the highest level of initiative and courage he could muster. "I discussed your proposal with Benedict Walker; he has no intention of selling to you or anyone else."

Bo-Bo was filled with rage, exasperated by Father Feely's response and infuriated with his inability to complete the sale. "Snuff him out like a candle . . . whack him," he rejoined with a menacing expression as a harbinger of impending doom, deadly serious about his intent.

Father Feely discussed Bo-Bo's hit order with Father Adam Baum before deciding on a course of action. The Padre reacted as if his thoughts had been premeditated, calculated, and rehearsed. "Benedict Walker is allergic to peanuts, and it would be a shame if he died from accidental anaphylaxis. A fatal condition in which the victim has trouble breathing because of constricted airways, increased pulse rate, and a sudden and drastic drop in blood pressure, followed by death. Murder is an unpleasant and vile task. Give Johnny Linguine a call. He's the leader of a small mafia group engaged in smuggling, racketeering, and trafficking."

Johnny Linguine was an exciting choice. A flatulent, obese middle-aged man who was a seasoned bullshitter and could tell a story in three different ways and draw tears. Johnny was drunk the day his old troubadour father got out of prison. His mother was a topless bartender with too many secrets up her sleeve. He responded affirmatively, without hesitation. "Professional hitman Billy 'Big Ears' Bellini from Kenosha has made a lot of hits for us. He can handle this matter discretely in a way that will make Benedict Walker's demise appear to be an accident. He'll ensure that no respiratory technicians show up to help the patient breathe before he goes into cardiac arrest. He's your man."

16

POISON CAKE

Benedict Walker followed the same daily routine of taking care of the grounds, janitorial duties, and property maintenance at the Hermitage for more than four years. The lease agreement with Father Feely and his band of priests was a perfect arrangement. He admired the hermitic, self-abnegating, and ascetic lifestyle afforded by the Hermitage. He had no reason to doubt the motives or sincerity of his clientele.

Life at the Hermitage was about cultivating sacred idleness and enlightened curiosity and tinkering with leisure pursuits. There were no cubicles, time commitments, or chores. Life seemed pleasurable and uncomplicated, free from the demands of duty, obligation, and daily tasks. "Leisure time properly spent is magical. Nobody at the Hermitage toils at a lackluster job. When we pursue the things of our choosing, time feels vast. Our activities provide amusement, entertainment, and pleasure, leaving us feeling refreshed rather than worn out," Father Feely had once explained to Walker.

During a routine inspection of the gas water heaters in the utility room, Sister Olivia Seno Grande roguishly opened her blouse, exposing her ample cleavage. She enticed Benedict Walker into the castle by twirling around and lifting the back of her skirt, exposing her red panties, and wiggling her fanny seductively.

"Follow me," she conveyed enticingly with a flirtatious flip of her long silky hair. Benedict was fascinated by her manipulative moves and kittenish charms. Aware that she was flaunting her robust figure for his benefit, he couldn't resist the overpowering appeal and luscious temptation. He shamefully succumbed to feelings of arousal and impulsive desire. Ignoring his guilt, he took the bait and followed her into the kitchen.

"Surprise!" Everyone yelled from behind the kitchen door.

Benedict staggered sideways with a startled look as the entire group burst into song: "Happy birthday to you, happy birthday, dear Benedict, happy birthday to you." Lova and Lola Kurvig from Sweden planted kisses on both his cheeks.

"Living at Gravestone Castle has been a glorious experience for all of us. Please accept these gifts and birthday cake as tokens of our appreciation for the incredible hospitality that you have provided us here," Father Cellophane feigned deceitfully. Gifts and cards included a bottle of shampoo from Lady Vanessa, a case of Italian noodles from Johnny Linguine, a box of Chrome Soft Callaway golf balls from a secret admirer, a bag of Werther's caramels from the priests, and a bottle of Woodford Reserve Kentucky Derby bourbon from the four nuns.

Sister Olivia distributed generous helpings of birthday cake and champagne glasses filled to the brim. Benedict graciously accepted many handshakes, congratulations, and pats on the back from everyone in attendance.

Father Adam Baum was profoundly immoral and wicked, reminding outsiders of someone willing to steal the Mona Lisa and get them involved in a Ponzi scheme. The villainous grin on his face betrayed all innocence and exposed his evil predatory nature. "Piety is a matter of the heart, and any outward expression without it is an empty gesture," the self-proclaimed Padre priggishly stated with an annoying moralistic attitude.

Feelings of lightheadedness and nausea suddenly overcame Benedict Walker. His meteoric heartbeat, rapid physical deterioration, and precipitating panicky behavior caused him to become disoriented, lose balance, and stumble on the steps. Constriction of the bronchioles in his lungs began to cause bronchospasm, sneezing, throat swelling, asthma, and shortness of breath. Itchiness of his skin and swelling of the face, followed by the eruption of eczema and stinging red blotches of hives, itchy burning bumps, and patches of migrating skin rash, quickly became unbearable. He politely excused himself and slipped out the back door.

Billy "Big Ears" Bellini, a longhaired tattoo-covered ex-con, lurked in the shadows with the stealth of a cat quietly watching its wounded prey ensnared in a trap. He had ordered two birthday cakes made with butter crème frosting and peanut flour—one for Benedict Walker's birthday and another for Angelina, his girlfriend.

Benedict hastened back to his apartment. He fumbled for his epinephrine auto-injecting syringe and injected the liquid contents into a vein in his left arm to counteract the severe allergic reaction. A hypersensitivity reaction of the immune system unexpectedly soared, radically increasing extreme abdominal pain, a catastrophic drop in blood pressure, vomiting, diarrhea, and cardiac arrest. Terminal bronchial secretions accumulating in the throat and upper chest, known colloquially as the death rattle, occurred shortly before Benedict's last breath.

The body was lying on the floor with a horrid grimace frozen on its face. The waxy gray-blue death mask was lamentable evidence of intense suffering and heinous pain. The lethal injection of peanut oil rushed into his bloodstream precipitated his brutal execution. Big Ears Bellini removed the discharged syringe of peanut oil from the victim's cold dead hand. He replaced it with the original syringe filled with life-saving epinephrine liquid.

According to Coroner Slaughter, the cause of death was accidental anaphylaxis, a severe allergic reaction to peanuts. "Benedict Walker had an allergic reaction to his birthday cake made with peanut flour. The onslaught of death was very rapid."

The chocolate cake with buttercream frosting from Holy Baloney bakery in Milwaukee, made with peanut flour, had a delicious flavor with a wonderful aroma, lingering taste, and overall richness. "I highly recommend the bakery," Father Baum declared to Deputy Sheriff Bud Light while displaying the sign of the cross.

Joey Linguine pressed the fingers and thumb of his right hand together, raised his hand to his lips, kissed the tips of his fingers, and joyfully tossed his fingers and thumb into the air, signifying the Italian gesture for *delicious*. "Delizioso! You must try it."

Baum had a toothy, graceless smile as big as a slice of watermelon. He looked like a caricature of an overly friendly drunk with learning disabilities; it was the first time anyone had ever seen him smile. He handed the deputy the last remaining slice of birthday cake and placed the remaining dishes in the dishwasher. Deputy Sheriff Bud Light licked his plate clean. It never dawned on him that he was eating the last crumb of evidence in a murder case.

Father Feely hastily summoned his lawyer to take advantage of the situation as prearranged. The two men spent the next twenty-four hours at the county courthouse intensely filling out legal forms, forging documents, clearing liens, and paying property taxes. The false property deed, identification cards, and legal certificates were forgeries designed to deceive. The serious offense they committed was punishable by the federal government as a felony in all fifty states. However, due to the complexity of such criminal cases, they were difficult for a prosecutor to prove in court. According to the false documents, Father Feely became the sole heir of Gravestone Castle upon the death of Benedict Walker.

Judge Geri Attrick declared the lease agreement, will, and real estate contract valid documents. She determined that probate court was unnecessary because no legal challenges were pending, whereby Benedict's needed to be verified.

Afterward, Father Feely's lawyer tossed a roll of hundred-dollar bills and two tickets for an all-expenses-paid world cruise into the judge's briefcase. "Thanks, good job."

Four years of sheer bliss had passed quickly at Gravestone Castle following the death of Benedict Walker. Nobody had challenged the judge's ruling or questioned the devil-may-care lifestyle of the Hermitage members living a luxurious and carefree existence in isolated seclusion. Vanity and complacency quickly displaced initial anxieties and lingering worries without any substantial care or wants to distract them. The web of connections between the Hermitage, Woebegone Dunes Resort, Ebony LLC, and the mafia became increasingly entangled through odious investments and confidential exchanges of luxury goods.

"As long as we have money to pay, they let us have our way. The best in the house is none too good for the easy, carefree life of Reilly," a gloating Father Feely recited with a satisfied tone of self-congratulation.

17

THE INVESTIGATION BEGINS

"*Thank you for* accepting my request to investigate the Hermitage in Wisconsin," Colonel Roberts offered in appreciation to Lieutenant Baron Dunning. "Meet me at Andrews Air Force Base at twenty-one hundred hours. I'll have a charter plane waiting to fly you and your new assistant, Emily, to Lawrence J. Timmerman Airport in Milwaukee," he directed posthaste.

That evening, Lieutenant Dunning arrived ten minutes early in a black chauffeur-driven limousine. Keen-witted, virile, iron-willed, and intelligent, he was constantly keyed up and ready for action. He was affectionately known as "the Velvet Steamroller" among his subordinates for his compelling powers of persuasion and vigorous pursuit of justice. He never failed to live up to his reputation as a man of action, ever vigilant in a quest for verity as a world-class detective. His fashionable appearance, elegant manners, and education were the result of being the son of a wealthy English hedge fund manager. He grew up in polite society in the Hamptons, a summer destination for affluent New York City residents. His trademarks included a dark trench coat, black leather gloves, long dark hair, broad shoulders, size fourteen shoes, and a Full Bent Billiard smoking pipe that he kept with him at all times. His refined palate and affinity for haute cuisine, characterized by elaborate preparations, high-quality table settings, and aesthetically balanced meals, were legendary.

"This is Emily, your assistant for this investigation," Roberts explained at the airport. "She will be accompanying you to Woebegone Dunes Resort. I'm sure you will find her entirely adequate when it comes to her investigative skills and analytical mind."

Emily wore tight black leather slacks with designer boots, a fitted black leather jacket that showed off her thin waist, leather gloves, and a colorful Laurel Burch silk scarf. On her shoulder, she carried a large cross-body bag made of aniline leather from Tuscany, Italy, with a strap pressing between her boobs. Her well-fitting clothes accentuated her curves in all the right places, and her high heels made her legs look longer and more attractive. She wore her hair pinned up in a bun, accented by a lovely pair of designer reading glasses. The way she carried herself demonstrated a high level of self-confidence with an air of mysteriousness, an incredibly desirable trait, the lieutenant thought. He could tell from how she presented herself—her bearing, attitude, and posture— that she was well educated and of high stature.

"Pleased to meet you, Emily." The lieutenant smiled while concealing his approval of her outward appearance. His first impressions were entirely positive, making his expectations extremely high.

Emily smiled. "Do you enjoy flying?"

"The idea of falling from the sky in a pressurized flaming aluminum container arouses me more than a colonoscopy, if that's what you mean."

The colonel paraphrased his final remarks to the investigative team. "The federal government faces a dilemma: Should we feign ignorance and insist that biological warfare doesn't exist and allow it to continue in secret if the results are favorable to our national interests? Or should we put a stop to the unethical practice for moral reasons?"

He promptly provided the answer to his question. "A continuing supply of rare-earth minerals like tantalum is our nation's highest priority. Cobalt is another essential element used in car batteries. More than seventy percent of the world's cobalt supply comes from the Congo, largely under the control of the Chinese. To obtain it, violent clashes, fatal accidents, child labor, human rights violations, environmental degradation, and corruption prevail. The federal government will never put Bo-Bo Bigelow out of commission. He satisfies a significant portion of our country's critical needs for essential rare-earth minerals. That's why our leaders have no desire to disrupt the political system of these countries, regardless of the number of atrocities committed."

Colonel Roberts placed his left hand on the lieutenant's broad shoulder and asked point-blank, "Are you sure you're the right man for this job?"

The lieutenant had perseverance, motivation, and problem-solving skills, and he eagerly accepted without reservations. "I wholeheartedly accept the challenge unconditionally. Nothing is holding Emily and me back or preventing us from assessing the current state of affairs. If there is a breakthrough assessment, we will initiate a case study to gather evidence and orchestrate a response."

With that, Emily and Dunning thanked Colonel Roberts for the assignment before boarding the chartered military aircraft, settling into their gray leather seats, and buckling their seatbelts with eager anticipation.

"What is your philosophy about fighting crime?" Emily immediately asked.

"The most difficult type of criminal offense to track is the one that has no motive," Lieutenant Dunning professed. "The detective's steadfast contribution to crime-fighting seems most worthy when the bad guy is fiendishly clever, a criminal mastermind, dangerous, and resourceful in every way. International finance, monetary interactions, and the manipulation of currency exchange rates arouse my curiosity. Still, what interests me the most is international trickery, deception by artifice or stratagem to conceal, escape, and avoid detection by the law. In this case, tracing the flow of Nigerian oil, rare-earth minerals, beehives, and money will certainly provide a ragbag of curiosities."

Emily nodded in agreement. "The Hermitage seems complicated—nothing seems right about it. It's very suspicious that persons living a monistic lifestyle can afford such lavish accommodations. I have the same concerns about the Royal Enouement Society. What is the mission of the club? What kinds of activities do they sponsor? Why do members insist on privacy? What is the best way to approach an organization with multiple players?"

"My philosophy is that there is always a mastermind behind criminal operations who creates the blueprints for crimes committed. Most operations quickly fail when you expose the leader and take the kingpin out of the loop. Ultimately, there is little difference in temperament between thugs who pickpocket other people's wallets and white-collar accountants who steal people's retirement savings. Avoiding danger is no safer for criminals in the long run than outright exposure. The fearful are caught just as often as the bold. The tragedy of life for the criminal mind is not rooted in failures but rather in complacency. Success leads to vanity, and that is what eventually causes criminals to expose themselves through unnecessary risks," the lieutenant explained.

"And who are the kingpin and antagonist?"

"Bo-Bo Bigelow from Nigeria is the obvious snake in the grass, an international playboy who is treacherous. Bo-Bo loaned Jack Daniels the money to build Woebegone Dunes Resort and gifted Father Feely the money to acquire the Hermitage at Gravestone Castle. Without Bo-Bo, there wouldn't be a demand for biological weapons. Father Feely is a secondary malfeasant at the source of problems yet to be defined. Without his cooperation and financial advice, Bo-Bo's entire international operation would collapse overnight."

18

SPECIAL FRIENDS

Later in the flight, Emily said, "I'm looking forward to a return to my roots. I have many fond memories of my early years in Milwaukee. Do you know anybody living there?"

"I had a notable encounter with a journalist from Wisconsin when I was in Nigeria recently," the lieutenant guardedly acknowledged without divulging if the contact had been a man or a woman. "We hope to see each other again this week if time allows."

After a long pause, he was forthcoming with a more truthful answer. "She's an international explorer, researcher, and writer for *National Geographic*. Her name is Crystal Glass. She's a graduate of the University of Wisconsin. The twinkle in her eyes and her authentic smile are her logos. She is very outgoing, attractive, and enchanting. There is something irresistible about her that makes her unique. She makes me feel like I hit an ice patch in winter. When I stand next to her, I feel off-balance and debilitated yet energized."

"She sounds enchanting and alluring. She must have put you under a spell because you seem moonstruck. But feminine intuition suggests you're not telling me everything," Emily accused.

The lieutenant continued waxing eloquently about Crystal's softness, grace, and charm as the epitomes of femininity. "She is as velvety as Hennessy whiskey, as sweet as Riesling wine, and as warm as a Wisconsin brandy old-fashioned in December. Maybe you're right—I'm stoned on her love."

"Perhaps your fondness for Crystal Glass is your motive for accepting this assignment in Wisconsin."

"Crystal's next assignment is an article on the Basilica of the National Shrine of Mary at Holy Hill in Erin, Wisconsin."

"The basilica is a heavenly place of special significance and worthy of religious pilgrimages. Visitors often remark about the serenity they find there. Tourists come because they are curious, and they leave feeling touched by something spiritual."

"I suggested she expand the article to include the Hermitage at Gravestone Castle as a sneaky, undercover way to gain insights into Father Feely and his companions. She agreed that it was appropriate to disclose something about the lives of individual priests who profess a vow of poverty, obedience, and chastity. Living the vocation of a consecrated life of religious contemplation is unique. The priests at the Hermitage claim to have formed a religious congregation with distinctive traditions as they strive to live a spiritual life of communion in goodness and righteousness. Referring to himself as the parochial vicar, Father Cellophane is the self-titled spokesperson for the Hermitage. There are no separate rules regarding celibacy for vicars. His duties include keeping parish accounts, chairing meetings, and holding fundraising events. Father Cellophane made Crystal promise to keep the location of Gravestone Castle secret and encourage the public to donate money to preserve the sanctity of the Hermitage."

The lieutenant continued to reflect on current institutional issues. "Religion has been plagued by increasing hypocrisy in recent years. People have been leaving organized religion in droves. There have been way too many public scandals. Too many priests preach about honesty but live a lie. Tolerance wears a bit thin when religious dogma is stripped of the caveats and nuances that more polished ecclesiastical dignitaries tend to employ. Too often in the corridors of power, a blind eye is turned to what goes on in private. When the bishop fathers a love-child, the institution throws up its hands in horror. 'We never even suspected,' they say. 'How could he have misled us so?'"

"Is Crystal Glass your special sweetheart? Your description leads me to believe that you perceive her as a valued treasure that you hope won't shipwreck. The idea of seeing her again seems to be dominating your thoughts. She subconsciously makes you smile."

The lieutenant seemed discombobulated whenever Emily mentioned her name. Allowing his emotions to be transparent left him feeling outwardly disconcerted and embarrassed. "She has a vital spirit and an eager mind. She has the alluring scent of a wild rose with a tidal pull on me. She holds the possibility of high adventure with certain wonders along the way."

"Feminine mystique is a problem with no name. A woman may forget what you said and what you did. Despite that, she will never forget how you made her feel," Emily tutored him, though she recognized feelings of covetousness rising to the surface.

"What about you? Do you have any special friends living in Wisconsin?"

"I'm a Wisconsin girl at heart. I graduated magna cum laude from Dominican High School in Whitefish Bay in North Milwaukee, an academic degree earned with great distinction. I lived on Danbury Lane one block from Lake Drive."

"Congratulations. The consumption of beer and brandy in Milwaukee is the highest in the nation—that's all I know. Get some sleep. It's going to be a long night," the lieutenant warned over the sound of the jet engines.

Emily knew the routine. She placed her chair in the full recliner position and removed a sleep mask of lightweight, breathable cotton, along with soft foam earplugs, from her carry pouch as a prelude for reaching the ultimate state of sleep.

19

ROGUE PRIEST

The droning hum and vibrations of the airplane engines relaxed the Lieutenant. He unlocked his black leather briefcase and removed a classified report from the Nigerian British Embassy: "Father Feely: The Chronology of a Rogue Priest" by British Agent Kingsley. The information was a thorough exposé of Father Feely's early life and work accomplishments while assigned to a religious mission in Nigeria. The young, inexperienced priest accomplished a remarkable number of projects. He built two churches and gave thousands of dollars in donations to the Vatican. He was highly influential in the hosting of the pope during his visit to Nigeria. Father Feely raised more money for charity in two years than most cardinals achieved in a lifetime.

"This is truly amazing. A harmless priest living an ascetic lifestyle in a remote hermitage in rural Wisconsin connected with an African cartel, defrauding the Nigerian government of millions of dollars in oil revenues," Dunning stated.

The report contained numerous dates and events: "During the twenty-four months Father Feely served with distinction as a visiting missionary in Nigeria, he made frequent trips to Europe, including Switzerland, England, Spain, France, and Italy. Passport records verify the dates and times of each trip. The justification for these expensive excursions and how he paid for them is the primary subject of this report."

Bo-Bo Bigelow hired Father Feely when he arrived in Africa. He directed Feely to fly to London to form Ebony LLC. This fateful event altered his destiny as significantly as winning the lottery. Father Feely presented a respectable and honest corporate image, concealing ownership and the source of the illegitimate funds. Millions of dollars from embezzled Nigerian oil sales quickly flowed into Ebony LLC bank accounts to purchase expensive real estate and luxury items. Bo-Bo's income increased twofold several years later. In exchange for a portion of the rare-earth minerals from Chinese mines in Africa, he agreed to subdue Muslim terrorists interfering with their operations. Bo-Bo and two of his partners purchased luxurious country estates in France with the help of Chloe Crouton and her second husband, Philippe Philoppe, the inventor of beach sandals. Bo-Bo drives a Lava Orange Porsche 911 Carrera 4S Cabriolet and has a large luxury yacht named *Ebony*.

Father Feely serves as a faithful docent, financial adviser, and figurehead for Ebony LLC. He is the chief financial officer responsible for purchasing real estate and expensive luxury items, including yachts and fine automobiles, and overseeing bank transfers.

Every year, large sums of money are transferred into Father Feely's International Heritage Endowment Fund, classified as a religious charity for tax purposes, in exchange for his services. Feely contributes to the Vatican, the Royal Enouement Society, orphanages, and other favorite charities every year. His contributions make the fund appear legitimate and avoid attracting the attention of the IRS.

The African experience was a significant turning point in Father Feely's life. But he has always been tight-lipped about his secretive life of luxury in the newly formed religious Hermitage founded with money given to him by Bo-Bo Bigelow.

After reading, the lieutenant locked his briefcase, crossed his legs, folded his arms, and closed his eyes to ponder what he had learned. He was abruptly awakened several hours later by the screeching sound of rubber tires hitting the concrete tarmac, with the airplane comfortably cruising to a stop at the end of the runway in Milwaukee.

He was eager to see the world-famous Whistling Straits golf resort sculpted into two miles of the Lake Michigan shoreline. Replicating the freshness of Ireland, it was known for multiple courses of dynamic contrast and world-class prestige defined by rugged and windswept terrain.

20

WHISTLING STRAITS

"Whistling Straits is home to major championships and the Ryder Cup," Emily reminded the lieutenant. "We should be there in time for lunch."

She was eager to sit behind the wheel of the atomic silver Lexus RX350 SUV with stratus gray leather seats parked beside the private airplane hangar. "There are numerous tourist activities taking place in Milwaukee over the next two weeks during Summerfest. Perhaps we'll be able to return for a day or two, if time allows," she expressed optimistically.

Now that he was in Wisconsin and one step closer to meeting with Crystal, the lieutenant became overly distracted. His mind was blank, and the relaxed sentimentality visible in his smile was out of character. The idea of seeing Crystal again excited his senses and dominated his consciousness. She was so delightfully chaotic, a mind-blowing feminine tease. She was a beautiful, mysterious, seductive femme fatale whose charms had ensnared him, an archetype of literature, film, and art. He was caught in an emotional whirlpool, daydreaming of her sweet little tortures. The idea of loving her seemed a splendid adventure.

Dunning and Emily enjoyed a leisurely detour along Lake Drive, with Emily acting as the tour guide. The continuous chain of mansions linking Milwaukee, Shorewood, Whitefish Bay, Fox Point, and Brown

Deer enhanced the experience. The Kohler Design Center, featuring exotic bathroom products, was very impressive. The luxurious, lavishly appointed, automatic electric toilets were particularly palatial. The Industry in Action guided factory tour ended with an inspection of the five-star American Club resort and a driving tour of the Harbor Center Marina in Sheboygan.

They arrived at Whistling Straits, perfect for a classic brunch beside the grand fireplace. The lieutenant ordered the fish and chips platter with a premium golden bottom-fermented lager beer conditioned at low temperatures. Emily relished a plate of mini-muffins composed of apricots, dates, ginger, and other secret ingredients as a prologue to lunch, accompanied by a Bellini cocktail of sparkling wine, lemon juice, and peach purée served in a champagne glass.

"Known for its good food and breathtaking views, Whistling Straits Restaurant has been honored with *Wine Spectator* magazine's Award of Excellence since 2001," the waitress informed them.

"I can see why. These muffins are delectable."

"The friendliness of the people is impressive. The facilities and quality of service, the cleanliness of the environment, and the commitment to excellence are of exceptionally high quality," the lieutenant remarked optimistically. "Our next stop is Woebegone Dunes Resort. I wonder how the two resorts compare? It's highly suspicious that none of the employees at Whistling Straits will admit to knowing anything about Woebegone Dunes Resort."

Emily exhibited high alertness. She was eagerly anticipating the adventuresome nature of the assignment, along with the opportunity to be mentored by a true professional and learn something she might not have had the chance to learn independently. "Everything about this assignment is difficult to understand and impossible to explain. The true identities and nature of the players involved are a mystery. There's something strange and unknown about people who live in a Hermitage and never come outside."

"Keep your eyes and ears peeled for anything unusual. Let me know if you overhear anything useful about the Royal Enouement Society, the secret organization headquartered at Woebegone Dunes Resort. It's one of the most obscure organizations on the planet, and members have the habit of discretion. Everything about them seems designed to be hidden and unexplained to elude observation and detection. Business is conducted in secret, remote from the public," Dunning reminded her.

"What's the purpose of the club? How long has it been in existence?" she asked.

"Nobody seems to know. It's a private organization veiled in allegory and illustrated by symbols like the Freemasons, Skull and Bones, Illuminati, Priory of Sion, and Bohemian Club. Membership is by invitation only. The purpose and function of the organization are unknown to outsiders. The members' names and functions are revealed only to the initiated.

"Hertz Von Rental the Third from Germany is another person the Colonel told me about. Hertz and Jay Walker were roommates at Lycée Jaccard High School in Switzerland. Hertz and Father Adam Baum share a passion for studying African killer bees. Adam Baum was caught illegally entering East Germany during the Cold War. He flooded a farmer's field known to contain land mines. After the water froze, he crawled across the icy surface during the night. His goal was to retrieve a highly classified document hidden in an abandoned subway tunnel in East Berlin. Soldiers followed his tracks in the snow and found him hiding in a forest. They broke a few ribs and dumped him back in West Berlin. When the Berlin wall fell, Father Adam Baum informed Hertz, and with Jay's help, they retrieved the records. Jay was wounded by gunfire but they escaped. The document describes chemical and biological weapons developed by the Nazis during World War Two. Millions of malaria-infected mosquitoes used as biological weapons exposed thousands of prisoners in concentration camps to lethal doses of the plague, cancer-causing viruses, and many more. German scientists living in a moral collapse worldwide were prosecuted, assassinated, or jailed following disclosure of the secret information."

Emily was amazed. "The adventure reminds me of a glittering spy-hall-of-fame movie. I would love to hear Jay's version of the events."

21

THE GERMAN

Jay Walker greeted his German friend Hertz Von Rental III from Germany at the airport with a Cheshire-cat-like smile and a heartwarming chamber-of-commerce bear hug. They were both looking forward to the trendy Summerfest activities in Milwaukee.

"It's great to see you again."

"Likewise. We have a lot of catching up to do."

The drive along the Milwaukee lakefront passed quickly as the topic of conversation ebbed and flowed back and forth between vintage school years together at Lycée Jaccard and current events. "Winning the high school hockey championship in Zermatt was exciting. The national rowing championship win over the elite students from Le Rosey boarding school on Lac Léman was especially gratifying," Jay recalled.

"The clandestine trip we took to Berlin to uncover Nazi World War Two chemical and biological warfare secrets changed my life. We dodged a lethal bullet—except for the small-arms fire that penetrated my calf muscle. My leg is weak but the scar is gone. I was placed under intense government surveillance and never told the truth to anyone about the military tribunal. The whole experience is outside the normal understanding of conventional criminal and civil proceedings. We were very fortunate that we didn't do hard labor in a Russian prison camp in Siberia. Talking about our escape is strictly *verboten*," Hertz stated.

Jay agreed. "I never talk about it either. Let's talk about our fondness for young French-speaking Swiss girls from Romandie, particularly the good skiers," he teased. "There will be plenty of beer-drinking, polka-dancing Wisconsin girls, who consider fun a core value, hanging out at the lakefront during Summerfest this week."

The men checked into the elegant Pfister Hotel and sat down to eat breakfast at the famous Pfister Café. Jay became emotionally distraught when Hertz asked about his summer job at Woebegone Dunes Resort. He slammed his fist down on the linen table cloth in anger, accidentally spilling his glass of water on his pants.

"I'm mad as hell about what happened to my father and family estate." Jay fumed at the arrogance of the priests that he accused of nefariously stealing his father's property. "What happened wasn't legal or ethical. I don't even know for certain if my father died of accidental causes or if someone intentionally poisoned him."

Hertz was unsettled by what Jay was telling him.

"I'd like to wring some son-of-a-bitch's neck. When my father Benedict died, Father Feely claimed to be the sole beneficiary—bullshit. I think it's a fraud. Father Feely and his lawyer must have forged my father's signature on a fake will. The only thing my father ever talked to me about was converting Gravestone Castle into a high-quality luxury resort hotel and restaurant. Father Feely said my father agreed to sell the property for a fraction of the appraised value. That's the reason Dad sent me to École hôtelière de Lausanne in Switzerland in the first place to get a degree in hotel and restaurant administration. I was planning to offer you a job at Gravestone Castle Hotel after graduation," he stammered, openly seething over the injustice and abrupt denial of an exceptional lifetime opportunity.

The more Jay talked, the more visibly agitated he became. "Four highly questionable dapper young men with stylish haircuts wearing formal business suits claiming to be priests appeared from nowhere. Four gorgeous, flirty women with beautiful faces, fit bodies, and expensive fashion choices, claiming to be nuns, joined them. The women look like contestants in a beauty pageant. The motley collection of infidels declared my family home to be a place of holy religious seclusion. I assume my father never told me about the Hermitage because he thought of them as temporary renters. The way he died is murky, and the unexplained appearance of the priests at the Hermitage is highly suspicious," Jay unloaded tempestuously.

"They confiscated my personal property and family heirlooms. The only thing the priests couldn't take away from me was the chalet on the adjacent farm. The owner was a widower from Germany who worked with my father at Gravestone Quarry. I inherited the property when he died. That's where I live now."

"You never appreciate what you have until it's gone. Toilet paper is a good example," Hertz suggested lightly.

Jay paused to take a deep breath, making an effort to act sensibly, bear down, and control his emotions. "I'm sorry for the emotional outburst exposing all my troubles and frustrations. The situation stinks, and there is nothing I can do about it."

Pausing to regain his composure, he intentionally changed the subject. "Tell me about your degree in applied entomology from the University of Hohenheim, Germany."

"Lithium chloride is the best way to kill menacing parasites that shorten the lifespan of honeybees. My research focused on diagnosing the effects of lithium chloride on honeybees to determine if the compound negatively affects their honey. Some of my studies took place in Africa, where parasites are especially harmful."

"That's interesting because Father Feely, the head priest at the Hermitage, and Father Adam Baum, the oldest priest there, both spent time in Africa. Father Baum is a former scientist who worked in covert operations. Rumors persist that he perfected using killer bees to assassinate foreign enemies in third-world countries. If any of his scientific breakthroughs were made public, it would cause mass protests, hysteria, and global political controversies."

Jay was eager to move on. "Milwaukee has numerous attractions, including the Lakefront and harbor marina, the art museum, war memorial, Pabst Mansion, Marquette University, the Mitchell Park Conservatory Domes, and the Harley Davidson Motorcycle Museum. Dinner at Mader's famous German restaurant will be particularly refreshing. Tomorrow morning, we'll head up to Gravestone Castle, where I grew up, and visit Woebegone Dunes Golf Resort, where I work."

"Playing tourist with you today has been enjoyable," Hertz remarked at the end of the day.

"Before heading back to our hotel, I would like to stop for a brandy Manhattan cocktail at the SafeHouse Restaurant. There is wall-to-wall spy memorabilia for those enamored with a life of espionage," Jay explained on the way.

After Jay provided the coded password, they entered the spy-themed restaurant through a private rear entrance in a darkened alley adjacent to The Newsroom Pub. Hertz was intrigued by the old black-and-white photographs and descriptions of events leading up to the collapse of Nazi Germany and the Berlin Wall, the life-saving airlift, and various Cold War incidents after the war. "These photos are a vivid reminder of the trouble we got ourselves into—experiences that we have agreed to never talk about."

A tall, muscular man was seated at an unlighted corner table. Bruno Greco was a professional thief. He dressed, talked, and acted so as not to attract attention or arouse suspicion. Stealing was an addiction. He vigilantly stayed on the lookout for small, high-value items for which there was an accessible resale market. He never resisted the impulse to steal other people's money and valuables with no additional motivation than the feckless thrill of it. He was intrigued when he overheard Hertz telling Jay that he always paid with cash. He observed as Hertz removed his black fitted European-cut blazer and hung it on the back of his chair before darting into the restroom. Bruno acted with the stealth of a cat burglar, removing the black blazer from the chair and seamlessly slinking out the back door. He heisted an iPhone, a passport, and a wallet filled with one-hundred-dollar bills before he randomly tossed the blazer into a dumpster and disappeared into the shadows.

When Hertz returned to his seat, he was startled to discover that his most valuable possessions were missing. "My identification, money, passport, and iPhone are gone. Call the police."

Hertz was traumatized. He felt guilty being the victim of a crime, knowing that he could have prevented it. It was depressing and sad to begin a vacation this way. He was eager to have the situation resolved, but at least he was happy to be reunited with Jay Walker.

22

SYSTEMATIC EXAMINATION

Emily was eager to get started on the investigation. She had already begun making observations, gathering facts, preparing data analysis, forming a hypothesis, and proceeding with a systematic examination of the situation. She opened the discussion with a question. "How do you know death was caused by a criminal act when it appears to be accidental? I'm thinking of Benedict Walker and his death due to a peanut allergy four years ago. My intuition keeps triggering suspicions that his death was intentional—causing me to wonder if anyone living at the Hermitage today is guilty of murder."

The lieutenant's response spilled out as if he had been anticipating this line of questioning. "Most victims are murdered due to a bad business deal. Premeditated murder takes calculated planning and willful indulgence stimulated by a profitable award. Master assassins are adept killers who avoid raising suspicions. Their actions are assumed to be the result of natural causes. The opportunity to fraudulently seize control of Gravestone Castle is a worthy financial objective. Avarice is a surreptitious motive for murder. Still, the insufficiency of admissible evidence caused the court to dismiss the case."

"Who would do such a thing—a priest using cleverness to bring about the defeat of an enemy through bewildering and confusing methods without a trace of evidence?"

"Many priests tend to be men normally incapable of violence who are more likely to use poison than physical force. The use of a cold-blooded hitman would be more likely, a cruel killer who excels at his craft and operates quietly without incident. Assassins are never suave, suit-wearing types romanticized in the movies who operate with the drama, professionalism, and glamour that mob films and spy novels afford them. A professional hitman is more likely to be an ex-con with a potbelly. The hitman strikes a deal, and he receives a partial payment and the remainder after death is confirmed."

"I have a hard time imagining anyone meeting your description. I have more experience with thieves with power and money, status and influence—white-collar criminals who commit theft, bribery, and graft."

"It's difficult to study the misdeeds of malfeasances and lawbreakers living in a secret world to which we have no access. There are occasional bumbling performances by novices hired by contractors with lame motivations that are easy to interpret. From my experience, there are four types of hitmen: the 'novice' is a total fledgling; the 'dilettante' is a bumbling idiot without much skill who is desperate for money; the 'journeyman' has access to criminal networks and usually gets nailed because he lives in the same area as the victim; and 'trained masters' with paramilitary experience from a different geographic location—individuals prone to use cleverness rather than brute force. Whispered meetings are private. With precision and grace, no one witnesses the execution or the escape. The hitman flies into a select area, kills, and departs immediately, making them less likely to be thwarted by law enforcement."

"What can you tell me about our hosts?" Emily asked.

"Wayne and Kate Kennedy are the owners of Shadow Structures Inc. They are close friends with Colonel James Roberts, and their company does a lot of business with the Defense Department. They should be arriving shortly."

23

PLANE CRASH

Wayne and Kate Kennedy were hopelessly lost. "I have no idea how far we are from Woebegone Dunes Resort. The road is not on the GPS map because it's private," Kate remarked with frustration. "We need to be there in time to greet our guests. Colonel Roberts speaks very highly of them. I wonder what brings them to Woebegone Dunes Resort?"

"If Colonel Roberts wanted us to know, he would have told us," Wayne surmised. He pulled his world-class Red Porsche 911 Carrera 4S Cabriolet to an abrupt stop at a fork in the road deep in the forest of northern Wisconsin, jumped out of the car, and looked around. There were no street signs, stop signs, mileage markers, or identification signs of any kind. He couldn't see more than a quarter-mile in any direction due to the thick, overhanging forest canopy and the continuous curvature of the winding road. Kate tapped her fingers on the center console, biting her lower lip and beginning to sound worried.

"Have you noticed how few road signs there are in this part of the state? The lack of directional signing is almost as bad as rural Nigeria. Suppose we buy Woebegone Dunes Resort and Gravestone Castle and build a luxury motor coach park. In that case, we'll have to work with the county commissioners to improve the road signage and cell phone coverage," Kate suggested.

Kate's alcohol-induced forgetfulness was beginning to agitate her husband. "Have you forgotten that Colonel Roberts rates Gravestone Castle as a good property to shelter from a nuclear attack? High security and longevity are positive reasons for moving to Wisconsin. Confusing winding roads through isolated forested lands adjacent to Lake Michigan make this area a perfect hideout."

Wayne's engaging warmth, youthful enthusiasm, perpetual optimism, and positive attitude were contagious. "Jack Daniels has nominated me for membership in the Royal Enouement Society—a very exclusive and prestigious organization. As a condition of the nomination process, I have to submit an essay to the board of directors describing my philosophy, with an emphasis on entrepreneurship, business ethics, and financial risk."

"That shouldn't be difficult for you. You are known for your love of wisdom and the habit of theorizing about fundamental issues and abstract topics, thinking logically to analyze and solve problems. You can write and speak clearly and attend to details when assessing new ideas and alternative solutions. Your way of critical thinking is fundamental in this age of disinformation. I admire your ability to make a smooth transition from philosophizing to implementation in a way that encourages people to associate our achievements with high moral and ethical values."

A red Porsche 911 Carrera Cabriolet had been speeding through the forest. Billy "Big Ears" Bellini mistakenly assumed it was Jack Daniels. He pulled back on the throttle to reduce airspeed. He circled his airplane around to gain a better perspective through the forest canopy. Billy was a contemptible soldier in the mafia with family connections to the despicable old-time Italian mob from Kenosha, Wisconsin. He had a mile-long rap sheet, arrested nearly a dozen times for auto theft, robbery, assault, battery, false imprisonment, kidnapping, and manslaughter. Miraculously, he was never convicted, primarily because every critical witness had committed suicide, mysteriously disappeared, or refused to give testimony.

"Listen! I hear an airplane coming," Kate remarked while cupping her ear.

A low-flying Cessna 172 slowly circled back and flew directly overhead, dangerously close to stall speed at treetop height. The pilot opened the side window, stuck out his arm, and fired a Ruger 7000 .38-caliber pistol at the red car below, striking the right rear fender.

"Who the hell was that?" Wayne stammered in total disbelief.

"Oh my God! What just happened?" Kate screamed.

Big Ears checked the navigation display showing the current route, information on the next waypoint, slip-skid indicator, and magnetic direction indicator. He adjusted the azimuth five degrees north, increased altitude, and maximized airspeed. He kept his eyes on the directional gyro and rate of turn indicator until they aligned. He was headed northeast with his left hand on the wheel and his right hand on the throttle when the bomb in the back of the airplane prematurely detonated at exactly 10:52 a.m.

Boom!

A terrific explosion, an orange flash of light, and a slowly rising column of muted smoke were barely visible above the tree line in the direction where the airplane had vanished below the horizon. The explosion blew a giant hole in the aircraft's right side, harmlessly expelling a thousand nails and a bucket of Super Soft Callaway golf balls into the air. A man's frozen chopped-off right hand flew out of an exploded Styrofoam cooler, making a high-pitched whistling sound as it soared a hundred feet horizontally through the air like a spinning frisbee. It ironically landed on the forest floor with the thumb sticking straight up as a clear sign of positive achievement and success.

A cluster of nails shattered the flight instruments on the instrument panel that provided the pilot with information about the flight situation of the aircraft. A chocolate cake with buttercream frosting splattered across the inside of the windshield, obscuring visibility. A smattering of nails stuck in the back of Billy's skull, right triceps, hamstrings, and calf muscles. The intensity of the blast lacerated the back of both ears.

The tympanic membranes in his ears were perforated, ruptured, and punched out in a ragged fashion, resulting in a complete loss of hearing followed by a discharge and bleeding, acute unbearable pain, and disequilibrium. It was impossible to see through the shattered windshield smeared with chocolate cake frosting. He panicked, closed his eyes tightly, unbuckled his seatbelt, and instinctively waited for the crash.

Metal fatigue in the horizontal stabilizer jackscrew caused the component to fail. Damage to the back edge of the wing altered the angle of the aileron, pitching the aircraft downward in a slow right-hand arc toward Lake Michigan. A ruptured fuel line sprayed aviation fuel on the underbelly of the plane. Static electricity accumulated as the aircraft's speed increased, causing the spent fuel to ignite. The wing tip fractured and broke off as it clipped the uppermost branch of the tallest Eastern white pine for miles around. Another towering pine tree caused the left wing to shear off, resulting in a tremendous crashing sound in the forest. The airplane's nose was stalled in midair and pushed down by the fierce resistance of evergreen branches. The momentum of the tail section continued to drive the aircraft forward. The fuselage somersaulted upside down and flipped backward, catapulting Billy Big Ears through the windshield and into the air, fifty feet above the ground.

The blunt force trauma rattled his skull. He experienced a temporary loss of consciousness as he tumbled like a rag doll through a maze of intertwined evergreen branches. He had the sensation of being thumped with sledgehammers as he slipped through the tightly interconnected tree limbs. Overlapping evergreen branches gradually slowed his descent until his body finally reached solid ground. A swampy three-foot-thick bed of moist greenish-yellow sphagnum moss floating on a marsh softened the impact. The momentum of the arm-twisting high-velocity contact-collision caused him to roll over three times before finally coming to rest on his back on a bed of soft pine needles.

His lifeless body lay in a sprawled, contorted position, his left arm wedged behind his back and a tree root holding up his right knee. His clothes were shredded and torn. Nails were sticking out of his skull, the back of his right arm, and his right leg.

The burning fuselage of his wingless airplane was dangling upside down, wedged between the forked trunks of a very tall pine tree forty feet above the ground. Hundreds of golf balls, broken honey jars, and a shattered wooden box containing a dozen Maker's Mark whiskey bottles indiscriminately scattered on the forest floor. His well-worn brown leather bomber pilot jacket, holding a Ruger pistol, a pack of Cuban cigars, a pair of aviator sunglasses, and a wad of hundred-dollar bills, hung on a tree branch. A frozen right hand in a leather glove with the thumb extending upward as a universal sign of encouragement, approval, and acceptance lay beside him.

A frightened ground-dwelling chipmunk, filling his cheeks with chunks of chocolate cake sticking to the back of Billy's head, chittered a warning.

24

DISBELIEF

Kate stared in the direction of the explosion in astonished disbelief, clueless and confused, with her mouth unsophisticatedly wide open, resembling an ignorant, slack-jawed, inbred yokel.

"Did you hear that awful noise? I can't believe what just happened. We need to call an ambulance, inform the fire department, file a police report, and call our insurance company as soon as possible," Kate screamed frantically.

Wayne jumped in the car, spun the tires, and took off down the road. They successfully navigated the winding roads without a street sign, a map, GPS, or an entrance sign to guide them. A mile further down the road, they accidentally discovered an inconspicuous small brass plaque on a large rock signaling the entrance to Woebegone Dunes Resort.

"We finally have cell service," Kate exclaimed, glancing at her iPhone in a black leather sequined flip case. She dialed 911 and frantically set about providing an elaborate but disjointed explanation about what she had witnessed.

"Did you see the airplane hit the ground? Was the sun shining in your eyes? Are you certain it wasn't someone's model airplane or a drone? How much alcohol have you consumed this morning? Have you also seen da Turdy Point Buck?" Tammy at police headquarters quizzed doubtfully, assuming the caller was drunk.

"No! I don't have a detailed description of the airplane. We don't know anything about the identity of the pilot or why anyone would shoot at us," Kate frustratedly exclaimed. "We don't even know where we were when the incident happened."

As a minor consolation, Tammy agreed to dispatch a police officer to investigate the incident. "Deputy Sheriff Bud Light will be contacting you at Woebegone Dunes Resort today or tomorrow with some follow-up questions. Have a nice day. Goodbye!"

Kate furiously shook her head from side to side. "What's he going to do? Give me a breathalyzer test?" She exhaled. "Model airplane? What about the bullet hole in the rear panel of our car as evidence?" Kate mumbled angrily under her breath.

Deputy Sheriff Bud Light received a call from the dispatch office. "This is Tammy at police headquarters. I have a report of an 11-78 aircraft accident somewhere north of Woebegone Dunes Resort."

"Uff-da—oh crap!"

Radio reception was poor—something about an airplane (model airplane or drone) that may have crashed into Lake Michigan north of Whistling Straits. Bud Light never bothered to get out of his car. He randomly drove around in circles for two hours without knowing where he was as he scanned the horizon for evidence of an airplane crash. Without visible signs of fire, smoke, or oily scum floating on Lake Michigan as evidence, Bud casually retreated to his favorite camouflaged parking spot. He pretended to be watching for speeders, but his real intention was to hide from the public. He backed his patrol car under a stunningly pervasive billboard displaying two naked people sitting in twin bathtubs staring at the sunset on an isolated beach in Mexico as marketing for Cialis, a cure for erectile dysfunction.

The deputy sheriff opened his lunch box, removed an antique silver flask engraved with a bald eagle from a purple velvet bag with a gold tie string, and took a slow, tantalizing sip of Korbel XS extra-smooth brandy.

"This brandy is phenomenal and amazingly smooth—well worth

the price," the deputy stated emphatically to nobody other than himself. "I love the nutty flavors and vanilla notes, and there is even something minty going on and something surprisingly chocolaty."

Deputy Sheriff Bud Light grinned as the alcohol took effect. He took another sip, turned off his radar, closed his eyes, relaxed, and fell asleep—the same routine he had followed every afternoon for the last five years. A red four-hundred-horsepower Porsche 911 Carrera Cabriolet traveling thirty-five miles per hour over the speed limit flew past. A quiet tension building in the bass tones of the engine produced marvelous goose-bumping sounds reminiscent of a race track, prodding race fans to stand and cheer. The engine growled as if rounding a curve on the Elkhart Lake race track as a red blur flashed past the deputy's hiding spot without detection.

25

SELF-DOUBTS

"Maybe we shouldn't be buying property anywhere in the land of the Cheeseheads," Kate said with a scowl and a furrowed brow. "What kind of deranged psychotic lunatics live around here anyway? Jeffery Dahmer, 'the Milwaukee Cannibal,' was a serial killer and sex offender who committed seventeen boys' rapes, murders, and dismemberments. He was from Wisconsin. And what about Steven Avery, the main focus of attention of the Netflix series 'The Making of a Murderer,' convicted of the rape and murder of Teresa Halbach? He was from Manitowoc; that's not far from here. And Ed Gein, Wisconsin's most notorious serial killer who used human body parts to make furniture and lampshades?"

Kate's complexion was a whiter shade of pale. "Jesus, I sure hope Colonel Robert's prediction about the US Department of Justice seizing control of Woebegone Dunes Resort and Gravestone Castle are true. Whatever happens, they are both exceptional, valuable properties in a prime location. Even if the resort doesn't become available, I still want to acquire Gravestone Castle and build a motor coach/country club/luxury RV resort."

Wayne agreed. "Whistling Straits, the nonpareil host of the Ryder Cup and President's Cup, and the Open Championship at Erin Hills are shining examples of the growing popularity of championship golf in Wisconsin. The American Club in Sheboygan is a premier five-star American resort that is a much better investment than dumping more money into speculative real estate in Green Valley, Arizona. I do agree with you, though, that I don't want to live in an area inhabited by a bunch of nuts and fruitcakes. I'm not backing off until I learn with certainty the truth about the Royal Enouement Society," he added with grave apprehension.

"Where do you think Jack Daniels stands on all of this?"

"It's my understanding that he has become somewhat of a recluse since his beloved wife died from breast cancer two years ago. The unspoiled, harmonious forest wilderness is his cultural refuge. He spends most of his time at his isolated rustic cabin on a property he refers to as the 'heart of Arcadia.' It's a place where he feels at peace in the forest setting, sheltered from the influences of urban civilization."

Far in the distance, Jack thought he heard a muffled explosion followed by a rudderless airplane in distress with several sections of aluminum paneling violently flapping in the wind. Intense heat from the engine manifold ignited gasoline draining out of the aviation fuel tank. Flames blackened the underbelly of the single-winged aircraft. It gradually changed azimuth from north to due east toward Lake Michigan. A puff of gray smoke briefly billowed into the air before extinguishing with the aid of the automatic Halon fire extinguishers. The sky was suddenly eerily quiet as if nothing had happened—the last place on earth without human noise.

Jack mounted his ATV and headed toward a bluff overlooking Lake Michigan to investigate. Finding no signs of debris floating on the water surface, he assumed that if it had been an airplane, it sank immediately. Jack made a hasty decision to ignore the possible crash of an aircraft, thinking there were no survivors, to avoid calling public attention to his private property. He opened the throttle, spun the knobby tires on his

ATV in the sand, and raced along the water's edge of Lake Michigan on the way back to his cabin.

He casually showered and put on a crisp dark-gray business suit before heading to Woebegone Dunes Resort to welcome Wayne and Kate Kennedy to his elite resort.

26

WOEBEGONE DUNES RESORT

Wayne and Kate Kennedy were enthusiastically greeted at the front door of Woebegone Dunes Resort by president Jack Daniels and CFO Lady Vanessa. Prideful of his ability to attract diamond investors to his private club, Jack thought his newest guests were precisely the type of clients he was seeking. He preferred middle-aged, educated, independent world travelers who were fabulous, clear thinking, and eager to support traditional values and invest in new things.

"Welcome to Woebegone Dunes Resort. I look forward to discussing membership benefits with you after you have had a chance to look around. We hope you enjoy our hospitality and find our luxurious resort to your liking," he declared. "Our mission is to provide our guests with warm welcomes, magic moments, and fond farewells. Lady Vanessa will give you a tour of the property and explain a few of the introductory details of membership to you."

Vanessa tossed her blond hair back and aggressively inserted her hand into Wayne's palm. She seductively pressed her ample breasts against his chest, forcing him to smell her perfume. "I'm Lady Vanessa, the indispensable chief financial officer. I'm pleased to make your acquaintance," she conveyed warmly with a fake Polish accent and a haughty, self-satisfied Botox grin. She was a mirror image of Kate, smartly dressed with straight posture and the same height, weight, general appearance, and hair color. Her obvious charisma and charm seemed the skills of a celebrity gold digger, reminiscent of a Renaissance courtesan with high-quality features and clients.

Turning to face Wayne with a glint in her eye, she gently placed his hand on her hip with the subtle persuasion of a professional ballroom dance instructor. She tossed her hair back and flashed a smile, capped with a prideful wink. She exuberantly wrapped her arms around his neck with a steamy high-society hug reminiscent of a scene from *Fifty Shades of Gray* that left Wayne blushing red. "Welcome, cowboy," she expressed, triggering sexual innuendo alarms in his head and heart. In true Hollywood fashion, she kissed him on the cheek, signaling unabashedly, "I'm available." With a mischievous fake smile as fresh as a ripe mango with overly white teeth, she spanked his rump like it was a Mexican piñata.

Lady Vanessa was fully aware that knowledge was power, particularly in large organizations. Her career-savvy communication skills at ferreting out semi-hidden information were uncanny. She had incredible success in discerning the deeper reality behind situations and events around her, primarily by using seductive strategies through an astonishing array of tactics. Her university thesis, "Sexual Economics Theory," identified numerous ways for women to increase attraction in the workplace by making their product more attractive than their rivals'. Included was a list of bonus tips on sweetening the deal by offering additional incentives and concessions; the primary factor when seeking wealth and power is attracting the wealthiest men.

Kate was an astute judge of character. Vanessa was a voluptuous, alluring blond bombshell with a shamelessly overbearing personality. Her façade deceitfully concealed her dishonesty and personal insecurities, smiling in the morning as if she had been crying all night. Kate ritualistically squeezed the back of Wayne's arm, signaling to him that he was already married and that he should stop unabashedly paying an excessive amount of attention to Lady Vanessa in her pale-pink loose-fitting silky wrap blouse enhanced with a Duchess of Cornwall's four-strand pearl choker with a vintage tiered diamond clasp radiating out from the central diamond between her cleavage.

"Welcome to Woebegone Dunes Resort. When are your guests,

Lieutenant Dunning and Emily, arriving?" Lady Vanessa asked with a relaxed, breathy, seductive voice, contributing to a perception of exceptional femininity. Inherently intertwined with her way of communicating were mischievousness and playfulness. She never played the waiting role. She was never passive, knowing that sexual excitement is always most prevalent in the hunter than the hunted. She subtly touched Wayne's arm every time he spoke as a warm gesture. When he said something funny, she laughed and hugged him suggestively. From Wayne's perspective, there was a lightness in her step and spirit, making her attractive to be near. A vision entered his mind of her seductively removing her clothes for his enjoyment, piece by piece in a provocative manner to the accompaniment of music with an erotic plumage-shaking fanfare.

Kate could read his mind. She kicked Wayne in the back of the leg.

"The lieutenant and his assistant will be along shortly. They stopped to take the Industry in Action Kohler Company factory tour," Kate responded bluntly with a jealous glance.

"If there is anything you need—anything at all—let Lady Vanessa know, and she'll personally take care of it for you," Jack assured them. "You will enjoy our secret earthly paradise and harmonious retreat thoroughly, isolated and hidden away here deep in the woods of northern Wisconsin, far from the pressures of the modern world. It's a romantic setting, a place of great happiness where everything is as you would like it to be, a land of contentment, luxury, and fulfillment. We take care of all the details and make everything as simple and easy as possible for our members."

"Even our toilets open and close automatically," Lady Vanessa boasted.

"I suggest you have lunch at your own pace. We'll get you on the golf course with your guests as soon as you are ready," Jack suggested. "The dramatic design of the golf course is one of the most fascinating you will ever see. It has tight fairways and greens surrounded by trees dangling above sheer drop-offs. To hold their nerve, players must study the course to game-plan ahead of time before committing to specific lines before swinging away. The adrenaline-fueled first-tee frenzy is unparalleled. The visual drama conveys thoughts and feelings alternating between smiling, laughing, shouting, crying, and excessive pouting. Fairways zigzag between natural forest openings and rock outcrops across a series of undulating terraces and ravines, where you can watch the action unfold below. Large rock outcrops cause explosive ricocheting fireworks. Sand traps are burial grounds for golfers lacking mental toughness who tend to shut down in the clutch when the match is on the line. The seventeenth hole, named 'Herniated Disc,' is a cauldron of pressure that increases tension, pinched nerves, stiff necks, and mental anxiety. The eighteenth green sits well below the landing area, a sheer drop into oblivion. There is always a tragedy when the wind blows."

"We will be relying on our caddies to guide us through the labyrinth."

"Your caddy's name is Jay Walker. He has excellent knowledge of the course. He gives sound advice and is especially good around the greens. As a psychologist, he is helpful on the mental side for boosting his clients' morale, stroking egos, and elevating everyone's game by promoting positive thoughts. He will keep you calm and advise you when to take a risk. Jay will remain in your shadow like a good friend, a valet, a coach, a parent, and a confessor, a local guy who knows what to say and when to say it. Most importantly, when not to say anything. His knowledge about the resort and the history of this part of Wisconsin is immense. He grew up on the adjacent property at Gravestone Castle. He is very familiar with the golf course and the entire surrounding countryside. Check with Lady Vanessa after you have finished lunch. She'll introduce you to your caddy and get you on the golf course when you are ready."

Wayne and Kate were eager to get started. "Thank you for the exuberant welcome. Kate and I are thrilled to be here, but we are very concerned about a significant incident that happened this morning. When I stopped the car to get our bearings, a man in an airplane shot at us, and a bullet pierced the rear fender of our new car. A few minutes later, we heard a muffled explosion and assumed the airplane exploded."

"I need something to calm my nerves," Kate reminded herself.

Lady Vanessa validated Kate's emotional suffering and acknowledged her fears by gently taking her by the arm and escorting her to the rose garden on the Sol de Terrace overlooking the Holy Fountain sculpture. Wayne followed close behind, enjoying how the women leisurely sauntered in a slow, graceful, feminine manner. They gave the impression of extreme confidence with long catlike strides used by models to demonstrate clothing during a fashion show.

Vanessa politely escorted them to a table under the shade of a patio umbrella. She offered them a complimentary glass of champagne along with a basket of grapes, a slice of cheese, olive oil, and warm French bread. A small ensemble on the lower terrace provided background chamber music.

"I'll be waiting for you in my office," Lady Vanessa promised. With the assistance of a listening device, she hovered out of sight, ducking behind walls to eavesdrop on conversations she was not entitled to hear. One discreet click of her stylish executive voice recorder spy pen was all she needed. Vanessa grossly infringed on their privacy by stealthily listening to their private conversation from behind closed doors without their consent as Kate unknowingly exposed their intentions.

"This resort is peerless. My first impression is heavenly and mystical, exceeding my wildest dreams. I've never seen anything like it. It's highly comparable to Whistling Straits. Owning Woebegone Dunes Resort would be a dream come true," Kate openly expressed, exposing her deepest desires. "Living in Gravestone Castle as our primary residence would be the crowning glory of my life's ambition—a perfect blending of an exclusive luxury resort with a significant historic property."

Vanessa gnashed her teeth with frustration behind closed doors, releasing an obscene string of profanities.

Kate was openly optimistic about the future, enthusiastic, sparkling, and effervescing with positive energy, like her Waterford toasting flute of crystal glass filled with bubbly champagne. She nudged closer, squeezed Wayne's hand, demurely looked him in the eyes, and smiled—the same reassuring image she had outwardly projected when they first met. "My life with you has been a total joy. Everywhere you take me, flowers bloom, the water glistens, and the sun twinkles merrily on little waves of the sea of tranquility. You do to me what nature does to fruit trees in the spring. Our marriage has been exceptional, an emotional experience filled with mysteries, hazards, and pitfalls. You have a charming way of always coming out on top. You're a consistent winner and a keeper— that's what I like about you most. I trust you explicitly and will always be your forever partner."

"I love you unconditionally," Wayne replied, reaching for Kate's hand and smiling.

Kate perused the lunch menu bound in tanned shell cordovan equine leather, known worldwide for its toughness, longevity, and protective qualities. "I'm pleasantly surprised at the fabulous selection of wines and the great variety of lunch items on the menu," she exclaimed eagerly, rubbing her palms together with anticipation. "The signature dish of creamy cauliflower leek soup infused with fine sherry, the regal crown roast of pork with lady apples and shallots, and warm sticky figgy pudding for dessert sounds wonderful."

Kate had a sophisticated way of dressing for the country club scene. She smoothed her cream-colored pleated skirt boasting an advanced design with a slimming princess fit. Her luxurious light-yellow Florentine top with mesh shoulders was highly flattering. Expensive Italian designer eyewear encrusted in precious gemstones covered her twinkly blue eyes, a frivolity and an indulgence crafted for the highest-end clients in the haute fashion world. Long-legged, five feet six inches tall, and naturally blond, Kate was the charming, forthright CEO of a rapidly expanding international plastics manufacturing business, Shadow Structures Inc.

Her husband, Wayne, was muscular and Hollywood handsome, a Cary Grant movie-star lookalike, tall with white teeth, dimples on cheeks and chin, dark hair, and a mustache. After a torrid love affair in college leading to an accidental pregnancy, they were happily married.

Wayne seldom showed enthusiasm for working out at the fitness center. Still, he somehow managed to watch his weight and keep his slender, muscular build.

Lady Vanessa had already found everything she needed to know about Wayne and Kate Kennedy—two thumbs down. Her intent was utterly clear. "There is absolutely no way I'm going to allow any potential buyer to join this club. Anyone who wants to purchase Woebegone Dunes Resort and make Gravestone Castle their home is not welcome here." Slipping into the rear service entrance leading to the back of the kitchen, Vanessa deviously removed a small container from her pocket. She poured half a bottle of triphala, a three-fruit liquid extract from India, into Kate's leek soup.

"Give this bowl of cauliflower leek soup to Kate Kennedy at table seven. She is the woman in the pale-yellow designer blouse," she instructed before quietly slipping out the rear service exit door.

27

THE CABIN

Whack!

A single hailstone rudely smacked the forehead of the seemingly lifeless body lying on the forest floor. The central nervous system issued an abrupt brainstem reflexive reaction to protect vulnerable body parts. The automatic startle response agitated Billy "Big Ears" Bellini as he opened one bloodshot eye resembling a fried red tomato. Unable to perceive clear or sharp images, he stared blankly at the blurry vastness of the wild blue yonder and the blackened hull of an airplane fuselage suspended in the trees above him.

There was no feeling in his left arm. He couldn't move. Something sharp was poking the back of his head, and he had a stabbing pain in his hip. He hurt everywhere, acute pain in his wrist, an excruciating headache. He squeezed his fist and flexed his left knee. He forced himself to roll onto his right side with great effort, allowing him to pull his numb left arm out from underneath his aching back.

He spent the entire afternoon in a catatonic state of semi-consciousness. Intense beams of sunlight penetrating the forest canopy as the storm clouds dissipated warmed his contorted, battered body. Suddenly, the forest floor cooled as a fleeting billowy white cloud with gray undertones drifted slowly across the deep-blue sky, exhausting the sun's warmth. A sudden drop in ambient temperature awakened his senses.

Little by little, he slowly opened one crusty, swollen, bloodshot eye discharging yellow mucus. A fair-weather cumulus cloud directly overhead was expanding like heaping piles of cotton balls and fluffy white pillows of cotton and transforming into an ominously threatening dark-gray nimbus storm cloud.

Cold pallid skin, irregular breathing, rapid pulse, dilated pupils, and a fall in blood pressure marked his acute medical condition. The fall from the sky had caused a life-threatening emergency state of circulatory shock resulting from low blood perfusion to tissues, resulting in cellular injury and impaired tissue function.

His clothing was tattered and torn. Blood dripped from his hair. Foamed saliva ghoulishly drooled from one side of his mouth. The survival instinct triggered excited delirium, automatically producing a biological mechanism leading to hysterical strength. He grasped a low-hanging branch with both hands and miraculously pulled himself to a sitting position. He was dizzy, and he couldn't hear. He had a terrible headache, a nagging toothache, and a possible broken back.

"*Merda! Che cavolo.* Holy crap!" he yelled in agony as he pulled several three-inch nails out of his leg and arm.

To orient himself, he scanned his surroundings, observing the sun in the sky and green moss growing on the shady side of the trees. Deliberately placing one foot in front of the other, he staggered forward in a northwest direction. Inch by inch, one unsteady step at a time, dragging his brown leather aviator jacket behind him.

One mile from the crash site, he ran across a fresh set of ATV tracks in the forest. He followed them directly to Jack Daniels's authentic storybook log cabin surrounded by evergreen trees. The log structure with a sod-covered roof blended perfectly with the forest environment.

He painfully reached above the doorframe and discovered the key to the front door on the first try. The cabin's interior with a black bear theme was honeymoon perfect with all the comforts of home, complete with a coffeemaker, fireplace, satellite television, gas grill, a liquor bar, plush towels, two bedrooms with king beds, and comfy leather recliners. The well-stocked pantry and refrigerator were like money in the bank.

Big Ears stripped off his tattered clothes in the master bathroom and carefully placed them on a bath towel. He stood naked in front of the mirror. Bruises, lacerations, and contusions covered his entire body. He removed three nails from the back of his skull before cautiously stepping into the warm shower and delicately washing the bloodstains from his skin. He discovered a pair of freshly pressed dress slacks in the master closet. A fancy white shirt with gold cufflinks, a blue velvet smoking jacket, and a couple of caramel brown leather Italian shoes all fit perfectly. He took three pain pills from the medicine cabinet and lit the fireplace.

A German crystal glass stein with an anchor pewter lid and engraved crest on the bar's top shelf attracted his attention. Knowing that Jack Daniels was a beer lover and competent judge in all manners of taste, he opened the bar fridge and peeked inside. Astonishingly, it was filled with craft beers from Bent Barley Brewing Company in Aurora, Colorado, famous for its exceptional hop aroma and flavor. He selected an American Imperial IPA and poured it gently into the glass stein. He swirled it gently and smelled it before taking a sip and swallowing. The aroma was intense. The upfront taste on the tongue was robust, owing to the superb combination of the base malts. The finish was smooth, pure, and balanced, demonstrating true craft in the selection of the hops. The beer was definitely big, coming in at around 11.5 percent alcohol by volume. The deep gold color, head, and carbonation were perfect. His enjoyment was immense. He gently eased himself into a heated brown leather ergonomic recliner and lost consciousness.

He was gently awakened at the dim light of dawn by the poignant liquid coolness of the haunting trill of a wood thrush singing in the forest.

Ping.

A message on his Iridium Extreme satellite telephone startled him. His girlfriend, Angelina, called from Curl Up and Dye hair salon.

"Am I going to see you tonight—just wondering? Love, Angelina."

Big Ears immediately tweeted a response.

"Pick me up at the following coordinates after dusk. Don't let anyone see you coming."

Angelina entered the coordinates and asked the computer to calculate the driving time from her beauty shop to the pickup point.

Big Ears searched every file drawer and closet to see what he might discover. He photographed all items of interest, including a map of future acquisition properties between Sheboygan and Door Counties. He carefully and methodically avoided disturbing or destroying anything in the cabin. He carried a dishtowel in each hand, ensuring no fingerprints were left behind and taking care that nothing was moved or left out of place.

He changed into black dress slacks, a black leather alligator belt, classic shoes, a gray Purple Label Aston French-cuff dress shirt and a double-breasted tailored black Heritage trench coat. The hematomas surrounding both eyes were hideous-looking, and aviator sunglasses with a large lens only partially concealed them. He took two more prescription pain pills, rolled his ragged, bloody clothing into a ball inside a bath towel, placed the entire bundle in a navy-blue bed sheet along with his shoes, and tied all four corners together.

He meticulously wiped down every part of the cabin to remove any evidence of trespass. He replaced the key above the front door and limped at a slow, steady snail's pace down the long winding driveway as the sun's disk disappeared below the horizon. A belligerent herring gull with a red bill dive-bombed him to warn that he was too close to her nest, forcing him to hide under a large spruce tree with low-hanging branches. Using the rumbled bundle of clothes as a soft pillow, he waited attentively by the elaborate wrought-iron gate as the evening sky faded from light pink to brilliant orange.

The familiar, soft, throaty exhaust of Angelina's black Mercedes 450SL convertible awakened him.

"*Dio Mio! Grazie.* Oh, my God! Thanks for coming to my rescue."

Big Ears crammed the bundle of bloodied clothes into the trunk and groaned with pain as he eased himself into the low-riding passenger seat.

"*Partire!* Go! Drive as fast as you can. Keep your headlights off."

Angelina was acquainted with the routine. Alarmed by the dreadful appearance of her boyfriend, she peered straight ahead into the darkness, concentrating intently on the curves in the narrow country road. She was fully aware that it was inappropriate to be overtly interested in asking her Italian goombah lover too many prying questions.

The agonizing pain and distress radiating from every vital part of his anatomy caused him to feel faint. He grimaced whenever he spoke, gestured with his hands, and attempted to move.

"I have a terrible headache. I slammed my forehead into the windshield when my airplane hit a tree. I need a secure, secluded location to recover for a few weeks."

28

BUILD THE CASINO

Life at the Hermitage had been stress-free for nearly four years, reminding the inhabitants of the carefree days of summer before school starts. Father Feely was free of care, happy and relaxed, detached from reality, unconcerned about the usual pressures of everyday living. Lucrative profits from stolen Nigerian crude oil and rare-earth minerals continued to flow into his International Heritage Endowment Fund each year. The easy money caused him to become increasingly submissive to Nigerian playboy Bo-Bo Bigelow. His bank account swelled to several million dollars in less than ten years. The carefree lifestyle he lived had progressively become a hammock, slowly lulling him into vanity and complacency.

Bo-Bo's message had been brief, and the intent was inescapable. "I want you to begin construction on a casino—now. My bodyguard Burly will be contacting you shortly."

Despite the seeming urgency of that weeks-old message, Sundays were Father Feely's favorite day of the week—a time of excitement focused on the Green Bay Packers football team. He loved it when the frenzied hometown crowd in green and gold jerseys flowed out of Lambeau Stadium in a cheerful, celebratory mood following an exciting win over the Chicago Bears. The expressions of shock and awe on the faces of Chicago fans after the Packers scored two touchdowns in the final two minutes of the game were comical.

"This win calls for a celebration with a raspberry-filled glazed donut and a hot cup of coffee," he bellowed loudly with a glory-of-God intensity. "Jelly-filled donuts for breakfast are sublime. Glazed and cream-filled donuts are beautiful and tempting for lunch. Chocolate frosting is for dinner. Changing the routine is what produces the greatest thrill," he explained to the teenaged girl behind the counter, wearing a mid-thigh silky black dress with a white apron and a tiara crown. Father Feely greedily stuffed a raspberry jam-filled donut into his mouth with both hands. His broad, unrestrained grin of sensual gratification signaled boyish joy.

A malicious stranger unexpectedly approached from behind. With the fingers of his left hand, he applied vice-like pressure to the back of Feely's neck, inducing fear, alarm, and psychological trauma. Father Feely grimaced. The man resembled a weightlifter of intimidating physical size with a glowering countenance. His face was exceptionally dark. A distinctive knife wound on his left cheek was infected with a slimy yellow gob of viscous substance that dripped from the fibrous tissue, which had not healed properly. He wore dirty black combat boots and a dark-green camouflage uniform with a rope tied in a slip noose around his neck. The black beret on his head contained a sinister-looking patch with a black shield and menacing skull and crossbones. His manner of speaking and unusual accent led Father Feely to believe he was African. Father Feely was terrified about what might happen next.

"Ouch! That hurts. What do you want? Is your name Burly?" Father Feely gagged in a muffled voice with his cakehole dripping gobs of red raspberry jam on the floor. His brain was on hyperalert with pupils dilated and weak knees. His breathing intensified as his heart rate accelerated.

"Bo-Bo is becoming exceedingly impatient with your lack of progress on the casino. The sooner it gets finished, the easier it will be for him to conceal the profits from his rare-earth mineral export business."

"It's not that simple, and the approval process is a lengthy, complex political labyrinth."

"Get it done quickly—or else," Burly ordered with a repulsive acidity in his voice and the lingering aroma of pungent-smelling Nigerian curry chicken. "I need another shipment of killer bees. The insects are wreaking havoc and inflicting great harm to the Muslim rebels in northern Nigeria. Bo-Bo wants the bees delivered to an oil tanker in Houston-Galveston, Texas, leaving for Nigeria in two weeks," he threatened. "The scientific techniques Father Baum developed to assassinate the highest-ranking enemy officers with killer bees are working extremely well. Send another shipment of rainbow herbicides and biological weapons with the next shipment of bees. No excuses and no delays," the ill-tempered, repulsive stranger threatened as a foreboding harbinger of future events.

Father Feely instinctively covered his face with his hands, speaking nervously through his fingers. "I am a simple priest. I live a quiet ascetic life, isolated in a holy place of religious seclusion," he pleaded, making the sign of the cross. Muscle spasms caused intensely painful cramping and involuntary tightness in his neck. "I am under intense surveillance by the federal government," he admitted nervously.

"Bo-Bo has made you incredibly wealthy. He finances your charities in exchange for reinvesting money in legitimate businesses—he fully expects that relationship to continue. Still, things are going to be different now. Two of his partners from Nigeria were arrested in France by Interpol recently. US Marshal Lieutenant Baron Dunning is increasing tension and drama with law enforcement. Don't be surprised when you see me eliminate the problem."

Without warning, the intimidating brute punched Father Feely with a closed fist in the soft underbelly beneath the rib cage. The ensuing force pressing upward on his diaphragm led to a sudden expulsion of air from his lungs, leaving him helplessly defenseless. "If you cooperate in any way with the FBI or Interpol, I will personally hunt you down and make you eat a giant hogweed plant."

The muscles in Father Feely's arms went limp. He gagged and choked. Globs of red raspberry jam mixed with chunks of half-chewed, soft, sticky, glazed, gooey doughnut dough driveled out of his mouth onto his shirt and pants. A giant blob of drool oozed from his open mouth onto the glass display case in front of the horrified teenaged clerk. Projectile vomit spewed his retched stomach's entire gastric contents, splattering all over the cash register, countertop, and floor. The teenaged clerk cried as she unsuccessfully attempted to wipe the vomit off her soiled uniform.

The dark stranger with a black shield with skull and crossbones tattooed on his left forearm kneed Father Feely in the groin, causing him to drop to his knees. The man grabbed the raspberry donut out of the father's hand, pressing it firmly into the priest's face with the butt of his hand. The bright-red raspberry filling residue was all over Father Feely's face, stuck in his ears, eyebrows, and nose hairs.

"I'll kill you with my bare hands if you fail to meet Bo-Bo's requests," the menacing stranger growled as he stormed out the door, leaving no doubt about his convictions.

Visibly shaken, Father Feely retreated in agonizing pain to the safety of his car. The ecclesiastic expressions of joy on his face had vanished in the blink of an eye. After a brief loss of consciousness, he stared into space with a flabbergasted look of exasperation.

"What happened? Did you have an accident? You look terrible," Sister Olivia Seno Grande proclaimed back at the Hermitage. "I'll run a warm bath for you."

She handed Father Feely a sip of wine and instructed him to relax in a chair until the bath was ready. She moved with the grace of a model posing for a photographer in an haute couture assemble. She was well-proportioned, dangerously curvaceous, seductively attractive, and enticing. Her hair was a rich light cappuccino brown with golden highlights, flattering for every skin tone. Her hips swayed with a natural grace and sensual pleasure as she placed one foot in front of the other, walking with long, smooth strides, with her arms at her sides and her hands relaxed. She grabbed an oversized luxury Wellington bath towel, dimmed the indirect lighting, instructed Alexa to play Johnny Mathis, and lighted several beeswax candles. She filled the simulated-rock bathtub basin with hot water and a fantastic amount of bubble bath oils before guiding Father Feely into the spacious crystal bathtub.

"Glory be!" he exclaimed.

Her slow movements were luxurious and exquisite. Her touches made Father Feely's skin feel tingly in a pleasurable way. Her sensual touching with a bar of soap shot off incredible sensations, leaving him aroused and incredibly excited. An electrifying spark of anticipation and a passionate fire lighted his imagination. A captivating rush of desire, fantastic feelings of sexual delight, incredible fireworks, and fulfillment stimulated his imagination. Father Feely leaned back, relaxed, and fell deeply asleep with a smile on his face.

Erotic dreams filled his imagination. He visualized Sister Olivia dropping her bathrobe on the floor, allowing her breasts to dangle in his face. They appeared twice as large as they hung down from her chest, reminding him of tasty ripe passion fruit, big, round, and juicy. His eyes twinkled as she traced her cute pokey nipples over his face, across his forehead, eyes, and lips. Exotic dreams of a heart-pounding, breathtaking, passionate love affair stimulated his imagination. Ardent desire and toe-curling emotional touching led him to lean forward and kiss the twin sisters salaciously. Dancing dreamily around the room in an intimate embrace, their bodies were perfectly attuned to each other. His moaning and groaning became alarmingly louder as he neared the culmination of his wish fulfillment.

His pervasive and exhaustive dreaming entertained Sister Olivia. She surmised that she was the object of his longing and the primary actor in his nightly naughty fantasies. She, too, often daydreamed about bathing naked with Father Feely, with nothing on except the radio.

He was abruptly awakened from his raging sexual fantasy as he frantically splashed water out of the tub. He tossed his arms in the air and impulsively yelled, "Ah, la, la!"

Sister Olivia offered the aroused priest a towel to conceal the glaring potency of his loins. His sexual arousal was an emotional contagion that caused amusement and excitement. The spontaneous convergence of her reflexive desires produced uncontainable arousal. She felt as if her body was falling off a cliff into an earth-shattering pile of tingling ecstasy as they headed to the bedroom. Greenlight moaning, groaning, authentic erotic sounds of pleasure and screams of animalistic delight without inhibition escaped the bedroom chamber. They echoed down the hall, signaling that something felt good and worked very well.

Father Adam Baum was roused from his chair, knowing that a porn scene was taking place right next door. He could hear and imagine it all. Denied his rest, he ate a spoonful of honey, did deep-breathing exercises, and lifted weights to reduce his acute uncontrollable compulsions and urges. The Padre abruptly switched on his computer and ordered a very expensive crossbow on the internet using Father Cellophane's credit card.

29

FATHER CELLOPHANE

Father Cellophane had never been one to rush. Warm morning rays of sunshine triggered bliss and cheerfulness, stimulating him to whistle as he walked through the forest primeval without a care in the world. He had very few commitments or responsibilities, and his life was stress-free. He lived in luxurious surroundings without concern for others, a semi-solitary existence of seclusion and self-indulgence. It was a fabulous arrangement endowed by wealth, a lifestyle that was the epitome of unsustainable living.

He walked at a leisurely pace through the ancient forest, listening to the sounds of the leaves rustling in the treetops, marveling at the heavenly wonders of the massive billowy white clouds overhead. A woodpecker tapped a message on a hollow tree as a healthy red fox nervously crossed his path. Pausing briefly to pull a few weeds in the Walker family burial plot, he glanced at Benedict Walker's gravestone. The laser-engraved image of his face in the black granite was haunting. The eyes were vacant, providing a window into his soul, exposing a mixture of pain and confusion and betrayal, a lingering timeless message of despair that resonated more powerfully than words. The silhouette seemed like an ominous premonition of death and destiny.

Jack Daniels fidgeted. He was irked. "Where the hell is that son-of-a-bitch priest? Would you please give me a glass of Maker's Mark VIP Kentucky Straight Bourbon Whiskey? I want that in a European-style crafted crystal glass with unique pineapple cuts," he demanded of the waiter.

Father Cellophane casually strolled into the Amber Room without a care in the world. A large bouquet of pink, yellow, and white fresh flowers graced the center of the table, covered with a light-yellow tablecloth, antique china, and freshly polished Maryland Engraved silverware. Radiantly lit lead oxide crystal chandeliers from Venice provided decorative lighting. Original oil paintings of the gentrified English landscape graced the dark walnut wall panels.

Jack Daniels was unapologetic about his desire to convert Gravestone Castle into the headquarters for the Royal Enouement Society. "How are you? How was your swim in Lake Michigan this morning?" he inquired politely, falsely pretending to care.

Visions of Lola and Lova Kurvig entered Father Cellophane's consciousness, two naked beauties impiously and irreverently sprawled between the sheets in the flickering candlelight of his bedroom—the real reason for his delay.

Father Cellophane was a master of deflection. "Very invigorating—makes one feel strong, healthy, and full of gusto," he falsely exaggerated. "The lamb is primal, and the table setting is elegant. My blessings to the chef," he casually complimented after tucking in. "Don't assume you are the only person trying to acquire Gravestone Castle," he reminded Jack. "The others are just as passionate and wealthy as you."

"Who the hell are they?" Jack demanded with hostility.

"Bo-Bo Bigelow wants to convert Gravestone Castle into a playboy mansion. He intends to gift a portion of the land to the local Indian tribe in exchange for a casino, a gas station, a trap and skeet club, and a tax-free smoke shop. Preliminary discussions have already taken place."

Jack exploded in a fit of rage. "I won't stand for it! A casino next door would destroy the character and atmosphere of Woebegone Dunes Resort."

"Wayne and Kate Kennedy are also hoping to buy Gravestone Castle and convert it to a palatial estate. They want to develop a luxury RV campground," he confided, ignoring previous guarantees of privacy.

"Members of the Royal Enouement Society are attracted to Woebegone Dunes Resort because of the isolated forest setting on the shore of Lake Michigan. Woebegone Dunes Resort rates highly compared to the Yellowstone Club in Montana, the Hermitage Club in Vermont, and the Caribou Club in Aspen, Colorado. Investors are standing in line to purchase a limited number of one-hundred-thousand-dollar gold star memberships at my posh resort. A casino and an RV park on the adjacent property would destroy the ambiance of the landscape setting and reduce the incentive to join."

30

INDOORS GOLF

Jack glared at Father Cellophane, falsely giving the appearance of losing interest in Gravestone Castle and villainously shifting his thoughts to indoor golf.

"CFO Lady Vanessa is waiting downstairs to show you our new simulator. The latest indoor golf experience is the video golf simulator with dual tracking technology trusted by the pros that offers meticulous course reproduction. It delivers a fluid real-time environment with real-istic, smooth, and precise ball flight and data feedback that matters," Jack boasted with pride.

Father Cellophane was a fan of Lady Vanessa and a sucker for new technology. He was a short hitter and a bogey golfer accustomed to tak-ing at least one mulligan and one "gimme putt" on nearly every hole. He loved his Garmin GPS watch. He monogrammed his golf balls with a three-bar patriarchal cross. If things went wrong, he blamed his caddy for giving him bad advice, the weather, the wind, divine providence, and flaws in the architectural design of the golf course.

Professional golfer Bruno Greco was already working up a sweat in booth number one, crushing one ball after another into the strato-spheric. Bruno was thirty-two years old; six feet, five inches tall; stat-uesque; muscular; and mustached. He was the Wisconsin long-drive champion known for his exceptional driving distance, a crowd favorite sponsored by Woebegone Dunes Resort, and a significant threat to win the national championship in Las Vegas.

"Amazing! This simulator is a lot classier than the wooden platform we have at the Hermitage overlooking Lake Michigan," Father Cellophane asserted amusedly.

Lady Vanessa transitioned to her female persuasion side, constantly flickering close to the surface inside her. She automatically turned men on, lighting them up as efficiently as the lighting of an automatic gas fireplace. She was charming and wise, knowing and witty, purposely elegant and dazzlingly persuasive. Her success in life was all about power by knowing how to make men believe they were heading down the most exciting path of their life. Common gossip indicated there wasn't a local male who could resist her charms. She was irresistibly alluring. Men felt giddy, dazed, and confused in her presence. Insincere promises of seduction made their heads spin. She was a sultry, erotic seductress eager to have her flame fanned.

Her breasts were a source of fascination that Father Cellophane couldn't resist. Her cleavage was so ample and unconstrained by the lack of a bra that he was confident her jiggling boobs would fall out of her blouse the next time she leaned forward. Her breasts simultaneously bounced up and down and sideways, a complex figure-eight motion that caused his eyes to cross. The excessive sway and Jell-O bounce-like effect were like riding in a car with soft springs.

Her invitation to Father Cellophane to visit the golf simulator was enticing. He readily complied when she suggested he sit on a stiff-backed wooden chair with his back to the video screen. Bruno unexpectedly lurched forward, grabbing both arms while Lady Vanessa wrapped black Velcro strips around his torso. Father Cellophane was uncertain how to respond. He had never been bullied or coerced into doing or saying anything against his will. Sensing that something was dangerously wrong, the priest violently kicked Bruno in the chest as an act of desperation to prevent his legs from being secured to the base of the chair.

Bruno gritted his teeth and sneered. "Do you know who I am?"

"You're the Australian dwarf-tossing champion. I saw you competing on television, and the objective was to see who could throw the dwarf the farthest. I saw you dislocate a man's arm."

"That's true, but that's not what I'm talking about—I'm the Wisconsin long-drive golf champion."

Before placing a golf ball on the tee, Bruno lit a cigar before taking a series of violent practice swings with tremendous swing speed. He rotated his shoulders and chest backward, tightened his muscles, and raised both arms above his head as far as he could reach. Recoiling with tremendous force and swinging the club with all his might, he rotated cleanly across the tee with both arms. Upper-body centrifugal force caused the fiberglass shaft to flex. The golf club's head whipped through the air at maximum speed, creating a vortex at the apex of his downward swing. The explosive force of kinetic energy in the clubhead released at the exact instant of impact, causing both feet to lift off the artificial grass mat on launch impact. The golf ball compressed in slow motion, resiliently rebounding off the clubface and whizzing past Father Cellophane's left ear at a terrific velocity, only two feet from his head.

He had never heard a golf ball make such a loud, thundering, whistling sound. He was suddenly unnerved, realizing the perilousness of the situation.

Lady Vanessa shook a quick claim deed in Father Cellophane's face with one hand. She poked him in the chest with the other as she demanded, "Sign this property deed immediately, or you'll be very sorry."

"My hands are tired," Father Cellophane stated defiantly.

"Wrong response," Bruno said, blasting another wild shot dangerously close to Father Cellophane's kneecap.

"For God's sake, please don't do that again," he pleaded mercifully. "It would be dangerous for you to oppose Bo-Bo Bigelow. If he wants to build a casino on the Gravestone Castle property, I doubt if you could stop him. Opposing him would automatically lead to bitter hostility and unwinnable conflicts."

"Don't hit him, for goodness' sake," Vanessa whispered in Bruno's ear before setting a timer for one minute. "You have exactly sixty seconds to agree to sell Gravestone Castle. You have reached the point of no return. This contract is your Rubicon. If you sign this document today, we will release you and never bother you again. You will be able to enjoy a full, long life of luxury living as a monk in a hermitage in Sheboygan, Kenosha, or Milwaukee, wherever you choose. Your fate is in your hands—you decide!"

Father Cellophane's sallow complexion washed out. His shoulders sagged, and he appeared mentally defeated on the verge of physical collapse. Still, he resolved to continue resisting and was unwilling to comply with her demands.

"Father Feely is responsible, and he will have to decide," he protested.

Bruno lost his patience. The priest's abject refusal, insolent behavior, and self-abasing response upset him. "Last chance, and here's one more ball to let you know what I think of you."

Hastily placing a golf ball on the tee, he flexed his muscles and recoiled. He paused briefly at the top of the backswing before unleashing the clubhead with the full force of his entire body. The head of the oversized competition driver caught the ball squarely in the middle, causing it to explode off the face at two hundred miles per hour. Bruno was overly exuberant and forgot to aim.

The golf ball crashed into Father Cellophane's head with the full force of an elephant gun. It struck him in the face, shattering the bones surrounding the left eye socket into a dozen fractured pieces. The eyeball exploded like a water-filled balloon. The broken cheekbone and rapid accumulation of blood caused the left side of his face to sag toward his chin. The intraocular jelly and clear vitreous fluid lining the eye's ciliary body spurted out of his eye socket onto his cheek. It drained down the side of his face into his open mouth, followed by a mass of ocular tissue and a stream of red blood. Blunt-force trauma fractured the frontal vertical bone plate in his forehead. The brain crashed backward inside the skull cavity on impact, causing traumatic subarachnoid hemorrhaging.

Numerous small arteries tore, and blood vessels ruptured, causing inflammation and bleeding in the brain. An uncontrolled flow of blood spread over the surface of the brain tissue inside his skull, causing wide-spread effects. A hematoma began to solidify, displacing the yellow brain fluid, forcing it toward the right side of the head. Father Cellophane lost consciousness and listed to one side. Heaven remained silent.

"Oh my God, he's unresponsive, disabled, and lifeless. You killed him. Jack Daniels is going to be furious. Roll the body in a rug. Hide it in the janitor's closet. Come back after midnight and toss the body in Lake Michigan," Lady Vanessa advised. "Everyone will assume he drowned."

Bruno rummaged through the contents of a cupboard drawer in the corner. To throw Deputy Sheriff Bud Light off track, he randomly selected an iPhone and a German passport heisted from the SafeHouse in Milwaukee.

Lady Vanessa turned off the light and quietly bolted the door behind them.

31

TWIN BOYS

Twin thirteen-year-old boys living on a farm two miles north of Jack Daniels's property ignored the bright-yellow "No Trespassing" signs and cautiously climbed over the barbed-wire fence. They nervously continued walking until they eventually stumbled across a massive stash of Callaway golf balls indiscriminately scattered on the ground.

"These golf balls are brand new, worth a dollar or more at the farmers' market," Gary remarked as they eagerly rushed to fill their backpacks. "We better not tell Dad where we found them."

"What's that shiny thing in the tree?" he said, pointing to a twelve-foot-long piece of blackened aluminum stuck in a large evergreen tree.

"It's the wing of an airplane," his brother Larry surmised on closer inspection.

The boys were caught up in the moment and having so much fun dragging the wing out of the tree that it never occurred to them to look around for additional pieces of wreckage.

"I've got a cool idea. Let's drag it to the top of the dune and pretend it's a sleigh. We can sit on it and slide down the beach."

Larry carefully positioned the tip on a fallen log and jumped on the wing with a great force three times in succession until the end bent upward to form the shape of a sleigh. The two boys positioned the sled at the top of a sandy couloir with no tree roots, rocks, or shrubs below to obstruct them.

"Hold on tight."

"I feel like Evel Knievel preparing to make one of his famous motorcycle jumps. Is this a bad idea?"

The two brothers rocked back and forth, inching forward little by little until the wing eventually lost traction and steadily gained downhill momentum. The dry sand and grasses offered very little resistance, and the speed of their descent was much faster than anticipated. When the sled hit the shoreline, there was a giant watery explosion, followed by the makeshift toboggan effortlessly continuing to skim across the surface of the lake. As forward momentum gradually decelerated, the wing listed to one side, and the boys sluggishly fell off in slow motion in five feet of water.

"Wow!"

They knew this moment would be a lifelong childhood memory they would never forget. Hysterically belly laughing, doggy-paddling to keep heads above water, and gulping mouthfuls of lake water, they reached the shore.

"What a hoot! I can't stop laughing. That was funnier than a barrel of monkeys," Gary screamed, slapping his brother on the back.

Their clothes were soaking wet as they crawled out of the water, thigh-slapping, dancing in circles, and uproariously laughing.

Air trapped in the wing allowed it to continue floating on the surface of the water, gradually drifting out of sight, pushed by a slight southwest breeze bobbing along in the shoreline drift waves.

Larry's boots made a loud squishing sound when he walked, triggering more raucous laughter. At the top of the dune, they retrieved their lunches, took off their shirts and pants, and hung them on a tree branch to dry.

"What is that small red thing over there?"

Gary strolled over to the tree and picked up a squarish bottle of

Maker's Mark premium Kentucky bourbon in a broken wooden crate. He broke the red wax seal and removed the cap. He pretended to take a big swig and passed the bottle to Larry to see what he would do. "Here— taste this. It's good," he feigned with a smile.

Larry swallowed a large mouthful of whiskey. He staggered sideways and then stumbled forward onto his knees. "Wow! That burns," he screamed as he erupted in a giddy fit of laughter. "That is the first time I ever tasted whiskey—it's horrible!"

Gary cautiously followed suit with a small sip as they alternately swallowed increasingly more enormous swigs of whiskey from the bottle.

"You look like an apple-faced monkey," Larry slurred hilariously in a fit of laughter while taking a big bite of his peanut butter sandwich. The sandwich awkwardly missed his mouth and hit him in the face, leaving large globs of brown peanut butter clinging to his cheeks.

Gary fell on his back, laughing so hysterically that he could hardly get the words out of his mouth. "You eat shit," he said in a gut-busting belly laugh, pointing to the brown-colored peanut butter dripping from his brother's face. "You look like an ignorant booger-eating butthead."

Insults continued to be hurled back and forth in an intense bout of nonsensical name-calling, triggering even more commotion followed by more uproariously boisterous laughter.

"You're nothing but a big Oscar Meyer Wienermobile driver."

Larry jerked his head up as if tasered into temporary submission. "Look beside you. The pilot's hand is giving us a thumbs-up gesture," he announced with an overpowering sense of wonder and amazement, setting off another round of rowdy behavior.

Gary swallowed some air and forced out a large belch, followed by Larry squeezing his hand under his armpit, producing a rude sound.

"I feel dizzy. My stomach is churning. I drank too much. I'm going to take a nap," Larry drunkenly mumbled as he lay down on his back under the shade of a tree.

"I can hardly walk and speak at the same time," Gary said, cluelessly smacking his forehead with an open palm. He closed his eyes and fell asleep in grinning ignorance. Two hours later, sunburned, dizzy, and feeling yucky, the boys gathered up their belongings and staggered toward home.

"It's getting late. The shadows are long, and the sun is beginning to cool. We better get home before dinner, or we'll be in big trouble. Leave the alcohol here. I don't care if I ever drink whiskey again," Larry slowly drawled with slurred speech.

"Don't tell Dad we trespassed on Jack Daniels's property. He won't like it," Gary mused. "Don't tell him we drank whiskey either because he'll ground us indefinitely."

"Wait," Gary whispered. "Someone is coming." The boys concealed themselves behind a large tree and peered into the forest. "Notice the way he's dragging his back foot and limping and breathing like he has broken ribs. Have you noticed that he has big ears? I think he's a thief planning to break into Jack Daniels's cabin."

The boys watched the stranger remove the keys above the door header and unlock the front door. "Let's get out of here before we get caught." When they arrived at the northern property boundary, Larry snagged his flannel shirt in the barbed-wire fence as he drunkenly tumbled face first into the dirt.

A large rogue wave from a passing freighter from Sturgeon Bay washed the aluminum airplane wing up on the beach later that evening under the glow of a full moon. It temporarily snagged on a small rock outcropping, three miles south of where it had initially entered the water.

32

SCIENCE AND TECHNOLOGY

Bo-Bo Bigelow was the world's largest purchaser of killer bees for assassination purposes, and Father Adam Baum was the only source. Johnny Linguine routinely trucked the beehives to Houston-Galveston and loaded them on oil tankers returning to Nigeria. Father Feely processed the orders, facilitated the process, and collected the money.

Father Baum was lurking in the shadows by the entrance to Gravestone Castle, waiting to fill a nonstandard order. He was peering into the murky black void through military-grade night-vision goggles when a black Hummer emerged from the forest primeval with its headlights extinguished. A man with a very dark face and a scar on his cheek lowered the passenger window and peered into the red sunset. The jaundiced yellow glow of his eyes from under his black beret signaled a hauntingly animalistic warning in the foggy darkness. Father Baum materialized from out of the shadows of the elaborate iron entrance gate like an apparition backlighted by the fading rays of the setting sun.

"You startled me," the African admitted in a deep, low-pitched voice. "Bo-Bo Bigelow wants me to snuff out a narcotics informant cooperating with law enforcement. The victim is an illegal alien from Sinaloa, Mexico, a landscape maintenance worker at Woebegone Dunes Resort."

Baum had a pessimistic view of the future of humanity, gloomy sneering disbelief in sincerity and integrity—dominated by an affliction for distributing pain, distress, grief, and misery to others. The Padre was habitually dishonest. He delighted in misfortune, sadistically relishing the bad feelings of others without boundaries. He slipped a black plastic bag containing a poisoned hat through the driver's side window. "Keep the bag closed at all times. The victim will be trimming trees on the fifth fairway of Woebegone Dunes Resort tomorrow afternoon. Insert the iPad in the glass window of the beehive and press 'go.' A prerecorded movie of bees doing a figure-eight waggle dance lets the rest of the hive know the exact direction and distance to the victim. The angle of the bee dance related to the sun's position indicates direction. The duration of the waggle dance signifies the distance, and the intensity signifies urgency. The entire swarm will become agitated. Fifty thousand killer bees functioning as a single organism will swarm out of the hive. They will viciously attack the victim when they smell the chemical phero-mones on the hat."

The driver handed the Padre an envelope filled with hundred-dollar bills. Father Adam Baum cupped his hands together and steepled his fingers, not to pray but as an outward expression of confidence. He had a malicious grin; a shallow smile with deep, piercing eyes; and an evil consciousness that betrayed all innocence.

The Hummer eased into the stagnant night air smelling like rotting vegetation and foul water. A lone white gull broke the stillness of the darkness by adding an eerie overture to the forest primeval with a raspy, croaking call.

33

CANADIAN CLUB CHAMPION

Lady Vanessa marched boldly into the Amber Room restaurant. "Your guests, Lieutenant Baron Dunning and Emily, are waiting for you at the driving range. I'll walk you over there now," she informed the Kennedys. She exhibited aloofness and disdain, deliberate indifference, and callous disregard. The cold-shoulder treatment she gave them and the outward demeanor she displayed were precisely the opposite of her former bubbly mood.

Lieutenant Baron Dunning concentrated on finessing his short irons to create backspin while alternately creating hooks and fades. "Thank you for hosting us at Woebegone Dunes Resort this week," he stated vigorously at first glance when the Kennedys arrived.

"It was very gracious of you to offer to be our hosts," Emily remarked politely. "This resort is enchanting. The beauty of the forest setting enhanced with random wildflower gardens is glorious. The architectural designs of the buildings and golf course are very harmonious. All of the human-made elements blend perfectly with the landscape. The understated natural beauty of the forest setting arouses my senses and piques my interest."

Kate extended a warm welcome to Lieutenant Dunning with angelic assertiveness and divine confidence. "This is the perfect place for an affair of the heart," she radiantly enlightened Emily. The lieutenant admired her enthusiasm. She seemed to be embracing her creative energy, moving intuitively with the flow of life, flowing like water in a river, radiantly drawing in success without any of the usual hustle and grind.

Caddies Jay Walker and Chris P. "Crispy" Bacon wore white long-sleeve performance coveralls that were freshly pressed.

"Glad to know you, Jay and Crispy," the lieutenant stated warmly. "We have heard many glowing endorsements of your talents, and our expectations are very high. We know that a good caddy can take four or five strokes off your game—we hope you are those guys," he said smoothly while extending the palm of his right hand with a friendly smile.

"Inside the mind of every golfer is a better one. The way to get started is to quit talking and begin doing. You can count on me as your caddy—at least five strokes—but only if you do as I say," Jay coached. "Woebegone Dunes Resort is a golfer's paradise, yet it remains one of Wisconsin's best-kept secrets. It's similar to Whistling Straits and Erin Hills in that regard," he said, waving toward the finely groomed fairways and sloping hills. "Very few people have had the privilege of playing golf at Woebegone Dunes Resort. There is no advertising because it's a members-only club on private land hidden in the forest, unknown to outsiders."

"The profuse wildflower gardens with countless varieties of plants and topiary are stunning. Sculptures and terraces randomly placed in unexpected and surprising locations throughout delight the senses by adding visual excitement and an element of surprise," Crispy elucidated.

"Our first impression is overwhelmingly positive," Kate remarked. "The stone clubhouse with its colorful snapdragons, petunias, alyssums, geraniums, and impatiens is stunning."

"Did you know that my wife, Kate, is the Canadian Club Champion?" Wayne boasted.

"Wow, Kate, you must be an outstanding golfer. It's an honor to caddy for you," Jay replied enthusiastically. "I knew you were an excellent player when I saw the Callaway Rogue ST driver with the Tungsten

Speed Cartridge, Jailbreak Speed Frame, and Flash Face in your golf bag. Engineering for maximum speed with exceptional levels of forgiveness is what Callaway does best."

Kate grinned with a wink and a smile as she reached into her vest pocket for a silver flask. "My friends do call me the Canadian Club Champion. It's the premium whiskey that keeps my arms loose and the wiggle in my fanny lubricated," she explained with a sexy little shimmy of her hips and shoulders.

The lieutenant summarized his philosophy in a fatherly way: "Alcohol adds a little tailwind to your sail, but more sailors drown in a barrel of rum than the ocean. My sweet mother's eyes were the color of Scottish whiskey. Every day she added nips of the Famous Grouse to her tea like salty old sailors, soldiers, and rodeo clowns."

Jay grinned amusedly. "Let's walk over to the first tee. First, I will explain the lay of the land to you. After that, we will follow these four gentlemen and caddies."

Caddy Dusty Rhodes was wearing his traditional white caddy jumpsuit, a prized element of the marketing image of Woebegone Dunes Resort. Still, to the Linguine brothers, he looked like a guy hanging around waiting to paint a house.

Johnny Linguine was puffing on a smelly cigar while talking on his Apple watch. "Golf is the most fun my brother Joey has without taking his clothes off."

Joey looked irritated. He was fuming about something other than golf, aggressively flailing about with his golf club, carelessly swinging the driver back and forth as a warmup routine.

"Joey, you look like a caveman trying to kill your lunch with a club," his brother Johnny teased.

The club accidentally hit the ground with a big thud. A huge chunk of wet sod flew through the air, splattering mud all over Dusty Rhodes's white caddy uniform, hat, and sunglasses. Dusty had been holding his cheeks tightly together for a good reason. The impact caused his sphincter muscles to relax suddenly, and he unintentionally let out a stinky ripper. The fat man with the big cigar, Johnny Linguine, spontaneously laughed heartily, lost his balance, tripped, and nearly tumbled on the ground.

"Joey, what an asshole you are. Your caddy looks worse than Bastardo the Greaser, the mechanic down at Carmella's garage, all covered in grease and oil. And we haven't even teed off yet," the fat man with the gunmetal toupee mocked as his words dissolved into laughter.

Dusty Rhodes was embarrassed by the unkempt appearance of his dirty and disheveled caddy uniform. Mud smeared on his sunglasses, blurring his vision, and dirt ruined the looks of his new red hat pulled down over one ear. He stuttered through his buck teeth, "P-p-please be c-c-careful."

Joey Linguine never apologized. Instead, he stealthily snuck up from behind and quietly slipped a sleeve of three Warbird Callaway golf balls into Dusty's hip pocket. "Make sure I don't lose any golf balls today. My brother Johnny keeps track of how many golf balls I lose to make sure I'm not cheating," he whispered with his hand over his mouth to conceal his words, faking a sneeze.

Jay cautiously held back his group. "Give them space. Johnny Linguine owns Linguine Trucking, Storage, and Excavation. His brother Joey is called 'the Tooth.' He bit a guy on the arm during a fight, and the wound became infected, and the victim had to amputate his right arm. Jimmy is the youngest brother. Their cousin Alfredo Casseroli is highly volatile and unpredictable. But he's a great chef when he's sober."

"Watching you guys putt is more painful than picking a broken nose," Johnny Linguine bumbled awkwardly. "If profanity affected the trajectory and flight path of a golf ball, you would win a lot of money. Remember not to pick up the ball when it is still rolling—that's bad sportsmanship."

"Have you ever noticed the uglier a man's legs are, the worse he plays golf?" the lieutenant gaffed in a rare breach of etiquette. "Most of the balls you find in the woods are from big hitters. The average golfer thinks they are concentrating when they're merely worrying. The Linguine brothers are like children, unable to count past five."

Emily ignored the Lieutenant's silly misguided attempts at humor. Instead, she was obsessed with Jay Walker. She observed him intensely, how a scientist records data with all available senses during an experiment. She was intrigued by him, the way he looked, moved, and talked. He seemed so unblemished, manly, and virginal. The instinctive sidelong glance he gave her in return appeared to be part of a pattern of courting behavior, signifying intense interest. She checked her feelings, knowing his response indicated mutual attraction. They seemed to be on the same emotional wavelength, having an internal dialogue without words. Perfect!

When their eyes met, he looked up innocently, returning her fixed gaze, signaling a romantic desire. The twinkle in her eye caught his attention and captured his imagination how a round-cut brilliant diamond signals alternating flashes of spectral-colored light. Emily had a beguiling smile on her lips, a lightness in her step and spirit, and a spark of something alluring that triggered lingering eye contact. She was nurturing, spontaneously wild, free, with abundant feminine energy. Her words were innocent, but there seemed to be an oblique allusion, a hint of a veiled sexual innuendo in her body language and the tone of her voice. Were her feelings a harbinger of exciting things to come? Was she subtly attempting to draw him closer?

"This place is magnificent. I'm fascinated by the grandeur," Emily commented sweetly with a honeyed look in her eyes, showing intense interest in Jay as a distinguished gentleman around whom she was comfortable. Her words were syrupy. In Jay's eyes, she was drop-dead gorgeous with her long, luxurious hair that was well kept. Without hesitation, she seemed so earnest and sincerely devoted. She had Jay's wholehearted approval and attention.

Jay's brain was hardwired to focus on one thing at a time, leaving him temporarily oblivious to the others. When the Mob Foursome was out of sight, he suddenly regained consciousness and began his rehearsed marketing speech. "There's a great deal of speculation about what goes on at the Hermitage. There are rumors that Father Cellophane enjoys running around in a speedo swimsuit while drinking multiple glasses of Chianti wine. He loves it when the nuns bundle him up in bubble wrap, roll him around on the bed, and pop all the air pockets. He says a little prayer on Friday nights and gets a free meal at Our Lady of the Immaculate Reception fish fry. Avid Green Bay Packer fans comprise the congregation. There is no Sunday mass during football season. Everyone is either in Green Bay watching the football game or hanging out at Linguine Brothers Sports Bar and Grill watching the big-screen TV."

Each time Emily looked at Jay, she smiled with a spontaneous public display of affection and startling desire for courtship. Jay responded by extolling the virtues of northern Wisconsin with the flowery praise of a seasoned advertising and marketing director by expressing admiration for the excellent gold-class qualities of Woebegone Dunes Resort. "Corporate Pro Colorado is responsible for the design of the resort. The stellar condition of the golf course, the health of the forest, the profusion of wildflowers, the superb quality of the resort facilities, and the beauty of the natural setting are glorious. The history of the Native Americans, early pioneers, and military in this region is also intriguing."

Kate took another swig from her silver flask before taking the mink headcover off her Callaway driver and plucking a titanium Tour TDS golf ball out of her golf bag. "What's the name of this fairway?" she inquired as she steadied the ball on a plastic Martini golf tee.

"On the Rocks," Jay responded with a smile. "I was reluctant to tell you."

Kate was ecstatic. She had brilliant white teeth and a compelling, powerfully irresistible smile, reflecting her admirable good nature and self-confidence. She mesmerically smiled as she reached into her vest pocket and took another swig of confidence.

Emily's head was in the clouds, disconnected from the present, thinking erotic thoughts and daydreaming about pleasant things that might happen in the future. She fantasized about being alone with Jay in a romantic setting, sitting beside him with a glass of wine, her head on his shoulder in front of a roaring fire on a cold winter's night. The thought of being swept off her feet by Prince Charming was becoming a reality.

34

HARUM-SCARUM

Jay smiled, cleared his throat, pointed to the next hole, and spoke his rehearsed remarks. "Hole number two is named 'Stairway to Heaven.' Walking up the steps is strenuous but well worth the effort. The view from the observation deck is panoramic, and you can see all around. It's also a good place to get oriented."

The innocent forest scents were bewitching, deep luscious green trees and berries anchored by somber forest wisdom. Emily was having an uninhibited fantasy, twisty, steamy thoughts that stirred her imagination and aroused her sensibility. Jay seemed imposing but kind and selfless, just the kind of man that attracted her. She quietly daydreamed about spanking him and making him beg for what he wanted, things that she was too ashamed to mention. She had erotic visions of coming together in a warm romantic embrace, holding each other tightly, warmly kissing, and erotically touching.

"I can see why this place is difficult to find," Lieutenant Dunning said, rupturing her fantasy, scanning the horizon for signs of human habitation. "The property is surprisingly isolated between mature woodlands and water. I don't see a single farmhouse, power pole, church steeple, water tank, or any signs of civilization—just big trees and keyhole glimpses of Lake Michigan."

Wayne and Lieutenant Dunning took the lead with magnificent long arching tee shots that seemed to float on air as they slowly drifted down from the deep-blue sky into the valley below. Kate and Emily followed two fine fairway shots of their own, despite Kate's slight alcohol buzz, sheepish grin, and diminishing attention span. They approached the green, walking in unison in good spirits, high on the fresh air and sunshine. Jay instructed Wayne to place the golf ball closer to his right foot and use his fairway hybrid club to drive the ball low and roll it up to the green to avoid hitting a large overhanging tree branch. Thanks to his guidance, Wayne hit a perfect shot.

"We're on a roll—four pars. It doesn't get any better than that," Kate said while contemplating the idea of using a little more swing oil to celebrate.

Crispy warned alertly, "The next hole is called 'Harum-Scarum.' There are numerous hazards. You need to pay attention and plan your strategy carefully. The fairway is a mini canyon beside an abandoned arm of the stone quarry. Steep vertical rock walls confine both sides of the fairway, and large rock monuments protrude out of the fairway randomly and in odd places. Be careful not to get injured by balls ricocheting off the rocks. The green is a peninsula on the edge of Gravestone Quarry filled with icy cold spring water," he cautioned.

"If you overshoot the green, your ball will roll into the water and be impossible to retrieve," Jay explained, setting fear into his clients' mind.

Emily aimed and fired. Her ball glanced off a large rock, altering the trajectory and rewarding her with an extra thirty yards of distance. Kate's ball collided with a large rock and came screaming right back at her. She shrieked, dropped her club, twirled around, and instinctively covered her head with both hands. The ball landed at her feet, exactly where she had hit it. She picked up her sorry-looking golf ball and scrutinized the damage. "It has road rash on one side and a big smile on the other," she declared optimistically.

"Turn your ball upside down—it's a frown, not a smile," the lieutenant teased. "Bad things happen in threes. If you have a fourth bad shot, you know it's the beginning of a new group of three."

Kate tossed the damaged golf ball into a squirrel hole and grabbed a fresh ball out of the box. Following Jay's advice, she hit a heavenly fairway wood the second time, followed by a hundred-yard chip shot that slowly circled the flag before spiraling into the hole. "Woo-hoo!" she whooped as an expression of exuberant delight and self-approval.

Wayne's second shot was ideal—majestically high and mighty. It was just the kind of trajectory he had seen professional golfers hit in the PGA Championship at Whistling Straits. The ball landed softly on the back of the green, bounced twice, and plunked into the pond behind the green. Tiny white bubbles in the center of an ever-expanding concentric ring of ripples were the only remaining evidence.

Emily had a solemn, phobic, sinking feeling triggered by a compulsive fear of deep dark water. "The water is dark and foreboding. I wonder what lies below the surface, beneath the water's edge in the mysteries of the dark abyss."

"Gravestone Quarry Lake is larger and deeper than it appears from this vantage point. Fingers of the quarry extend into multiple fairways, providing a highly intimidating hazard," Jay explained.

With warm, fluttery internal sensations bubbling up inside as evidence of a glowing spark of secret desire for a romantic friendship, Emily inquired curiously, "Do you miss Gravestone Castle?"

Jay had a secret desire to hold Emily in his arms. She had balanced extroversion and self-confidence, large eyes, a big smile with white teeth, healthy hair, and glowing skin. He found her attractive beyond belief, with many beautiful highlights, positive features, a youthful appearance, and awesomeness. He had a secret admiration, infatuation, and fondness for her, a strong desire to be with her at all times. He greatly appreciated the attention she gave him, the way she explicitly offered gratitude, praise, advice, and words of affection.

His passions swelled as he began speaking with increased enthusiasm, expelling his true feelings. Exposure of his inner self caused his voice to quiver. "My father and I shared the dream of turning Gravestone Castle into a classy five-star hotel and restaurant specializing in weddings and group events. My father's incentive was to send me to Switzerland's best hotel and restaurant school. I was devastated by the unexpected loss of my father and greatly disturbed by the cause of death. Since then, everything that has happened has been heartbreaking and distressing—my life is upside down. Tragically, my father died on his birthday from a severe food allergy. The priests at the Hermitage presented him with a birthday cake made with peanut flour and peanut oil," Jay informed her, emotionally choking on his own words.

"Everyone was acquitted. Still, I believe Father Feely and his lawyer forged my father's last will and testament. How they persuaded him to gift Gravestone Castle to the Hermitage is a complex mystery to me," he confessed wearily. "I attended university in Switzerland when it happened, so I don't know any of the details. My expensive European education is wasted, my lifetime dream of owning a premiere resort in northern Wisconsin rudely extinguished."

With a sorrowful expression, Jay stared in the direction of the massive stone structure that had been his esteemed family home as a tear migrated down his dusty cheek. "I apologize for feeling sorry for myself and distracting you from your golf game," he intoned with a fall in the pitch of his voice.

Feminine intuition drove Emily to offer comfort and assurances. She had a strong desire to help, stimulated by a readiness to take action—a cognitive and genuinely compassionate empathy. She hugged Jay tightly, longing to soothe his troubled soul. She spoke softly with her lips close to his neck, whispering encouraging words in his ear as an act of kindness and compassion. Her hug was romantically more profound and lingering than a passionate kiss.

A single whiff of Emily's lavender perfume made Jay's heart do somersaults, and these olfactory cues stimulated a biological response affecting mating behavior. Thoughts of being with her consumed his focus and drive. Standing next to her was like drinking two shots of tequila—pleasurable excitement followed by euphoric feelings of sheer bliss. Jay openly exposed his feelings by exhibiting a new puppy's adoring, worshipful cuddly affection. The overt sense of intimacy left them feeling connected, romantically warm and fuzzy. He tightly squeezed her hand as a clear sign of a budding romantic relationship.

35

DEADLY ATTACK

Herding the flock in the direction of the next tee, Jay explained, "The name of this fairway is Waterloo. More birdies and bogies than pars on this hole—it's either a feast or famine, the way that Phil Mickelson attacks a golf course. The fairway forms a horseshoe with a double dogleg to the right. It's the only hole that heavily favors slicers. The green isn't visible due to the dense evergreen forest and protruding rocky ledge that parallels the lake until you reach Ascension Point. The safest way is the longest, and it's also boring. It's a hundred yards shorter if you're willing to take a blind shot across the quarry lake through a narrow gap in the trees. You have to be very accurate to avoid the water," Jay explained.

A terrifying swarm of angry bees forming a small dark cloud obscured the sun as they streaked past overhead a mere ten feet above the ground. "They seem like predators out for blood," Emily screamed. The sound of her voice shattered the silence of a peaceful summer afternoon by the lake. The high-pitched buzzing sound of an angry swarm of bees stimulated an intense fear of predation. She sucked in her breath, subconsciously afraid that someone might be dangerously in peril. Her stomach muscles tensed. She had a visceral, intuitive feeling the insects were aggressively targeting someone.

"The sound of bees swarming is eerily frightening. They remind me of scary animal sounds in the dark that intuitively reaches deep inside us, automatically triggering primal fears and survival instincts," Emily warned.

The interruption caused by the passing of the bees ended with a horrifying, bloodcurdling, primeval shriek of a desperate man in danger of being killed. A maintenance worker was violently stomping up and down, swatting bees away from his head and face, frantically waving his arms in the air, signaling a life-threatening attack. The nightmarish swarm of angry killer bees was unmercifully assaulting him from every angle. The expression of sheer terror on his face was difficult to discern through the mask of angry crawling insects covering his head and face.

Emily nearly fainted. Anxiety-induced chills, nausea, heart palpitations, and shaking accompanied her feelings of dread.

A fellow worker yelled, "*Saltar al lago*—go jump in the lake."

Lieutenant Dunning reacted with the demeanor of a professional fireman blindly rushing into a massive life-threatening blaze without fear, hoping to be a hero by saving an unfortunate victim in peril. Jay followed close behind, with Emily stumbling along after him. The target of the attack was a Hispanic male wearing a black Whistling Straits golf hat. The victim flailed his arms in wild desperation. He stomped his feet, recklessly spinning around in circles, frantically attempting to tear large clusters of angry bees off his face.

When he screamed, gobs of bees flew into his mouth. His frantic attempts to separate himself from the attacking swarm angered the vile insects even more. The accumulative pain of multiple stings stimulated his adrenal glands, resulting in a superhuman burst of life-saving energy. He ran recklessly through the forest in a desperate attempt to escape the unrelenting attack. He accidentally slammed his head into a tree trunk, adding pain and confusion. He forced his way through the forest like a wild animal on a rampage, pushing aside low hanging tree branches that blocked his vision. Without warning, he blindly stumbled headfirst into a steep rocky crevice, releasing a haunting primal scream that lingered in the air as he tumbled out of sight. He expelled a projectile vomit as he bounced head over heels off the last remaining overhanging rock ledge, free-falling more than thirty feet into Lake Michigan. Torn flesh from his arms dangled like potato skins on thorny bushes and sharp protruding rocks. His body landed with a sickening thud on a large boulder, smashing his skull and breaking his back, killing him instantly. The violently disturbed swarm of angry bees aggressively continued stinging the corpse without mercy. They clustered around the eyes and ears and crawled under his clothing, eventually attacking the anus, the last remaining portion of the body floating above the surface of the water.

Red blood mixed with cranial brain fluid and hundreds of dead bees stained the rocks on the shoreline of Lake Michigan. Emily peered over the edge of the cliff in disbelief. The psychological fear of death catatonically traumatized her. "I feel sorry for his unfortunate widow and children," she mumbled almost unintelligibly.

Her eyes remained transfixed on the body drooped over the rocks, reliving the experience, internalizing the feelings and actions of the victim in the final moments of death. She watched as the corpse sluggishly slid off the inclined rock into the water, leaving behind telltale red skid marks. His hat bobbed up and down on the tranquil capillary ripples of the surface of Lake Michigan. There was no solace or relief from grief in her altered state of anxiety. Her knees were weak. She felt dizzy and faint. Vivid flashbacks of the nightmarish event produced distress, melancholic sadness, disturbing thoughts, and intense emotions that traumatized her. Her skin was cold and sweaty, and her eyes dilated. Her face was pale and sallow. Her pulse was rapid, her breathing shallow. Her blood pressure dropped precipitously.

Jay embraced her from behind as a sign of comfort and consolation in her time of distress and sadness. He had a manly desire to reduce her stress and shelter her. Emily felt sorry for the victim and his family and friends. She twirled around, stood on her toes, put her arms around Jay's neck, and warmly planted a kiss on his cheek in appreciation of his emotional support.

The lieutenant called Deputy Sheriff Bud Light to report the fatality location. "Emily and I will remain here at the scene of the accident until the deputy arrives. Jay should return to the fairway and explain what happened to Wayne and Kate Kennedy, who will be eager to learn the outcome."

36

I QUIT

Jay emerged from the forest, emotionally traumatized by the chaotic and tragic death he had just witnessed. He had reluctantly departed the scene of the accident and returned to his guests. "The poor man died after falling off a cliff trying to escape from the chaotic swarm of killer bees. They continued stinging him unmercifully, even after he died," Jay explained.

"We're so sorry for his friends and family," Wayne and Kate conveyed.

Joey Linguine's words rudely interrupted them. "Hit until you're happy, boys!" he hollered unequivocally from the next fairway.

Johnny, Joey, and Jimmy Linguine, as well as cousin Alfredo Casseroli, had never completed a round of golf without an incident. There was always a kerfuffle, followed by an accusation of lying and cheating. They continually argued over the rules, cussed creatively, and exhibited rude behavior. Most rounds ended with disputes over lost balls and damage to the golf course. Maintenance issues invariably prevailed: nasty cigar butts littering the greens, footprints menacingly left in the bunkers, divots in the sod, and scuff marks on the fairways proved their passing on every hole.

Joey took several firm practice swings, lacking both finesse and accuracy, using way too much brute force. He chicken-winged his left elbow at the top of an overly fast backswing, causing his club to slam down into the turf behind the ball on the downswing. The golf ball popped straight up in the air as a massive chunk of muddy sod flew sideways and smacked his caddy, Dusty Rhodes, in the crotch for the second time.

"Another camel-ass shot—it's high, and it stinks," he bellowed with a laugh.

"The problem with your golf game is you stand too close to the ball—after you hit it."

Joey made a second attempt. He hammered his Callaway Apex 5-iron into the dark-green, perfectly manicured, finely clipped turf, resulting in an enormous divot in the fairway.

As they approached the hundred-yard marker, Johnny received a telephone call from a client asking about a costly oil painting. "Yes, Father Marcello discovered the antique painting in a European monastery in Italy. It has an extraordinary backstory. He asked me to broker the sale to raise money for the Hermitage. Meet me at sunset by the elaborate wrought-iron entrance gate to Gravestone Castle. I only accept cash," Johnny stated.

Caddy Dusty Rhodes stood unobtrusively in the background, subtly eavesdropping on the conversation, feigning not to hear.

"We're going to make a fortune when our client from Atlanta shows up to buy that famous oil painting stolen by the Nazis during World War Two." Johnny smirked derisively after hanging up. "Any dummy could sell that painting on Craigslist for one hundred fifty grand or more. Father Marcello is an excellent forger. He created a believable back story, painted it himself, and appraised it for two hundred thousand. The jaw of a pearl-clasping, super-rich woman in Georgia dropped when she found out it was available for such a low price."

Dusty's head swirled with the dream of owning a small log cabin isolated in the forest under the shade of tall evergreen trees, far from the city and the audaciously disrespectful Linguine brothers. *If I hid in the woods by the entrance gate before Johnny arrived with the painting, I could steal the buyer's cash and the painting at the same time. I could buy myself a nice cabin with the money,* he impulsively planned in the background.

As the group of four rounded the last bend in the fairway and approached the green, it became glaringly apparent that the balls had disappeared. While they aimlessly wandered around poking the bushes and peering into the bottomless lake, Dusty stealthily dropped one of Joey's spare golf balls on the edge of the green.

"Hey, J-J-Joey, I found your golf ball," Dusty announced, smiling and winking nefariously, prematurely assuming that his actions would increase the size of his tip.

"Your golf balls are in the bottom of the lake. Give me your money, you cheap bastards," Joey chuckled dishonestly, reaching out a greedy palm with dirty fingernails.

Dusty bent over to tighten his shoelace.

Wham!

A golf ball exploded out of the trees, unexpectedly blasting Dusty in the buttocks. In super-slow motion, the ball disappeared, paused for multiple seconds, and then miraculously popped back out.

"Ouch!" he screamed.

"Wow! Did you see that screaming line drive explosively smack Dusty in the rectum?" Joey marveled. "Rectum? It damn near killed him," his cousin Alfredo Casseroli chuckled.

Dusty spasmodically threw up his arms, accidentally knocking his hat into the water. His hips awkwardly thrust forward as if an electric cattle prod had poked him from behind. He arched his back with his hands on his hips, lost his balance, tripped over a rock, stretched his hamstring, and tore the double-seamed crotch in his caddy uniform. He bloodied his elbow on a sharp tree branch. He stumbled into the quarry lake before slipping and falling in the mud, destroying the white caddy uniform. Joey had soiled his uniform on the first tee with a chunk of flying wet sod. His appearance was shoddy and slipshod. He was soaking wet, besmirched, grass-stained, and his uniform torn. He was a disgrace to the professional caddy world. Hunched over, humiliated, and rubbing his sore butt, throbbing with pain, with both hands, he remorsefully limped away in the direction of the clubhouse. He paused, twisted his rubber neck backward, and shouted, "I q-quit! You try carrying your own damn golf bags," he stuttered with a severe lisp.

"What a loser! You stutter, you talk with a lisp, and you limp. You're as worthless as the G in *lasagna*. Don't forget your hemorrhoid donut cushion, you caddy shack fucker," Joey teased.

"He's a *wampus*, a strange and objectionable individual perversely acting to the extreme inconvenience of others," Johnny added.

Dusty Rhodes snapped. He was sensitive about his appearance, and his pride was hurt. The other boys in the orphanage had teased him all his life about his red hair, buck teeth, protruding ears, and a speech impediment. He had finally reached the breaking point, and he wasn't going to allow others to push him around and tease him anymore.

Dusty exploded. "Think fire! You're all going to burn in hell—sooner than you think," he threatened menacingly. "You sons-of-bitches are con men and art thieves. I hope you go to jail," he barked as he stormed away. With his back turned awkwardly, he stomped in the direction of the clubhouse. He violently wormed his way through a patch of red tulips, aggressively kicking and crushing the colorful flowers. He deliberately went out of his way to trample with heavy footsteps a beautiful patch of showy yellow and purple iris flowers. His words of intimidation had a credible ring of truth. His threats lingered in the air after he was gone.

Joey Linguine disingenuously laughed at his caddy's misfortune. With a muffled snort, he hollered, "You short, fat fannies are playing way too slow. Pick up the pace and get the hell out of here before someone else gets hit by a golf ball." With that, he led the disheveled procession to the next tee.

Dusty arrived back at caddy shack headquarters, covered from head to toe in filth. He had pond scum smeared on his sunglasses, mud dripping from his crotch, dirt stuck in his ear, and blotchy dark stains all over his face. His hat was missing, and his red hair was tousled and untidy. His uniform was disheveled, and he was bloodied and limping.

"You look like a farmer that fell off his tractor and got run over in the ditch. What's the matter with you?" Without any outward display of empathy, his uncaring supervisor yelled at him, "Don't even think about coming back to collect your paycheck."

37

CONSEQUENCES

Jay realized too late the major blunder he had committed by encouraging his clients the Kennedys to hit blindly across the lake through a narrow opening in the forest into a foursome. A good caddy would have climbed up on a rock or a tree to get a better view to make sure the coast was clear to avoid the risk of hitting another golfer. Concerned about what might happen next, he instinctively realized that Wayne couldn't have slammed into a worse group of loudmouthed gangbangers. He was worried that if the Linguine brothers failed to respond immediately, they might find a worse way to get even later. Everyone knew they were notorious for holding grudges and maliciously attacking people they didn't like. Jay cautiously led the twosome on a delayed march to the green, secretly hoping that one of the Linguine brothers wouldn't kneecap him in the parking lot or blow up his car.

Kate took another swig of Canadian Club whiskey from her silver flask, making it harder for her to think clearly and move with coordination. She was impulsively feeling sexually adventuresome and uninhibited. When it was Wayne's turn to putt, she pulled up her skirt, sat down on the green with the cup between her legs, and spread her legs far apart. Jay was stunned by the view of his client's yellow lacy panties. He feigned interest in the sound of an owl in the forest, purposefully averting his eyes in the opposite direction. Wayne got down on his hands and knees to get a better perspective of the slope of the green. Kate lifted her top and flashed him at the midpoint of his backswing. Wayne was stunned and temporarily blinded by the distraction. He nearly missed the golf ball completely; it glanced off Kate's left thigh and softly deflected directly into the hole for a birdie.

"Bravo, Wayne," Kate congratulated him with enthusiasm.

Back at the clubhouse, CFO Lady Vanessa summoned Bruno Greco, long-distance drive champion, to the high-tech indoor virtual simulator. The infrared sensors tracked each ball's spin, speed, and trajectory against a backdrop of actual courses from around the world.

"Did you toss Father Cellophane's body in Lake Michigan as planned?"

"Not exactly. I was afraid someone at the Hermitage would see me, so I buried him in the sand," Bruno explained, shrugging his shoulders as if it didn't make any difference.

Carefully adjusting the camera angle on the simulator to project the view from the seventh tee to the fifth green, Lady Vanessa put forward a sinister offer. "Wayne and Kate Kennedy are planning to buy Gravestone Castle and build a trailer park next door. Their proposal is incompatible with the objectives of Woebegone Dunes Resort. Do whatever it takes to make them forfeit the entry fee, resign their membership application, and leave this state forever," Lady Vanessa mumbled under her breath. "I'll give you a hundred bucks if you can hit one of them with a golf ball."

"From where?"

"From right there," Vanessa explained, pointing to the parking lot.

Bruno's experience in the army as a long-range sniper came to mind as he walked to the back of the parking lot. He took a dozen flashy practice swings to stimulate the fast-twitch muscle fibers in his chest, arms, and shoulders before aligning the ball with the target.

Swish!

The golf ball made an extra-loud *ping* as it compressed on impact, exploding off the club's face and screaming toward the target with hypersonic speed like a torpedo with an explosive warhead. It was a potential kill shot hurtling through the air, simulating steam escaping from a pressure cooker as a direct indicator of lethality.

38

SHANGRI-LA

Whoosh . . . thud!

A golf ball from an unknown origin flashed over Wayne's head like a heat-seeking missile, leaving behind a directional whistling sound that lingered in the air like the contrail of a jet airplane. Its flight abruptly terminated in a sand bunker with the dull sound of an object with a solid mass at the core, landing with some degree of force like a foot beater pounding a two-headed bass drum.

Wayne had recoiled in response to the threatening incoming sound. Instinctively forming a tight ball, he covered his head with his hands and rolled on the ground as an avoidance maneuver. Kate's frightening, ear-piercing primal scream caused Jay to overreact in a knee-jerk fashion, instinctively jumping out of his skin.

"Where the hell did that ball come from? I don't see anyone behind us," Kate quizzed.

Wayne sputtered angrily, picking himself up from the ground and dusting himself off, reflexively tightening his fists and squinting into the forest. "I saw a dark shadow duck behind the trees near the parking lot. I assume Joey Linguine hit that golf ball at us as a brutal act of retaliation for accidentally hitting his caddy."

Jay worried the confrontational situation would escalate into a hostile head-to-head skirmish with guns blazing. Annoyed at the intense emotional distress his clients were suffering, he called the clubhouse to report the incident.

"Someone viciously hit a golf ball at Wayne and Kate Kennedy, intentionally hoping to injure them. We have good reason to assume it was Joey Linguine. Send Ranger Fox out immediately to put an end to Joey's hostile behavior before the situation escalates out of control."

Ranger Fox fearlessly sprang into action with the powerful heart of a former ultimate fighting champion. Sneaking up from behind, he unexpectedly enveloped his left arm around Joey Linguine's head and neck with clenched fists. Tightening the stranglehold headlock grip between his elbow and the side of his body like a powerful bear trap, he twisted the body around with a hip toss. Vigorously rubbing his knuckles across the top of the skull caused excruciating Dutch-rub scalp pain, causing Joey's eyes to water profusely. He grabbed him by the underpants for good measure, lifting his feet off the ground and giving him a hanging wedgie. The prolonged strain caused significant discomfort and annoyance to the victim.

"Ouch! Damn it, you popped a hernia in my groin," Joey groaned with a prolonged expression of physical pain while attempting to stabilize his balance.

"I don't care if you popped multiple hemorrhoids. That's what happens when men wear thong underwear. I've had it with you assholes. We don't tolerate your kind of behavior, and nobody should intentionally try to injure another golfer. Take your golf clubs and leave the property immediately. You're no longer welcome at Woebegone Dunes Resort," Ranger Fox ordered, pointing to the parking lot with the take-charge authority of a forceful leader.

The minute Joey and his gang were out of sight, Ranger Fox waved to Jay Walker, signaling an end to the dispute. He immediately reached for his cooler and rewarded himself with a bowl of rich, creamy ice cream churned into a smooth consistency with hot fudge, caramel, and nuts.

"Brain freeze," he muttered under his breath, smiling brightly before continuing his routine patrol.

Wayne was duly impressed, quick to forgive and forget, and happy to see the situation deescalated. "Abundant sunshine is the best medicine and a harbinger of optimism," he reminded the others as the clouds slowly unfurled, exposing the warmth of the sun.

Kate agreed. "The panoramic view of the rocky coastline is postcard-perfect. The meticulously manicured, undulating green fescue fairway surrounded by dozens of monster sand bunkers contrasts agreeably with the misty deep-blue waters of Lake Michigan and the wispy white clouds drifting slowly overhead."

Jay furled his eyebrows and faced into the breeze to estimate the wind speed and direction. Reaching into Kate's golf bag, he extracted a high-launch fairway wood, wiped the handle with a damp towel, and handed the club to Kate. "The Heavenwood produces a high, towering ball flight, which lands very softly, the perfect club for this shot. Keep it low. Aim for the right side of the green. Everything slopes to the left toward Lake Michigan."

Kate loosened her sweater, pushed up her sleeves, bent from the hip, took a wide stance, adjusted her grip, waggled her backside like a duck, and took a deep breath. Her ball rolled up the right side of the fairway before diagonally crossing over to the lakeside of the green, just as Jay had predicted it would. She smiled demurely.

"Wow, nice shot. That was a humdinger, better than most golfers I've caddied for," Jay exclaimed, secretly worrying with lingering uncertainty about the dangerously errant golf ball.

"Thanks for the good advice. Best round of golf I've played in a long time."

Wayne stroked his chin with his right hand, tightened his golf glove, glanced at his GPS watch to calculate the exact yardage, and estimated the wind speed and direction. He licked his lower lip. He lifted his shoulders, puffed up his chest, took two silky-smooth practice swings, and caught the ball perfectly at the apex of his swing. The ball arched spectacularly high into the air before drifting slowly back to earth, where it landed softly on the edge of the green. The ball spun backward and rolled within six feet of the hole. He completed the swing in a perfect comma position with his belt buckle facing the flag. He was beaming with an air of exaggerated swagger.

Kate's eyes twinkled. Caught up in the moment, she smiled and gave him a congratulatory kiss on the cheek. They lazily lagged behind the caddy, holding hands, chatting, and enjoying the beautiful scenery, the exceptional weather, the perfectly sculpted golf course, and the wonderment of a perfect outing. Kate passionately loved her man.

"Golfing at Woebegone Dunes Resort is truly a glorious day in paradise. I feel just like when we were dating in college," Kate reminisced nostalgically.

Wayne smiled and patted her behind. "Beyond doubt, this is what God would be doing today—if he could afford to hire a caddy and had the time to play a round of golf at Woebegone Dunes Resort."

"This is such a beautifully sculpted, harmonious landscape—a magical, idyllic setting, an earthly paradise hidden away in an isolated part of the country, far from the troubles of the real world. This valley feels like a mythical kingdom and a place of refuge for holy people. 'Shangri-La' is the perfect name for this fairway," Kate waxed lyrically.

She dramatically threw her hands up in the air as if competing for points on *Dancing with Stars*, joyfully twirling around in a complete circle, admiring the entire panoramic landscape scene. Startled by what she saw concealed in the forest high on a hill in the distance, she quietly exhaled before exclaiming, "Look at that old stone building nestled in the trees at the top of the hill. It reminds me of the romantic village in the Himalayans in the book *Lost Horizon* by James Hilton, where the inhabitants were free of war and enjoyed unheard-of longevity. Perhaps that's why they named this fairway Shangri-La?" she revealed pensively.

Wayne put his hand up to his forehead to shield the sun. Squinting with both eyes to improve his focus, he peered into the forest to distinguish between the moss-covered stone building and dark forest shadows. "It is very imposing from this angle. It reminds me of a medieval fortress, an executive prestige property inspired by folklore."

Jay shrugged his shoulders. "You're looking at the back of my historic family home—Gravestone Castle."

"It's a magnificent fortification that stirs the imagination. It brings to mind princesses, knights, horses, and pervasive tales of chivalry. You had a very unique and privileged childhood, Jay," Kate stated emphatically, putting herself in his shoes.

"Gravestone Castle was my heritage, designed and constructed by my father and grandfather. The architectural theme is Bavarian. My grandfather Hans Walker became very wealthy during prohibition. He hid his highly lucrative bootlegging operation in the underground quarry. Significant changes took place when the federal government leased the property. It was quadrupled in size and upgraded numerous times. The larger and more fortified the buildings became, the more rent my father was able to charge," Jay reflected. "Gravestone Castle is a hermitage now. It's a place of religious seclusion suitable for the ascetic lifestyle of a small group of priests and nuns. Supposedly, they meet with their brethren for communion, for shared meals on holy days, for nature walks, and for having simple discussions about the spiritual life. But I think that's a misrepresentation, a false front meant to mislead the IRS."

"Look!" Wayne interrupted loudly. "Someone is holding a high-powered rifle looking at us through a hunting scope, or is it simply a reflection of a tree branch on the window?"

"The thought of someone pointing a gun at me makes my blood run cold, leaves me wet-pant scared, and gives me the heebie-jeebies," Kate admitted.

"That's Father Adam Baum keeping vigilance. He seems to have lost some clarity, self-control, and emotional stability in recent years. He hates poachers and trespassers that approach the castle without permission, especially anyone who dares to encroach from the lakeside."

"Stay calm and rational. Act normal. Pretend not to notice. If the Padre wanted to kill us, we would already be dead," Wayne contributed.

Jay showed composure and spoke calmly as if this were routine behavior for the so-called Padre. "Security was a major contributing factor in the selection of Gravestone Castle as a government research center," he explained. "Enthralled with the remote location, the access to Lake Michigan, and the proximity to the anti-aircraft missile base at Camp Haven, the government was very pleased with the arrangement. The original stone farmhouse gradually evolved into a large militarized fort with multiple buildings. Eventually, the entire complex was neatly contained within a large outer perimeter wall, making it easy to defend against a small-arms attack. My father designed it to look like a medieval castle with everything except a moat filled with water."

The others were overly curious, eager to learn more. "My parents and I were the only civilians allowed to live on the property. My father supervised the stonemasons and the construction of the buildings. My mother was in charge of the kitchen and cleaning staff and homeschooled me in her spare time. We never went anywhere or took vacations. Our family home was a separate building, so we seldom interfaced with the scientists. Security guards and temporary construction workers arrived after dark in unmarked security vans. We were completely isolated. Even our neighbors didn't know the place existed."

Kate was overly distressed, knowing that a perverted priest was deliberately spying on her through a telescope. Carelessly maneuvering to the back of the green to get a better view, nausea and vertigo overcame her as she peered over the edge of the steep hillside below. She felt unsteady, lightheaded and faint, with a sensation of spinning. The vanishing horizon line between the deep-blue white-capped waters of Lake Michigan and the hazy blue sky blurred.

"Be careful!" Jay shouted, suddenly aware of the perilousness of her situation.

"Oh, my God! I'm going to be sick," Kate howled. Overcome by vertigo, she staggered sideways, doing the crab walk and holding her backside with both hands.

"I have an urgent need to pass gas. Whoops! It's the pernicious Hershey squirts," Kate screamed with embarrassment, jerking down her underpants.

39

SAND BUNKER

"Don't look!" Kate screamed as projectile diarrhea sprayed across the manicured green. Her knees buckled as nausea overcame her. She lost her balance, staggered sideways, and tumbled down the steep embankment head over heels, awkwardly cartwheeling into a sand bunker. The scene ended grossly with a crescendo of a pinwheeling, watery explosion. She landed on her backside with a terrific thud like a sack of potatoes falling off a concrete loading dock.

"I think I broke my leg. I can't get up," Kate shrieked with humiliation and embarrassment, feeling dishonored and diminished in the eyes of others. Covered from head to toe in grit and sand, grass stains, and smelly brown filth, she lay on her backside with a considerable grimace of pain and disgust on her face. Her skirt had ripped, and her blouse was in tatters. Her blond hair was tousled and dirty. Her golf glove was lying off to the side, and her expensive designer sunglasses had twisted egregiously.

"Something hasn't been right ever since I ate that damn leek soup the murderer in the kitchen served me for lunch," she shrieked even louder.

Wayne threw down his putter and slid down the steep embankment into the sand bunker, into what looked like an explosion of nuclear waste combined with the scent of pond sludge. The sight of his lovely wife sprawled and lying helplessly on the ground unnerved and disheartened him. Kate was slovenly filthy, untidy, twisted, and contorted into an awkward position. He covered her privates with his jacket, placed a golf towel under her head for comfort, and handed her the umbrella to shield her eyes from the sun.

Jay's mouth was agape, thinking about the wildly contorted X-rated flying cartwheel his client had accidentally performed. Knowing that her behavior resulted from drinking too much alcohol, he described the situation to Dr. Pepper in exact detail with a giddy smile on his face. "This an emergency," he hollered into his radio, trying to sound concerned. "My client Kate Kennedy is in a deplorable state of untidiness. You will need to wear disposable full-body bacterial protection. Bring a leg splint, extra blankets, rubber gloves, towels, and a clean white caddy jumpsuit for her."

Wayne was suddenly and unexpectedly speechless with alarm, and his brain froze with fear. He stood still, catatonically pointing to a man's hand sticking out of the sand at the far end of the bunker, the way a prized hunting dog reacts when flushing a pheasant.

Kate egregiously twisted her head around, coming face to face with the shocking revelation of a human hand heinously protruding from the sand. The nightmarish realization of what she saw triggered extreme emotional anxiety and panic. Suddenly energized to get on her feet and remove herself from the bunker, she screamed, "Oh, my God! Get me out of here!"

Jay called Deputy Sheriff Bud Light to report the bizarre, extraordinary discovery of a dead body in the sand bunker.

Paramedic Dr. Pepper arrived wearing rubber gloves, a head covering, and a protective ensemble resembling a full-body hazmat uniform. He wiped Kate down with a damp towel and helped her climb into an extra-large one-piece caddy jumpsuit. "I've been a paramedic for thirty years, and I've never seen such a shocking event. Fortunately, I think you only sprained your ankle. I'll take you to the medical tent, get you cleaned up, and transport you to the clinic for an X-ray."

"No! Take me to my car so that I can fetch clean clothes. After that, I want to go directly to the clubhouse," she demanded rudely.

"Perhaps you shouldn't venture into the clubhouse in your sullied condition?" Dr. Pepper suggested. He was fervently hoping to keep up appearances by dissuading Kate from exposing herself to the other club members in her current disturbed state of mind and outwardly disheveled appearance.

40

NAKED WHITE WOMAN

The oversized caddy uniform dragged on the floor as Kate limped through the main hallway of the quaint stone clubhouse leading directly to the gift shop, restaurant, and bar. She brushed up against every wall and held onto every chair and table for support along the way, leaving a trail of telltale smudge marks on everything she touched. Patrons gasped at the sight of her scruffy, tousled appearance. An awful smell lingered in the vestibule behind her.

"Where's the bathroom?" she crudely demanded with startling abruptness, exceeding the code of behavior for polite society. Once there, she turned on the fancy brass Kohler water faucets full blast and filled the Gilded Meadow gold conical bell vessel sink with water. The sink provided an exquisite focal point with the carved floral pattern and precious gold accents on a translucent background.

Kate stripped naked in front of the rose-colored mirror, tossed the oversized caddy uniform in the wicker wastebasket, and dropped her designer apparel in a helter-skelter heap directly on the tiled bathroom floor. A clean bathroom towel was ideal for giving herself a full-body sponge bath. She gargled with the complimentary mouthwash and sprinkled ample amounts of cologne on her neck and breasts.

Recently returned from a marketing tour of South Korea, Jack Daniels had three unsigned membership contracts in his hand. He was eagerly looking forward to the arrival of the potential new members and the extra cash flow they would provide.

Three buoyant Korean women enthusiastically darted into the women's restroom on the way to the dining room. Expectations were high. They had been eagerly looking forward to visiting the gold-class American resort since watching the PGA Championship at nearby Whistling Straits and the United States Open at Erin Hills.

"What intrigues me the most is the signature dish of goose comfit de canard served over forbidden rice and mango coulis sauce with haricot vert and marinated tomatoes. For dessert, I want the lemon-berry ring cake soaked in liqueur-flavored syrup," the largest of the plus-sized elderly women exclaimed.

The four ladies squeezed through the restroom door, eager to wash their hands and relieve the stress of the long drive from Milwaukee before being seated in the dining room. The lady in front abruptly stopped in her tracks. Her jaw dropped. Widening her stance and firmly planting her feet, she extended her arms with the palms facing backward, blocking the other women from entering.

"A naked white woman is standing in front of the sink washing her bottom with the guest hand towel," the puzzled South Korean woman shrieked in disgust. With a collective gasp of communal disbelief and neck whiplash, the women clumsily collided with each other. They stumbled in four different directions, like four electric dodgem cars slamming into each other at the fairgrounds. They recklessly tumbled out the exit door ass over teakettle, erratically spilling into the lobby, causing one of them to fall on the floor. Indignantly, in high-pitched screams, they muttered vulgar expressions of annoyance in a foreign language only their bewildered husbands could understand.

"No membership for us—we're leaving on the next plane," they snipped in unison at Jack Daniels. "I should have taken a video to share with friends on Facebook to expose your farcical American customs and ghastly bathroom ethics."

Kate slipped into a fresh set of designer golf clothes and dialed the resort spa and beauty parlor. Her tousled hair was an absolute mess. In response to Lady Vanessa's strict instructions, the hotel reception-ist smugly provided a rehearsed negative response. "I'm sorry, we have no vacancies for women's hair treatments this afternoon. Suppose you have an immediate need for attention. In that case, I suggest you contact Angelina, the owner of Curl Up and Dye beauty salon."

Kate jotted down the telephone number, made an appointment, and informed Wayne of her decision. "I am leaving immediately to get my hair washed and set. I'll meet you back here for dinner," she offered as she determinedly limped out the front door.

With nothing else to do, Wayne headed to the spa for a steam bath and a massage. "It's twenty dollars extra for a happy ending," Suzan Wong, the massage therapist, explained in broken English.

41

BODY IN THE BUNKER

The process of extracting the corpse from the sand bunker was erratic. Deputy Sheriff Bud Light was a decent cop but a lousy detective. Hovering over the corpse like a vulture circling someone dying of thirst in the desert, the deputy was overly eager for the victim to be officially declared dead. He verbally exaggerated the extraction process with the bombastic enthusiasm of a Las Vegas boxing promoter, inflated and high-sounding but with little meaning.

"The body belongs to a ghastly, bloated, overweight male weighing in at one hundred and ninety pounds. He is a slightly balding middle-aged man with pasty, unhealthy white skin—a dead ringer for Father Cellophane at the Hermitage," he announced with surety.

"Uff-da!" Forensic archaeologist Sean Flanagan curiously remarked. "The crime scene reeks of sewerage sludge," he complained as he gridded off the burial scene with wooden stakes and white string to frame the crime scene accurately.

The lieutenant was broad-shouldered, muscular, and preternaturally spry. He possessed the visage of a detective accustomed to evaluating forensic evidence with an intense inquisitive gaze. His assistant, Emily, approached wearing a luxury Lizzie Driver high-end golf ensemble with luxurious handcrafted Italian golf shoes fabricated of stingray leather.

Deputy Sheriff Bud Light ignored the formality of the time-consuming methodical forensic procedures as he rushed to roll the body over and unwind the bubble wrap surrounding the torso. "Approximately forty percent of the bubbles are flat," he observed, eagerly looking forward to popping the remaining ones.

"Wait!" Emily flailed her arms in desperation. She jumped into the bunker and snatched the plastic out of the deputy's arms to protect it from further damage. As if participating in a parlor game of charades, she dramatically raised the bubble wrap above her head for everyone to see. The audience gasped when they realized the value of her astonishing discovery. The popped bubbles formed a Latin aphorism message: "Carpe diem. Those who cannot remember the past are doomed to repeat it."

The entire group stopped dead in their tracks the way a crowd reacts to gunfire—unsure about what to do or say next and worried about the significance of the bizarre message. Forensic archeologist Sean Flanagan removed an oversized diamond-studded Super Bowl ring from the victim's finger. He placed it in a small evidence bag and attached a label with the finding's date, time, and GPS coordinates.

The deputy took advantage of the pause in the action to indiscriminately hand out Green Bay Packer football schedules to everyone in attendance before continuing with the investigation. "I suspect foul play. How else could the body have been buried under three feet of sand?" he suggested, manifestly stating the obvious.

Sean Flanagan made an astonishing observation. "The victim is wearing a skintight yellow speedo."

"That's a bright-yellow Solid Jammer speedo swimsuit. It has the exclusive nine-thread flat lock stitching technology for a custom fit with optimal stretch," Deputy Sheriff Bud Light declared upon immediate recognition.

Emily was open-mouthed and dumbfounded, wondering how the deputy knew this information. Her eyes rolled back in her head, anticipating additional titillating observations and details.

"There is a high-quality Green Bay Packer logo patch sewn on the left side. The vivid green, lustrous gold, and arctic white color are authentic team colors," the deputy spewed enthusiastically. "Someone autographed the back of his tight-fitting yellow speedo," he added with his head only inches above the victim's backside. "The autograph belongs to Ben Dover, a recent graduate of Notre Dame University. He's the third-team punter for the Green Bay Packers on the practice squad. Ben used a Sharpie permanent black ink marker that can stand up to the harsh conditions of industrial work in northern Wisconsin for his signature."

"Look what else I found," Sean remarked, holding an iPhone and German passport from the bottom of the sandy grave above his head for everyone to see.

The deputy sheriff immediately confiscated the evidence. "Both items belong to Hertz Von Rental the Third," he announced as he placed the phone in an evidence bag.

"Hertz is a friend of Jay Walker," someone informed him.

A hippie-looking reporter named René Malarkey, reeking of smelly cannabis, grimaced when he saw the corpse. "The poor guy looks like he was hit in the face with a hockey puck. He suffered severe facial trauma from an intense, violent force, fracturing his cheekbones, crushing the eye socket, and breaking his nose."

The reporter forced his way into the sand bunker, carelessly tripping over Sean Flanagan's strings and accidentally jerking several stakes out of the ground. A golf ball lodged in the victim's left eye socket had broken all the bones on the left side of his face. René rudely poked at the shattered eye socket with his pointer finger before declaring, "Yuck! The bones in his forehead are all soft and mushy."

Deputy Sheriff Bud Light had seen enough. He coarsely dragged the corpse out of the sand bunker by the ankles using multiple short, violent tugs. He used his foot to leverage, how professional chiropractors contort patients into extremely awkward positions to relieve back pain. With great effort, he forcefully stuffed the body into a tight-fitting black body bag. It took even more vigorous physical exertion to squeeze the body into the patrol car's backseat for transport to the coroner's office for a post-mortem examination.

The highly aroused, attack-trained, aggressive nature of the inherently dangerous police dog already occupying the backseat caused spontaneous mayhem. The police dog knew how to kill perceived hostile targets on instinct. He snarled and growled menacingly before attacking the victim's crotch with a bite force exceeding 320 pounds of pressure, violently shaking the body bag from side to side. "My dog doesn't like the smell," the deputy rationalized the animal's uncontrollable behavior as he departed the crime scene.

"We should conduct a thorough walk-through on the beach to search for additional physical evidence and seek out potential leads," the lieutenant stated. Emily agreed.

42

WHITE CLERICAL COLLAR

The lieutenant marched with vigor, taking long strides in the soft sand as if striding over puddles. Emily followed closely behind with a curious mind, putting her problem-solving skills to good use by checking for hairs, fibers, impressions, tool marks, footprints, residue, and other potential clues. "Look, there are some clothes neatly folded on the beach."

Lieutenant Dunning rubbed his chin and tugged his earlobe as he made an inventory. "There's a black shirt with a white clerical collar with a small white square at the base of the throat, a pair of shiny black shoes, black pants, and a beach towel neatly folded and stacked in a square bundle. The waist in the pants is five inches longer than the inseam, and the neck size is seventeen inches. These priest clothes belong to Father Cellophane."

Emily ambiguously scratched her head. "The circumstances of Father Cellophane's death are uncommonly queer. Ten feet to the left is a crumpled one-piece caddy uniform similar to those worn at Woebegone Dunes Resort; it is wrinkled, dirty, and wet. There are drops of blood on the sleeve and a tear in the crotch. The right leg is inside out. Someone hastily removed the uniform and randomly tossed it on the beach. The name tag says 'Dusty Rhodes.' There are two new golf balls in the left front pocket. Father Cellophane may have been accidentally struck in the eye by a golf ball when he was preparing to go for a swim. After the injury, the perpetrator may have panicked and rushed to bury the body in the sand bunker," Emily surmised. Despite her professionalism, her radiant skin had a dazzling, glorious, illuminating inner glow. Lake Michigan was as calm as glass. Light rays from the sun, reflecting on the surface of the water, profoundly mirrored the curves of her hourglass silhouette.

Continuing the investigation farther up the beach, they stumbled on the scene of the killer bee attack at the base of a cliff. "The primal screams of the victim as he tumbled down the rock cliff have been a terrible reoccurring nightmare for me. Watching the poor victim floating face down in the water is the most gruesome thing I have ever witnessed. I feel like a war veteran hypersensitive to danger overcome with post-traumatic stress, dilated pupils, and rapid heartbeat. Flashbacks and troubling thoughts about the traumatic circumstances of the horrendous death have overwhelmed me."

"When you are the target of a swarm of killer bees, there is no escape. Even if you jump in the water, they will continue circling overhead until you surface. Africanized killer bees have killed over one thousand humans, horses, and other animals in this country. Before the onslaught of uncontrolled death throes, victims become afflicted with delirium, violent seizures, vomiting, and purges. They suffer incredible agonizing pain. They hear everything you say until the very end because the ears are the last organ to die."

Emily was meditatively reflective on the breathless trauma of past events, profoundly absorbed in deep thought, wondering what future challenges lie ahead.

43

A WALK ON THE BEACH

Lieutenant Dunning stopped abruptly, executed an about-face, and began walking rapidly in the opposite direction a half-mile down the coast. Twenty minutes later, he and Emily discovered hundreds of golf balls indiscriminately scattered in the sand.

"Follow me. I want to see where these golf balls came from," the lieutenant announced without hesitation as he headed up the steep embankment.

Emily followed closely behind. She clung to every exposed tree root and branch with both hands to keep from slipping backward as the sandy soil continually eroded beneath her feet. The sudden drop in temperature and the unfamiliar smell of decaying vegetation on the wet forest floor produced an earthy aroma that gave her goosebumps. "This is a ghostly place. The forest spirits seem to be exuding an eerie sense of tormented anguish. The trees are past their prime, slowly losing vigor with age and atrophying in place."

Detective Dunning crawled on hands and knees near the summit of the steep bank to keep from slipping backward. He reached back and nearly pulled Emily's arm out of the shoulder socket by jerking her up and over the top.

"This place is creepy," Emily worried suspiciously, eyeing the vines covering the castle walls and the creepy forest surroundings. "The upper window on the left is where Wayne and Kate Kennedy saw someone spying on them through a high-powered rifle scope. I'm not comfortable here; we should leave before anyone catches us trespassing."

The lieutenant pointed to a circle of gray rocks containing ashes from a recent campfire. "There's a broken Woodford Reserve whiskey bottle, a pile of cigarette butts, half a dozen Chianti wine bottles, several half-smoked cigars, and pink lacy panties." He removed a magnifying glass from his pocket and bent down on his hands and knees to take a closer look. "These are Cheeky Lace Panties with all-over lace in bella donna pink by Victoria's Secret. My sister has the same pair in cornflower blue—don't write that down. I detect a slight scent of Body Fantasies Signature Japanese Cherry Blossom body spray."

The lieutenant peered through a group of tightly spaced lilac bushes. "Look what I found—exactly what I was looking for: a wooden platform used as a golf driving range. Someone standing on this platform may have struck Father Cellophane in the eye with a golf ball. When they realized an irresponsible act of involuntary manslaughter had fatally wounded him, they must have panicked. Hoping to make the body disappear as quickly as possible, they rushed down to the beach to conceal any evidence of wrongdoing, and the cover-up suddenly became more serious than the original crime."

"Is this the detective's dilemma you have been telling me about— killers who cover up their crimes to thwart the police?" Emily inquired. "I wonder if there were any witnesses."

44

AIRPLANE WING

Emily stood on the wooden platform and scanned the shoreline of Lake Michigan through the telephoto lens of her camera, looking in both directions from the top of the peninsula. "There's a damaged aluminum canoe a mile up the beach stuck in some rocks. We should investigate."

Detective Dunning slipped on his black leather gloves and pulled his socks up to his knees for protection from thistles and poison ivy before retreating into the vegetation-clogged ravine above the sandy beach. "Be careful. Don't slide, and don't cut yourself on a piece of rusty metal. Watch your step on the way down. Stay directly behind me for safety and especially be on the lookout for giant hogweed," he warned.

Emily complied, slipping and sliding down the steep bank, staying directly behind him and moving in sync, as if attached at the hip.

Expectations were high as they approached the shiny metal object on the beach. "I was certain it was a crushed aluminum canoe, but I see now that it's the wing of an airplane. Aluminum is a silvery-white, nonmagnetic, ductile, lightweight metal that resists corrosion. It is not radioactive, and all living plants and animals tolerate it well. I wonder why it was assigned the unlucky atomic number thirteen," the lieutenant remarked as they approached the shiny piece of metal stranded on a small rock outcropping.

"I see an enormous dent with splinters of wood lodged in the metal that smell like a pine tree. The wing may have been violently sheared off with great force before the fuselage crashed into Lake Michigan. There's a suspicious-looking set of boot marks in the aluminum. The tread pattern is unique to the Boy Scouts of America. These are hiking boots that are approved and uniform-ready for various environments; they are lightweight and nonslip, designed for outdoor activities."

The lieutenant lifted the wing to observe the underside. "These long lineal scratches down the entire length of the wing puzzle me. Did the wing slide a long distance on the sand before ending up in the water?"

"I'll do some research on the prevailing wind and lake currents to see if we can determine the exact location of the crash site," Emily offered. "Bud Light may have some suggestions when we meet with him tomorrow."

45

DUSTY RHODES

The next day, Deputy Sheriff Bud Light was in the process of tossing a pile of crime reports, urgent requests, and reports into a cardboard box on the floor as the lieutenant and Emily entered. He greeted them warmly before sitting down and tapping a wobble-head Packer doll on the head.

The lieutenant expelled a thick ring of pipe tobacco smoke with touches of sweetness and spice before speaking. "What are your theories about Father Cellophane's bizarre death?" he wanted to know.

"I fear Dusty Rhodes may be guilty of manslaughter, resulting from felonious actions taken with reckless disregard. I think Dusty accidentally killed Father Cellophane while hitting golf balls onto the beach from the wooden platform on the hill behind Gravestone Castle."

"Do you think his actions were a deliberate act of intimidation and retribution intended to harm? Was Dusty smart enough to steal Hertz Von Rental's wallet, iPhone, and passport and bury them with the body to divert suspicion from himself? I read Dusty's police profile. He is a unique and unpredictable character, extremely lacking in self-confidence. He is highly troubled by failure, socially withdrawn, and permanently in emotional turmoil due to low self-esteem. He is irrationally hostile toward others, sensitive to criticism, and overwhelmed by mental anxiety. Dusty has the motive to be culpable—he very well could be the murderer."

Deputy Sheriff Bud Light agreed. "Dusty was in a vindictive, excitable mood when he stormed off the golf course that day. He was soaking wet, dirty, and humiliated—mad as a wet cat. He probably walked to Gravestone Castle to collect Father Cellophane's money. Dusty maliciously hit a few golf balls at Father Cellophane as a desperate act of frustration, accidentally striking him in the eye. He rushed down to the beach, recklessly tore off his caddy uniform, and tossed it in a heap on the beach. Uncertain what to do next, he hastily buried the body in the bunker with a sense of urgency."

"Then what happened?" Emily queried.

"Dusty Rhodes's luck unexpectedly went from bad to worse in one deplorable day. Getting fired from his job as a caddy at Woebegone Dunes Resort was devastating. His highest-tipping client, Joey Linguine, called him a prick and laughed at his severe stuttering, buck teeth, and childhood behavioral problems. Globs of wet brown mud stained his white uniform. He tripped and fell in a lake, scratched his glasses, tore his caddy uniform, cut his elbow, and was severely humiliated in public. He had a terrible hangover from drinking too much brandy. His hemorrhoids were swollen and excessively itchy, resulting from an explosive blindsided hit from a high-velocity golf ball. Nothing could be worse. He has no family or friends, and now he is the prime suspect in the felonious assault of Father Cellophane," the lieutenant reported plausibly.

Emily was impressed. The lieutenant had excellent mental acuity, perspicuous lucidity, and witticism. His ability to express his ideas clearly and transparently was exemplary. She was eager to interview the suspect in person.

"I arranged to meet with him at the police station to answer some questions," Deputy Sheriff Bud Light informed them.

Dusty limped into the interrogation room with a stretched hamstring muscle, a severe groin strain, a scratch on his cheek, a fresh white bandage on his elbow, and a Band-Aid on his forehead. He sat awkwardly on his hemorrhoid donut ring, intentionally listing to one side to avoid putting pressure on his bruised buttocks. He reminded Emily of a sailor leaning as far as possible to one side as a counterweight to keep the sailboat from capsizing in the wind.

Deputy Sheriff Bud Light quizzed him extensively about his background, work experience, relationship with the Linguine brothers, and Father Cellophane. Dusty was at a loss for words, tongue-tied, and unable to respond spontaneously. The fast-paced interview continued, with one strongly worded question fired at him after another without waiting for a response. "Why did you discard your caddy uniform on the shore of Lake Michigan? Have you ever met with Father Cellophane in any capacity other than as a caddy? Have you ever been to the Safe House restaurant in Milwaukee? How do you know Hertz Von Rental the Third? Did you steal his passport, wallet, and cellphone? You admit that the uniform found on the beach was yours, but you have no idea how it got there. Do you deny accidentally killing Father Cellophane?"

Dusty was startled by the accusatory tone they were using, distressed by the allegations of lying, and rudely awakened by accusations of murder. He denied ever seeing anyone hitting golf balls onto the beach. He denied having anything to do with the death of Father Cellophane, and he claimed to have never met Hertz Von Rental III. Bud Light tugged on his earlobes to express his annoyance at the lack of responsiveness.

"Do not leave town," the deputy sheriff ordered after threatening to submit a written affidavit to a judge establishing probable cause. "I found your uniform at the crime scene. You had a motive to threaten Father Cellophane because he owed you money, making you the prime suspect in his death."

Choking on his saliva, Dusty summed up his situation in one word. "My whole life is *caddywampus*. Nothing is normal. Everything was screwed up when my parents abandoned me, putting me in an unfortunate, disadvantaged situation. An alcoholic nurse dropped me on my head when I was a baby. I had permanent brain damage that triggers cockamamie feelings of being out of step and ridiculously off-kilter. That's why my eyes are farcically misaligned and my eyebrows are crooked. My teachers considered me abnormal, and they said I operated without controls."

Dusty despairingly kept his head down in the dumps while heading for the exit after the first coherent thing he had said all day.

Emily waited until the door was closed. "I feel heartbroken. Dusty's hapless journey through life and bleak prospects for the future are disparaging. Abandonment by his parents at an early age caused a severe deviation of his life's trajectory. His trivial existence epitomizes the word *woebegone*."

The lieutenant capped her sentiments with an observation of his own. "What made Milwaukee famous has made a loser out of Dusty. Mixing misery with brandy and cheese curds and talking nasty to himself pretty much defines his doleful, crestfallen existence."

46

RETRIBUTION

Dusty Rhodes kicked open the door of his tiny camp trailer, barely large enough for sleeping and eating. His whole life had been an unsettled mess. The tire on one side had gone flat, causing the floor to tilt severely. Bathing and washing took place at the prefabricated shower building and portable toilets across the alley on the edge of a rocky mosquito-infested riverbank. The extreme humiliation and embarrassment he was feeling had finally pushed him over the edge, outside the bounds of morality, acceptable behavior, and all sense of sound judgment. Getting fired from his job was a transformational event. The merciless insults hurled at him by the Linguine brothers created intense feelings of anger and vengeance. Being hauled in for questioning by the police was the last straw, and he snapped. Retribution was his only solution.

He opened a bag of warm, musty cheese curds and a crumpled bag of broken pretzels before taking two large swigs of brandy from a bottle. The pretzels and cheese curds stuck together in his mouth in big clumps, filling the gaps between his crooked teeth with globs of phlegm-like porridge. The three warm beers he drank in his truck on his way home from the golf course gave him a sudden urge to go to the bathroom. He bolted through the squeaky spring-loaded screen door. He removed his shoes and rushed across the alley to the purple plastic outhouse in his stocking feet.

Four teenaged pranksters from the adjacent neighborhood were having a smoke and a laugh behind the shower building when Dusty arrived. They quietly crept up to the outhouse and, with one big unified shove, tipped it over backward. The lightweight plastic structure hovered briefly at the balance point before tumbling down the steep embankment toward the river, haphazardly flipping end over end, bouncing randomly down the hill the way a Mexican jumping bean moves when exposed to heat. Erratically glancing off the rocks and rolling over three times, the outhouse made loud crashing sounds as it cascaded over a pile of boulders, leaving big dents in the sides of the toilet.

"That was the best one ever," the boys screamed with glee as they took off, running down the street in raucous laughter.

There was a long quiet pause. Muffled scratching sounds from inside the toilet eventually broke the silence. Dusty awkwardly struggled to turn himself around inside the cramped, darkened space filled with stench. He unlocked the latch and forcefully flung the door open with a bang, revealing what appeared to be an abandoned coffin lying on the ground. Dusty slowly poked his head into the darkness with an astonished look of disbelief. He had lost all sense of orientation. Excrement covered his head. It was behind his ears, in his nostrils, under his shirt, in his hair, and between his fingers. He cautiously eased himself out of the casket, took off his shirt, dropped his pants, and tossed them in the river. Blue and yellow stains and semisolid chunks of brown feces stuck to every part of his torso.

A wave of blood-thirsty mosquitos covered his entire body, sucking his blood until they burst. Hundreds of itchy, pink, puffy insect bites caused his eyes and ears to swell. A giant leech attached to his groin wiggled as it sucked his blood, causing intense fear and panic. Dusty grabbed the squirmy little bloodsucker by the tail and squeezed it tightly, causing the fat wiggly black worm to vomit into the suction point.

Struggling to climb up the steep rocky bank on his hands and knees, he staggered past his neighbor's trailer, wearing nothing but dirty underpants and one brown sock. His neighbor, Carly, and his girlfriend were sitting on the patio enjoying a six-pack of beer, listening to country music, and laughing their heads off.

"Hey, Dusty?" Carly called out with a smile. "Shit-faced drunk again, I see."

Dusty stubbed his toe as he stumbled into his trailer and took another long snort of brandy. Without forethought and preparation, advance thinking, or evaluation of consequences, he ripped through a cardboard box under his bed filled with dirty clothes. Dusty impulsively jerked out a dingy pair of fireproof Nomex pants and a wrinkled dark-green camouflage shirt. He impetuously stuffed a pistol into his belt and crammed the flask of brandy into his front pocket. Slamming the screen door caused it to fall off the hinges. A storage shed sat caddywampus on a cracked concrete slab behind his trailer. He excitedly fumbled for the keys before dragging out a stolen government-issued fire-starting drip torch. Dusty was on a mission, and nobody was going to stop him. He tossed the torch into the back of his rusted-out hulk of a little brown Datsun pickup truck with a cracked windshield.

"This is the end of the r-r-road for the L-Linguine brothers and the p-priests at the Hermitage. Johnny Linguine is planning to sell a forged oil painting for two hundred grand tonight, and I'm going to be waiting for him. Everyone living at Gravestone Castle deserves to d-d-die," he stuttered insanely.

He pulled off the road in a sheltered location near the entrance to Gravestone Castle. He hid his truck between a cluster of closely spaced evergreen trees half a mile away. He crept through the woods, dragging his well-used fire-breathing drip torch behind. Stealthily, he hid in the shadows of the stunning wrought-iron entrance gate with distinctive scrolls, spear points, and timeless classical design. He crouched beneath a mature spruce tree and waited, trying to recall everything Johnny Linguine said about how much easy profit there was in selling forged paintings. His strategy was to confront Johnny when the buyer for the picture arrived, rob the cash from the man from Atlanta, and steal the painting from Johnny. He had made up his mind—he would kill both men and set the woods on fire. Everything seemed to be coming together precisely as planned.

Johnny arrived in a luxurious black Range Rover with oversize chrome wheels. He was wearing a black trench coat with the collar turned up and carrying a large black canvas pouch secured with a long leather strap over his shoulder. The stranger from Atlanta arrived in a Mythos black metallic R8 Audi. He was wearing a black leather jacket and dark-gray Tyrolean hat and pulling a small wheeled suitcase filled with cash. The two men eyed each other suspiciously before shaking hands and exchanging packages.

Dusty stealthily crept out from under the low-hanging tree branches and peered through the darkness. With perfect timing, he leaped out from behind the trees, waving his revolver above his head. Dusty used a quick-draw technique romanticized by gunslingers' infamous historical gunfights in western movies. He fired his gun directly into the faces of Johnny Linguine and the stranger from Atlanta at point-blank range, killing both of them instantly.

Two short pops shattered the forest's silence but went unnoticed in the Hermitage. A detective movie was showing in the soundproof movie room. Popcorn was popping, appliances were humming, and windows were whistling in the wind. There was clanking in the dishwasher and ambient background noises coming from the furnace.

Dusty threw the leather case containing the oil painting in the back of his compact truck and stuffed the suitcase in the front seat. Recklessly racing home to the trailer park with his priceless booty, he tossed the oil painting on the bed and dragged the bag of money through the spring-loaded door. The weight of the suitcase against the sharp edges of the screen door exploded his circular donut-pillow hemorrhoid seat cushion. He dragged the well-used seat cushion outside, tossed it on his neighbor Carly's concrete patio, and lit it on fire.

Second thoughts filled his head. He had forgotten to light the forest on fire. He had even failed to retrieve his drip torch from under a tree. His fingerprints were all over the applicator. What if the police found it? They would know it was him. He panicked before taking two more swigs of brandy for extra courage before rushing back to the scene of the crime to retrieve the drip-torch canister.

47

PARALYZED

The trauma of killing two men caused Dusty's heart to race. He was nauseous and filled with excessive feelings of worry. Apprehensiveness and emotional panic resulted in cardiac mitral valve prolapse, when heart valves refuse to close correctly.

Strong, gusty winds blowing across the highway made driving unsafe. Loose steering caused by worn chassis components, control arm bushings, ball joints, and gear linkages connecting the steering column to the sockets in the front wheel assemblies were radically worn. A threatening cold front as part of a supercell was rapidly forming overhead. Dense, towering vertical clouds, carried by powerful upward air currents filled with water vapor, blackened the sky, signaling pending tornadoes, hailstones, lightning, and dangerously severe rain. Rising air parcels caused wind shear inversions and unbalanced electric charges between anvil-shaped cloud domes in the tropopause.

Dusty concealed his small truck deep in the forest beside an old tractor tire rotting on the ground. He walked in a direct beeline through the darkness, haphazardly pushing and pulling tree branches out of his way to prevent them from scratching his face. He darted wildly between trees, bushwhacking his way through the underbrush. "Where's my damn drip torch? I better find it soon. I can't be fiddle-farting around here all night."

Armageddon, the guard dog, growled nervously at the front door as an early warning sign of a possible intruder outside. Father Adam Baum retrieved the crossbow from the closet. He stepped into the darkness to determine the source of the disturbance. A marauding black bear appeared to be wandering through the forest. The German Shepherd darted into the darkness toward the trespasser. Father Adam Baum aimed the crossbow in the general direction of the dark shadowy figure, with eyes wide open. A dangling pine needle scratched a corneal abrasion on his left eye, causing significant discomfort, tearing, and blurred vision. A flash of lightning, followed by a deep rumbling thunder, caused him to accidentally discharge an arrow into the darkness as Dusty cautiously navigated between the trees.

An electrostatic thunderbolt of lightning from the atmosphere came crashing down from the sky, accompanied by the emission of extremely bright light. The rapid expansion of the lightning bolts and dangerously hot air created a sound wave, causing a thunderous sonic boom. Simultaneously with the sharp, loud crack of thunder, Dusty was unexpectedly hit in the back of the neck with great force without warning. His head violently jerked forward, causing him to lose his balance and awkwardly lunge forward. His arms remained impassively dangling at his side, offering no resistance or protection to his face. He came crashing down into the ground face first, breaking his nose and chipping his front teeth. He was completely hidden from view by a dense patch of five-foot-tall cinnamon ferns.

The menacing, militaristic German Shepard attack dog, Armageddon, rushed forward. Expressing dominance by exhaling his stinky breath in Dusty's face was a highly effective sign of intimidation. The dog released a primeval, menacing growl before bolting into the darkness.

The intruder was much too close to the rookery. An overly excited gull dive-bombed and screamed at the intruder, making unbearable noises as he avidly nuked the potential threat with all the ammo he had. He incessantly stabbed Dusty in the back of the head with its sharp beak, ripping his shirt and pecking his ears. Dusty tried to yell for help, but no words came out of his mouth. He couldn't move. His eyes blinked slowly, but nothing else worked. He was agonizingly incapable of the slightest voluntary movement. He panicked. Anxiety overcame him, knowing that he could think but not speak, call for help, or save himself. His mind had an alarming sense of detachment from his body, like a decapitated chicken in a farmyard. An uncontrollable fear overcame him, knowing that he was paralyzed—at the mercy of the gods.

The forest was still. There was nothing but darkness, dead silence, and cold. A hard rain began to fall, conjuring up images of a storm that would destroy everything and wash everything clean.

Father Adam Baum sat on the ground with his eyes closed to reduce the irritation in his eye, babying the severe abrasion on his eyeball to stop the stinging. There were no sounds or evidence of the bear. When his eye finally stopped tearing, he rushed to the entrance gate to see if he could detect the cause of the disturbance. In the middle of the driveway, he discovered the body of Johnny Linguine sprawled on the ground. A stranger lay dead beside him. Both men had been shot point-blank in the head. The black Audi was still idling.

Father Baum was resilient. When timely decisions were essential, he chose wisely, especially during traumatic incidents and periods of extreme danger, when critical life-saving actions were needed. He knew how to avoid conflict, while others fumbled, unable to act rationally or decisively. Intuition saved him.

The Padre called Joey Linguine to report the bad news. "Your brother Johnny is dead, and I have no idea who shot him. We need to get both bodies away from Gravestone Castle to prevent the cops from snooping around and asking questions. Bring two helpers and get over here as quickly as you can. Lock the bodies in the trunk and abandon both vehicles in Estabrook Park in Milwaukee. Remove the license plates and toss them in the Milwaukee River. Jimmy will pick you up at Estabrook Beer Garden and drive you out of town to create a valid alibi."

Dusty Rhodes lay face down in the ferns on the wet forest floor, hidden from view in the darkness. He listened as the Padre barked orders. In a short time, the cars drove off, and then there was silence.

Events unfolded in Milwaukee exactly as the Padre predicted. Teenagers were always alert for the possibility of finding an unlocked car. "Hey, look at this—two unlocked cars parked side by side. Let's take them for a ride."

The oldest boy draped Johnny's trench coat over his shoulders. He arrogantly strutted around the parking lot like a male peacock showing off his plumage. Another boy stole the shoes, while others fought over the remainder of the clothes. They grabbed Johnny's naked corpse by the arms and legs and heaved it into the Milwaukee River. They argued over seating arrangements in the new ride before setting out to impress neighborhood friends on Capital Drive.

A dishonorably dressed female hitchhiker seeking excitement was quick to accept a ride. Big Willie, with a chip-toothed grin, coveted the black Audi. "This Audi is a damn fine pimpmobile," he bragged. The gang laughed and passed around a bottle of Jamaican rum to celebrate their new wheels. With every swig of alcohol, the laughing became louder and the swearing more vulgar.

The fun ended when they were T-boned by a drunk driver in a Ram 2500 running a red light at Capitol Drive and Fond du Lac Avenue. They abandoned the accident scene, painfully limping into the shadows. Loud hip-hop music was still blaring on the radio when the police arrived a few minutes later, flashing red and blue lights. A half-naked shoeless body was locked in the trunk, brutally executed by a single gunshot to the head.

Police discovered Johnny's luxurious black Range Rover crumpled around a tree in Brown Deer Park the following morning. No witnesses came forward to assist with either investigation.

Children playing on the bank of the Milwaukee River downstream from Estabrook Park poked the bloated, decomposing cadaver with sticks, releasing distinct odors smelling like rotting fish and feces. Microorganisms were beginning to digest the body, excreting foul-smelling gases that caused the torso to bloat. The skin was loose and turning black. Warm temperatures accelerated the decomposition process, liquifying the tissues. Turtles and other scavengers in the water contributed to the decay. Thousands of blowflies were laying their eggs in open wounds and orifices. The size of the soft-bodied legless fly larva found in the decaying matter was an indicator of the time of death.

The insurance companies declared both vehicles a total loss. They were hauled to a recycling center and crushed. A report of a potential airplane crash on the shore of Lake Michigan remained a priority.

48

MISSING AIRPLANE

It was a miracle that Billy Big Ears had survived the nightmarish airplane crash. He spent the next three weeks relaxing in Angelina's backyard, hanging out by the swimming pool, sleeping, reading magazines, and cooking rib-eye steaks on the outdoor grill. Abundant sunshine, ibuprofen, large doses of vitamin C, ice packs, and painkillers hastened the healing of his life-threatening injuries. "If anybody sees me, tell them I fell off a ladder."

His unshaven facial hair concealed numerous scratches, cuts, and bruises. It was much too painful to shave. He abandoned his usual routine of raking his hair straight back with the teeth of a comb to create the stereotypical Italian hairstyle. He changed his appearance by combing his hair forward. He swooped his bangs across his forehead to cover a severe contusion above the left eyebrow and hide the ugly red scabs on his ears. New sunglasses with large dark frames hid his black eyes. A black long-sleeve turtleneck covered cuts and bruises on his arms and neck. The overall makeover radically changed his outward appearance.

Angelina spoiled her man with love and attention. She enjoyed pampering and overprotecting him and showing deep care and appreciation. She loved having him with her at home. Angelina gussied up in a gimmicky way with mirrors and lights whenever Billy was in the house, dressing in expensive, ostentatious clothing and bling jewelry.

She always tried to make herself more attractive to create higher sexual arousal and excitement.

She unbuttoned her blouse, rubbed his shoulders, and kissed his neck. "You are such a virile, masculine man. I love it when you chase me around the house, tear my clothes off, and do all those naughty things," she remarked with an artificially white smile.

Big Ears was eternally grateful, and when he felt sufficiently healed, he ignored the pain and hugged her anyway.

After several weeks passed, he called Joey Linguine to explain his disappearance.

"What the hell happened to you? I thought you got cold feet and skipped town," Joey scoffed derisively.

"I have a good excuse," the prodigious braggart boasted. "The bomb that I was planning to use to blow up Jack Daniels in his cabin exploded prematurely, causing my airplane to fall from the sky and violently smash into a tree. The day before I crashed, I whacked the right hand off a trash hauler from Chicago that owed me money. When the cops find his hand at the crash site, they'll take fingerprints and automatically assume he is the one that stole my airplane."

Joey Linguine interrupted with urgency. "Bo-Bo wants to buy Gravestone Castle and build a casino. Jack Daniels is competing to buy the same property. Bo-Bo still wants you to whack Jack to eliminate the competition. He will give you an additional five grand if you don't leave any evidence. You're creative; make the bastard suffer."

"I accept."

Billy Big Ears waited two more weeks for his external wounds to heal before calling the police or going out in public to avoid arousing suspicion. "Someone stole my Cessna 172 airplane, and I'm hoping for a quick reimbursement from the insurance company," he fabricated.

Tammy at police dispatch was disrespectful and blatantly rude, unimpressed with his plea for assistance. She reluctantly set aside her emery board nail file used to grind down and shape her fingernails and touched up her red lipstick before taking a slow sip of stale, rancid coffee. She casually jotted down the make, model, and tail number and, with a frustrated look of exasperation and disbelief, tossed the missing property form on the top of Deputy Sheriff Bud Light's desk between an Aaron Rogers bobblehead doll and a ragged homemade cheese hat made from cutting the foam rubber out of his mother's living room couch.

49

THE REAR WINDOW

Emily sat by the window, evaluating the day's events, thinking about the horrors of crashing an airplane. It was a warm evening. A cool breeze caused the bedroom curtain to flutter. The sound of a cocktail glass breaking on the concrete pool deck below caused an exaggerated acoustic startle reflex. Emily was jumpy. She sat up in bed, cupped her hand by her ear, and listened intently.

In her suite at Woebegone Dunes Resort, the rear window looked out onto a courtyard encircling a freeform dark-blue lagoon-style swimming pool with waterfalls and fire features, rocks, flowering plants, and a cave-like grotto. She could overhear a man and a woman whispering directly below her window. Morbid curiosity led her to spy on them through a slit in the curtain. The simple act of voyeurism created a pleasurable tinge of excitement. Watching and wondering if the couple was engaged in sexual activity, she assumed the conversation was about the passionate joys of seduction and conquest.

The woman wore her underwear like a second skin of silk and satin, so sensual, so inviting, releasing delicate bows and straps from hidden places. It was as if she was opening an antique music box, slowly exposing all of her secrets, scents, and fantasies one at a time. Visions of a man and a woman undressing with deliberation in a public place were like a steamy romance novel. They were revealing their hidden treasures with an air of mystery, unfolding as the first step of a wondrous journey.

Low-luminary landscape lighting cast a shadow of an attractive hourglass-shaped woman on the patio wall, her silhouette on full display. The elegant curve of her back beneath the wavy folds of the draped fabric of her dress was mesmerizing. She had a deep purr in her voice. The top of her warm, soft breasts was erotically alluring in the moonlight, underneath her cleavage a tantalizing dark shadow.

The woman possessed a false modesty. She knew that she was beautiful to the eye, with sleek, well-toned, attractive curves, tight thigh and calf muscles, and well-built shoulders with an elongated neck.

Watching Lady Vanessa remove the wrappings from the treasures they were concealing, discarding her wardrobe for the man's pleasure, was highly erotic, stimulating, and sexually exciting. Their passions rose, building momentum as they slowly undressed as a form of seductive striptease. It was like opening the drapes in a darkened room to gaze upon Adam and Eve in paradise.

Bruno Greco was handsomely sculpted, reminding Emily of Apollo, son of Zeus, king of the gods. He was entirely focused on Vanessa, telling her what clothing items to take off and discard, piece by piece. He tempted and teased her. He took time to appreciate her good looks, creatively figuring out her sensitive zones while stripping off her clothing one piece at a time. He shamelessly referred to her as a goddess. He was highly motivated but resisted the urge to speed up the process by tearing off the wrapping paper and letting it rip, not wanting to pay for the cost of replacing her clothing. He was a little too drunk to remain goal-oriented. When his pants came off, intuition colored the entire romantic adventure that followed, leaving a lasting impression burned into Emily's consciousness with no doubts about the ending.

The excitement of watching two attractive people writhing with pleasure like two intertwined snakes was much too tempting to resist. The sexual pleasure derived from watching another couple engaged in lovemaking was invigorating. The sequence of events that had just happened outside her window lingered in her imagination. The storyline had evolved significantly from the opening of the erotic foreplay process, eventually unfolding in a bonfire of passions bearing little resemblance to the initial flickering flame.

The excitement of watching two impassioned adults engaged in a spirited frenzied sense of arousal precipitated a delightful sense of pleasurable titillation, curiosity, and emotional stimulation. However, the intense joy she experienced as a first-time voyeur abruptly turned stone cold when she overheard her name spoken. A subjective sense of apprehension and dread overcame her, an uncomfortable fear that something dangerous, painful, and threatening was about to happen. Her instinctive reactions were anxiety, nervousness, and self-preservation, accompanied by emotional distress, panic, and excessive worry. Her heart and mind were racing. Was something creepy and potentially dangerous about to happen? Insomnia caused by stress and anxiety caused her to toss and turn and lie awake until dawn.

Emily was eager to share her experience with Lieutenant Dunning. She arrived an hour early for the planned breakfast meeting. Too much coffee caused caffeine overstimulation, trembling, and dizziness. Heart palpitations, heartburn, and shivers followed. Emotional agitation led to abnormally rapid speaking and a reduced ability to think critically, clearly, and rationally. It was difficult for her to express her ideas in a straightforward, simple manner. Her thinking skills needed to explain logical connections between ideas became uncoupled. The lieutenant was caught off-guard. It was difficult for him to decipher her words and unravel the link between the indecent public nudity and her energized emotional response to a perceived threat of bodily harm. Emily had never lost so much credibility, made so many misstatements, or sounded so logically fallacious—errors in reasoning that rendered her ideas invalid. Her exaggerated hand gestures, off-kilter body language, and excessive talking were clear indicators of restlessness, irritability, and anxiety. Her mind was racing in crisis mode. The unnatural shrillness in her voice and inner tension made it challenging to communicate effectively.

Feeling isolated, disconnected, and vulnerable, she took several deep breaths, relaxed her shoulders, and consciously thought about the message she was trying to convey. "Vanessa and Bruno sat wrapped up in a blanket below my rear window for over an hour. Vanessa is worried the IRS might conduct an audit of Woebegone Dunes Resort. She and Bruno Greco plan to leave for Switzerland at the slightest provocation to escape the law. Vanessa is doing everything she can to disincentivize Wayne and Kate Kennedy from becoming members of Woebegone Dunes Resort. You and I are labeled 'undesirable' guests. We need to keep our eyes wide open because I'm sure they are conspiring to create an unfortunate accident for us."

Emily was irritable, anxious, and stressed. Anxiety triggered mood swings, memory loss, concentration problems, and compulsive behavior. "I hate feeling threatened. Knowing that someone wants to bash our heads in is a genuine criminal threat of violence. Where's my dark chocolate?"

"Your feelings are valid. Let's sort through this together."

To appease, pacify, and calmly soothe her hyper state of anxiety and mollify her worries, the lieutenant offered reassurance by pouring her another cup of coffee. He smiled politely, glancing around the room and admiring the meticulously organized place settings with colorful flower bouquets and precisely aligned high-back chairs.

"Wayne and Kate Kennedy should be arriving soon," she reminded him.

"Enjoying the daily moments that bring us great joy is a requisite for healthy living. When we dramatize our emotions, we lose perspective and become somewhat unbalanced. Happiness comes from taking time to appreciate the good things in life, the daily moments that bring us great joy—like having another cup of Black Forest coffee."

50

AMBER ROOM BREAKFAST

Wayne and Kate entered the dining room the way actors walked onstage, full of confidence and rehearsed, quintessentially knowing what they wanted to accomplish. Wayne was an understated, subdued, unassuming masculine man of good character. Being well read, intelligent, extremely wealthy, a world traveler, and the holder of a dozen patents, he exuded politeness and charm. When others were agreeable, Wayne automatically assumed control. He had the natural ability to speak spontaneously to an audience onstage at a moment's notice.

Lieutenant Dunning was overwhelmed by the fashionably elegant, high-class cuisine served in the Amber Room Restaurant at Woebegone Dunes Resort. He lowered his face to the level of his plate. He inhaled deeply to expose the delicious smells to the olfactory nerves in his nostrils before taking a bite. His delectable Edwardian breakfast of bourbon fried pork chops, maple peaches, Johnny-cakes, a mild hors d'oeuvre, fancy blackberry brie omelet with honey-baked ham in a hash brown nest, served with a Tequila Sunrise, was delicious. He removed the white cloth napkin from under his chin before inviting Wayne and Kate Kennedy to voluntarily unload their observations about their experiences at Woebegone Dunes Resort.

Wayne vented in detail. "The day we arrived, a stranger fired a gun from an airplane that severely damaged our new car. A maintenance worker died on the golf course after being stung by a thousand angry killer bees. I accidentally hit a caddy in the back, and an errant golf ball nearly hit me. Kate had food poisoning, nearly broke her leg, and we discovered the body of a self-proclaimed priest buried in a sand bunker. All of these distressing incidents and threats to our safety have sent our minds into overdrive, leaving us feeling anxious and worried."

The lieutenant responded to Wayne's demeanor. He was a master at soothing frustrations. Approaching matters at hand with a sense of elegance and grace, he had a genuinely compassionate approach to ease the hardships and negative feelings others might be experiencing. "Are there any details about these incidents that would benefit from an additional inquiry from a detective's perspective?"

Kate had an immediate response. "Before I fell into the bunker, I saw someone looking at me through a high-powered rifle scope from a window in the back of Gravestone Castle. It was very frightening. Luckily, I wasn't seriously injured when I rolled down the hill," she explained, holding up her shapely leg with both hands and deeply massaging the calf muscle.

Lieutenant Dunning showed composure, poise, agility, and patience to minimize the impact of uncertainty. His ability to make people feel safe and secure in response to growing pressures indicated his leadership preparedness, maturity, and insight. His composure was reflected in his attitude, body language, and overall presence. He placed a pinch of aromatic tobacco in his pipe. Projecting an air of omniscience, as if he already knew the answers to the questions he was asking, he cross-questioned, "Tell us about your company and future intentions."

Wayne was happy to comply. "Kate and I are hoping to buy both properties—Woebegone Dunes Resort and the Hermitage at Gravestone Castle. We want to maintain the privacy of the luxurious golf resort and convert Gravestone Castle into our primary residence. The name of our company is Shadow Structures, Inc. The Pentagon is our largest client. We hold a dozen patents, but most of our products are top secret. That's how we know Colonel James Roberts."

Not much later, the meeting concluded with a handshake from Wayne and a hug from Kate before they left. The lieutenant paused to gain composure, tugging on his earlobes before asking Emily, "What do your instincts tell you about Wayne and Kate?"

"They are a wealthy and intelligent husband and wife team who built their company from scratch with personal initiative. They have an excellent reputation, an exceptional record of accomplishment, innovation, and profit. They seem to be effortlessly gliding through life, moving smoothly and quietly at their own pace without worries, with everything coming up roses. Wayne is charming, articulate, and genuine. He is a sophisticated gentleman and a masculine role model, admired by men and stalked by women, delicious in his male variations. Kate has integrity. She is honest, soft-hearted, and has balance in her life. Lady Vanessa is the opposite, an inherently dishonest person, corrupt at the core, willing to commit immoral acts for personal gain without apology, like a virus that'll make your computer crash."

"What are your plans for this evening?" he asked.

"Jay and I have finally agreed to meet after work at the bar for a potential romantic encounter."

51

JAY WALKER

Jay could sense her proximity and feel her warm breath on his skin while sitting closely beside Emily, holding hands in a private booth. Emily stared intensely into his eyes with a captivating Mona Lisa smile. She met his gaze for a few extra seconds, a seductive feminine approach sure to awaken sultry passions. The radiance of her smile and the pleasant, alluring trace of her perfume temporarily distracted him. A portion of his brain-processing ability and cognitive functioning deteriorated into a state of temporary decline.

Emily sensed how Jay was feeling, making her want to reach out empathetically and give him a big, fussy squeeze. It was her way of offering solace and emotional comfort to relieve his distress. "Gravestone Castle is the most mysterious private estate in Wisconsin, more fortified and beautiful than the mansions on Lake Drive. The fairytale image of your family home, ideally suited for European royalty, enthralls me. My imagination is filled with fanciful and wondrous characters, leaving me spellbound thinking about the possibilities and wondering what it was like for you as a child."

Jay felt safe sharing his deeply personal thoughts and emotions with Emily because she cared about him sincerely.

"Tell me about your childhood," she politely encouraged.

"My life has not played out as expected—fate has turned against me," he poignantly revealed. "My father was planning to convert Gravestone Castle into a luxury resort after I graduated college. I'm baffled why he inexplicably donated the property to the Hermitage. I suspect foul play, but Judge Geri Attrick said the terms of the will are legal and enforceable."

He lowered his head. Rolling his eyes as an expression of exasperation, he explained, "My mother died of breast cancer when I was a child. My grandparents died the same year, and I was heartbroken."

Emily amorously placed her hand softly on his thigh and gazed warmly into his eyes, smiling outwardly as a heartfelt expression of empathy. She felt sad knowing that Jay's mother had died at such an early age, and it was tragic that his grandparents had passed away the same year.

Jay despondently shrugged his shoulders. "After my mother died, my father sent me to Lycée Jaccard. It's an elite boarding school for boys in Lausanne, Switzerland, located in an idyllic setting and learning environment in the heart of the Swiss Alps. Skiing and other sports were an excellent distraction. I loved the mountains, chocolate, wine, cheese, and Swiss culture. I even liked a few of the girls I met on the ski slopes," he gushed with emotional nostalgia, thinking about the heady days of youth, when everything was possible.

His emotions peaked, and his shoulders sagged. His voice wavered as tears welled up in his eyes. He seemed to be giving up, gradually slipping into a depressed state of despair. "I rushed home from Switzerland to discover religious strangers living in my house. My vision of a secure future shattered. My family home was ransacked and taken from me with pretext and without forewarning. I was emotionally distraught and unprepared for what had happened."

Emily's kissable pink lips and warm brown eyes with long dark eyelashes were powerful distractors. The erotic feelings and emerging fantasies she stimulated in his brain were causing a significant loss of concentration. Emily tilted her head and leaned in close. Her silky hair was smoothly hanging down, signaling interest and engagement as a sign of primal feminine magnetism. She could sense that his heart was aching—while hers was racing. Her maternal instincts bubbled to the surface. She reached out with both hands to express how much she cared for him.

Jay was captivated by her presence, causing him to lose focus. The erotic aphrodisiac stimulant in Emily's perfume was sexually arousing, a love potion that positively influenced his male brain. Fragrance chemicals affected his conscious perceptions and expectations, resulting in an immediate change in mood, evoking a relaxed sense of calmness.

Emily was wholly absorbed in Jay's life experiences. She was happy to know that he trusted her enough to share his innermost personal thoughts and feelings with her. He seemed vulnerable, seductive, irresistible, provocative, and exciting, like walking dangerously close to a precipice. She daydreamed about his masculinity, honesty, and authenticity, imagining their futures together with a single-mindedness. Erotic fantasies, portending a discreet romantic fling with Jay, filled her mind with a dizzying resoluteness. She was dedicated, willing, energized, and motivated for a private rendezvous—a romantic affair with her paramour.

The illusion of spending nights with Jay under a warm blanket calmed her. The comforts of commitment, a positive relationship, and a change in routine seemed profoundly satisfying and transformative. Thinking about Jay romantically stimulated a feeling of bliss, a sense of security, and passionate excitement. Was her lucid dreaming a sign that he was having the same dream, she wondered.

Hours later, the sound of her alarm jolted her awake from a deep sleep, shattering her romantic fantasy of an exciting life together.

Showering was a luxurious experience that awakened her to reality and positively influenced her mood. She had been eagerly anticipating the meeting with Sister Olivia all week.

52

THE NUNNERY

The lieutenant arranged a meeting with Sister Olivia to inquire about the workings of the Hermitage. Olivia was in a surprisingly good mood, leading the lieutenant and Emily to wonder if she had put whiskey in her coffee that morning.

"Tell us some things about yourself and the other nuns living at the Hermitage," Emily inquired.

Her response rocked the boat. "I am the Sister Superior at the Hermitage. When Father Feely announced a crusade to hold a virtuous beauty pageant for women desiring to become nuns, many hotties accepted the invitation to compete. Most of us were praying to protect our virtue at the same time. I was a high-school cheerleader with a boyfriend and entered on a whim. I had to undergo a few erotic indignities that included going topless for a Japanese movie company. Overall, the event was a tremendous success. I was the pageant swimsuit winner. First prize was an opportunity to become Sister Superior of the Hermitage at Gravestone Castle."

Emily was in awe of Sister Olivia's life experiences, curious to know if the judges were distracted by her exceptionally sexy figure and provocative dressing style. The lieutenant casually remarked that Sister Olivia "breathed" well.

"I offer full-fledged membership into a convent of colorful women whose mission is to look fabulous while spreading joy and absolving guilt. I am the gatekeeper of the Irredeemable Sisters of Everlasting Merriment. My group of sisters evangelizes. We entertain unsuspecting audiences with flamboyant flourishes while fallaciously preaching love and acceptance to unbelievers—imagine doing all of this for only a small fee. We don't dramatize, criticize, or compromise, and we certainly don't circumcise. The video will answer all of your questions."

The recruitment film was a slick, commercially produced, professionally edited movie with a musical tribute to religious life. "Many breezy young women wholeheartedly and enthusiastically embrace our way of living. After a two-week internship, they vivaciously throw their weight behind the benefits of the Hermitage lifestyle."

The opening scene showed young women in the springtime of life, espousing a typical day in the life of a nun: a girl walking on the beach, another soaking in a bubble bath, praying and preparing an elaborate feast for a group of handsome young priests on an exquisite banquet table suitable for a king. Background scenes with music included panoramic landscapes at the peak of the fall season in splendid autumn glory. There was a warm glowing fireplace, water lapping on the sandy shores of Lake Michigan, and deer grazing in a meadow filled with wildflowers.

Speaking softly in a calm voice, the narrator made a convincing pitch for new members. "You don't have to be a virgin to become a sister or a nun. We don't ask you to cut your hair. It's okay to have tattoos, and you're not even required to wear underwear or be one hundred percent female. Our only requirements are to avoid cursing and spitting in public and taking a ten-day vow of stability. If you make good on your temporary vows, you're ready for the religious life."

The following vignette was an evocative account of a hypothetical scene designed to provide a visual context. The camera focused on Sister Olivia standing behind a desk in the library. "The lives of nuns can be surprisingly rich and not just with spiritual experiences. The discernment process can be completed online for a small fee by email and by attending virtual webinars every Tuesday. Join us in the privacy of your own home by the magic of online communication for a special group retreat, hosted lovingly by us for you."

The video smoothly transitioned to a scene of a relaxed young woman sunbathing by a swimming pool in a brightly flowered hipster bikini as a potential recruit for nunnery school. She carefully placed the racy romance novel she was reading on the side table before sipping an ice-cold mint julep served in a frosty copper mug. "How much does it cost to become a nun?" she inquired.

A slick, prerecorded voiceover from an unseen announcer supplied the answer. "Cost is never a consideration when choosing a religion. If you feel that you are a good fit, you will be able to spend time living with us at the Hermitage right away. Some of our newest members support the Hermitage by selling products they make or providing special favors to the priests. Those who work outside the Hermitage donate their income for a monthly stipend. Very importantly, luscious desserts are served with every lunch and dinner."

The voiceover then stated that being sent to nunnery school by loving parents is the best present many women would ever receive. "Simply put, Gravestone Castle nunnery school is the way real women learn about religion. Our clients learn to never wait for a miracle or covet a special way of life, never swear when nobody is listening or debate whether smoking, drinking, and kissing boys is worth doing. Sooner or later, you have to decide between Ft. Lauderdale, bikinis, and sunshine for spring break and volunteering to work at the Salvation Army on Saturday nights."

"What's the difference between a sister and a nun?'" asked an attractive brunette with a gorgeous figure. She was wearing white shorts and a pale-pink cashmere sweater exposing abundant cleavage.

"A nun removes herself from the world, remains cloistered, and has limited interaction with friends, family, and others. A sister does the opposite. She has a professional calling and frequently engages with the outside world," Sister Olivia replied.

"How long does the process of becoming a nun or a sister take?" inquired another potential client wearing a cheerleader sweater and displaying silky brown hair in twin ponytails.

The narrator explained, "Your training is a four-stage process divided into the spring, summer, fall, and winter quarters. At the end of each season, you will receive an official document attesting to your status and level of achievement. The different levels you progress through have no set time limits, and you are not required to pass beyond a certain stage. If you prefer to remain a sister, we will give you counsel. After six months, you will take your vows, agreeing to live a contemplative life based on a vow of stability."

"Will I receive a diploma or some certification?"

"For a small fee, recruits receive a framed diploma signifying that they are nonordained sisters. They become members of the laity that are not part of the clergy, subscribers of a religious institute validated by the Hermitage at Gravestone Castle. You will make peace with your past when you finish your lessons. You will be able to use words like *holy*, *exalt*, *glorify*, *behold*, *blessed*, *grace*, *sinner*, and *holiness* in full, coherent sentences. You will learn how to trust the process, clear your resistance, ask the universe to deliver what you want, and keep your vibration high."

The recruitment video concluded with Sister Olivia bragging about the financial success of her charity. "We receive many contributions, cash donations, and precious works of art each year. We have a highly diverse assortment of women willing to provide the Hermitage with a fixed sum each month to qualify for participation in our online webinars."

The lieutenant communicated his response nonverbally. He folded his arms, leaned back in his chair while projecting a false smile, and rolled his eyes as an expression of disbelief. Sister Olivia reacted favorably, incorrectly assuming that eye-rolling was an acknowledgment of her feminine beauty and a modern form of flirtation. The masculine way he looked at her subdued and distracted her, his big brown eyes probing into her as if he approved of everything she held inside. She paused to look back over her shoulder on the way out the door. Smiling coquettishly, she departed with a lustful air of excitement, sexual fantasy, and desire resulting from a sense of arousal provoked by the lieutenant's masculine physical stimuli.

Emily rudely shattered the lieutenant's dreamy fantasy of a castle in Spain. "Would you like to continue undisturbed with your lustful day-dream involving Sister Olivia, or would you like to assist Deputy Sheriff Bud Light with his search warrants? Bud Light is expecting us to help him with the investigation of Dusty Rhodes's trailer."

The lieutenant was jolted off cloud nine and unnerved by Emily's acute feminine awareness of his aspirations and ambitions. He resisted the urge to deny her observations by immediately straightening his posture and adjusting his bearing to project a more professional, business-like temperament.

53

THE WARRANTS

The day held the potential for the most excitement the deputy could remember since joining the police force ten years earlier. Deputy Sheriff Bud Light was on a mission. He marched with an overinflated sense of self-importance. He reminded Emily of a pompous college drum major strutting with his feet out, elbows up, and head back. With a no-knock search warrant confidently in hand, he pranced with a swagger into the trailer park where caddy Dusty Rhodes lived. His objective was to collect fingerprints, footprints, tire tracks, blood, body fluids, hairs, fibers, and debris. Field-detecting drugs and explosives as admissible as testimony in court to show evidence of a crime was a potential outcome.

"Are you certain that Dusty lives here?" the lieutenant wondered. "There is no evidence of recent occupation, and there are no footprints or tire tracks in the sand since it rained ten days ago."

The teardrop-shaped trailer Dusty Rhodes called home was the smallest ever manufactured. It had an average height of about five feet, making it impossible to stand up and hard to move without staying hunched over and bumping into everything inside. The lack of cooking facilities, a sink, and a toilet made the space highly unlivable. A crystal chandelier found at the dump dangled obnoxiously from the highest part of the ceiling, just below a water leak. There was a significant number of design and construction flaws. Deputy Sheriff Bud Light accidentally bumped the chandelier with his forehead, causing an abrupt high-voltage electrical discharge, flash of light, and sharp sizzle sound. His eyebrows flamed for an instant before disappearing. The interior wall panels were impossible to repair due to delamination and wood rot. The entry door had fallen from its mount, and the latch would not lock. The air was stale.

Taking the trailer out on the road was a source of trouble. A sudden gust of wind generated by a semi-truck had caused it to porpoise, shimmy, and fishtail wildly before a slight bump in the road caused it to become unhitched. It spun all the way around, flipped onto the left side, and slid into the ditch, leaving the rear axle bent, the frame radically caddywampus, and the door five degrees off-kilter.

Deputy Sheriff Bud Light was genuinely interested in the availability of the low-priced trailer. "Tammy would love this trailer for deer camp. I wonder if I could buy it for her for a low price at the police auction."

Emily observed an empty bottle of brandy on the bed, a bag of warm cheese curds, and a Ruger revolver designed for concealed carry use. On closer examination, she noticed the gun barrel showed signs of being fired recently.

The black leather portfolio contained an original oil painting of the Castle of Chillon in Switzerland, one of the most visited castles in Europe. "A single garrison could control access up the Rhone Valley into France, Germany, and Italy," Emily announced, confidently knowing that she was contributing to the investigation.

The deputy tossed a small suitcase onto the bed to check the contents. He was astonished to discover thousands of dollars neatly wrapped and stacked inside.

The lieutenant was greatly surprised. "I'm amazed that Dusty Rhodes could possess what appears to be an expensive original oil painting and so much cash. These are astonishing finds incongruous with his lifestyle, leaving me to assume this is stolen property."

"The picture frame is old and weathered," Emily observed.

The lieutenant perked up. "Old dusty frames are the perfect disguise for deceitfully hiding counterfeit works of art. Many dealers and auction houses are overly eager to accept forgeries as genuine to assure a quick profit. There are giant pools of money sloshing around Manhattan and London for such purchases. The super-wealthy are always looking for creative places to park money by diversifying their holdings. Rich people buy more art than ever before and stash it in strange places. The upper crust of society knows that if a work of art is perceived to be legitimate, it can be hawked as an asset—bought and sold with no questions asked."

The others were eager to learn more. "Carrying out an art scam is relatively easy. Most importantly, you have to create a believable backstory. The forger needs to select the right materials, choosing the paint pigments wisely. He has to pay attention to detail. Weathering a painting outdoors in the elements is a common practice in the world of forgery. The best trick is to create fake 'missing' paintings from a famous artist's body of work and make up a story about how the painting changed hands over the years. Fraud has followed the art world because values have gone through the ceiling. Investors have created a financial froth in the art world, and very few are interested in tipping off law enforcement. Only a fraction of art undergoes robust due diligence before being sold."

"Are you telling us that there's nothing morally wrong or illegal about copying or imitating a famous work of art?" Emily inquired.

"If a forgery is highly exacting, experts are seldom aware and reluctant to admit deception. From a legal perspective, art is never fake, but a forged statement of authenticity for financial gain is illegal."

"I wonder how high Father Marcello would appraise this painting?"

Feeling claustrophobic in the confined space and eager to exit the trailer, Bud Light stumbled and accidentally forced his hand through the flimsy screen door.

"What's that awful burned-rubber smell?" he casually inquired while pointing to a circle of gooey plastic on the neighbor's patio.

"It's a hemorrhoid seat cushion. Remarkably, someone popped it and set it on fire in the neighbors' front yard," Emily observed on closer examination. "Probably the same one Dusty used to relieve pain and itching."

The deputy poked it with a stick before leading the investigative posse to the Hermitage under the authority of the second warrant.

54

FORGERIES

On the way to Gravestone Castle, the lieutenant offered Emily some strategic advice. "Pay special attention to personality and nonverbal cues. Learn to ignore any preconceptions that stop you from seeing clearly. Listen to your intuition. Body language and voice tone represent a significant portion of what people think. Outward expressions of disillusionment, emotional suppression, sentience, and gut feelings are often just as important as physical clues," the lieutenant explained while tugging on his earlobes.

Emily thought intensely about the lieutenant's advice. Her initial visceral reaction to Father Feely in the first meeting was subliminal. She shared her past impressions and personal feelings without hesitation. "The tone of Father Feely's voice is abrasive. His expensive Italian shoes indicate excessive wealth. The dazzling gold cross pendant and thick gold chain dangling from his neck override any semblance of spiritual leanings. His eyes suggest concealed secrets, tension, and mistrust. His deep frown lines suggest worrying and overthinking. He appears contained, highly independent and detached, challenging and skeptical, and prone to whingeing and hypersensitivity. He has no clear sense of direction and struggles to work in teams. He regularly overlooks important facts and practical details," she added with confidence.

"Excellent," Lieutenant Dunning exclaimed with a rare smile as an outward expression of approval. "Stay focused on the reason Colonel Roberts sent us to Wisconsin in the first place. Our objective is to observe the spending habits of Father Feely to determine how he can afford to live such an impressive and elaborately lavish life of luxury."

Deputy Sheriff Bud Light dauntlessly led the procession through the heavy arched wooden doors leading into the chapel. Residents of the Hermitage had been hastily assembled in the chapel to explain the reason for the unannounced investigation. Tangled cobwebs between the candlesticks on the altar, stagnant air, and a thick layer of dust on the pews proved the chapel had been vacant for many months.

Emily glanced around the room to test the lieutenant's hypothesis about nonverbal clues. Father Adam Baum sat rigidly aloof, haptic, and isolated in the back row, an austere figure with an agitated side-eyed deportment. His expression was inscrutably tight-lipped, stark, and poker-faced, reflecting an unpleasant cryptic demeanor that was impossible to read.

Father Marcello slouched with his arms indecently draped over Sisters Lova and Lola Kurvig from Sweden. "We serve humbly in love," Lola improperly professed with a titillating sense of mischief.

Father Feely directed the group into the library, a gorgeous room with dark-wood paneling, floor-to-ceiling bookshelves, a fireplace, a gray slate floor with an orange rug, ornate ebony, an ivory chess table with matching chairs, and subdued indirect lighting. Emily was immediately attracted to a classic oil painting of Chateau de Tourbillon in Sion, Switzerland, constructed in 1308 by the Knights Templar. She secretly noted the frame and the color and texture of the pigments, remarkably similar to the painting discovered in Dusty Rhodes's trailer.

"The Castle is a Swiss heritage site of national significance built on a prehistoric Neolithic dwelling dating to the fifth millennium BC," Father Marcello stated boastfully. "The painting was missing for many years, and it has a terrific backstory," he added.

"I have an oil painting in police custody the court would like appraised," the deputy encouraged politely. "It looks very similar in style and colors to this one."

Lieutenant Dunning had an intuitive, razor-sharp ability to identify counterfeits quickly and without evidence. He insightfully cast a side-long glance at Father Marcello, flashing an expression conveying doubt, suspicion, and scorn. "Paintings and costly works of art appear to grace every room of Gravestone Castle. The Hermitage must be a favored institution of religious-minded philanthropists," he insinuated, suggesting the existence of a covert operation promoting extremely lucrative forgeries.

Father Marcello's emotional response was ominous. His blink rate increased, his head position changed with shifty eye movements, and his breathing was inconsistent. There was a distinct change in the tone of his voice, and his bodily expressions didn't seem to match what he was saying. The direction of his eyes was remarkably counterfeit.

Emily observed Father Marcello's behavior with a discerning eye, the way the lieutenant had previously advised: "Guilt is a powerful weapon, linked to pervasive feelings of inappropriate behavior, and many priests know how to wield it skillfully. Watch for an elusive blank stare with a far-away look in the eyes. Changing head position, loosening the collar to get more oxygen, and repeated phrases are other predictable behavior and ways to discover the smell of deceit."

Father Feely gloated over the high-priced art collection with excessive pride. His repellent bragging about his prestigious accomplishments related to accumulated wealth, intended to make himself look smart, were vain and immodest. As the conversation toiled onward, it soon became apparent that Father Feely arrogantly thought of himself as better than everyone else. He believed that his sole reason for existing was to bombard listeners with envy-provoking snippets of his bodacious lifestyle.

"It's true—religious people are more giving than others," Father Feely admitted. "Itemized deductions for charitable contributions of art in this country exceed $1.5 billion a year, significantly more than the value of donated mutual funds. Father Marcello has exceptional skills as an authentic, registered, highly qualified, certified art appraiser. He works closely with CPAs advising taxpayers with the requirements for appraisals and IRS policies and procedures for valuing artwork to establish a fair value for each donated item. Selling art is a lucrative business. Whenever Father Marcello discovers a rare painting in London or New York for a good price, we buy and sell it for a profit to pay our operating costs."

The lieutenant saw below the surface pretense. "You appear to be skilled at underhandedly seducing seasoned curators and collectors into acquiring faux works of art that have everything they are seeking. The market seems ripe for artful financial deception and trickery."

Father Marcello nervously reacted with a sudden burst of heart palpitations and a spark of emotional excitement. Cautiously slanting his head as an outward sign of distrust, he flashed a half-wink at Emily from across the room as a distraction and a universal symbol of flirtation. His behavior was quick, discreet, and suggestive, and his eyes were the medium through which he expressed his inner thoughts. Even in a crowded, noisy room, a message reeking of deceit secretly broke through the secret cone of silence.

"Which rooms belonged to Father Cellophane?" the deputy inquired.

55

THE CROSSBOW

Deputy Sheriff Bud Light led the procession with the search warrant authorizing him to search Father Cellophane's apartment. Father Feely and Sister Olivia directed the group into the hallway and up the stairs to his palatial suite, where the search began in earnest. The living room had attractive luxury furniture, wingback chairs, polished wood tables, an ornate grandfather clock, a floor lamp with an exquisite full-sized sculpture of a naked lady, and a glass cabinet filled with expensive Hummel plates and figurines costing thousands of dollars.

On the opposite side of the room were a dining area, kitchen, two bedrooms, and two bathrooms. There were four new golf putters in the hallway and an advanced executive putting green, and one of the putters was gold plated.

Sister Olivia pointed to a picture of a young boy in an ornate picture frame. "This is Polpetta, Father Cellophane's illegitimate son. Polpetta lives in an orphanage in Milwaukee because the mother was only a teenager when he was born."

"The boy looks every bit as mischievous and coarse-speaking as Huckleberry Finn," Emily remarked with a genuine interest in the topic of adoption. "The book next to the picture, *Adoption Detective: Memoir of an Adopted Child* by Judith Land, is an adoption story that belongs in the Parthenon of adoption classics. I highly recommend it."

Lieutenant Dunning pointed to the shoes in the bedroom closet. "You can tell a lot about a person by their shoes. A good detective can accurately guess the gender, age, social status, and various personality traits, including where they've been and where they're going. Expensive shoes belong to high earners, flashy and colorful footwear belongs to extroverts, and older shoes in good condition belong to conscientious types. Reformists and progressives tend to wear shabbier, less expensive shoes denoting a personality of chaotic domestic habits, probably best avoided. In this case, I would say Father Cellophane lived a promiscuous, dissolute life. He was a lecherous rogue lacking moral constraints."

Deputy Sheriff Bud Light embarrassedly glanced down at the brown unpolished scruffy work boots he was wearing outside standard police uniform protocol and rules of conduct.

The deputy poked his military-grade flashlight under Father Cellophane's bed and pulled out a flirty pink lace Victoria's Secret bra. Emily's eyes widened in astonishment, knowing it an exact match to the cheeky lace panties previously discovered outside the castle wall next to the stone fire ring.

Sister Mary Pompino's voice quivered, failing to confess or acknowledge ownership. She tossed her long, beautiful, auburn-colored hair over her shoulder and wiped false crocodile tears from her eyes. "I'm going to miss Father Cellophane. His favorite activity was walking along the shore of Lake Michigan in his yellow speedos with his hands behind his back," she confided.

"Look what I found in the closet," Bud Light interrupted as if discovering something of exceptional value. "Wow, I have always wanted one of these," he exclaimed excitedly, cradling a large flat cardboard box with both hands. "It's an empty container for a very expensive crossbow, powerful and accurate enough to bring down a grizzly bear."

Emily perused the datebook. "Possible bear sighting near the entrance gate—epic rainstorm with lots of lightning and thunder."

Sister Mary Pompino explained. "I assumed a client wanted to purchase an indulgence the night when he went out in the rain. Indulgences were Father Cellophane's way of promising atonement for sins of the flesh. Recipients pray and pay one hundred dollars to Father Cellophane for mercy and forgiveness. Each time he sold one, he celebrated with an age-worthy bottle of Chianti wine," Sister Olivia added with a guileful wink.

The deputy opened a letter addressed to Lady Vanessa from Father Cellophane. "'Dear Vanessa, Dusty Rhodes is a despicable caddy and a loathsome human being, and I refuse to tip him. He adds ten strokes to my game every time I play—he should be fired immediately.' The lack of tipping was a serious reason for Dusty to be angry with Father Cellophane," the deputy self-righteously deduced. The attention he was receiving caused him to puff up his chest with a sense of grandiose self-importance.

The lieutenant observed that the deputy's powers of deduction weren't always reliable, and the supposition theories he exhibited weren't always praiseworthy. Still, he had a tenacity and never gave up.

"We discovered Dusty's caddy uniform near the crime scene, haphazardly discarded in a crumpled heap on the shore of Lake Michigan. I need to arrest him before he skips town," the deputy stated with a glint in his eye, fumbling with his handcuffs and revolver.

"Be patient," Lieutenant Dunning cautioned, conservatively giving the baseball "safe sign" with both hands. "Always get your ducks in a row before requesting an arrest warrant authorizing you to take him into custody for probable cause," he reminded him, implying preparedness and efficiency.

56

CAMP HAVEN

With the investigation complete, Emily pointed to two wooden Adirondack lawn chairs in the courtyard, eager to explain what she had gleaned from various historical sources.

"Europeans flocked into Wisconsin territory after the Indians signed a treaty in 1883 relinquishing all lands on the west shore of Lake Michigan. A religious group from Europe unwittingly used headstones from ancient graves to construct a large stone church in the vicinity of Gravestone Castle. When the leader died, the congregation lost their way, abandoned the unfinished church, and moved to Fargo, North Dakota.

"Jay's grandfather, Hans Walker, purchased the vacant land eighty years later. He had the mind of a German engineer and the persistency of a mule. He thrived during Prohibition by manufacturing whiskey in a secret underground quarry, distributing boatloads of whiskey up and down the shore of Lake Michigan, as far south as Chicago. He was young and energetic with a passionate boyhood dream of building a castle. After nearly two decades of continuous building on the stone foundation of the original church, Gravestone Castle eventually evolved into a substantial structure."

The lieutenant placed fresh English-made Marcovitch smoking tobacco in his pipe. He blew a perfect smoke ring that lingered in the air, crossed his legs, and resumed listening intently, pondering the perplexity of the situation.

"The US government leased three farms north of Sheboygan in 1940. They built an army antiaircraft missile base at Camp Haven, the exact spot Whistling Straits golf course occupies. At the same time, the federal government leased Gravestone Castle for use as an ultra-secret science laboratory. Hans Walker negotiated a lucrative long-term contract to serve as the construction superintendent. They had one son, Benedict Walker, and one grandson, Jay Walker."

"Have you found any historic photographs?"

"Photographs were prohibited. The original house was gradually transformed into a large fortified complex, resembling a medieval fortress linked with tunnels and a high rock wall. All of the activity occurred at night to avoid suspicion. Vines were planted on the exterior walls to conceal the structure within the forest setting. The entrance road was torn up and made serpentine. It was relocated under the heaviest forest canopy to avoid detection from airplanes. Accommodations ranged from large comfortable suites for the top scientists to simple dormitories for the younger military guards. Other rooms included a large dining room with a commercial kitchen, meeting rooms, recreation room, theater, library, multiple garages, storage rooms, greenhouses, offices, labs, and a chapel. The fortified complex, designed to defend against a small-arms attack, had defensive gun ports integrated into the thick stone walls. There were numerous booby traps, hidden tunnels, storage compartments, and priest holes. Strategically placed secret doors, hidden hallways, and a warren of interconnected tunnels helped provide maximum security. Scientists stored classified research documents underground with hazardous materials, munitions, and explosives," Emily informed Dunning with a high level of intrigue.

There was a high level of intensity and vigor in her voice as she continued speaking with an undiminished force. "Scientific research at Gravestone Castle was primarily aimed at destroying enemy food supplies. They researched ultra-secret biological and entomological weapons, more advanced and lethal than anything the world has ever seen. Unfortunately, there is no evidence to prove that any of this activity ever took place."

Lieutenant Dunning was intensely curious. He displayed an uncanny knowledge of the covert elements of asymmetrical warfare designed to exploit the enemy's weakness in response to the highest order's political provocations and power dynamics.

"The public was acutely aware of the national missile defense system at Camp Haven north of Sheboygan. Submarine lore preserved in a museum in Manitowoc, Wisconsin, is highly interesting. Still, Gravestone Castle remains an enigma, mysteriously absent from the wartime record. Gravestone Castle nearly became a secret standalone massive national computer data repository storage facility designed to support the US intelligence community. But the proposal was scrapped when the Haven Nuclear Power Plant at Whistling Straits failed to materialize."

"Is there any data to back up that claim?" he asked.

"There has never been anything sinister in the public record about Gravestone Castle. The fear of accidentally trespassing on haunted ancient Indian burial grounds is a significant public deterrent." Emily paused for effect. "There's a mystery here. Would you please explain something to me? I searched Google Earth to see if I could find Woebegone Dunes Resort and Gravestone Castle. Mysteriously, neither site appears anywhere in the satellite database—they don't exist."

The lieutenant contemplated the significance of her words and the potential world-changing consequences of past events. "The government can restrict aerial photography and satellite imagery of sensitive sites. Vice President Dick Cheney's residence remained obscured for his tenure in the office. Aerial coverage of the entire country of Israel is suspect. The government can realistically manipulate images to show nothing, a different layout, vegetation or to hide weapons installations. The technology is widely used in espionage to swap features as a form of image trickery, removing structures and replacing them with greenery. Just because you can't see something in an aerial photograph from space doesn't mean it doesn't exist."

Emily was shocked, astonished, and appalled. "I feel a little worn and frayed on the edges. I guess computers and satellites trained in artificial intelligence can do just about anything. The forest seems so wild and primitive in this region, resembling the earliest ages in the history of the world. I like the isolation from the influences of humanity. The murmuring pines and hemlocks bearded with green moss, softly lighted by diffused sunlight, standing like soldiers of old with voices sad and prophetic seem so natural."

Dead silence followed. The absence of noise was awkward and scary, sending a powerful message communicating deep thought, the intensity of emotion, and astute profundity.

Emily was in a problematic mood. "Do you mind if we take a short walk to the entrance gate for a bit of fresh air before we leave?"

57

DEATH BY DEHYDRATION

Once outside the confines of the protective castle wall, the lieutenant followed a narrow winding trail through the forest leading to the elaborate wrought-iron front-entrance gate. Soft pine needles embellished the forest floor and muffled the sound of their footsteps. Emily marched in sync directly behind the lieutenant, glancing from side to side, admiring the impressive height of the evergreen trees. The air was cool and fragrant under the shade of the forest canopy. Intermittent rays of sunshine at irregular intervals flickered through the trees. A quarter-mile from the castle, she paused, squinting intensely and cupping her hands around her ears to increase focus. A noisy murder of crows displayed unusual antics and made loud raspy signature calls.

"There is a murder of crows riding a thermal air current in the distance, all squawking at the same time," she observed with a modest degree of nervous alarm.

"The appearance of a large number of crows congregating in one place is an omen of death. We must be close to the cemetery," the lieutenant remarked alarmingly. "Ravens and crows are scavengers associated with dead bodies, battlefields, and cemeteries. They tend to circle above corpses and dying animals, waiting for them to cross over the mythical rainbow bridge. There is probably a dead animal carcass attracting their attention somewhere in the forest nearby."

"Oh, my God!" Emily gagged. "Crows are eating the decaying flesh of a dead human. Death can happen in many forms. What is the worst way to die? Is one form of death worse than another? The brutality of death disturbs me, regardless of the method of destruction. There are a million ways to die. What's worse is that beheading, drowning, getting thrown out of an airplane, or being burned to death all have the same effect. I am completely unprepared for what I see before us on the forest floor on this gloomy day. Who is it?"

The lieutenant bent down on one knee to examine the body. "The smell is worse than a stinking corpse lily, a rare flower found in the jungles of Indonesia. The victim appears to have been killed by a bolt fired from a crossbow. The arrow penetrated the spine in the back of his neck and instantly paralyzed him. He may have lay in this position for ten days, tortuously dying of thirst before dying. Terminal dehydration to the point of death is grossly horrifying and morbidly agonizing with headaches and muscle cramping. His eyes are red and yellow and sunken deep into his skull. His nose and lips are bluish-gray and appear overly parched. Wherever his skin dried and cracked, it bled," the lieutenant observed.

"Starving to death is no picnic," he continued. "The victim would have lost half his body weight before he died of thirst. Cells throughout the body begin to shrink as water moves out of them. Brain cells stop operating, leading to mental confusion. Shrinking of the brain causes it to disconnect from the skull, leading to the rupture of multiple blood vessels. The victim would have suffered massive personality changes and seen things that didn't exist."

Emily winced. Her stomach was in a knot, and the stench of a rotting human corpse lying face down in the ferns made her vomit.

"Eventually, he would have reached the point of no return, when nothing could rehydrate him. His blood pressure would have fallen when his kidneys stopped functioning, and cellular waste would have quickly accumulated in his system. He would have suffered a great deal from delirium and hallucinations as his organs slowly and painfully began to fail before he eventually succumbed to terminal death by dehydration. Stiffening of the joints and muscles would have occurred before rigor mortis eventually froze his body in the current anatomical position unless he took antibiotics at the time of death. In which case, there would have been a delay in bacterial-mediated putrefaction," the lieutenant theorized.

"Did he have the ability to cry for help?" Emily empathetically whispered in a low somber tone.

"Hallucinations would have caused him to make terrifying involuntary primal sounds. Especially when ants began crawling into his mouth and ears, while ravens and small animals nibbled on his fingers and buttocks."

The lieutenant was careful not to disturb the body. "I didn't recognize the victim at first because of the enormous weight loss he has suffered, but I'm certain now this is Dusty Rhodes. His facial features are pretty recognizable with those buck teeth, freckles, and red hair. His chipped teeth are protruding so far forward it looks as though he could eat an apple through a tennis racket."

"I recognize the shoes he is wearing because they are the same ones he had on during our interview," Emily observed.

The lieutenant removed a well-worn leather wallet from the victim's back pocket to prove his identity. "Dusty's wallet is like an onion; when you open it, it makes you cry. There's nothing in it."

"Dusty was woebegone and low-spirited, a wretched soul bruised by adversity. He had an inferiority complex, a severe lack of self-worth, and sorrowful feelings of not measuring up to standards. Conditions that drive afflicted individuals to overcompensate, resulting in either spectacular achievement or extremely asocial behavior. Whatever shortcomings Dusty was feeling, he had to have a strong motive for sneaking around the Hermitage at night like a professional cat burglar. Why do you suppose he was here?" Emily wanted to know.

"Most murders can be classified under three motives—money, love, and power—which leads me to assume Dusty was hoping to steal something valuable. Can you think of anything at the castle that Dusty may have coveted?" the lieutenant asked.

Emily slowly shook her head and then asked, "How did Dusty get here? Where did he leave his truck?" She continued expanding the search outward from the crime scene. "Oh my! What is that odd-looking canister laying on the ground next to the body?"

"Smell that? Nothing else in the world smells like victory in the morning more than napalm," the lieutenant responded with his best imitation of Robert Duvall in the movie *Apocalypse Now*. "That's a drip torch used by firefighters for wildfire suppression, starting controlled burns, backfires, and hazard reduction burning. The device spits flaming fuel oil that instantly ignites vegetation. It's a civilian form of napalm."

Emily removed her digital tape recorder and camera from her cross-shoulder carry bag. She began dictating her observations, starting with the date, time, and GPS coordinates. "The body of a man appearing to be about twenty-five years old was discovered lying face down in the woods about a half-mile west of Gravestone Castle in the vicinity of the elaborate iron entrance gate. A steel bolt pierced the victim's spine, resulting in full-body paralysis. The victim is of average height with a ruddy complexion and fiery red hair, freckles, protruding ears, and large upper teeth projecting over the lower lip. He is hollow-cheeked. His body is withered. He may have remained alive for over a week before dying of thirst. Dusty Rhodes, an employee of Woebegone Dunes Resort, was recently fired. We know that he had verbal altercations with Father Cellophane and the Linguine brothers recently."

Emily paused to fill her lungs with fresh air, followed by a shallow sip of refreshing ice water. "The Super Sniper Whisper Apocalypse Predator Crossbow shipping container discovered under Father Cellophane's bed may have contained the weapon used to kill Dusty Rhodes. I wonder where the crossbow is now?"

"Dusty Rhodes was thriving in a life not worth having. He worked seasonally for the forest service as a firefighter, leading me to believe that he was familiar with the function and use of drip torches for igniting fires," the lieutenant surmised. "If Dusty was a night prowler, one of the priests may have legitimately assumed it was a bear and fired the crossbow in his direction, accidentally killing him."

"Do you suppose he was planning to burn down Gravestone Castle as a way of getting back at Father Cellophane?" Emily inquired.

"Dusty may have been planning to break into the Hermitage and burn the place down as an act of vengeance, but never rule out theft as the most common reason for trespassing. I assume he collapsed in the ferns immediately after being struck in the spine, leaving the shooter to assume the trespasser was an animal that darted away into the darkness unharmed."

Emily unexpectedly lost her composure in a noisy act of spontaneous combustion as a way of releasing excessive internal pressure. "Fiddlesticks! What a bunch of nonsense. I'm baffled, bewildered, and perplexed by all this malarkey. We'll never be able to ask Dusty Rhodes if he killed Father Cellophane."

58

BEFUDDLED

"Everything about this situation is caddywampus—in disarray like a lop-sided bicycle wheel. What a bumfuzzled set of incoherent events this investigation is turning out to be, proceeding in such an erratic and feeble way," Emily indignantly remarked like a goose sputtering fat in the oven. "The bizarre deaths we have witnessed this summer leave me feeling off-balance and confused. It feels like a bad case of jet lag, the way daylight savings throws everybody off kilter," she prattled.

"I volunteered for this assignment optimistically, aspiring to learn some things about international money laundering, clever criminals, and Ponzi schemes. I was expecting to travel to Europe and Africa to observe the lifestyles of celebrity one-percenters. Instead, we are caught up enigmatically in the aberrant investigations of multiple freakish deaths, leaving me feeling like an undercover queen for a day. First, we learned about a man with a peanut allergy that died four years ago. A golf ball killed a priest of questionable character. Then a maintenance worker was stung by killer bees. Now we have a dysfunctional caddy shot in the back with a crossbow—and we don't even know at this point if any of these incidents were accidents, manslaughter, or premeditated murder. Were any misdemeanors or felonies committed?" she lamented. "Deputy Sheriff Bud Light has never even mentioned manslaughter without malice or intent."

Emily was in emotional labor, eviscerated in a state of steady decline, exhausted and lamenting about the entire dynamic. Panicked breathing produced wheezing sounds, chest rattling, and obnoxious whistling sounds. She seemed in desperate need of a therapist to unload her troubles and all the messy baggage in her life.

"I apologize for my rueful and petulant self-pity. I must learn to keep my emotions in check to appear outwardly unruffled. Staying calm in the face of dramatic disturbances isn't easy. Rejecting the feelings of vertigo when you are approaching the edge of a psychological abyss isn't easy. Our investigation has turned into a never-ending wild goose chase, an unreasonable search for something nonexistent and unobtainable. Our quest is a hopeless enterprise like searching through flotsam debris for a building demolished in a title wave. I still have so many lingering questions. My mind is a swirling vortex of motives and emotions. Were the deaths rare, freakish accidents or deliberate, cold-blooded murders? Who killed Father Cellophane? Who wrapped him in bubble wrap and buried him in the sand bunker? Why was he wearing a yellow bikini speedo? How did Dusty's caddy uniform and Hertz's passport end up next to the body? There are way too many hanging chads and lingering questions—everything about this investigation is askew. Our scientific approach to this investigation has ended with more questions than answers," Emily sputtered feebly in an incoherent burst of steam.

"Your breathing reminds me of an overheated engine, spasmodically emitting soft explosive sounds just before it quits working. Take some deep breaths. Stressing out about the situation won't help," the lieutenant stated amusedly to soothe her anxiety and increase her well-being.

"The serotonin in my brain is completely depleted, leaving me feeling like an afterglow of the person I used to be. I'm hovering unconsciously in the same place with no clue about what to do next, ruminating on worries that linger beneath the surface in the mind and spirit but barely in the realm of conscious thought. Every death precipitates another senseless pursuit of a red herring, an endless search of a hopeless enterprise surrounded by a basket of deplorables," she lamented.

Turning his focus inward, the lieutenant tapped his prefrontal cortex with his left pointer finger, the brain region responsible for complex thought unique to humans. "Being a good detective is having the wisdom to comprehend the limits to the amount of discourtesy, discrimination, and unfairness that an individual can tolerate. Dusty Rhodes may have flown into a rage resulting from excessive maltreatment and lack of tipping by his clients. It is our job to predict the consequences and disclose the alternative outcomes of various scenarios," the lieutenant advised, validating her feelings and acknowledging them as necessary.

"Be careful not to overthink or torment yourself when the answers to a problem don't come easily. Learn to keep an open mind. Know that imagination can create conscious expositions, discern intent, and generate new alternatives and motives that are not readily apparent from the physical evidence. Life is an ongoing trial, and death is a certain verdict. Pain teaches you more than pleasure, and adversity teaches you more than comfort. Even a small glimmer of hope, tantalizingly far in the future, can help you overcome the anxieties and traumas of daily living. Centuries ago, bereaved survivors would fully succumb to their grief, wearing black mourning clothes for months at a time. Whereas society today expects us to dust ourselves off, put on a clean shirt, and get back to life as soon as possible."

The lieutenant's words were reassuring. He acknowledged Emily's feelings and reminded her to take deep breaths, practice guided imagery, and exercise mindful meditation.

"Thanks for listening. You have a way of responding in clear terms."

"Before we leave, I would like to determine where the shooter was standing to see if we can discover any evidence or detect anything unusual or suspicious."

59

THE STATUE

The lieutenant peered through the trees in the direction he believed the shooter might have been standing. "There is only one obvious line of sight through the forest leading back to Gravestone Castle."

"After you, Lieutenant," Emily suggested, pushing back a tree branch to prevent it from scratching her face. "Bushwhacking through a dense forest by cutting through tree branches and bushes while stepping over fallen logs and rocks is strenuous—not my favorite way of hiking."

The lieutenant pointed to several broken branches and sticks lying on the ground fifty yards from the body. "I assume the shooter was standing in this spot when he shot Dusty. There's enough disturbance and broken branches to make me think the shooter stumbled and fell or accidentally sat down in this spot."

Emily glanced behind the lieutenant with a sudden look of terror on her face, noticing something shocking and frightening that excited her. Her reflexive, fully adrenalized, animalistic scream was bloodcurdling. Her mouth was wide open with a look of amazement as she pointed to a realistic sculpture of a man walking with his hands behind his back. Her heart fluttered. Cold shivers left her shaking like a leaf. "The statue behind you reminds me of a sinister dude in the subway with anxiety disorders and schizophrenia that exhibits purposeless agitation, hears voices, and experiences delusions."

The lieutenant approached to take a closer look. "It's a life-size statue of Father Cellophane going for a relaxed stroll in the woods. Fiberglass is a very durable material that will bond to almost any surface. The inherent corrosion-resistant characteristics of fiberglass make it an ideal hobbyist material that is cost-effective, strong, and lightweight. Other than cheap bristle paintbrushes and plastic trowels, no special tools for applying the resin and metal rods for strength are needed. When finished, paints simulate bronze or marble," the lieutenant explained.

Emily was apprehensive. "I think it's eerie and disturbing—frightening even. Father Cellophane looks grotesque. His physique is disjointed, lacking a coherent wholeness. His limbs are normal in dimension but awkward in position and angle, twisted at the wrong angles with one shoulder higher than the other. His spine is bent. His knees are too close together, and his wrists and elbows are at unnatural angles. It appears the sculptor tried to force the human figure into position after rigor mortis. It's creepy. It makes my flesh crawl, causing freakish thoughts to worm their way into my brain. The statue of a German Shepherd dog standing beside him looks extremely lifelike."

Emily was a bundle of nerves. "His limbs are crooked and out of kilter, and his head is off-center and caddywampus. The left cheekbone and eye are too low, making it look like the bones in his face were broken, and the taxidermist tried to cover it up."

"Father Adam Baum has a long history of making statues of dead people. There's an irony of a statue with bird poop on its head—exactly what his adversaries had in mind," the lieutenant stated, reaching out and touching the surface of the statue. "Did you know that people with schizophrenia tend to have a high rate of irritable bowel syndrome?"

Emily's skin was pale. Her stomach churned. "We are becoming entangled in a never-ending clandestine story of secret schemes. All this leads me to believe that we will never solve the riddles inherent in any of these deaths. Everything that has happened since our arrival in Wisconsin stimulates my curiosity. My vigilance to avoid possible danger and difficulties lures me deeper into an increasing number of suspense-filled horror tales. All the fuss and nonsense are finally getting to me. This investigation has been such a rambling, unsystematic series of unrelated events. We spend more time brainstorming than investigating. We've learned almost nothing about Father Feely's finances and Father Adam Baum's biological and entomological weapons. We have no idea where events are leading us. Our investigation is nothing but an unsolvable puzzle—an incoherent, jumbled storyline leading us deeper into a series of mysteries and red herrings. The motives are never clear. We keep turning the pages, uncovering incoherent clues, and finding unsupported evidence in unexpected places."

"You need a milkshake, a box of chocolates, and someone to hold your hand and tell you how nice you look, Emily. Some days you have to work harder to find the sunshine. Learning to be a detective is not about memorizing all the facts but the training of the mind to think. Evidence and logic go hand in hand. When things seem to be falling apart, they may be falling into place. Handle clues delicately. Immerse yourself in the story. Pace yourself and stay engaged," the lieutenant suggested encouragingly.

Emily was slightly embarrassed by her fear of statues, her low spirits, and her negative attitude. "What does it say on the pages of the book Father Cellophane is holding behind his back?"

"It says 'Carpe diem, quam minimum credula postero'—it's Latin, a reminder that encourages youth to enjoy life before it is too late. Seize the day or die regretting the time you lost. Strain your wine and prove your wisdom; life is short; should hope be more? Drink in the sunshine before the day passes away because you will never experience this moment again. In the moment of our talking, envious time has ebbed away. Seize the present; trust tomorrow because you only live once. It's the same message we found in the bubble wrap."

Emily reluctantly explained what she was thinking. "The teeth in Father Cellophane's mouth are very true to life, and the dog's bite is incredibly graphic and realistic. When the historical society was restoring several eighteenth-century religious sculptures in Mexico, they became very suspicious of the source of the statues. As it turned out, the teeth were real. They murdered the victims, wrapped the corpses with wire mesh, covered them with cotton gauze, and coated the cadavers with plaster to hide the bodies in plain sight. I think someone made the statue of Father Cellophane and the dog using a similar technique, wrapping the body with wire and cotton and coating it with fiberglass. We should investigate to see if there is a body under the fiberglass coating."

The lieutenant pensively tugged on his earlobes in support of her request. "I'll ask Coroner Slaughter to prepare an X-ray to determine if your assumption is valid."

60

FIREWORKS

Bo-Bo Bigelow was infuriated to learn that Jack Daniels was still alive. He picked up a candlestick, snuffed out the flame, and spit on the floor, flagrantly symbolizing his intended actions. Liquid wax vaporized in the flame's intense heat, leaving behind a malodorous wisp of smoke as smelly and disgusting as the criminal act of murder. His intent was clear. Tapping his fingers on Father Feely's chest as an act of intimidation to emphasize the urgency of his request, he said, "I want Jack Daniels snuffed out like a candle. Whack him." Father Feely nervously agreed to comply with Bo-Bo's heinous demand out of fear for his own life.

Assassin Billy Big Ears Bellini had spent his entire adult life involved in nefarious criminal enterprises. Big Ears arrived in Sheboygan at Harbor Centre Marina, a clean deep-water port in a beautiful park setting on Lake Michigan, for a prearranged meeting with Father Feely's newest henchman, Joey Linguine.

Linguine was the first to speak. "Nigerian playboy Bo-Bo Bigelow is furious you failed in your first attempt to assassinate Jack Daniels. He doesn't care that the bomb went off prematurely, causing your airplane to crash. Jack Daniels is still actively preventing Bo-Bo from buying Gravestone Castle and building a casino. Bo-Bo is pissed, outraged, and frustrated. He wants Jack Daniels snuffed out immediately—this is your last chance," Joey threatened.

"I promise I won't fail this time. Jack is having a new golf cart delivered this week. When golf cart batteries run dry, they are highly susceptible to exploding. Each battery packs the explosive power of a grenade. Six golf cart batteries exploding simultaneously under Jack's seat should do the trick. I'll mix in a few fireworks, mortars, skyrockets, and TNT to create screamers and explosions to increase crowd reaction. There won't be any evidence, and everyone will assume it was an accident."

"Make sure you're successful this time."

Long-drive champion Bruno Greco arrived at Woebegone Dunes for his routine monthly golf outing with Jack Daniels. Lady Vanessa was there to intercept him. "Jack sends his regrets because he has other commitments and is unavailable for golf today. He asked me to take his place."

Bruno had skipped town immediately following the accidental death of Father Cellophane. He was eager to learn the fate of the police investigation. "Does Deputy Sheriff Bud Light have any cockamamie theories about who hit Father Cellophane with a golf ball and buried him in a sand bunker?"

"The deputy is completely in the dark—confused and befuddled. I slipped him a couple of bottles of brandy to fog up his brain. Why did you bury the body in the sand? Why didn't you toss him into Lake Michigan to make everyone assume he drowned?"

"I was preparing to dump the body in Lake Michigan when flames from a giant bonfire behind the Hermitage illuminated the beach. You could see up and down the shore for half a mile. Several tawdry nuns were singing karaoke and dancing topless around a campfire. One of them was Sister Olivia, the nun with the big naturals—big bazookas. A drunken barefooted teenaged girl was screaming at the moon and yelling, 'Glory be.' Father Feely was drinking, smoking a cigar, and playing honkytonk outlaw-country dance music real loud. When the fire flared up, I panicked because I thought they could see me, so I dragged the body into the shadows as quickly as I could and buried it in the closest sand bunker."

"Be quiet; keep your voice down," Lady Vanessa warned. "Let's continue this conversation on the golf course. Jack has a new golf cart. He got satellite radio, a humidor, chrome wheels, air conditioning, and an electric beer cooler. Fetch the golf cart. I'll meet you back here in a few minutes."

Bruno Greco opened the garage door on the east side of the storage building. Numerous unmarked cardboard boxes lined the walls. He climbed into the driver's seat of the fancy new golf cart with oversized chrome wheels and metallic gold flaked paint, placed the key in the ignition, and turned the key.

Kaboom! Bang, bang, bang!

The explosion shook the ground a mile away. There was a horrific display of noise, light, smoke, and burning wreckage with brightly colored sparks of red, orange, yellow, green, blue, and silver confetti tumbling down from the sky. Aerial skyrockets with propulsion shot into the air with the force of a mortar shell in a tremendous display of smoke and fire. Pyrotechnic stars lighted the afternoon sky. Chlorine strengthened the color of the flames, and oxidizers increased the fuel combustion, intensifying the light. Skyrockets assembled with potassium compounds exploded with a thunderous noise and brilliant purple hue. Boxes of cherry bombs tossed high in the air by the explosion began exploding like machine guns firing the entire nine yards.

Deputy Sheriff Bud Light was the first to arrive on the scene after the explosion. "Holy shit—a fireworks display went wildly wrong." A fancy chrome wheel from a golf cart was spinning around on a broken axle. Small bits of leather upholstery and a steering wheel dangled overhead from a broken tree branch. Large chunks of torn fiberglass paneling spread across the debris field. Large blobs of red blood and intestines were dripping from the walls and ceiling. Golf clubs randomly scattered in a big pile resembled a giant game of pick-up sticks. A man's severed arm lying on the pavement appeared to be giving Bud Light the finger. A torn piece of a man's golf shirt was slowly dissolving in a puddle of bubbling hot battery acid.

Bud Light immediately dialed the lieutenant. "Illegal fireworks exploded at Woebegone Dunes Resort. A golf cart blew up with the force of a hand grenade, killing at least one person. The air smells like rotten eggs. Body parts lying all over the ground on the east side of the golf cart storage barn are unidentifiable."

"We'll be right over."

Bud Light curiously reached down and removed a cigar from a wooden humidor lying face down on the ground with the lid blown off. He cut the wrong end of the cigar off with his pocketknife and began to smoke it.

Coroner Slaughter arrived at the scene to view the carnage. "The body is unidentifiable. The skull is fractured, and the dura membranes surrounding the brain and spinal cord are shredded. Dental records and DNA may be the only way of verifying the identity of the body," he explained.

Emily and Dunning arrived not much later. "This is one of those cases with many of the mysterious elements of fiction," the lieutenant said as he reached down to pick up a man's golf shoe wedged up against the wall with an amputated foot still inside. "Size fourteen," he observed. Using a stick to drag part of a man's shirt out of the pool of battery acid, he exclaimed, "Extra-large."

Deputy Sheriff Bud Light was becoming visibly nauseated from inhaling cigar smoke combined with the smell of gunpowder mixed with blood and guts. "If you're going to vomit, get the hell away from the crime scene," the lieutenant ordered. The deputy's face looked drained as he began rocking back and forth on his heels, looking up at the sky.

CFO Lady Vanessa approached the explosion scene, shaking in her boots, wide-eyed with trepidation. "What happened?" she stammered in stunned disbelief with a stupefied expression on her face. "I sent Bruno Greco to fetch Jack Daniels's golf cart less than ten minutes ago."

Deputy Sheriff Bud Light took a deep drag on the expensive imported cigar dangling from his lips, burning his eyes as his lungs filled with smoke. He casually stifled a cough, accidentally expelling an ill-formed, unsymmetrical smoke ring into the air. "There's been an explosion. One of us will need to inform Jack Daniels about the accident," he stated with a sense of self-importance.

61

DEATH BY ELECTROCUTION

Jack Daniels felt a tightness in his chest. News of the golf cart explosion and the terrible loss of life of his friend and long-drive golf champion Bruno Greco was bound to trigger high levels of emotional distress, terrifying nightmares, and disrupted sleep patterns. He deliberately separated himself from the group to avoid social engagement, retreating to his cabin as a place of solitude. He impulsively called the Sheboygan toilet factory to make an unplanned comfort purchase of an automated, streamlined one-piece toilet with integrated steam cleaning.

"I want to buy a toilet with the vitreous china enamel coating with an automatic open and close lid, self-cleaning wand, pre-mister, rear cleanser, front cleanser, dryer, deodorizer, and the elongated bowl offering added room and comfort, including a heated seat with adjustable temperature settings. I want a tankless design with a direct water supply. The one with dual flush and stainless-steel wand offering adjustable spray, shape, position, and water pressure with temperature, pulsate, and oscillate functions," he demanded. "Add the deluxe hammered copper toilet seat. The famous design with your secret jewelry chemical formula that produces a dark-blue and green patina tarnish color with the automatic multicolored water glow nightlight feature."

"Our installer will arrive tomorrow morning at nine o'clock. Thank you for your business."

The morally corrupt salesperson telephoned his friend Billy Big Ears Bellini to report the purchase. "I finally perfected the wire harness you asked me to fabricate last year that converts a heated toilet into an electric chair. Are you still interested? It'll cost you a thousand bucks."

"Are you sure it fits the toilet you claim Jack Daniels ordered recently?"

"Yes!"

"Okay, I'll meet you at the 8th Street Ale Haus in Sheboygan on Sunday afternoon. There is going to be a band, and the food is great, and they have some excellent beers on tap."

Big Ears drank a pitcher of beer and paid his friend a thousand dollars in cash before leaving with the one-of-a-kind macabre electric harness.

One week later, when he was sure the coast was clear, Billy snuck into Jack's woodsy cabin with the intent to kill him. He removed the key from above the front door, removed his shoes, put on latex gloves, and attached the preconstructed electric wire harness to the back of the copper toilet seat. Confident that the wires were sufficiently hidden, he secured them to a pressure switch and plugged the device into the power source.

Jack ordered a supersized porterhouse steak. The chef covered it with caramelized onions, red and yellow chili peppers, and mushrooms. He had Anasazi corn, pinto beans seasoned with chili pepper, bacon-wrapped jalapeño peppers, and a spicy salsa red beet salad, washed down with four shots of Don Julio Anejo Tequila and three mugs of Dos Equis Amber Lager beer. For dessert, he ate half a dozen sugar-coated sopaipillas, dripping with Tupelo honey.

When he was sufficiently satisfied and everyone had departed the dining room, he returned to his cabin. He removed the gold cufflinks from his white dress shirt, unbuckled his black crocodile leather belt, and dropped his navy-blue pleated dress pants with pin striping to his knees.

"This toilet is fit for a king," he mused to himself. He happily admired the one-of-a-kind blue-green patina copper finish as the seat cover automatically lifted as he approached. The water in the toilet alternately glowed bright red, green, purple, and gold.

When he sat down, the twenty-pound pressure switch exceeded the weight limit. An electric current surged around the copper toilet seat. He never had a chance to scream. The AC electric current caused his muscle fibers to twitch twenty times per second. His involuntary response to the electric surge was to jerk forward in a fetal position. He tightly grasped the toilet seat with both hands, increasing the duration and intensity of contact with the source and worsening the injury. The electric current remained concentrated at the primary contact point with the skin, where the most cell damage was taking place. The more Jack strained, the more gases he forced out. Smelly flatulence, resulting from gases trapped in the digestive system, made a loud, obnoxious thunder-like rumbling sound, ten times louder and longer than a whoopee cushion, followed by a high-pitched whistling sound as the remaining flammable hydrogen sulfide gas, smelling of rotten eggs and vegetables, escaped. The combustible flatulent gases flared wildly, causing a brightly colored blowtorch effect that singed the wall behind the toilet, turning the paint brown. The tissue in his colon became carbonized, leading to bowel perforation and acute renal failure. Urine output surged. He listed slightly to one side as explosive diarrhea slammed into the wall like an urban fire hydrant on a hot summer Independence Day.

Pulsating hot water surged out of the oscillating nozzle at the end of the stainless-steel wand. An electric arc and a thermal flash spiraled around the toilet seat, igniting Jack's underpants on fire, causing severe thermal burns to his dangling testicles. Additional flash burns caused blunt trauma and injury to the central nervous system. His muscles contracted violently. Tetanic contraction of the rotator cuff muscles caused shoulder dislocation and severe damage to the central nervous system. Cutaneous burns scarred his face; there were corneal burns to his eyes and intraocular hemorrhage. Retinal detachment caused blindness.

Violent muscle seizures and extreme muscle contractions caused ligament tears to his spinal cord and paralysis. Between episodes, he was in an altered state of mental confusion. His breathing stopped as respiratory arrest resulted from a contraction of the diaphragm. Cardiac arrest from atrial and ventricular fibrillation and myocardial infarction, as well as heart vessel rupture, caused his heart to fail. Jack Daniels was dead by electrocution. His face was distorted and bent out of shape. His chin and lower teeth were brutally hanging down in a rigidly contorted, inflexible expression of sheer terror and horrifying pain—a horrific frozen image of death.

Shortly before bedtime, Lieutenant Dunning noticed a brief electrical interruption at the main lodge at Woebegone Dunes Resort. The ceiling lights flickered, and the television went blank for a few seconds. He was curious about the reasons for the brief power outage. He alertly made a mental note of the exact time that it occurred.

Billy Big Ears quietly stepped out of his secret hiding place in the master clothes closet to admire his work. He snapped a ghastly portrait of Jack's horrified facial expression before shutting off the main electric circuit breaker. He tiptoed to the opposite side of the toilet to avoid leaving footprints in the stinky filth on the floor. He detached the improvised electric harness from the copper toilet seat and placed it in a disposable plastic bag.

As a special gift to Deputy Sheriff Bud Light, he inserted a photograph of a Taliban soldier having sex with a goat in Jack's right front shirt pocket. "This will mess with the deputy's mind." He tossed a woman's vintage earring on the bed to create a second red herring. After checking twice to make sure everything was in its original place, he locked the front door and hurried through the woods to the entrance gate.

Angelina was dutifully waiting in her black Mercedes 450 SL convertible with the headlights turned off. The classic car silhouetted against a backdrop of wispy white clouds radiantly glowed under the light of a brilliant red sunset. Billy sucked in a deep breath, twisted his neck to one side, and painfully compressed his torso before backing into the front seat. His cell phone fell unbeknownst out of his coat pocket into the ditch.

Early the next morning, Lady Vanessa expressed her concerns to the lieutenant. "Have you seen Jack Daniels?" she inquired. "He's more than an hour late for breakfast; he hasn't answered his phone all morning." With a heightened level of unease, she added, "Jack has never been late for a breakfast business meeting, and he is always punctual and calls to let me know if he will be late. His lack of response this morning is very troublesome. It's possible he overslept because he had a lot to eat and drink last night, but I doubt it."

"He's probably stuck on a long-distance telephone call informing Bruno's family members of the tragic explosion. I'll call Tammy at police dispatch and ask her to radio the deputy sheriff to see if he is available for a routine house call."

62

ROUTINE HOUSE CALL

Tammy applied fresh red lipstick, twirled her strawberry blond hair with one finger, and blinked her false eyelashes before switching the police radio to transmit. She intentionally articulated her message in a strong, soothing, sultry voice. Bud Light was sitting in his patrol car beneath a billboard in a shady spot under the trees.

"Bud, Lieutenant Dunning suggests you make a house call to Jack Daniels's cabin. He hasn't checked in at Woebegone Dunes Resort this morning as expected, and he hasn't answered his telephone for more than three hours."

"Are you talking about Area 51? I've never been there before. What's up there?" Bud worriedly requested to know. "Is this a missing person investigation? Should I use the siren and flashing lights on the patrol car on the way up there?"

"No, that won't be necessary. There's nothing to be concerned about—just a routine visit to an old log cabin surrounded by undeveloped forestland. Go in quietly to avoid attracting attention to yourself," Tammy suggested. "You can't miss it. The elaborate iron entrance gate is fit for a temple. It's always locked, so leave your car there and walk in on foot. It's only a couple hundred yards to the cabin. We have no suspicion of foul play. Try not to startle Jack or any of his guests. Just make a routine inquiry to let him know that others are concerned about his well-being and remind him about his meeting with Lady Vanessa this morning."

"Roger that. Bud Light here on a 10-57 missing person investigation. Over and out," he stated loudly over the public airwaves with a nervous air of apprehension.

A farmer, a motorcycle mechanic, a hairdresser, and a newspaper dispatcher monitoring the police channel intercepted the radio transmission. Angelina heard the communication over the radio at her beauty shop and repeated the information to her customers. The farmer on the adjacent property drove his tractor to the far end of his field to see if he could spot the patrol car coming.

The local newspaper editor dispatched René Malarkey to the scene to discover what a 10-57 missing person incident was all about. "Weird stuff like this happens on a regular basin in Aspen, Colorado, where I used to live," René remarked. "Hunter Thompson and other notorious characters thrived there in the glory years."

Deputy Sheriff Bud Light was nervous and hesitant to act alone. He was intimidated by the lack of an armed partner to back him up. Rumors swirled about hazardous waste disposal; prison labor camps; scary, inbred, mentally unstable people; African monkeys living in the trees; and mad scientists working for the government conducting medical experiments on the insane.

The closer Bud Light was to his destination, the more nervous he became. "I wonder if any of the rumors are true," he asked himself. He parked his patrol car beside the locked entrance gate, tightened his holster, and fidgeted with his revolver. He adjusted his darkened aviator sunglasses, took a deep breath, puffed up his chest, smoothed his mustache, straightened his police badge, and stuck out his chin before placing his stiff-brimmed patrol hat on his head and walking in on foot. He ducked behind a small tree when he spotted the cabin in the woods. When he was confident the coast was clear, he advanced stealthily, cautiously crouching down behind alternate trees in a zigzag pattern.

Observing nothing of importance and seeing no signs of occupancy, his confidence steadily increased. Peeking through a window into the living room, he noticed that the television was on.

He knocked firmly on the front door, tapped on the window, and hollered, "Mr. Daniels, come out with your hands up. Whoops! What I meant to say is are you home?"

Hearing no response, he knocked twice more and loudly tapped the glass windowpane with the barrel of his gun, accidentally cracking the glass. Uncertain about what to expect, he circled the cabin looking for signs of life. He checked the front, side, and rear doors, seeing and hearing nothing other than a dove eerily cooing in the forest. Finding no other way in, he cautiously entered the screened porch, slid open the sliding glass door, and tiptoed inside.

He had never expected to see so much luxury and wealth on display in an isolated woodsy cabin in the forest. It was interesting to see how the rich and famous lived, but the putrid smell inside was distressingly sinister. He wondered if the stuffed animal heads and safari trophies from Africa covering the walls were the cause of the terrible stench. Delicate ivory and ebony woodcarvings of African tribesmen and naked women garnished every nook and table. A beautiful one-of-a-kind carving of a gazelle and an African lion graced the mantel above the fireplace.

He visually inventoried everything in the living room before peeking into the guest bedroom, kitchen, pantry, and wine cellar. He glanced into the master bathroom, where the most potent, unpleasant, moldy, burned, rotten odor originated.

He gasped in astonishment at the sight of a dead body leaning forward and straining with all his might, holding on tightly to a toilet seat with both hands. His first impression was of Satan sitting on a throne of hot decaying onions and sea lion farts. The victim's eyes were glazed and shockingly wide open, his body catatonically frozen in time with a horrifying primal scream etched into his burned face with his lower jaw jutting out defiantly in a severe projection of the lower teeth beyond the upper. Suddenly aware of the reason for the putrefied burned stench, he darted back into the family room and immediately contacted Tammy on the radio.

"Tammy, this is Deputy Sheriff Bud Light on the 10-57 missing person case in Area 51. You won't believe what I found."

Pausing to gasp for a deep breath of fresh air, he anxiously continued, speaking with a nervous twitch.

"I discovered Jack Daniels dead in his cabin, electrocuted. He's dead as a doornail. He's in a horrifying unresponsive stupor. He is sitting catatonically on an electric toilet, slumped forward, tightly clutching the toilet seat with both hands. The inside of his house smells as bad as a rotting whale carcass. It's a barbarically chilling scene. The poor man's deformed face is ghoulishly diabolical, frozen into a deformed caricature of his former self. His expression reminds me of Eddie the Eagle, the ill-prepared Englishman and Olympic daredevil, going off a ski jump at sixty miles an hour. There is diarrhea all over the place. His underpants are all burned up. Bits of corn, beans, beets, peppers, carrots, chunks of fatty steak, and a hundred other things are dripping from the wall," he explained exhaustedly. "The night-light in the toilet bowl is alternating colors, blinking blue and red, resembling patrol car emergency lights."

Bud took another quick series of deep breaths. His face was pale; his lips were blue; his eyes were bloodshot and yellow; his breathing was shallow. He was feeling intensely green around the gills with an inclination to vomit. Bud leaned forward and put both hands on his knees. He vomited on an ornamental dwarf bonsai pine tree harmoniously growing in a small black ceramic pot. It was a symbolic arrangement ceremonially presented to Jack Daniels by the Japanese ambassador to symbolize peace and friendship.

"I'll send Lieutenant Dunning and Emily over immediately to help you with the investigation. Wait outside and don't touch or disturb anything before they arrive," Tammy ordered before signing off.

63

ELECTRIC TOILET

Lieutenant Dunning and Emily were greeted at the gate by a farmer wearing a big straw hat, sitting on a noisy diesel tractor with his twin boys. A smiling young man with a fresh haircut laughed and spoke on the phone with Angelina, who was at her beauty salon. A heavily tattooed muscular biker on a rough-sounding Harley Davidson motorcycle in need of a tune-up was revving the engine nearby. Twenty-two-year-old rookie newspaper reporter René Malarkey reeked of cannabis. He had long hair, a silver earring, and an oversized baggy yellow T-shirt printed with bright-green marijuana leaves and sporting many red wine stains. He was positioned outside the ornate iron gate, actively interviewing the other spectators to learn what they knew about Jack Daniels.

"This is private property. Nobody is to advance beyond this point," the lieutenant ordered, pointing at the front entrance gate before briskly marching up the driveway. Emily followed behind wearing trendy high-heeled black leather boots for fashion-forward ladies, walking nearly twice as fast, breathing deeply, and trying not to fall behind. Bud Light escorted the lieutenant to the screened porch behind the cabin. His skin was yellowish green. The front of his patrol uniform was stained, and he was having difficulty speaking coherently. He was nauseous and stated that he preferred not to accompany the investigators inside.

"Jack's cabin smells beastly inside. It's brutal," he stuttered after making a face and waving his right hand in front of his turned-up nose. "I'll stay here and guard the door."

Emily and the lieutenant put on paper shoes and latex gloves before entering the cabin. Emily exercised extreme care to avoid disturbing any of the many precious artifacts on the sofa tables while taking pictures to record the arrangement of the rooms and contents of the entire cabin. Lieutenant Dunning's nostrils flared to let in more air, reminding Emily of a grinning bear smelling a honeypot. He sniffed the air in every room. "Pew!"

He sized up the entire scene before turning on all the lights, opening the windows, and setting the ceiling fans on high to let in some fresh air.

"This is an obvious case of electrocution—most likely caused by faulty wiring," Lieutenant Dunning explained at first glance.

Emily was pale as a ghost, experiencing intense queasiness.

"According to this billing receipt on the counter, installation took place ten days ago. I wonder how many times he has used it since then," Dunning speculated pensively. "The factory owner, the engineer who designed this diabolical device, the plumber who installed it, and the heirs to Jack's fortune have a lot at stake in this case. If a faulty part or installation error causes the toilet to malfunction, the media will have a field day. It's going to take an entire team of electricians, engineers, lawyers, and insurance claims adjusters to prove how this accident happened. Lawyers are similar to wolves. They always hunt in a pack, but when food or money is available, they attack each other to gain possession and then gorge themselves."

"Jack is an important person. His death is going to attract a lot of media attention," Emily predicted. "What about this?" she asked, pointing to a priceless slant-style Japanese bonsai plant in the family room. "It's a beautiful specimen of the informal upright-style juniper—how unfortunate that it's dripping with acidy vomit. Bonsai can live for eight hundred years and sell for a million dollars," she exclaimed, focusing her iPhone camera on the poisoned miniature plant.

Lieutenant Dunning cleared his throat and breathed deeply through his nose to increase his olfactory acuity. His nose twittered, reminding Emily of a rabbit smelling fresh carrots in a verdurous garden. Leaning a little closer, he took two more deep breaths into and out of his nasal passages and several more sniffs of the aesthetic award-winning dwarf bonsai. "I detect the fruity smell of brandy in the vomit. I want a DNA test on this bonsai tree immediately; even a few cells can provide a profile," he declared affirmatively.

"Look at this," Emily exclaimed serendipitously, acting as though she had discovered a valuable ancient treasure map. She dramatically and delicately extracted a book from the shelf as if handling a priceless ancient manuscript. "This rare book appears to contain answers to everything you ever wanted to know about the Royal Enouement Society."

The lieutenant was highly engaged. He carefully perused the mission statement and fawned over the navy-blue leather-bound manual with gold script. "I'll examine it thoroughly with attention to detail back in my room and report back on the contents."

64

MEDIA INTRUSION

Unexpectedly hearing voices outside, the lieutenant pulled back the curtain and peered out the window to see what the commotion was all about. Half a dozen strangers were mulling about, eager to learn something about what was happening.

The obnoxious, scruffy, muscular Harley-Davidson biker boldly tore the "No Trespassing" sign off the fencepost in an act of defiance. He led the entire procession to the cabin. He was spitting large chunks of soggy brown tobacco pellets on the front porch and peeking in the windows. The smiley-faced young man with the fresh haircut took pictures with his cell phone, laughing hysterically and texting Angelina at the beauty shop to keep everyone updated. The farmer wearing baggy denim coveralls stood off to the side with his two boys, clutching a loaded shotgun across his chest, suspiciously eyeing the others.

Reporter René Malarkey peppered Bud Light with a chain of rude questions about the reasons for the lurid smell coming out of the cabin. He was putting words in the deputy's mouth, twisting his responses, and making repeated requests for more sordid details about the bizarre method of electrocution.

"What kind of toilet was it? What adjectives would you use to describe the putrid smell? What caused the man's underwear to catch on fire? Could you tell what the victim had been eating based on what was dripping off the walls? Was the victim wearing boxers or briefs? What color were his underpants? Were they Haines, Jockey, Fruit of the Loom, or Duluth Buck Naked stink-free underwear? How many other victims have you found electrocuted while sitting on a toilet with their pants down? What is your favorite toilet nightlight color—red or purple? How would you describe the victim's facial expression—was it contorted and ghastly, gruesome and gut-wrenching, or just gray and waxy?"

When the young reporter called his editor, he stopped the presses and relayed the information to a local Green Bay television affiliate. Breaking-news headlines reading "Owner of Woebegone Dunes Resort electrocuted on an electric toilet" were spreading like wildfire. Within twenty minutes of discovering the body, the news was already making headlines on live radio and television stations across the Midwest.

Coroner Slaughter casually added to the media frenzy. "This is the most bizarre, eccentric, freaky, unconventional death I have ever seen in my twenty-year career as a mortician."

The farmer's twin sons, Gary and Larry, agreed that writing an anonymous letter to the police department was the safest thing to do without admitting they had been trespassing. "Dear Police: An airplane crashed into a tree on Jack Daniels's property. The pilot's severed hand was lying on the ground below the wreckage. Several hours later, we saw a man walking with a limp with long brown hair and big ears break into Jack Daniels's cabin. We ran away without being seen, Anonymous Birdwatchers."

Tammy at police headquarters placed the letter on a stack of unopened correspondence beside a plastic bag filled with warm cheese curds. She harshly admonished the deputy. "You look like an intellectually challenged stroke victim. Your mouth is wide open, your eyes are closed, and your facial muscles look paralyzed. After you finish your nap, you need to prepare for probate court tomorrow to help the judge authenticate the rightful heir to Woebegone Dunes Resort. It is very likely to be a contentious hearing."

65

PROBATE COURT

Judge Geri Attrick opened the proceedings with a formal announcement. "The granting of probate is the first step in the legal process. We are here to administer the estate of Jack Daniels, distribute his property under a will, and resolve all claims related to the ownership of Woebegone Dunes Resort."

Local newspapers had been overly lurid in their overstated descriptions of the torment and suffering Jack Daniels had endured. The disgusting sketch of Jack by René Malarkey circulated widely on social media. It was a gruesome, ghoulish cartoon of a dead man sitting on a toilet screaming. The victim leaned forward, straining and grasping the toilet seat with both hands. His lower jaw protruded forward with an exaggerated, tortured, diabolical expression. Dozens of colorful T-shirts displaying the disgusting event were extremely popular. They sold out quickly during the first week of Milwaukee Summerfest. Sales of electric toilets plummeted overnight. Numerous lawsuits were pending.

Deputy Sheriff Bud Light was in charge of courtroom security. There was a hint of brandy on his breath. He google-eyed the women and scrutinized the behavior of everyone else. Amused by what he was thinking, he whispered in Tammy's ear, "Poor Jack Daniels—the brown slurry-like, putrid, foul-smelling filth on the wall behind the toilet reminded me of my Scottish grandmother's haggis recipe."

Tammy nearly vomited with visions of the gruesome bathroom scene in her mind, the body catatonically frozen in time on the electric toilet seat, recoiling in horror.

Motley discontents, zealots, lawyers, curious looky-loos, and news media representatives occupied all remaining seats.

Bo-Bo Bigelow and his powerfully built bodyguards arrived early, escorted by three hawkish attorneys in black suits, and assertively occupied the entire front row. The quarrelsome mood they projected foretold of a potential ass-kicking event. Team members wore a distinctive bluish-gray bracelet made of the rare-earth mineral tantalum, valued at over fifty thousand dollars.

"To control tantalum is to control the world's supply chain," the lieutenant quietly conveyed to Emily, pointing out the unique ornamental bracelets with diamonds. "Bo-Bo is a free-spirited individual living a carefree life of alcohol and open sexual freedom. He lives an unconventional lifestyle, barely adhering to any world conformities. He is fearlessly vocal about his intentions, believing that he should have the right to do as he pleases. He is constantly traveling, leading a life of luxury. He has political friends in high places. Never cross him, or you'll disappear."

Joey and Jimmy Linguine and cousin Alfredo Casseroli were together in public for the first time since they had disposed of the two bodies in Milwaukee. They conspicuously entered the courtroom together, acting somewhat suspiciously, sensitive to the effects of every action and nervously looking over their shoulders. They were wearing matching navy-blue suits and dark sunglasses with their hair heavily oiled and slicked back. The tallest member of the Singing Supremes tribute band, wearing a short sparkly mini-dress, quietly hummed a tune.

Wayne and Kate Kennedy intermingled with a large entourage of nameless members of the exclusive Royal Enouement Society. Father Feely and his band of priests and nuns, wearing long, loose-fitting black robes, were huddled together on the far side of the room. Father Adam Baum sat in the back row, scanning the audience, seeking a competitive advantage. A smattering of worried insurance adjusters, nitpicking real estate appraisers, and money-grubbing lawyers with argumentative clashing points of view merged with a posse of engineers and contractors from the toilet company. Jay Walker and his German friend Hertz Von Rental III were the last to enter. News reporters gathered behind their hero René Malarkey.

Freelance reporter Crystal Glass from *National Geographic* looked attractively out of place. Lieutenant Dunning smiled and nodded his head approvingly in her direction to acknowledge her presence. Crystal flashed a flutter of excitement with her twinkly eyes, sending the lieutenant strong feelings of attraction and affection. In response, he exuded a euphoric sense of relaxation and infatuation, conveying deep feelings and emotions as if seeing the person of his dreams for the first time. Emily jealously strained her neck to better view the two lovebirds. The unspoken, subtle attraction they had for each other signaled the beginnings of a steamy romantic relationship.

66

EXECUTOR OF THE WILL

The judge spoke directly to Lady Vanessa. "As the executor of Jack Daniels's last will and testament, you are responsible for collecting all of his estate assets and transferring inheritances to the beneficiaries as directed by the will. Your legal duty is to act in the estate's best interests and the beneficiaries'. Legal notices need to be published and creditors notified. You can expect multiple lawsuits. When you've paid the debts, filed all necessary tax returns, and settled all of the disputes, you're ready to distribute the remaining property to the beneficiaries and close the estate."

Lady Vanessa wore a tight-fitting black and gold shimmering party dress with enhanced low-cut cleavage. A fashionable sparkling diamond necklace dangled like bait in the hollow between her breasts. She expressed no remorse over the death of her boss while egotistically enjoying the exceptional attention she was receiving.

The lieutenant lasciviously whispered in Emily's ear, "Lady Vanessa is a seductive type of woman that could cause a bishop to spill his red wine and kick a hole in a stained-glass window. She's hotter than a two-dollar pistol—a sexually hot woman who knows how to turn a flicker into a flame by doing all the wrong things right. I have never seen a woman in a tight dress with such a whacked-out wiggle when she walks."

Vanessa replied rhetorically, excitedly knowing that she was entitled to at least 4 percent of Jack's estate as payment for carrying out the executor's duties. "I will do my best to carry out Jack's wishes objectively." Her lawyer startled everyone by smiling and rudely clapping his hands in approval. An angry stranger shoved him in the back from behind. The exasperated judge reprimanded them and threatened to throw them both out of the courtroom in retaliation for their uncivil behavior.

"The court predicts challenges to the validity of the will by a large number of persons claiming a portion of Mr. Daniels's assets for a variety of reasons," the judge explained.

Emily quietly whispered to the lieutenant, "Lady Vanessa is such a diva, a self-important temperamental woman, a waspish character who is difficult to please. The short skirts, titillating open blouses, and sexy clothing she wears are deliberately provocative, intended to arouse desire in men. When she walks, her hips, spine, and shoulders move in circles, swirls, and serpentine undulations like a snake lazily gliding through the grass. Men may forget what she said, but they will never forget her sweet temptations and how she made them feel at the peak of a launched rollercoaster, replaying her actions, the kind you see in movies, over and over in their mind until their next encounter."

"Cleavage is nothing to look down on, Emily. But cleavage in the court or on the court is never a good idea. She is a self-absorbed, selfish woman—a petulant diva, a smartly dressed, sexually provocative floozy with many faces and casual partners. She is primarily motivated by fame and money," the lieutenant promptly rejoined.

Penny Pincher, a female representative of the IRS, wearing a conservative black dress and high heels, was the first to address the court. She spoke in generalities, portending of something catastrophic that was about to happen. "The word probate strikes fear into the hearts of the executor of every estate because if the challenge is messy, it can go on for decades. In this particular case, the scale of Jack Daniels's estate is immense."

She was temporarily distracted by laughter coming from the front pew. Rumbling flatulence sounds thundered off the ceiling as one of the

Nigerian bodyguards intentionally leaned to one side. Lingering mal-odorous smells permeated the courthouse.

"What kind of beans has that guy been eating?" Joey Linguine mumbled.

Chloe Crouton rolled her watery eyes and waved a white lacy hanky as a gesture of surrender. The audience coughed in unison as a sign of breathing malfunction.

Penny Pincher struggled to regain her composure before continuing. "Jack Daniels maintained the illusion of a prosperous, sustainable business for a long time. Now that he is deceased, we will discover the truth," she conjectured before laying out her suppositions. "Litigation is likely to expose fraud, abuse of powers of attorney, and denial of creditors' claims. In concise language, the process of inventorying, cataloging, and dissolving Jack's financial assets will be predictably burdensome. Everyone should prepare for the worst. It is very likely the court will initiate the clawback provision to recover money already dispersed to many of you in the audience," Penny articulated with unsettled apprehension.

The audience groaned inharmoniously as an expression of anger and disappointment, triggering numerous side conversations. Joey Linguine kicked the wooden pew in front of him and angrily slammed his fist down to express his frustration.

Chloe Crouton took a deep breath, waved her handkerchief in disbelief, and nearly fainted. "Investing money with Jack Daniels was the best investment my husband and I ever made."

When the lengthy and contentious hearing ended, Lady Vanessa stepped out of the courtroom arm in arm with her lawyer with the formality of a cheap Las Vegas wedding. She was wearing glitzy, oversized, Hollywood-celebrity fashion sunglasses with a broad grin on her face as an expression of immodesty and an air of smug arrogance. Her rehearsed sexually stimulating multidirectional walking style was outwardly indicative of a whole life experience. She reminded the audience of a female sauntering on a public promenade who turned heads and captivated the attention of everyone.

The lieutenant indignantly whispered in Emily's ear, "Lady Vanessa has a special talent for juggling with hot money, a sleight-of-hand illusion like pole dancing in front of a mirror. Her charms are primarily illusions, frivolously bending the facts to make them rhyme. She possesses arrogance and an overbearing character. She's manifestly deceitful, vain, and egotistic."

Lady Vanessa arched her spine and shoulders in response to her lawyer's gentle touch, the way a cat expresses contentment. "I don't care if someone sues. The longer it takes to resolve the will in probate court, the more money I'll get paid," she happily announced to the admiring crowd in the hallway corridor.

She applied fresh lipstick to her full luscious lips, looking as if they had been stung by bees. She unbuttoned the top of her glittery party dress to appear flirtier, younger, and more feminine before stepping outside to face the cameras. She effectively swiveled her head horizontally from a fixed position; the way starlets are trained to pan for the camera without blinking to achieve that flawless look. Pretentiously knowing how gorgeous she was and how to make herself look more fun, she pushed her hair to the side, showcasing the whole length of it.

Reporter René Malarkey peppered her with questions in a vain attempt to evoke a response. "Do you find it hard to talk to the media about your sexuality? What is your favorite thing to do by yourself?"

67

FORENSIC EVIDENCE

The lieutenant and Emily walked directly from the courthouse to Coroner Slaughter's laboratory. A plethora of diagrams and charts cluttered the walls. He spread X-rays, showing slices of Father Cellophane's brain, across the table.

"The death of Father Cellophane was caused by a hemorrhagic progression of a cerebral contusion delivered by a golf ball. The cerebrovascular damage was excessive, and continued bleeding in the brain caused his death. The splatter patterns of the fluids that inflate the eyeball prove the ball speed was forty percent higher than the swing speed of an average golfer."

"Did Father Cellophane flinch to avoid being hit?"

"He was sitting down and leaning back."

"Sitting on the beach? Can you prove where the incident occurred?"

"I'm glad you asked. Contusions, lesions, and discoloration of the arms, wrists, ankles, and neck show signs of a struggle shortly before the time of death. The evidence leads me to believe someone tied him to a chair before hitting him in the face with a golf ball. Blood splatter patterns on his shirt, pants, and neck prove that he was dressed and bound to a chair at the time of impact. I assume he was transported to the burial site after dark when the golf course was closed. Someone removed his clothes, folded them neatly, and placed them on the beach.

They stripped him down to a yellow speedo and wrapped him in bubble wrap with the words '*carpe diem*' punched out in the plastic bubble wrap. Is someone leaving us a message?"

Emily felt a bit queasy, and she had already made up her mind. Pathology was at the bottom of her list of desirable professions; the study of laboratory samples of human body tissue for diagnostic and forensic purposes made her want to vomit.

"The contents of a victim's stomach are a valuable tool in the pathologist's arsenal, which may prove to be the difference between accidental death and foul play. One hour before his death, Father Cellophane consumed a thin-sliced grilled spring lamb with lesser calamint herbs and violet mustard with strained yogurt and rosemary. He had a wild strawberry tart with a scatter of clover, rose petals, and lavender for dessert—a signature dish served only at Woebegone Dunes Resort. The assailant may have lured Father Cellophane into a false sense of security by having a meal with him. The evidence leads me to believe someone at Woebegone Dunes Resort is responsible for his death, probably due to manslaughter, murder committed by an act of violence."

68

X-RAY

Coroner Slaughter explained, "The X-rays of the fiberglass statue you requested were highly revealing. They prove that the decaying corpse of Father Cellophane was dug up and stolen from the cemetery. Steel rods were strapped to the skeleton and forced into shape for strength and rigidity. The body was then wrapped with wire mesh and cotton and covered with fiberglass."

"The statue realistically captures a moment in time—as if the soul is trapped inside and hoping to escape. It's an imposing, hyper-realistic figure of a living person that tricks our minds by blurring the line with reality, despite reeking of unpleasant fetidness," the lieutenant philosophized.

Emily was curiously wondering who would commit this type of crime. "The statue reminds me of an insane psychopath obsessing over the corpse of a dead relative, offering them alcohol and cigarettes and treating them as if they were merely sick. Is there a law against wrapping a dead body in fiberglass and making it into a statue? Since ancient times, Egyptians embalmed the corpses of nobles as mummies and stored them in luxurious sarcophagi."

"Father Adam Baum is a renowned taxidermist. He has a history of preserving family pets, animals without a purpose kept for love and amusement that act as nonjudgmental witnesses to our lives. Touching a stuffed animal, especially for those with low self-esteem, helps relieve existential angst. The Padre once admitted to stuffing a woman's pet dog for her, but she later complained that her new pet kept humping it."

A wave of emotional distress of immobilizing intensity caused Emily's heart to pound. She was experiencing anxiety, lightheadedness, nausea, and vertigo in anticipation of stomach bile reflux. She had a sense of losing control. A sudden episode of intense fear reminded her that a panic attack was imminent. Her mouth filled with saliva to protect the teeth from stomach acid. She was green about the gills. The emotions of stress, excitement, and anxiety triggered queasy, stomach-turning nausea.

Unaware of her condition, Coroner Slaughter placed the X-rays in the file drawer before removing a notebook from the bookshelf describing Jack Daniels's electrocution.

69

CORONER SLAUGHTER

"Electrocution is an excruciating death. The body swells up, and boiling blood pours out of every orifice. The eyeballs pop out, and flames burst from under the skin. The body temperature is so hot that the flesh cooks and falls away."

Emily sipped a cool glass of water to settle the sickness in her stomach.

Deputy Sheriff Bud Light interrupted. "Two anonymous bird watchers claim to have seen what appeared to be a homeless man with big ears, shaggy hair, and torn clothing break into Jack's cabin. According to the informants, his left shoulder sagged, and he dragged his left leg as if his hip had dislocated."

Coroner Slaughter removed a photograph from his evidence case file and laid it on the table for everyone to see. "I found this picture of a Taliban soldier standing behind a goat in Jack Daniels's shirt pocket."

The deputy removed it from the table and examined it closely. "I recognize the person in the photo—that's René Malarkey, the reporter dressed up as a Taliban soldier. He was released from the army six months ago. Look closely under his robes; he's wearing that same yellow T-shirt with the bright green cannabis leaves that he still wears today—the one with the burn holes exposing his stomach."

Coroner Slaughter paused to allow everyone ample time to scrutinize the disturbing image before continuing. Emily refused to look.

"The vomit on the priceless Japanese bonsai tree in Jack's cabin matches your DNA," Coroner Slaughter stated with a stern look in the direction of Deputy Sheriff Bud Light. "The contents of the digestive system indicate a high consumption of alcohol, proving that you were legally drunk."

The lieutenant blew a giant smoke ring, calmly watching it uncurl in the air before asking, "Do you have any additional thoughts about the death of Dusty Rhodes?"

"Dusty died of dehydration, surviving for at least one week after being paralyzed by a bolt from a crossbow, exactly as you assumed. Feces material from the bowel was in his hair, under his fingernails, behind his ears, and under his chin. He fell into a septic tank or rolled down a hill in a portable toilet. Either way, he was having a truly crappy day." Coroner Slaughter smirked.

"What about peanut allergies and the death of Benedict Walker?"

"Peanuts are the number-one cause of death related to food-induced anaphylaxis. The peanut butter 'kiss of death' that killed Benedict Walker causes victims to die from anaphylactic shock. There is an immediate drop in blood pressure and fainting. The hypersensitive immune system releases chemicals that flood the body. Airways dangerously narrow, blocking normal breathing. Hives and wheezing lead to dizziness and confusion, followed by nausea, vomiting, abdominal pain, and diarrhea. Without immediate medical attention, death is inevitable. Benedict had severe eruptions of atopic dermatitis of the inside creases of his arms. His face swelled. His skin was pale, and his lips were blue. The syringe lying on the floor beside him could have saved his life, but he was unable to discharge the life-saving contents into his bloodstream."

Emily was feeling rather anemic and washed out. Her dilated eyes were wide as saucers, brimming with amazement as she pondered the events that may have transpired immediately before death. She held her breath to stifle a wheezing attack.

Dunning was eager to express his opinion. "Your sophisticated scientific analysis is changing my perspective, knowing that devilish premeditated precautions would be needed to slay someone using this method. To intentionally cause Benedict Walker's death, the perpetrator would have been an insider aware of his allergies and daily routines."

The lieutenant raised his eyebrows and tugged on his earlobes without speaking. It was as if he was trying to pull words out of his mouth, exasperatingly rolling his eyes as an unpleasant sign of intrigue. "The world has many conniving, money-hungry people who jealously covet property belonging to others. Morally repugnant individuals with an extreme will to make money tend to ignore right and wrong and choose wealth over conscience dictates. Gravestone Castle is a one-of-a-kind classic gem—a scarce, intriguing property of high value, a crown jewel and a prize worthy of a compromise in ethical judgment."

Coroner Slaughter continued with his discoveries. "Billy Big Ears Bellini died of bacterial meningitis. It's a deadly disease that develops very quickly and causes brain damage, loss of vision, paralysis, and stroke, followed by death within four hours. Meningitis causes inflammation of the tough layer of tissue surrounding the brain and the spinal cord, leading to brain swelling, resulting in permanent disability and coma. Initial symptoms include head and muscle aches, sensitivity to light, neck stiffness, and malaise, followed by altered mental status, seizures, and focal neurological deficits. Untreated bacterial meningitis resulting from sinus infections and skull fractures is contagious and almost always fatal. Survivors face permanent disabilities, including brain damage, hearing depletion, loss of kidney function, and limb amputations."

"Do you have any idea how Big Ears contracted the disease?"

"An X-ray of his skull shows a recent skull fracture in the bones that form the cranial portion of the skull, resulting from blunt-force trauma to the forehead. The force was excessive, fracturing at the impact site, resulting in damage to the underlying structures within the skull, including the membranes, blood vessels, and brain. The back of his ears showed severe signs of recent skin tearing and scarring, similar to injuries sustained from explosions. His girlfriend, Angelina, blames Billy's injuries on a fall from a ladder several weeks ago."

Deputy Sheriff Bud Light interrupted. "The fuselage of Billy's stolen airplane was found wedged between the branches of a forked tree on Jack Daniels's property. I assume the pilot was forcefully blasted into the sky over Lake Michigan due to an explosion louder than the sound of an engine backfiring. The aircraft spiraled into a wildly uncontrollable nosedive. The noise on impact with the trees would have been incredible. The pilot's hand was torn off in the explosion, appearing as if a madman had hacked it off with an ax. That's how I was able to get his fingerprints," he stated proudly.

Emily felt hopelessly disconnected, dizzy, and nauseous, classic symptoms of complex post-traumatic stress from exposure to nightmarish events leading to multiple grisly deaths.

The coroner spoke directly to her. "The pilot would have had one hell of a bloody face, a massive headache, a punctured lung, broken ribs, and a lot of physical and mental trauma. He would have been sick to his stomach from the strong smell of gunpowder, organic waste, burning machinery, and sparking electric wires. When a colossal fireball of burning fuel blew through the cabin, it would have melted his clothes to his skin."

The image of a man on fire with his arm chopped off repulsed Emily.

The coroner summarized the situation. "Our efforts keep reminding me of two people making a debacle of trying to fit a couch through an apartment door on the second floor."

Coroner Slaughter shifted gears, making an anticipatory drum roll before removing a mysterious photograph from an envelope on his desk and placing it on the table. "Two days after the electrocution, reporter René Malarkey found a cell phone lying in the ditch at the end of Jack's driveway. He extracted several photos of the crime scene before it became locked, preventing the police from identifying the owner.

The lieutenant processed the information slowly, cautiously anticipating the revelation of clues to a previously unsolvable puzzle that had suddenly become clear. The transition from no understanding to spontaneous comprehension was accompanied by exuberance when the solution proved true. He reminded Emily of a jack-in-the-box toy ready to pop open when least expected. His joyful enthusiasm, liveliness, and emotional exhibition always preceded the revelation.

"Sociopaths, arsonists, rapists, and serial killers are known for having a strong desire to return to the scene of the crime. It is common in police dramas for a detective to arrive at the scene and immediately focus on a person in the crowd who is acting strangely."

Deputy Sheriff Bud Light was ready for immediate action. His face lit up. "In that case, I think I know who the murderer is. The pot-smoking reporter René Malarkey from Colorado with the yellow cannabis T-shirt is an ambulance chaser. He's always Johnny-on-the-spot and the first person to arrive in an emergency." The lieutenant disagreed. "René monitors police radio with a scanner religiously. That's why he shows up so quickly at the crime scenes, but if you think he has something to contribute, go ahead and interview him."

70

BUMFUZZLED

Coroner Slaughter dropped a bombshell. "The bodies of two men with a similar modus operandi and cause of death were recovered in Milwaukee last night. Children discovered Johnny Linguine's body floating in the Milwaukee River downstream from Estabrook Park. His Range Rover crashed into a tree in Brown Deer Park. An Audi A8 with a Georgia license plate was involved in an accident at Capital Drive and Fond de Lac Avenue in Milwaukee on the same night. The body of an art collector from Atlanta was shot in the face and locked in the trunk. According to the ballistics report, the revolver we discovered in Dusty Rhodes' trailer killed both victims."

Emily was shocked to the point of speechlessness. She was experiencing an epiphany, a rare sudden and striking realization that the investigation was suddenly headed in a different direction, much more complex than she had anticipated. "Dusty Rhodes's actions seem irrational yet plausible. The cash, the painting, and the gun we discovered in his trailer are highly incriminating evidence linking him directly to both of these murders."

The lieutenant practiced mindfulness, taking his time to process the information and drudge up just the right words. "This is a notable game-changer worthy of attention that changes our previous assumptions. I never suspected Dusty Rhodes of being the treacherous renegade this evidence makes him out to be. He may have shot them during the exchange of money for the oil painting. The discovery of two abandoned cars in a city park with the keys in the ignition would have been difficult to resist by teenagers with a passion for joyriding."

Emily slumped in a chair, overtaxed with nervous tension and anxiety. Her skin was pale, an obvious sign of dehydration and emotional stress. Persistent negative thoughts were cause for concern, as Colonel Roberts had warned in the beginning.

"My heart feels like the ashes of a dumpster fire. The hideous smell of death is hindering my breathing and causing acid reflux indigestion in my esophagus. Father Cellophane died due to being hit in the face by a golf ball. Father Adam Baum or some other immoral, corrupt degenerate dug him up and made the corpse into a fiberglass statue. What the hell was the perpetrator thinking? A course worker at Woebegone Dunes Resort fell to his gruesome death trying to escape a swarm of angry killer bees. The death scene was terrifyingly sickening and appalling. Dusty Rhodes died from dehydration after being hit in the neck and paralyzed by a bolt fired from a crossbow. On the same day, he shot two people in Estabrook Park on the east bank of the Milwaukee River. Somewhere before all this took place, Dusty fell in a septic tank. He died a horrible, agonizing death," Emily summarized hopelessly, playing with her hair and rubbing her palms together.

"Bruno Greco was violently blown to smithereens, minuscule pieces that could never be recognized or put back together again. Jack Daniels died hideously, clinging to a malfunctioning electric toilet. A stranger shot at Wayne and Kate Kennedy from an airplane, and Kate rolled down the hill with her underpants pulled down to her knees. Before we could interrogate him about his stolen airplane, Billy Bellini died of meningitis. His airplane wedged into a forked tree, and the police found the pilot's right hand in a leather glove on the ground below the wreckage. Bizarre! Is this what our investigation all comes down to at the end of the sidewalk? What else could go wrong? We have no idea why these deaths occurred. Our investigation has opened a troublesome can of worms more complicated, unpleasant, and difficult to solve than I ever imagined with issues whose resolutions are unintelligible and contentious. Dusty Rhodes stole an oil painting and killed two men, and we still haven't even found his truck. We have no idea who shot at Wayne and Kate Kennedy from an airplane. The cause of the electric toilet failure that killed Jack Daniels is incomprehensible. Weeks have passed willy-nilly, without a plan, substance, or consequence."

"At least you haven't shot anyone yet," the lieutenant opined as a way of dispersing her doubts. "Where this investigation goes depends on how many slams remain in the old screen door."

Emily changed her tone of voice a full octave as a sign of exasperation. "The future viability of Woebegone Dunes Resort is in jeopardy. Yet you have nothing but praise for the Royal Enouement Society members that we have yet to investigate. What have you learned about the secret society from the handbook we discovered in Jack Daniels's cabin?"

Emily was stressed and impatient. Her emotions were intense, and her behavior disconcerting. She continued venting impatiently without listening for a response. Most of her sentences ended with a slight wheezing sound. "The uncertainty of this situation gives me the collywobbles. Everything is in disarray, disorganized and awry, unsymmetrical and discombobulated. Nothing is lining up squarely. Everything in our world is off-center and caddywampus. I feel like an intoxicated performer in the circus: a person spinning plates, bowls, and other objects on poles combined with contortion and acrobatic skills. When the audience thinks we have all we can handle, someone throws us another object to juggle. Events are irredeemable and disastrous, the way a bad performance at a junior high school talent show unfolds."

The lieutenant empathetically concurred. "This inquiry started with a trip to Africa to expose massive oil theft, Chinese investment in rare-earth minerals, and biological warfare against guerilla terrorists. And now we seem to be caught up in several of the most bizarre, outrageous deaths and human carnage scenes in the history of Wisconsin. We are both in need of a day off to recoup our energy and enthusiasm. Perhaps you should accept Jay Walker's offer to visit his chalet."

"What are you planning to do this weekend?"

"I'm planning to spend the day with my friend Crystal Glass."

"The precocious reporter that put you under a spell in Nigeria?"

"A day off would be good for both of us. It would help you reduce your stress and anxiety, increase your productivity and focus, and let yourself fall in love with your job again."

Emily's sense of joy, happiness, and exhilaration spiked, knowing something positive would happen. She enthusiastically raised her hands above her head, spun around, and offered the lieutenant an appreciative hug—an act of friendship that was long overdue.

A day off? Emily was excited about the possibilities. She was eager for something positive to happen, impatiently desirous of a day of peace. It was a time of high expectations to let her hair down and behave freely, to have some fun and relax. At the top of her fantasy wish list was a private *sub rosa* romantic rendezvous with Jay Walker.

"Enjoy the day but don't get too relaxed. Colonel James Roberts grows weary of our investigation's continuously unabated rising action. He is eager to wrap up our mission and expects a resolution soon. Tomorrow night, we have a dinner reservation at the Fox and Hounds Restaurant and Tavern in Hubertus, Wisconsin. Wayne, Kate Kennedy, Deputy Sheriff Bud Light, and Tammy will join us. The colonel is expecting reasonable answers to some difficult questions."

71

BIG NIGHT OUT

The following morning, Lieutenant Dunning greeted Crystal warmly in the lobby of Woebegone Dunes Resort with a romantic hug and a kiss on the cheek. Crystal was radiantly fizzing with enthusiasm. She leaned her head on his shoulder and then gently touched his cheek before slowly pulling away.

"You seem to be emanating great joy this morning. The pleasant-smelling fragrance of the perfume you are wearing is a mood enhancer that makes my heart sing. Your presence causes my brain to bypass its normal functions. You seem to be leading me to places that I haven't been before, a world that is naturally intriguing, interesting, and engaging—more luscious than I ever imagined."

"I have been thinking about you every day since our chance encounter in the jungles of Nigeria. At first glance, you reminded me of Tarzan standing naked on the side of the road."

"Even a battleship looks small against the backdrop of the ocean," the lieutenant countered in defensive of his manhood, visualizing hugging her in a hot soapy shower.

Her spirit was radiant, and her untethered, confident, and accessible feelings were beguiling. She vivaciously effervesced with sparkle. A perfect date, the lieutenant thought, animated, exuberant, lyrical, and full of life, leaving him with a self-satisfied expression that was a visual reflection of his cheerful disposition.

She wanted to know Lieutenant Baron Dunning based on a foundation of trust, intimacy, and mutual compatibility. Never before had she been so attracted to such a unique, masculine, intriguing human. The words "I now pronounce you man and wife" innocently flickered through her mind like an unexpected electric shock.

Intuitively, she smiled knowingly that Lieutenant Dunning was experiencing the same thoughts. Her nonverbal body language and happy, loving facial expressions unconsciously mimicked his behavior as a sign of attraction, drawing her closer to him. She remained focused and strongly engaged, a great sign to the lieutenant of the direction she wanted to go.

Strolling around the marina hand in hand as a sign of intimacy and newly found affection was thoroughly enjoyable.

I don't care what we do with the remainder of the day, as long as I have you to myself."

"This evening, we will be dining at the Fox and Hounds Restaurant in Hubertus, famous for its old-world charm, creative cuisine, and warm atmosphere. Colonel James Roberts; my partner, Emily, and Jay Walker; Wayne and Kate Kennedy; Deputy Sheriff Bud Light; and Tammy will join us. I'm sorry to drag you into a business meeting, but it's the best I can do."

The lieutenant gazed out at the deep-blue water of Lake Michigan. The aesthetically pleasing landscape contributed to his sense of well-being. "I love the water. I look forward to taking you on a cruise someday. The sea inspires visions that are haunting and alluring, especially at sunset. When I was in Spain, silver moonlight was shimmering on the placid combers of the briny deep. That's when I had a remarkably unexpected fantasy—a ghostly image of you, like an apparition of the Virgin Mary. I longed to hold you near and kiss you. It's hard to breathe when your heart yearns so much for someone so far away."

Crystal placed her hands on the lieutenant's neck and obsessively kissed him on the lips, triggering feelings of luscious passion. "Is this what you had in mind in your dream?" she enticed with a mysteriously attractive and fascinating acceptance. "I have an overwhelming sense of belonging with you, to talk with you, listen to your opinions, and understand the way your mind works." Grinding with her hips and pushing herself against him, her body language was persuasive. She had a solid willingness to satisfy her emotional desires driven by an intense craving for union and vibrant ecstasy. A feeling of euphoric arousal and exhilaration overcame her, along with a racing heart and accelerated breathing. Curiosity, intrigue, and supercharged hormones gradually seeped out, propelled by fantasy. She self-consciously blushed, admiring the spirit, sparkle, and panache the lieutenant exhibited in public.

"You have an uncommon flair, a dash of vivacity, stamina, and vitality. You feel like a roaring fireplace on a cold winter's evening whose flickering flames draw me in and captivate my heart. I'm enjoying this experience of being with you in a way that I can't recall ever happening before. The feelings I have for you are overwhelming. I feel secure and content when I'm with you, the same way I feel during a storm when I'm comfortably warm and well-protected in bed."

"I feel the same way. I have this intense yearning that I can't disguise that won't subside. I feel the magic between us. I fantasize that you will be mine tonight, forever, and always, until the end of time." He wrapped his arms around her waist and kissed her on the lips as he gallantly opened the backdoor of his car. She was naturally drawn in by a bouquet of fresh flowers and a box of gourmet chocolates neatly centered on the back seat like a block of cheese in a mousetrap.

Inside, she cuddled with her head on his shoulder. She unbuttoned her blouse before allowing herself to slip down in the seat until her head was comfortably resting on his lap. The lieutenant ran his fingers through her silky hair, rubbed her neck and shoulders, and massaged her back. He marveled at the smooth surface of her milky skin and beautifully shaped breasts. Engorgement of her nipples caused them to visibly protrude beneath the surface of her blouse, reminding the lieutenant of the high beams on his Porsche. Hungry eyes, heavy breathing, involuntary moans, an urgent need for proximity, and an animated internal fire signaled to the lieutenant he was on the right track.

"I noticed that you carry a concealed weapon at all times," Crystal teased, taking note of more than one hard lump beneath his clothing. "The 'chairman of the board' appears full of vigor, bursting with good health and virility, pushing hard against your barn door and forcibly trying to get out. Shall I help him escape?" Crystal questioned with wide-eyed innocence and admiration.

The highly romantic mood collapsed at the height of emotional anticipation, like hot air escaping a balloon. The lieutenant's back stiffened. His senses were suddenly on startlingly high alert. The festive, cheery, optimistic mood flipped abruptly from happiness, sheer bliss, and passion to an eerie feeling of a potential external threat. An intuitive fear of something foreboding and creepy caused his mood to change abruptly, unexpectedly projecting intense awareness of everything around him and the reality of it.

"What makes you think something is wrong?"

"In my line of work, being able to detect threats and make correct split-second judgments is imperative. There are four sinister-looking characters in a black Hummer behind us. They are spreading out and walking in this direction. A person about to attack typically has their upper body poised forward, balanced over the toes the way a sprinter bursts off the line. Action is always faster than reaction. Being aware of early warning signs can cut down your reaction time, allowing you to respond and counterattack or escape more quickly."

Crystal nervously peeked in the rearview mirror to increase her situational awareness by keying in on unexpected anomalies. "Let's get out of here quickly," she agreed on immediate recognition of the potential threat.

"Tighten your seatbelt. The road may be a challenge," the lieutenant cautioned.

72

HOT TUB PARTY

Jay Walker's invitation had arrived at the perfect time. Emily felt sweet on Jay, and she had secretly been yearning to sneak off to be with him for any reason. Maintaining a polished, professional image every hour of every day was an emotionally draining and physically exhausting experience for her. Thoughts of an unfettered romantic affair with Jay had been filling her imagination for some time now. She was eager to let her hair down, drop her inhibitions, and cease acting formally and conservatively.

She eventually discovered the isolated country lane leading to his Swiss chalet through trial and error and dead reckoning. The quaintness and charm of the alpine structure nestled into the forest pleasantly surprised her. The architecture, the slate roof, the window shutters, flower boxes, and the exciting details carved into the wood were enchanting.

Emily was classy and elegant, a tasteful woman with good manners. She was polite, respectful, and courteous to those around her. She was always well-groomed and took pride in every detail of her appearance, including the clothes she was wearing and the way she wore her hair and makeup.

"Welcome to my chalet. I will be serving cheese fondue made with cubes of gruyere, cheddar, and Emmentaler cheeses for lunch. I have already opened a fine Swiss Chenin Blanc wine with distinctive character notes. I think you'll like it."

The first glass of wine was refreshing. The second glass was delightful. The third glass filled the room with happiness and laughter. Emily casually let her hair down, signaling old-fashioned informality, relaxed inhibitions, freedom, and a desire for fun.

"I'm enjoying the wine, but I confess that I never drank more than one glass at a time before," Emily responded with class and appreciation.

"I should have reminded you to bring a bathing suit so we could use the hot tub on the porch," Jay suggested remorsefully.

"Is the water warm?" she asked before testing the water with her fingers.

Emily was wearing a classic style of clothing made from high-quality satin fabric. Her tailored slim-leg capri pants, embellished with lace and diamond rhinestones, were stunning. "Like I said, this is the first time I ever drank more than one glass of wine." Casually slipping off her sweater and abandoning her elegant apparel in a heap on the deck, she tumbled recklessly into the steamy hot water.

"Come and join me. The water is enticing and alluring," Emily suggested seductively.

Jay was shocked by her playful way of talking; relaxed, suggestive behavior; and beguiling flirtation. He grabbed another full bottle of wine, unaware that alcohol had already reduced his motor skills, cognitive functions, and inhibitions. He stripped into his underwear before splashing into the warm bubbly water with steamy visions and fanciful notions of what might happen next.

"Wow, you remind me of the epic tales of the illustrated cartoon character Captain Underpants." Emily openly displayed her feminine attractiveness by messing up her hair, giggling, sticking out her chest, and making her legs more visible—behavior that was better blamed on the wine and entirely out of character with her strong moral beliefs and traditional conservative demeanor.

Jay took full advantage of the situation, teasing, flirting, and harmlessly charming her with gestures, provocative sign language, and erotic touching as part of the courtship game, hoping to excite her to the possibility of an actual intimate encounter. Emily was flattered by the attention, excited by his risqué behavior, and turned on by his flirtatious, amorous teasing.

"Jay, you need a spanking." She blushed before taking another sip of wine and puckering her lips as if to invite a kiss. Her eyes twinkled dreamily with a strong sense of desirability and provocative excitement. Her body language was sultry, candidly open, and hinting of physical intimacy. The sexy sheer lace bra she was wearing left nothing to the imagination. She seemed so highly exploitable and vulnerable to seduction.

Uncertain of the situational outcome, they covered themselves with dry towels, held hands, and tiptoed to the bedroom, leaving a trail of watery footprints. Locked together in a warm romantic embrace, they tumbled onto the bed in a mischievous avalanche of happiness.

Jay placed his head on the pillow, held her tightly, and closed his eyes. "I'm intoxicated with your love. I feel blissfully relaxed and mentally close to you. My heart is racing as if I'm at the top of the alluring descent of a rollercoaster. The euphoric sensations I experience when I'm with you are amazing. I want to be together all of our days, wake up every morning to your sweet face, and hold you in my arms forever and always. There's no way I'm ever letting you go."

Suddenly, out of the blue, they were rudely jolted by the University of Wisconsin fight song blaring on Emily's cell phone. The feelings of blissful happiness they had been experiencing shattered.

"I used to play the clarinet and march in the university band, and that's why I picked the fight song for my ringtone. The cadences are varied and exhilarating, and the music is highly stimulating. The intense vitality of a college marching band is always refreshing," Emily explained with pride before picking up.

"Hello, Emily, this is your mother. I didn't hear from you yesterday.

Silence isn't golden to a mother—it's suspicious. Ignorance isn't bliss. What have you been doing all day? I hear music in the background."

"I'm busy, Mom. I'm still on a special assignment at Woebegone Dunes Resort, several hours north of Milwaukee. The situation is complicated. I'll call you tomorrow—goodbye."

"No matter how old I become, my mother will always be watching for signs of improvement," Emily said, turning to Jay.

She removed Jay's navy-blue luxurious silk robe with braided gold trim from the closet and draped it over her shoulders. She flopped down on the living room couch with the front of the robe carelessly and invitingly open. Her lightly tanned, flawless, soft, smooth skin was essential to her overall attractiveness, indicating good health. Jay rubbed her back and said nice things in her ear before lying down beside her spoon fashion to keep her warm and make himself comfortable. There was barely enough room on the couch for two people, and he held her tightly from behind to avoid falling on the floor.

"The first day I met you, I dreamed about you. You are always full of energy, bright-eyed and bushy-tailed, and ready to have fun. You're the only girl that ever made me feel this way. You are the most glamorous, smartest, most beautiful girl in the world."

When Emily's cell phone unexpectedly rang a second time, Jay lost his grip. He tumbled off the couch, banging his elbows and hips on the hardwood floor. Emily laughed at the awkward, comedic misadventure. Jay's raised eyebrows signaled surprise and mild amusement. The peaceful romantic feelings they were experiencing in each other's arms came to an abrupt halt, as rudely as a cold bucket of ice water in the face.

The tone of Lieutenant Baron Dunning's voice was grave and urgent. "I need immediate backup. Four suspicious characters are following Crystal Glass and me in a black Hummer, and they seem intent on harming us. We are heading to the Fox and Hounds restaurant and will wait there until Colonel James Roberts and the rest of you arrive."

"What should I do?"

"I need you to put on a disguise and meet us at the restaurant immediately," he demanded explicitly. "Act quickly. The threat is grave, and the intention may be to inflict pain or other hostile acts of retribution. This seminal moment in our investigation may influence everything that follows."

"Jay and I will be there as quickly as possible."

Turning to Jay, she barked out an order. "Lieutenant Dunning is in big trouble—he needs our help. Run outside and retrieve the duffel bag in my car."

Jay was having trouble concentrating and keeping his balance. Alcohol stifled his reasoning skills, and his inhibitions and slurred speech were apparent signs of intoxication. He was feeling a little woozy as he rushed outside in his wet underwear to retrieve the cylindrical red canvas duffel bag.

73

FOX AND HOUNDS

Emily handed Jay a deluxe Beach-Boy style wig with gray hair and matching bushy eyebrows, wingtip shoes, and a brown suit with a checkered necktie and suspenders.

"Put these on."

"My thick-rimmed eyeglasses are crooked, and they make my eyes appear overly large and cross-eyed," Jay complained.

Emily purposefully left her underwear dangling in the bathroom because it was too cold and wet to wear. She slipped into a faded 1950s midcalf tea-length navy-blue dress with tiny white flowers. She stuffed a can of bear spray and zip-tie handcuffs into her purse, lifted the hemline of her dress, and tucked her Ruger 38 revolver into her concealed thigh holster.

"The grandmother wig on your head and wire-rim glasses on your nose look very authentic. We look like two sassy old people from Arizona, cheeky and full of spirit," Jay remarked as he raised the wig to expose his eyebrows.

The aftereffects of drinking too much wine left Emily thinking everything was hilariously funny, but she was feeling a bit woozy without knowing how to act sober. When they arrived at the Fox & Hounds restaurant, Emily scanned the parking lot before issuing orders. "Keep your eye on that black Hummer in the shadows. Don't let them see you.

Lieutenant Dunning has clandestinely probed deeply into the lives of many people suspected of every type of crime imaginable. It won't surprise me if he has become the target of retribution by someone hoping to redress past grievances."

Jay slid down in the seat to continue observing inconspicuously without being seen.

"The lieutenant expects us to hone our powers of observation by being mindful of our surroundings, sharpening our powers of examination, increasing our memory power, augmenting our investigative expertise, and enhancing our surveillance skills. He says to be proactive, observe the malfeasants as closely as possible without letting them know you are targeting them."

Emily stealthily worked her way behind the trees, keeping in the shadows to avoid being seen, until she found herself behind a dumpster adjacent to the rear service entrance. The front window in the Hummer was partially open. Chills shot up her spine when she saw the driver. The stranger had an ugly knife scar on his left cheek, the way the lieutenant had described the vicious Nigerian gunman who shot the African safari driver Noah. The same person was the group leader who stole the lieutenant's clothes and identification and left him standing naked on the side of the road.

She texted the lieutenant: "Four suspicious characters with distinctive physical traits and unusual personality quirks are sitting in a black Hummer in the deep shadows of the most remote corner of the parking lot." Using pure military-style language, she assigned a number, a nickname, and a visible physical identifier to each individual to make them easy to memorize. "The driver with the black beret is 'Scarface.' 'Red Beard' is number two. 'Chief Yellow Fang' and the 'Tattoo Lady' are three and four."

Scarface combatively barked out his final instructions. "We do this exactly as planned—we entice the lieutenant into the back room, drug him, kidnap him, drive him to the lake, and drown him. Everything takes place so quickly that nobody knows what happened."

Emily texted the lieutenant inside the restaurant: "Code red! Emergency evacuation! A combative three-person force is about to enter the restaurant. All three individuals are armed, and the driver is still outside sitting in the Hummer."

The lieutenant surreptitiously scowled in response to a potential confrontation as the three hostile strangers entered the dining room. He studied the body language and profiled the facial expressions of each individual before whispering to Crystal, "Red Beard is carrying brass knuckles and multiple concealed weapons. The Chinese man with the yellow teeth is a kung fu master, great for movies and acrobatic performances but bad for a fight. The woman is wearing faux hair extensions. The tattoos that decorate her arms and legs likely result from an impulsive drunken binge in Mexico. They are an eclectic bunch of morons that appear intent on doing us harm."

Outside, the driver stepped out of the Hummer to tighten his boot-laces. Emily pounced with the stealth and quickness of a cat, knocking him off balance and hitting him on the head with a rock. A quick chop to his throat resulted in difficulty breathing and swallowing and a complete lack of ability to speak or act. She discharged a cloud of liquid bear spray into his face, temporarily reducing his ability to see, breathe, and smell, leaving her in complete control. His evil eyes, brightly illuminated from an overhead security floodlight, were bloodshot and glowing bright red like a terrorized bull filled with rage. She locked her hands around his neck in an illegal chokehold and spiraled his back and shoulders around like an ancient twisted tree trunk. She lifted his shoulders slightly off the asphalt and flipped him face down on the pavement with brute force. She cuffed his wrists behind his back with disposable flex-cuffs and taped his mouth shut before signaling for Jay's help.

"Act. Never wait. Challenge your fears. Hesitation leads to anxiety, which is simply a fear of the unknown," Emily instructed, displaying a take-charge aspect to her personality that Jay had never seen before. With tremendous effort and teamwork, they hoisted the man to the top edge of the dumpster. He fell headfirst into a pile of rotten tomatoes, moldy dinner rolls, wilted lettuce, mashed potatoes, fish, spoiled melons, piles of spaghetti and meatballs, steak bones, mushroom soup, and other smelly day-old dinner scraps. Without hesitation, Emily followed up by removing the stem caps from the tires on the Hummer to let the air out of the tires.

Crystal sat quietly, worrying without speaking, picking her food without eating. "How do you know they're bad people? What should we do? Shouldn't we formulate an escape plan?"

"Take my car keys. Make everyone assume that you are going to the bathroom. When you get to the hallway, duck into the kitchen and exit through the service entrance as quickly as you can. Move smoothly without attracting attention to yourself. Don't hesitate, apologize, or pause to ask for permission. Go directly to my car and place the keys in the ignition. Get in the back seat, lie down, and wait for me."

When he was confident that Crystal had escaped without being detected, the lieutenant forced his cell phone to ring. "I'm in a restaurant. Please excuse me while I step outside to avoid disturbing the other customers," he stated furtively, pretending to be accepting a critical call. He calmly stood up from the table and quietly slinked out the front door with a fluid grace without attracting undue attention. He dashed to his car and sped off with Crystal sitting in the back seat, nervously eating a box of chocolates to fill an emotional need.

Newspaper reporter René Malarkey wore a ratty yellow T-shirt with bright-green cannabis leaves, blotchy wine stains, and multiple large burn holes exposing his stomach. He was standing by the entrance when he unexpectedly witnessed an eighty-year-old woman with no underwear slap a man in the face with the quickness of a cougar. The older woman lifted him above her head and rolled the menacing stranger into a dumpster when he stopped resisting.

Her impulsive actions left Emily feeling worried and guilty. The setting created uncertainty and an extreme sense of urgency. Her emotions were spinning out of control. Her pupils dilated, and her skin flushed. Her rapid heart rate and heavy breathing increased oxygen consumption.

Her muscles trembled, primed for action. Her sympathetic nervous system activated a sudden release of adrenaline in response to acute stress. Inner torment caused her to reach a high point of tension, propelling her to an emotional meltdown, like with the sinking of the *Titanic* or the fear of an angry grizzly bear in your nightmares.

A dread of other external conflicts brought urgency and complexity, automatically triggering an ancient fight-or-flight response. Emily's initial impulse was to run and look for temporary cover to hide from the potentially life-threatening situation. But the woods seemed unsettling, a creepy place full of foul odors, imminent danger, and a sense of the unknown. There was a clear and present danger—a defining point in the investigation, a down-to-the-wire feeling, and a gripping climax to the quest. A desperate sense of panic and horror causing a slow emotional burn overcame her, knowing that firmness of purpose was lacking. The situation was in desperate need of resolution.

74

GUNSHOTS

The three-person assassination team hired by Bo-Bo Bigelow to drown Lieutenant Baron Dunning was slow to react. The tattooed lady inconspicuously strolled into the restroom to find out why Crystal took so long in the bathroom. Finding no evidence of the woman she was following, she darted outside to look around.

She was shocked to discover that someone had handcuffed the driver before tossing him into the kitchen dumpster. Strips of lettuce, tomato, and macaroni noodles were clinging to his face.

Reporter René Malarkey snapped multiple pictures of the tattooed lady struggling to drag the flummoxed dumpster diver out of the rusty metal garbage bin. He rushed boldly into the restaurant, running from room to room shouting an exaggerated account of what had just taken place outside. "A little old lady beat the crap out of a muscle man in the parking lot. She sprayed him in the face with bear spray, handcuffed him, and rolled him into a dumpster. Fishbones, spaghetti, and watermelon rinds are all over his face. Come see for yourselves."

Several intoxicated celebrities pushed their way toward the front door en masse to determine what was causing the commotion. Red Beard stumbled and knocked over a pitcher of water, causing it to spill into the lap of an attractive young lady wearing a formal wedding rehearsal dress. Her fiancé smacked the clumsy intruder in the face with his elbow, causing him to fall to the floor in a semiconscious state of pain. Blood dripped from his broken nose.

Red Beard was furious and frustrated when he saw the handcuffs on Burly. The flat tires on the black Hummer infuriated him. He pulled out his gun as an act of revenge and exploded into an uncontrollable rage. He pointed the gun at the crowd, demanding to know who was responsible. When nobody confessed, he indiscriminately began shooting wildly at the cars in the parking lot. Bullets pierced the radiator of a Mercedes CLA 250, the windshield of a white Lexus LS500, and the gas tank of a KIA Telluride. A fourth shot sailed directly over Emily's head. She instinctively retaliated in self-defense by lifting the hem of her dress, removing the revolver from her concealed inner thigh holster, and deliberately shooting the perpetrator in the shoulder, the Tattoo Lady in the foot, and Yellow Fang in the knee before jumping into her car and speeding away.

Observers were amazed by the spectacle. The crowd was so excited by the sight of blood that nobody bothered to take notice of the color of her car or license plate number as she sped out of the parking lot. A crowd formed around the three wounded gunshot victims in obvious agonizing pain, dripping with blood, whimpering, and cussing loudly.

The scar-faced driver wearing the black military-style beret stepped to the back of the crowd unnoticed. He brushed several broken eggshells off his shoulders. He straightened his beret dripping with butterscotch pudding and pickles before stealthily climbing into the front seat of the black Hummer. He slowly eased out of the parking lot on four flat tires without attracting attention, shielded by darkened black windows. The Hummer was half a mile down the road without media attention or fanfare and entirely out of sight before the first ambulance arrived.

Emily raced down the windy country road, wondering what to do next. She impulsively whipped her car into the parking lot of a second-hand thrift store. "Let's change clothes and wigs so that I can get rid of this old-lady disguise."

At the bottom of the used clothes bin, she discovered a frumpy, unfashionable army green dress with an elastic waist and frilly sleeves. It was a tacky outfit with a dowdy lack of style.

"You look mumsy," Jay said, peering through his bent wire-rimmed spectacles. He selected an ill-fitting, unkept, wrinkled, unproportioned gray business suit with a wide pukey-colored yellow tie.

Lieutenant Dunning and Crystal were traveling in the opposite direction. Ten miles from the restaurant, they made a 180-degree turn and pulled off the road onto a wooded country lane. The lieutenant parked the car and reached for Crystal's hand. He self-consciously hugged her tightly to reduce stress and diminish her fears. His show of support eventually caused her to stop shaking. His intimate touch and soothing voice were a sophisticated way of communicating his love and assurances. She felt safe and confident in his arms. Twenty minutes later, the tension eased. Crystal was sufficiently calm; a news announcement was made on the radio reporting that three persons were shot and wounded in the vicinity. The lieutenant reluctantly picked up the phone to inform Colonel James Roberts about the unfortunate shooting incident.

"External circumstances have significantly altered the trajectory of the investigation, diverting attention away from the original action plan. I regret to inform you that there was a shooting at the Fox and Hounds restaurant. Four strangers were tracking me in what appeared to be a covert mission to do me harm. One escaped, and the other three were shot and wounded in the parking lot by a vigilante. Reportedly, it was an older woman. My date, Crystal, and I had already left the scene before the shooting took place."

The colonel interrupted. "Deputy Sheriff Bud Light has already briefed me. A reporter named René Malarkey witnessed the entire event. He saw everything and took numerous pictures to back up his statements. His report is on the national news. Thankfully, there was no mention of you and Emily," the colonel acknowledged. "Bud Light explained that an older woman shot three gangsters in the parking lot outside the Fox and Hounds restaurant in self-defense. She did the police a big favor. All three shooting victims are malicious international fugitives wanted for previous crimes, including assault, robbery, kidnapping, and murder. The shooter has become an instant national celebrity, a Wisconsin legend, a role model for women, and a hero to national gun-rights advocacy groups and defenders of the Constitution. She was an armed bystander acting in self-defense. Nobody in the crowd can identify her. The driver that got away appears to be Bo-Bo Bigelow's bodyguard Burly. We assume he is the same individual that attempted to kill you in Nigeria. It's doubtful he'll ever return to this country again."

"When will you be arriving?"

"I'll be there at six o'clock sharp, as originally planned."

The lieutenant and Crystal reluctantly returned to the restaurant and waited in the parking lot. He cautiously parked his car beside Deputy Sheriff Bud Light's patrol car. Emily and Jay arrived a few minutes later as the last ambulance was pulling out of the parking lot. The rowdy crowd slowly diminished after being asked to disperse. The lieutenant and Emily eavesdropped as local police wrapped up the shooting incident investigation. Reporter René Malarkey was the primary witness. He was wildly animated and amusing, waving his arms in the air, pointing to the fresh pools of blood on the pavement, exaggerating events, and enthusiastically describing the actions of the participants.

The reporter used a tremendous number of adjectives to describe the female shooter. He was fascinated with the flowing curves of her figure, pondering what she looked like under her clothing, hoping to satisfy his curiosity. He claimed the little old lady was "going commando," running around without underwear. He seemed fascinated by the wobble and shake of the elegant swells beneath her dress. He failed to look at her face. He described her actions as very decisive. "She acted swiftly with great force and foresight like a heroic action figure moving with the rehearsed motion of a highly tuned Olympic athlete. She acted in self-defense without hesitation. She's a pistol-packing mama, a self-appointed vigilante, and a morally justified patriot," Bud Light offered, unaware that Emily was the woman in the blue dress.

No one noticed the similarities, even though Emily was standing in plain sight. She stood motionless, listening intensely to the debate as the reporter described how she had subdued the driver. "She handcuffed him, raised him over her head, and tossed him into the dumpster with the help of her cross-eyed husband. Ten minutes later, she innocently shot the other three victims in self-defense."

Emily quietly eased behind the lieutenant without being noticed. Secretly hoping he would forgive her sins, she made the sign of the cross and piously prayed for a pardon, penance, and absolution. Emily breathed a massive sigh of relief when no finger-pointing connections were forthcoming between the identity of the little old lady and herself. She was deeply conflicted, knowing that confession was the appropriate response. Conversely, she had only acted in self-defense—intentionally wounding rather than killing the three villains. She remained quiet, worried that others would think negatively about her. When the time was right, she would face the colonel's criticism with fortitude, but in her mind, it was far better to confess to the lieutenant privately.

The ambiance of the evening disappeared in an instant, shattered by the pulsing sound of a helicopter making a landing approach in an adjacent field. The main rotor blades produced a loud whirring blade-slap clatter as the pilot flared the aircraft's nose to the right to kill speed. The pilot precisely positioned the helicopter over the intended landing area. The plane hovered temporarily before descending in a cloud of dust. Colonel James Roberts briskly departed the plane with his head down to avoid being decapitated by the swirling rotor blades.

"Welcome, Colonel?" Dunning expressed, doing his best to conceal his agitated emotional state.

The colonel shook hands but concealed his emotions and tight-lipped his verbal response. He trivialized the small talk and withheld his opinions until all members were comfortably seated at the dining table.

Emily sat in a chair at the opposite end of the table to avoid direct eye contact. She ordered a double vodka martini to reduce her stress. "Make it dirty," she suggested. Alcohol was a powerful sedative and depressant. The first two sips eased her fears and took her mind off her troubles, helping her feel less shy, giving her a boost in mood, and making her feel somewhat relaxed.

The colonel unexpectedly opened the meeting with a toast. "Please raise your glasses. I want to praise Lieutenant Dunning and his assistant, Emily, for the wonderful job. Here's to their bravery, boldness, tenaciousness, and teamwork. Emily, you have been heroic. Thank you for all you have accomplished."

The applause that followed was sincere but modest.

The colonel's prepared remarks transitioned from his speech to a question-and-answer session as smoothly as if continuing the conversation. Numerous perspectives and opinions about recent events added to their understanding. Deputy Sheriff Bud Light talked the most prolonged and loudest, answering some of his questions before anyone else could respond. However, his memory and concentration seemed somewhat lacking, his conclusions and rationale disjointed, awkwardly presented, and confusing.

"What's next on the agenda?" the colonel asked.

The lieutenant was quick to respond. "Emily and I are planning to attend an art auction and fundraiser at Gravestone Castle this weekend sponsored by the Hermitage. A formal masquerade ball, an orphan camp picnic, and a memorial service for Father Cellophane will be an excellent time for us to observe the lifestyles of Father Feely and Father Adam Baum up close. It will be fascinating to see who shows up to purchase Father Marcello's 'priceless' paintings."

75

NATIONAL NEWS

Realizing this was a front-page story, the young reporter eagerly responded to numerous television reporters and late-night hosts. Malarkey continuously embellished and overstated the details. "There was a huge *brouhaha* at Fox and Hounds restaurant in Hubertus, Wisconsin," he loudly proclaimed. "A little old lady with no underwear beat up a felonious gangster driving a black Hummer. She and her cross-eyed husband tossed him into a dumpster full of garbage. A piece of raw liver stuck to his shirt. Then she shot three people in the parking lot. I captured the entire sequence of events with my camera. Wait until you see this," he exaggerated, making a drama out of a crisis.

Headline stories throughout the country were a smashing national success with tremendous audience ratings, and newspaper sales surged. The accompanying photographs were copyrighted and sold to magazines across the country, including several millennial smut e-publications in Canada, Germany, Mexico, Japan, and other foreign countries.

"It was total bedlam," René declared with amusement on every celebrity late-night talk show, eager to explain a firsthand account of the bizarre shootings. "The *Washington Post* offered me a job. My reporting is exactly the type of obscene smut headline reporting they prefer," he bragged. The precocious reporter puffed up his chest with pride, showing off his new T-shirt. On the front, there was a hilarious sketch of a man in handcuffs wearing a black beret, wide-eyed and peering out of a dumpster through a fog of coffee grounds and yellow kernels of corn. An image of Jack Daniels sitting on a toilet, screaming, was on the back.

"My latest sketch is going to be another bestseller," he predicted. "It's a picture of a braless eighty-year-old-woman waving a gun in the air after handcuffing a hot-tempered muscle man. The gray-haired older woman has become a Wisconsin legend, but nobody knows her name.

The police are still waiting for her to claim her reward for actions leading to capturing the three felons she shot. Concealed thigh holsters for women to be worn under short dresses are selling like hotcakes. All three of my T-shirts are bestsellers at Milwaukee Summerfest. Walmart is planning multiple Halloween costumes to commemorate these events. An action-drama movie at the Sundance film festival is sure to be a hit," he enthusiastically projected.

76

FUNDRAISER

Father Feely gleefully projected a substantial financial windfall from the planned art auction. "The mere mention of Father Marcello's collection of historical paintings in press releases will be enough to attract wealthy buyers. When the bidding gets furious in high society, it's exciting to watch the behavior and lifestyle of the elite. Seeing bidders with the highest level of wealth and social status battle it out with their bank accounts is certain to bring in an influx of cash to the Hermitage."

Sister Mary Pompino appeared bright and cheery with her vibrant auburn hair. She was fully engaged, aiming to get the most out of life. "I volunteer to decorate the castle with lots of fabric, fresh flowers, mood lighting, and candles for the masquerade ball and auction. The Great Room is spacious and ideal for hosting a Venetian ball, and the conference room is perfect for the auction. We will need a live band for classical musical entertainment, including a string quartet and a harpist, and a magician to entertain our guests throughout the evening."

Sister Olivia Seno Grande was radiantly glowing with excitement. "I'll wear my Lady Godiva costume with a gold mask and lots of feathers. Father Marcello will attract attention in an Italian Bauta mask, a black cape, and a black tricorn hat. It's an original costume from the glamorous traditions of the Italian Carnival in Venice that highlighted the worldly exploits of Casanova."

"A Bauta is no mere mask but rather a whole costume, aimed not only at hiding one's face but one's social status as well," Father Marcello enlightened them.

Joey Linguine capped the excitement by volunteering to host a fundraiser for orphans. Father Feely advocated for an afternoon memorial service. "It would be appropriate to honor Benedict Walker, Father Cellophane, the Mexican golf course worker killed by bees, Billy Big Ears Bellini, Bruno Greco, Dusty Rhodes, Johnny Linguine, and Jack Daniels."

Sisters Lola and Lova Kurvig offered to assist the bartender. "We can attest to the fact that alcohol makes men more wide-eyed and intense, bigger spenders, and less sluggish in bed."

The group hugging, initiated by the sexy twins at the end of the meeting, triggered a collective happiness phenomenon that spread like an emotional contagion.

Lieutenant Baron Dunning sat in a comfortable chair in his suite of rooms at Woebegone Dunes Resort. He spent the entire afternoon intensely perusing the Royal Enouement Society handbook discovered in Jack Daniels's cabin. The lieutenant thrived in ambiguous situations, synthesizing and memorizing all of the information collected during elicitation activities. His methods were similar to a business analyst putting the puzzle pieces together in a meaningful way to create understanding and consensus. He was so happy with the contents that a soliloquy formed in his mind. "Reading a good book is like having a conversation with the brightest people of the last thousand years. It's highly motivating and empowering—definitely a keeper—a masterly tale of how to be a helmsman and steer your ship into port by using mindfulness in positive ways to achieve worthwhile goals leading to happiness and peace of mind. From a scholarly standpoint, this rare Royal Enouement Society manuscript has more treasure and knowledge than a sunken pirate ship in the Caribbean Sea."

When he was tired of reading, he opened the custom invitation to the Hollywood-style extravaganza events hosted by the Hermitage. The gorgeous uncoated cardstock with a fine linen texture had an expensive look and feel synonymous with a formal wedding invitation. He placed the invitation under a halogen incandescent light for a closer examination. He sprayed watermark fluid on the paper out of habit to uncover any invisible trademarks, embedded codes, or undetected digital forensic data unique to each invitation. A faint, lingering sweet smell of perfume that impregnated in the paper unexpectedly permeated the room. A ghostly semitransparent apparition manifested itself before his eyes. He looked carefully through a magnifying glass to decipher the words "Carpe diem! The future depends on what you do today. Yesterday is gone. Drink in today. Cherish your solitude. Make each day count. Live as if you were going to die tomorrow."

The message written in Latin read like a headless decomposing body found on the side of the road on a dead-end street, confusing and unsettling. The meaning behind the words was clear, but the motive for placing a cryptic message hidden from view on the invitation was vague, inexplicit, and perplexing, implying a purposely concealed meaning.

As a prelude to a creative thinking episode, the lieutenant exhaled pipe tobacco smoke out of the nose to experience the pipe's complex aroma and flavor. "Inspiration occurs most often when the mind stops concentrating."

He shifted gears by turning his focus to the planned art auction at the Hermitage by amusing himself with the emotional power of art as an expression of human creativity, imagination, experimentation, and self-expression. "Art strongly correlates with higher achievement in reading and mathematics, creativity, social development, and self-worth, as well as money, power, and beauty, but it is not essential. Art has no intrinsic, objective, declarative set commercial value. Art ranges from the ridiculous to the sublime. The objective is to achieve uselessness while prattling endlessly in the intuitive language of aesthetics, without saying anything of importance. The value of art depends on provenance and history and the notoriety of previous owners. Art sold at auction greatly increases the prestige of the winner that takes all and creates envy for the losers. Father Marcello seems to be one of the winners."

77

MASQUERADE BALL

A team of workers, caterers, chefs, musicians, and entertainers was busy rearranging furniture, putting up decorations, rehearsing, and preparing for the big gala event at Gravestone Castle. Father Feely praised their efforts and said a short prayer in eager anticipation of an expected charitable financial windfall. Sister Olivia, extolling the virtues of the Hermitage as a praiseworthy charity, raised eyebrows as she let down her long dark hair. She was persuasively exciting the male workers in her long silky black robe, like a whore soliciting money for a Boy Scout jamboree. "Good girls go to heaven; bad girls go everywhere," she superficially reminded them with an unconventional quirky smile that set her apart from the others.

Father Adam Baum selected a Zorro mask with a black hat and cape. He looked like a masked superhero leading a double life. He was wearing a green sash and holding a whip and a slender sharp-pointed rapier sword used as a thrusting weapon. The Padre was paranoid, reluctant to expose the sanctity of the Hermitage's inner chambers to strangers— something never done before in the castle's history. He remained tight-lipped, outwardly twitchy, and overwrought with apprehension. He obsessive-compulsively worried about opening the ancient, fortified, elaborate iron entrance gate, exposing the inner courtyard to outsiders for the first time.

In due course, Father Feely declared, "Everything is finally in place. It's time to open the gates to the castle."

Johnny Linguine's brother Joey was the first to arrive in a white rental van with a missing hubcap and a dented left rear panel. Indiscriminately blocking the front entrance, he slammed close the driver's side door, which was slightly out of kilter. He threw open the back double doors of the van to let everyone out. Without consulting the others, Joey took the initiative to add some entertainment to liven up the party. He hired three little female people to sing.

"They are famous for bringing their urban Motown sound to the stage as a tribute band to the Singing Supremes.

I couldn't find a magician, but I was able to find a homeless organ grinder," he informed the congregants.

An uncontrollable rambunctious monkey with a cleft lip and a runny nose appeared in the back of the van. It was annoying everyone by boisterously jumping up and down, banging a tin cup on the back of their heads. The monkey bolted out of the truck the second the rear doors opened, chattering a complex repertoire of sounds indicating annoyance, excitement, and freedom to explore. A toothless, unshaven organ grinder wearing a thirty-nine-dollar Walmart tuxedo costume jacket covered by a tattered overcoat grabbed his baggy pants, took a stance, and did the old soft shoe across the lawn before capturing the monkey with a butterfly net.

Joey gave each of the three female little people wearing glamorous tight-fitting gold and silver sparkling stage gowns a big hug, a kiss between the breasts, and a sexy pat on the behind before lifting them out of the van one by one. "I'm setting you girls up in the rumpus room next to the big-screen television and pool table," he declared. "I'll make sure you get plenty to eat and drink."

The driver raised the blinds on a chartered luxury bus as he drove through the massive iron entrance gates leading into the interior courtyard of Gravestone Castle. Sister Olivia wore a skin-colored one-piece spandex Lady Godiva birthday suit, a long blond wig, and a golden mask. She made a grand entrance on horseback riding through two parallel rows of flaming torches perched on wooden posts. Sitting astride a white horse decorated with long purple ribbons and a twisted unicorn horn, she drew everyone's attention.

Excitement was in her voice as she hailed the crowd. "Ladies and gentlemen, welcome to the Hermitage at Gravestone Castle. A warm welcome of friendship is yours. May you experience great joy, acquire many fond memories, and experience a superb evening filled with jubilation and great pleasure. This night is for you. The band is playing, and the castle is open. We expect you to have a wonderful evening." The guests were highly impressed with the bodacious entrance experience. They marveled at the mythical white unicorn she was riding, her sexy costume, and her extraordinary welcome speech.

Heavenly classical harp music in the antechamber room enticed the guests to enter the castle through the front entrance. They flowed into Benedict Hall, a great room with rock walls and an arched cathedral ceiling with multiple chandeliers. Father Marcello added excitement by simulating a formal red carpet experience by announcing each guest individually. "Lieutenant Baron Dunning in the black velvet tuxedo jacket is escorting Crystal Glass, wearing a black and gold mesh gown with floral appliqué embroidery, high-low silhouette, and sweetheart neckline," he announced proudly with a wink and a bow. "Next, we have Jay Walker, the former owner of Gravestone Castle, in an impeccably cut elegant navy tuxedo jacket with Hollywood glamour. His date, Emily, wears a royal blue lace off-the-shoulder gown with appliqués and a plunging neck."

"Welcome to the Hermitage at Gravestone Castle," Father Marcello expressed in a profoundly seductive, masculine voice with an Italian accent. He looked proud and self-assured. He inappropriately touched, hugged, kissed, and whispered lewd, sexually explicit comments to every female guest, suggesting a wide range of stiff alcoholic drinks.

Lieutenant Dunning admired the way Crystal carried herself. "Masks and costumes provide favorable opportunities for a woman to let her virtues and respectability slip. A mask is a pretense and a disguise that outwardly expresses the covert character of the person behind the cloak. This façade veils the true feelings and bitter taste of one's true personality.

"Father Marcello wore the Bauta costume, a most effective disguise belonging to the upper class and usually worn only by the main characters in theatrical dramas. The uniform was popularized by the Italian adventurer Giacomo Casanova from the Republic of Venice. He was made famous because of his complicated and elaborate love affairs with passionate women and subsequent arrest for affronting religion and common decency. Casanova was a disreputable rogue. Father Marcello plays the role of Casanova in a way that is lavishly expressive and naturally impressive. He's lax in his morals and addicted to every kind of dissolute living, don't you think?"

"He looks generous and delighted with himself," Crystal asserted, shamelessly casting her eyes on the prominent bulge in his tight-fitting black elastic tights.

A Spanish-speaking waiter directed them to the bar. He was a height-challenged illegal alien on roller skates with Napoleonic tendencies in bed, standing head-high behind the bar. He was wearing a Bucky Badger uniform, the official mascot of the University of Wisconsin. His arms and legs were much too short for the uniform. He ludicrously encouraged the three Supremes tribute singers to drink tequila. "It fights dementia, helps you lose weight, and kills coronavirus. One tequila, two tequila, three tequila, floor . . . "

The bartenders were a pair of conjoined Siamese twins attached at the hip named Lewis and Clark. Lewis was moody and fraught with severe emotional problems, including unpredictable bouts of distress and bad-tempered sullenness. He wore a French beret, talking to his poodle and nibbling on frog legs. Clark was a natural frontiersman and explorer who enjoyed wearing a hunting knife in his belt and a coonskin hat with a long bushy tail. "We only serve doubles, double your fun and double your pleasure in half the time," they stated in unison.

All eyes turned as the pope, upright and regal with a graceful stature and a compelling gaze, advanced toward the audience. "Hey, it's Father Feely disguised as the pope," Joey Linguine observed excitedly. Father Feely seemed to float on air as he moved toward the center of the crowd. He wore a white robe with an embroidered sash, a golden ceremonial scarf, red pope shoes with gold lace trim, and an ivory-colored pointed papal miter hat. He held out his hands with the palms open and smiled warmly. He elevated his arms to gather attention and quiet the audience, raised the cordless microphone to his lips, and formally addressed the crowd.

"To our esteemed guests, patrons of the arts, dignitaries, celebrities, philanthropists, athletes, scholars, fans, and everyone attending tonight, I offer you an appreciative welcome. On behalf of my brethren and sisters at the Hermitage, I wish you all a friendly salutation. The flags are flying. The balloons are ready for release. It's shaping up as a great evening, a memorable event that we've all been planning with great anticipation. We are going to have a merry and enjoyable time together. Ladies and gentlemen, tonight we have stars in the sky and onstage."

An orchestra divided into families of instruments with precise timing quietly filled the hall with a relaxed ambiance. The crowd reacted positively to a soothing classical soliloquy arranged by the orchestra.

Lieutenant Dunning displayed a broad smile indicating approval of the performers.

The voices of the Singing Supremes unexpectedly shattered the ambiance of a quiet interlude with "You Can't Hurry Love," "Come See about Me," and "Back in My Arms Again."

"Damn it, where the hell is that music coming from?" Father Feely was accidentally overheard muttering directly into the microphone. Carrying on with his remarks after the unexpected, chaotic distraction, he continued, "This is a superb happening, fit for royalty, and that's what you are to us. The auction room is now open for viewing."

78

THE AUCTION

The crowd was enticed into the auction room by an elegantly dressed sister nun trainee in a seductive satiny black evening gown with extreme cleavage, a slit leg opening, and famous starched "Flying Nun" head-wear. Standing beside her was her date, Ben Dover, the rookie backup kicker for the Green Bay Packer football team. Positioned between them on table number one was a large diamond-studded Green Bay Packer Super Bowl ring elegantly displayed on a white pedestal covered with a bolt of green silk cloth.

Emily seized on the perfect opportunity to interview Ben Dover. "Did you know Father Cellophane?" she inquired.

"Yes, ma'am," he responded with sass and excitement. "I knew him very well. He was a great athletic supporter. I sold him a six-pack of yellow speedo jammers containing two skintight stretchy Dancing Pants and two Prancing Johnny string thongs with the elastic pouch, one pair of Struttin' Stevies endorsed by the USC marching band, and one pair of Pinocchio Spanky spandex bum covers. He sent me a couple of autographed snapshots of himself sitting on a Linguine Brothers Sports Bar and Grill barstool wearing his yellow speedos. I posted them in the locker room at Lambeau Field."

Jay and Emily continued circumnavigating the auction room in awe of the semi-precious artworks and antiques for sale. Jay was shocked by the sight of a few of his mother's prized possessions for sale in the auction. "The rare green emerald and diamond antique brooch set in gold belonged to my mother. The Hermitage should not have ownership of possessions that were my rightful inheritance. They are profiting from the sale of items deceitfully obtained."

Three antique paintings owned by Father Marcello on display in the front of the room roused Emily's curiosity. "Each image has an illusion of reality, wonderfully detailed and precisely accurate. The subject matter is unembellished and depicted with great skill and care, honest representations of historical settings with excellent composition."

The black-tie, buttoned-up crowd settled into their seats to begin the formal bidding. The setting reminded Emily of an art auction in the movies, a high-end carnival act at Sotheby's London attended by millionaires. As the sleazy barker auctioneer, Joey Linguine kept up a constant patter of "I have one hundred thousand dollars. Do I hear two hundred?" Father Marcello's paintings sold for much more than anticipated. The audience enjoyed the pleasure of watching the equivalent of a small nation's GDP traded for some colored oils on cloth.

Lieutenant Dunning paid close attention to three wily bidders from Nigeria, London, and Hong Kong. He discretely forwarded pictures of the three unique bidders to Colonel James Roberts for real-time analysis and processing at the central hub of the Pentagon. "They are cunning individuals willing to use tricks to achieve an aim, clever persons of intelligence with high situational awareness of potential outcomes and scenarios and the people around them with all of the drama of a made-for-television investigation."

Colonel Roberts was thrilled with the results, and his response was encouraging and positive. "International investigations of this sort are a delicate business. The crimes of privileged individuals within the context of legitimate corporations and government offices frequently go undetected and unpunished due to the perpetrators' power, status, and political influence. The information you have provided provokes new lines of inquiry into securities fraud, embezzlement, corporate fraud, and money laundering. All three individuals have direct links to Bo-Bo Bigelow from Nigeria. Each individual represents an important branch of their company Ebony LLC: oil embezzlement, stolen rare-earth minerals, and Swiss banking."

79

MONKEY BUSINESS

The crowd dispersed toward the main auditorium in small groups to continue with the planned events when the auction ended. The scruffy tone-deaf organ grinder with messy hair wore a baggy jacket with deep pockets; he was an unfortunate representative of the lower class. His large barrel organ perched on a crooked wooden leg was out of tune, and the man lacked any sense of rhythm.

The nervous little white-headed Capuchin monkey sitting on his shoulder was wearing a bright red nutcracker-soldier marching band jacket with epaulets, a slanted gold banner, and black trim with a rimless silky black hat. The monkey disappeared under the elegantly decorated gourmet appetizer table draped with an ivory-colored linen tablecloth. Reaching blindly above his head, he stealthily dragged a wedge of choc-olate-covered banana across the tablecloth, leaving an unsightly brown stain. He sucked the coating off a banana and spat the entire gooey mess into the palm of his hand. He indiscriminately tossed the mushy glob of half-eaten chocolate banana across the room over the heads of the crowd.

A woman in the back of the room was randomly struck squarely in the face by the glutinous glob of vegetable matter. When she attempted to scrape the gluey substance off her forehead, the wet projectile streaked her eyeliner as it sunk deeper into her dignified hairpiece. The crowd in the back of the room watched in horror as globs of moist, sticky banana dripped down her forehead into her eyes. The shock of being rudely struck in the face by a mushy half-chewed chocolate banana missile came as a complete surprise. She accidentally spilled her pink cosmopolitan served in a chilled martini glass in her lap. She was mortified and shamed by the pink stain it left on her elegant white gown, which appeared to be a blood spatter.

The monkey heisted the lieutenant's favorite full-bend tobacco pipe out of his coat pocket. Crystal attempted to grab his tail, but he escaped. He jumped on the back of a dark-green velvet wing chair, where he casually taunted the lieutenant by pretending to smoke it.

"Hey, give me my pipe back, you harelip son of an ape—stop putting my pipe in your mouth," he hollered. The toothless, unshaven organ grinder took the lieutenant's pipe out of the monkey's mouth, wiped the excess chocolate saliva on his sleeve, and politely returned it to the lieutenant.

Chronically needing a cigarette and a hit of nicotine, the organ grinder stepped outside. Easing into the backseat of Joey's white van for a smoke, he poured himself an oversize Texas tumbler of Troubadour Whiskey.

Joey Linguine and his younger brother, Jimmy, slipped outside nefariously to rummage through the limousines and charter buses in the courtyard to see what they could steal. Joey was wearing a skintight bright-red fancy bullfighter maestro costume with lacy gold trim, a professional bullfighter's black hat, white knee socks, and black shoes. His brother wore a torero matador Spanish bullfighter fancy black suit with a red cape. "There's nothing of value to steal, other than a large bag of Skittles lying on the front seat of a black stretch limousine."

They were startled by a menacing whistling sound descending from the heavens. A frightening chunk of yellow, blue, and brown ice crashed through the roof of Joey's white rental van like an all-weather, long-range Tomahawk missile. A tremendous explosion occurred on impact with the top of the truck. Joey threw open the back doors to assess the damage. With only one breath, a pungent whiff of urine overcame him. The impact from a human waste meteor had blown a three-foot-diameter hole in the roof of the van. The giant ball of frozen lavatory excrement had exploded into hundreds of chunks of yellow and brown icy slush. Oily stains covered the light-gray carpet and interior walls of the van.

The organ grinder was disheveled. The giant ball of ice knocked his hat off, dented his forehead, broke his collar bone, and dislocated his shoulder. Blood dripped from his forehead, and his left eye was swollen shut. The injury to his brain caused him to speak with a hodgepodge English accent. "Take good care of my monkey and organ," he implored Joey, simulating the death rattle with his last gurgling breath before passing out from a concussion.

The mysterious explosion drew a small group of spectators outside to see what the excitement was all about. The crowd peered curiously into the back of the van to assess the extent of the damage. "A 'poop bomb' of frozen human lavatory excrement waste hit him in the head. Sewerage seeping out of the drain tanks in a malfunctioning commercial aircraft toilet fell from the sky midflight. Someone better call an ambulance. A meteor of frozen sludge and urine bombed Joey's rental van and wounded the unfortunate organ grinder," a retired airline pilot exclaimed.

The crowd was horrified by the egregious smell of the van's interior and the sight of the elderly gentleman with a bruised, bloody skull.

Drunken guests heavily sedated from drinking old-fashioned brandy cocktails began milling around, unsteady, staggering, laughing, and acting foolishly.

While the crowd outside fiddled irresponsibly with trivial matters in the face of an emergency, a female guest standing beside the snack table in the auction room reached across the table for a chocolate-covered strawberry. The sleeve on her evening gown brushed against a lighted candle. Her dress made of highly flammable material burst into surface flash flames as the outermost fiber material caught fire. Hot flames spread quickly, melting the fabric to her skin. Bystanders impulsively threw their drinks at her to put out the fire. Alcohol caused her heart to race and her eyes to burn. A chorus of ear-piercing screams sent fear through the crowd, attracting everyone in the immediate vicinity. The horrifying spectacle of a lady helplessly set on fire triggered group paralysis. The lieutenant returned to the main hall just in time to see the initial flash fire and hear the chorus of screams. He instinctively forced his way through the crowd, grabbing the punch bowl with both hands as he passed by. He poured the ice-cold liquid onto her head, showering her with juice to douse the flames. Multiple orange peels haphazardly dangled from her towering bouffant hair arrangement. A cluster of red cherries and grapes filled the top of her plunging neckline, amplifying the size of her abnormally large breasts.

"Stop! You're waterboarding me. I can't breathe," she cried out indignantly.

The restless monkey was a retired military combatant veteran with two tours in Afghanistan and a trained pickpocket of significant experience. He clicked his heels together and saluted a woman before reaching into her purse and heisting her iPhone. He randomly pushed buttons until making a FaceTime connection with the US president during a cabinet meeting. The monkey picked his nose and pretended to sing like Elvis Presley. In a clear case of monkey-see-monkey-do, he randomly texted gibberish, accidentally spelling out the message "WTF PU 911!"

"What a ludicrous clown, an entertainer, trying to be funny, a stupid monkey acting like a ridiculous buffoon," the president exclaimed with amusement.

When the monkey tired of texting the president, he haphazardly tossed the smartphone on the floor. The phone slid under a lady's miniskirt face up, where it continued to broadcast live-action video on the large-screen television at the president's cabinet meeting. The monkey impulsively changed his mind, jumping off the wingback chair and rudely pushing a lady backward to retrieve the cell phone. His crazy antics left the president completely baffled about what would happen next. He swiftly texted the monkey back "KUTGW" ("Keep up the good work").

The trigger-happy monkey impetuously swigged down Sister Olivia's brandy Manhattan before running around in eccentric circles, giving the crowd the middle finger. A few guests laughed hysterically, joyously filling the monkey's tin cup with hundred-dollar bills, assuming that his obnoxious behavior was part of the planned entertainment. He continued randomly pressing buttons until a wealthy widow from Sheboygan answered. The monkey held the camera up in the air to expose the crowd's faces while energetically running around in circles like a whirling dervish. When the lady on the other end of the telephone screamed, the monkey tossed the cell phone to conjoined twin bartenders Lewis and Clark. Lewis protected his face with his hand and ducked, and Clark assuredly grabbed it in midair with the other hand.

"An impetuous pip-squeak monkey engaging in ridiculous shenanigans made this audacious phone call." The explanation further stressed the nervous lady when she saw two strange talking heads speaking simultaneously.

The party was rudely interrupted by the approaching sound of a police siren with blue and red flashing lights. Deputy Sheriff Bud Light slid his car into the parking lot, with local reporter René Malarkey tailgating closely behind. The fenders of both cars clicked and then interlocked together as they came to an abrupt halt behind Joey's white rental van. "I'm here to investigate a malicious act of domestic terrorism—the bombing of an American-made Dodge van and the murder of an elderly navy veteran."

"What kind of bomb was it?" René Malarkey asked curiously.

"A huge 'poop bomb' falling from an airplane toilet blew a horrendous hole in the roof of Joey's van and killed the organ grinder," someone shouted.

"I think a UFO crashed," a retired science professor professed.

René Malarkey was eager to capture the police investigation on film. He was wearing a yellow T-shirt with a sketch of Emily in her eighty-year-old disguise shooting three villains in the Fox & Hounds restaurant parking lot. The three Singing Supremes tribute band singers eagerly complied when the reporter asked them to pose for pictures beside the van. The flashy sequin dresses alternately sparked red and blue, reflecting the emergency strobe light bar. Their melodious voices and seductive dance moves attracted a crowd as the trio burst into song.

The crowd trepidatiously moved closer to view the putrid-smelling van with the rough opening in the roof to determine the extent of the damage. The deputy sheriff filled a plastic bag with fragments of frozen urine and feces with his bare hands to preserve the evidence. "I'll take these pieces of evidence home and put them in my refrigerator for future scientific analysis," he proclaimed with due diligence.

An intoxicated man claiming to be a first responder forced the victim's shoulder back into the socket with the crude brutality of a professional wrestler. He taped the broken collar bone down with camouflage duct tape. He placed the organ grinder's arm in a sling made from Father Adam Baum's green sash, leaving the Padre holding his whip in one hand and his sword in the other. The doctor retrieved a large piece of smelly yellow ice from Bud Light's evidence bag and taped it to the older man's forehead to reduce the swelling above the eye. A bluish yellow liquid saturated the head bandage and dripped drown the victim's cheek as the ice began to melt.

Emily gasped in a fit of nervousness before emotionally unloading. "Why is there a hole in the roof of this van? The van smells like a men's urinal. Who is this older man with a bloody face with a bandage around his head? I've never heard of a frozen airplane 'poop bomb.' I think I'm going to vomit. This whole incident is chaotic—I'm so damn bumfuzzled, flustered, and confused. The idea of poop bombs indiscriminately falling from the sky gives me the heebie-jeebies. I feel like I'm going to have a panic attack. How far is the nearest hospital?"

"Hospitals are the only place where the word 'positive' causes dismay and alarm. They feed you Jell-O, white bread, and apple sauce and kick you out of your bed before you are well. Still, they won't let you go home until the computer allows it—at least nursing homes keep you there until you're dead," Deputy Sheriff Bud Light offered.

80

BOWEL OBSTRUCTION

The masquerade ball and auction provided a substantial financial windfall for the Hermitage. Sister Olivia planned an elegant commemorative celebration brunch for the following morning. She rushed in with some terrible news. "Father Feely died last night due to a bowel obstruction. He ate some unripe persimmons from China that caused his mouth to pucker. He developed a bezoar, a solid mass of indigestible material accumulating in the digestive tract, resulting in intestinal blockage and fatal, life-threatening complications. He became ill suddenly, and resuscitation was not successful. According to proctologist Dr. Seymour Fecal, Father Feely developed a toxic megacolon. It became dangerously distended due to abnormal dilation of the colon followed by a paralysis of the peristaltic movements of the bowel. Pressure built up, and his feces became overly hard and impacted. The bowel ruptured, leaking harmful intestinal contents and bacteria into his abdominal cavity."

Emily was startled by the suddenness of Father Feely's passing and the unconventional reason for his demise. Exasperated by the news, she threw her hands in the air. She rolled her eyes to express superciliousness, disbelief, and irony. "And now we have two more bizarre deaths to investigate and a lady that caught her dress on fire that has nothing to do with our original reason for being here in the first place. I never heard of a bezoar or poop-bomb before yesterday."

Lieutenant Dunning tugged on his earlobes. He stumbled at rationalizing the situation, knowing that Father Feely's felonious connection with Bo-Bo Bigelow was the primary reason for the investigation. "Father Feely's untimely death catches us off guard and leaves us with a vacancy and a dilemma about what to do next. Perhaps it's time to disband the Procol Harum investigative team."

Deputy Sheriff Bud Light interrupted. "Don't expect Dr. Fecal to solve your problems for you. He spends most of his time drinking shots of Old Troubadour whiskey. He hangs out with broken-hearted fools and hustlers singing country karaoke tunes at Linguine Brothers Sports Bar and Grill. He only has one eye and sings with a lisp. His glass eye is the one always looking to the left. He claims that a doctor only needs one eye to see through a colonoscopy scope. Most of his colonoscopy patients need at least three days of recovery in the hospital. Every Halloween, he hands out free instructional videos demonstrating how to provide a stool-based sample for the poop-in-a-box colorectal test."

The lieutenant ignored the deputy's indiscreet remarks. "Father Feely was an important person—the bereaved will have many ghosts to contend with. His death is a reminder of the importance of healthy gut flora that's high in friendly bacteria essential for overall health. Healthy intestines are important to combat the harmful effects of alcohol," the lieutenant counseled while pondering the significance of the situation. "Every investigative strategy needs to adjust to reality eventually. Death rides hard and fast when it brings its news of mortality, leaving us confused and unsure of our bearings as we flail about in the wake of its passing. Everything familiar becomes illusionary. The prologue to death is emotional suffering, downheartedness, and infirmity."

Deputy Sheriff Bud Light flippantly heisted one of the delicious-looking pepperoni sticks and popped it into his mouth.

"Father Feely had been self-treating with garlic clove suppositories in the rectum before going to bed to treat anal parasites. His feisty warning signs were anal itching, burning, and discharge. He had previously tried jalapeño suppositories from Mexico, but they were much too hot.

The suppository you put in your mouth is from a wet market in Wuhan, China. They helped Father Feely relax, but he said they made his bum burn."

"Tastes like crap!" the deputy shrieked as he made a horrible face and spat the entire mouthful into the wastebasket. His petulant behavior reminded Emily of a dog choking on a bone.

"Father Feely's eulogy will be lengthy and complex. He is a legendary figure in West Africa. He was very effective at promoting neo-colonialism, the practice of using capitalism, globalization, and cultural imperialism to influence developing countries instead of direct military or political control."

Sister Mary Pompino, with the radiant auburn hair, cheerfully volunteered to take charge of the funeral arrangements. "Your enthusiasm for planning extravaganza gala events, marching band parades, and fundraisers is boundless," Sister Olivia remarked.

"Let's stop gossiping and fiddle-farting around and turn this memorial service into a whiz-bang production."

"Time is of the essence," Sister Olivia agreed. "Be sure to include details about the time and location of the funeral service. But don't get snitty, huffing and puffing, throwing your weight around, and making good use of your lower lip."

"Father Feely was the glorious leader of the Hermitage at Gravestone Castle and the wealthy owner of the international Heritage Endowment Fund. I will begin by writing his obituary, giving a biographical sketch outlining important events in his life, emphasizing his positive qualities and generous charitable contributions."

"Be sure to include some photos," Sister Olivia added. "Try to find one where he's not holding a glass of wine. We should plan to host a hospitality event after the memorial service to honor Father Feely's main financial contributors. It may be our last chance to squeeze one last donation from them, and we should let them know that we will always hold a special space in our hearts for his friends and followers."

"We should hold the memorial service concurrent with the orphan camp picnic on Sunday afternoon. There will be lots of people in attendance and plenty of food, and it's the best chance to get everyone together on short notice," Sister Mary advocated.

"I'll ask Father Marcello to lead the memorial service."

Emily was soft on Sister Mary Pompino. "You have so much spunk and enthusiasm. I admire the way you assume control."

As soon as they got back to the car, Emily unzipped her emotional baggage and unloaded its entire contents. She was feeling overwhelmed by a rare state of pointless apoplexy. "The thought of analyzing another ludicrous and meaningless death during the ill-fated Operation Procol Harum investigation leaves me speechless. Emotional exasperation is causing me to lose consciousness. I'm feeling lonely and depressed, emotionless and hardboiled. The appalling, odious death of Father Feely epitomizes the meaning of the word *sad*. His suspicious, freaky, off-the-wall death leaves me feeling a whiter shade of pale. A lady's dress caught on fire at the masquerade ball. Frozen lavatory waste falling from the sky nearly killed the organ grinder. What's going to happen to his monkey?"

"Incontinence causes pathological laughter and crying out of proportion to the underlying mood. Exaggerated and tempestuous emotional outbursts are highly annoying to others. Facial expressions are involuntary, followed by pathological crying and laughing and wetting your pants. I hope that's not what you're experiencing," the lieutenant rationalized.

"I feel like wet firewood; there's no spark."

"It's impossible to be burned out unless you used to be on fire."

"I accepted this assignment to become the finest version of myself, hoping to achieve my goal of landing a high-paying job as a professional accountant with a top accounting firm. I never expected to be associated with a naked priest struck in the eye by a golf ball, a golfer blown into smithereens by exploding fireworks, or a resort owner electrocuted on a toilet. Killer bees chased an illegal alien over a cliff. A pilot lost his airplane and his life. Dusty Rhodes was covered in turds and shot in the neck by a bolt fired from a crossbow. Father Cellophane is a fiberglass statue, and Father Feely died from a bowel obstruction. My résumé is a joke—not the type of experience most accounting firms expect to see on a top-quality, professionally written CV formatted for success."

"I know that you may be feeling powerless during these times. Events such as these often color our worldview. Nobody expects to be killed by a frozen poo projectile jettisoned from an aircraft. It's important to internally process your feelings and let go of negative repeating thoughts. Working on your self-esteem and having space and time to figure things out will help you the most. Take all the time you need to clear your head," the lieutenant advised.

"I feel like I'm carrying a backpack full of troubles and emotions, living in the valley of the unconcerned. I've only been in Wisconsin a short time, and I'm already feeling sorry for myself."

"It's easy to succumb to your difficulties and retreat into the safety of your comfort zone. It would help if you learned to muster the strength and courage to move forward. You need to create a pattern of resistance where you struggle to see things clearly and objectively to gain a clearer picture of the situation, or you will wilt under pressure."

"My sincere opinions aren't easy to let go, but you make a good point. I can see that there are moments when it's beneficial to step back, to release all attachment and gain a proper perspective of the situation."

"Our investigation of Father Feely and his felonious exploits may soon be drawing to a close, albeit without certitude, declaration of guilt, or judgment," the lieutenant predicted. "By the time you are ready to apply for a job with a top accounting firm, your name will have already been widely circulated on a national basis. It's hard to beat a twisted ending for pure entertainment value. Suppose you bring the characters and conflicts to life in your résumé. In that case, your future employer and readers will care to know how everything worked out in the end. They will feel something when knowing which characters succeeded and who failed. You will become instantly famous if people find out you are the eighty-year-old gunslinger who wounded three people in the parking lot of a restaurant in Wisconsin. You could run for Congress. From that perspective, your résumé will stand out from all the rest and give readers a surprising jolt."

81

ORPHAN CAMP PICNIC

Joey's eyes twinkled. "An orphan camp picnic is planned as a great way of demonstrating public charity toward Christian children and the perfect way to showcase the Hermitage—and make some easy money. My standard finder's fee for matching a child with a prospective set of adoptive parents is ten thousand dollars."

"How will you distribute the funds you raise?" Emily wanted to know.

"I will donate a percent of the funds to the orphanage, minus my administrative fee that usually runs about ninety percent. A dodgeball tournament will be one of the highlighted events. The adults will be encouraged to bet on the winners."

Guests began arriving precisely on time. Joey threw open the main entrance gate and directed everyone where to park. The first rowdy ruffian off the bus immediately caught everyone's attention. He appeared to be about ten years old. He wore blue jeans, a tight-fitting white T-shirt, and a red University of Wisconsin baseball cap with a large white logo. His brown hair was overly long and combed back in a swooping ducktail. He was muscular and tall for his age. Joey Linguine was astonished at how much the boy had grown recently.

"Hello, Meatball! It's me, Uncle Joey," he hollered.

"This is Polpetta, Father Cellophane's kid. The police tricked Father

Cellophane into taking a paternal DNA test, and it matched with this boy. Social Services took him away from his mother because she was only a teenager when Polpetta was born. He recently formed a rock and roll band, and he has already written four songs: 'One-Eyed Trouser Mouse,' 'Pie-Eyed Patty Cake,' 'Hersey Squirts,' and 'Moonlight, Lace, and Sweat.'"

Polpetta turned his eyes toward the most attractive little girl in the crowd before making an astonishing pronouncement. "I hope you don't scream as much as the last girl I kissed. When you look out your window tonight, you might catch a glimpse of me. Don't worry; I'm not going to murder you."

The frightened little girl ran back to the bus and reached for Sister Olivia's hand. "I don't want to play with Polpetta—he scares me."

"Don't worry about him. He's a good athlete, and he will make a good partner for you in the three-legged sack race. There are many nice prizes, so you will want to have a good partner."

The famous racing sausages from Milwaukee Park—Bratwurst, Polish, Italian, Hot Dog, and Chorizo—kicked off the big charity fundraiser for orphans. "I bet ten bucks on the Italian sausage to win," Polpetta announced with confidence. He intentionally stuck his foot out and tripped the bratwurst, causing him to fall flat on his face ten feet from the finish line. The crowd reacted wildly and laughed hysterically. The Italian sausage ran somewhat erratically due to poor visibility. Nevertheless, he squeaked across the finish line in first place after deliberately stepping on the poor victim's head.

The injured party's head twisted around inside the bratwurst costume, making it impossible to see through the eyeholes. "Help! It's dark in here, and I can't see."

His Bavarian lederhosen suspender snapped loose from his pants. The metal buckle whipped into the crotch of the man in the hot dog costume. He tumbled to the ground writhing in pain, struggling and groveling around with frantic twisting contorted motions like a snake writhing out of the bushes.

"Always keep your wienerschnitzel above your lederhosen," Joey hollered.

The dazed chaperones stuffed in the racing sausage costumes covered with dust and grass stains smelled like vomit. "Help! Three of us puked inside our costumes. Get these damn helmets off us."

Polpetta calmly picked up a grapefruit-sized rock and casually heaved it blindly over the outer perimeter wall. The crowd heard a metallic thump as the rock landed on the hood of a red all-terrain Rolls-Royce Cullinan SUV parked on the shady side of the rock wall.

Polpetta turned his attention to the other children as he reached across the picnic table to swipe Joey's beer. "This West Coast style IPA beer from Bent Barley Brewing Company in Arora, Colorado, is delicious." He took three large swigs and spat a mouthful of beer into another little boy's ear. "It's okay. He's deaf; he can't hear," he explained to the other kids.

Joey cautiously approached the most promising-looking couple in the group sitting in the shade of a large oak tree. "If you're thinking of adopting a child, this is going to be the best day of your life. Just look around and see which kid appeals to you the most. Then, for ten thousand dollars, I can do all of the paperwork for you."

A neatly dressed, attractive young girl with dimples and white teeth politely spoke to several other prospective parents. "We are thinking about adopting a little girl, someone similar to that cute little girl with brunette pigtails over there."

Realizing that this couple was genuinely interested in adopting a child, Joey reached into his hip pocket and filled their glasses with whiskey from his flask. "Kids are like puppies—you should always take the one that comes to you first," Joey encouraged.

After having ferreted out the prettiest mothers and the couples with the most incredible wealth and the most expensive cars, Polpetta set out to aggressively conduct his interviews. He held his red baseball hat deceptively and humbly in his hands. With the utmost grace, politeness, respectful behavior, and consideration of others, he approached the couple from New Jersey with a contrite heart.

"Hello. My name is Polpetta Cellophane. How do you like me so far?" Projecting confidence and self-assuredness, Polpetta looked the husband forcefully in the eye and firmly shook his hand before reciting his prepared self-promoting marketing speech. "Given the right opportunity and environment, I'm certain I can become a positive, productive member of society and a proud member of your family and community. I always put others first. My preference is to be close to a library and a good parish church. Moreover, I'm sure I could pass muster if an attractive couple such as yourselves would approve of me as adequate and satisfactory."

After which he smiled warmly and greeted the man's glamorous wife by gently snuggling his face between her breasts, entwining his arms around her narrow waist, patting her fanny, and giving her a warm fuzzy embrace. "I would love to have you for my mother," he encouraged roguishly.

She was very impressed.

"Polpetta left us with very positive feelings," the wife was happy to report to Joey. "Polpetta seems like a very positive, polite, and ambitious young man. He touched our hearts today, and he might be a perfect match for us. Unfortunately, we have never had children, and we have no benchmarks for measuring expectations or achievement."

"Oh, you'll never be sorry if you choose him. He's very mature for his age, and he'll be ready and eager to drive your Rolls-Royce Cullinan SUV before you know it."

82

POISON HONEY

Polpetta enticed the little girl with the brunette pigtails to walk with him behind the garage. "Let's go exploring."

They continued wandering around Gravestone Castle until they discovered a large glass greenhouse isolated from the other buildings. "Look!" Polpetta said in astonishment, running across the lawn. "The greenhouse contains many flowers and thousands of bees." He tapped on the window with his knuckles and peered inside. When his face touched the glass, thousands of angry killer bees tried to sting him. He was tempted to break a few windows in the greenhouse just for fun but held back due to the fear of being stung.

There was a storage building in back of the greenhouse with a sign on the door that said "Danger—Keep Out." Polpetta removed a small tool from his lockpicking kit and inserted it into the keyhole. After several twists and turns, the lock opened.

"There's nothing but shelves of gooey honey inside," he remarked disappointedly. He grabbed a jar from the middle shelf, unscrewed the lid, stuck his pointer finger deep into the honeypot, and pushed it into the little girl's mouth. "Here, suck this."

"That's good honey," she exclaimed with glee, waving both hands in the air and wiggling her ears. "My face is all sticky now."

Polpetta had no trouble picking the lock on a gray government-issued metal cabinet in the corner. "More jars of honey," he exclaimed. "I never saw so damn much sweet honey."

"What does that sign say?"

"'Poison honey.'" He examined one of the jars to see if it looked or smelled different from the regular honey. Then, showing a fondness for causing trouble, he mischievously peeled the label off the poison jar of honey. He transposed it onto one of the regular jars before exchanging the container in the cabinet for the one on the shelf.

"What's the difference? They both look the same to me."

"Don't tell anybody. We could get in big trouble."

On the way out the door, Polpetta noticed a bright red gas valve labeled "Greenhouse Furnace, Do Not Touch." He took off his red baseball hat and set it on the laboratory sink before taking hold of the gas valve with both hands and wrenching it all the way open. Then, with no more mischief to create, he grabbed the girl by the hand and returned to the picnic. "I thought you were going to kiss me? I like kissing," she remarked in dismay.

"I prefer older women. Why don't you put some of this honey on your lips and see if one of the other boys wants to kiss you?" Polpetta explained while stuffing a bratwurst and bun into his mouth. "I wish we had these brats at the orphanage," he remarked grotesquely with bread-soaked saliva dripping from both sides of his mouth.

He told the most petite boy in the group to pull down his zipper and hang a raw bratwurst out of his pants for everyone to see. Sister Olivia laughed hysterically at the sight of all the little girls running away. One of the prospective parents standing in the shade of a tree screamed. She covered both eyes with her hands, lost her balance, and stumbled backward. She tripped over a tree root and accidentally tossed her lemonade into the face of a sensitive pale-faced six-year-old orphan boy, who immediately began to cry.

Father Adam Baum had no interest in socializing, especially not with the children. He preferred to remain as far away and isolated as possible. He was reserved and showed excessive nervousness and timidity in the company of young people. The obnoxious noises and frivolous commotion outside agitated him. They stirred his emotions to the point of forcing him to make a conscious effort to remain calm. "There have never been any children at Gravestone Castle—not ever. So why do they have to invite them here now? Somebody needs to get rid of Joey Linguine for causing all this unnecessary commotion," he grumbled dispiritedly.

During his routine midday stroll, the Padre paused at the greenhouse to admire his vast collection of precious golden-colored jars of honey. He obsessed over the slightest misalignment of the glass containers on the middle shelf. He compulsively straightened them one at a time before placing a precious jar of honey in his jacket pocket for personal use.

He casually slipped on his leather slippers and silky dark-green smoking jacket with black lapels to initiate his daily ritual. To calm his nerves, he heated a steaming pot of black tea and assembled a plate of dry bread. He spread a generous coating of honey on each cracker. He stirred four tablespoons into the teapot to sweeten the tea before reclining in his favorite leather chair. He took a sip of hot tea and exhaled a little steam, expressing delight in the deliciousness of the drink. He ate a bite of honey-coated dry bread and then another, quickly followed by two more. A horrifying sense of anxiety, restlessness, and overwhelming apprehension overcame him.

Excess saliva began pooling in his mouth and lungs. Carbon dioxide and other gases were building up around cells mixed with the fluid, forming a gassy, light-pink, blood-tinted mucus. The bubbly substance spilled out of his open mouth uncontrollably. Exposure to the air resulted in uncontrollable foaming at the mouth, an extremely uncommon symptom for healthy living and a sign of a severe underlying medical condition requiring emergency medical care.

Father Adam Baum smacked his lips and made false chewing movements like smelling something putrid and tasting spoiled food. He was nauseous. His forehead was wet, and his palms sweaty. His skin was cold and clammy. Infantile spasms attacked his arms and legs and then his fingers, causing his priceless heirloom teacup to drop and shatter on the floor. His body awkwardly stiffened before his neck suddenly went limp, causing his head to fall back. His eyelids fluttered due to rapid blinking. He stared blankly at the ceiling fan before starting to cry and then laugh out loud. He saw flashes of light, followed by feelings of increased dizziness. He was disturbed by psychogenic disorders reminding him of childhood traumas he had experienced earlier in life, leading to several lengthy full-body seizures.

Saliva pooling in the mouth involuntarily pushed through clenched teeth and onto his lips and chin, dripping like a leaky faucet onto his silky English smoking jacket. His heart and lungs began to fail, causing fluids to build up around his organs, starving his cells of oxygen. Manifestations of headaches, nausea, and convulsions swarmed over him. There was a bluish-gray tone to his face and skin. The tips of his transparent fingers were a deadly dark blue and gray when held up to the light. As he began wheezing and gasping for breath, feelings of suffocating and drowning increased exponentially. His cough produced frothy sputum tinged with blood. His lungs' impaired gas exchange caused the acute respiratory failure and cardiac arrest due to hypoxia—a cardinal feature of congestive heart failure.

A giant convulsion robbed him of his last breath. He awkwardly lurched forward, his body tumbling onto the floor in a big heap like a sprawling wet octopus as death swarmed over him.

83

DODGEBALL

"The plans are in place for Father Feely's memorial service ending with rum punch, cookies, a bonfire, and a pyrotechnic-fireworks display. Father Feely's ashes embedded in a massive shell will explode in the sky at dusk. It will be an explosive celebration of life, ending with a sensational bang of cremation fireworks that will make this an affair to remember," Sister Mary Pompino lightheartedly informed the others. "As our guests walk out of the chapel, they will feel the heat of a huge bonfire, topped by Father Feely's favorite leather recliner soaked with gasoline. The children will learn why the word *funeral* starts with the word *fun*."

The children peacefully relaxed on the lawn under the shade of a mature oak tree, listening to Polpetta extoll the virtues of a game they had never played. "Dodgeball is a systematized opportunity for bullies to target and humiliate weaker children—it's a ton of fun. So let's get this party started."

Emily indignantly inserted herself into the discussion, chiding Joey and his minions about the harms of fighting, feuding, rivalry, and excessive competitiveness. "Raising money by pelting adorable children in the face with a dodgeball is a questionable practice. Feelings may get hurt, and many schools have banned the sport."

Polpetta rationalized, "Dodgeball sounds bad to some people, but we are using American rules. In Africa, where the game originated, they use rocks and feces instead of a rubber ball. Joey is willing to pay if he gets a crack at the little bastards. He also wants the kids to wash his car, race dirt bicycles through the forest, and participate in a paintball war, allowing the adults to bet on which child wins. He's planning a fresh cow pie toss, plastic toilet seat redneck horseshoes, and a belly flop contest in the mud. He also likes the idea of having the kids paint self-portraits and then teaching them how to sell their paintings on eBay and Craigslist."

The youngest, weakest, and most minor children were terrified about what to expect as Polpetta grabbed the ball out of Joey's arms and made the first wicked toss. The violently thrown ball smacked a defenseless little boy on the side of the head. Dazed and nearly knocked out, humiliated, crying, and clutching his bright-red swollen ear with both hands, the boy fell flat on his face.

Polpetta jumped with glee. "I love this game. You're out! Get off the court, you little bastard."

Everyone laughed. Polpetta bragged loudly at the end of the tournament about all the "sissies," "suckers," and "pansies" he had eliminated with kill shots. He laughed about grabbing his teammates from behind and using them as human shields. He intentionally tripped a pale-faced "wimpy whiner," causing him to get slammed in the crotch with the ball and promptly eliminated. The humiliated losers continued whimpering, crying, blowing their noses, and rubbing their bruises.

Everyone looked forward to a warm cookie and milk following the trophy presentation and the enormous bonfire Joey had promised. Stolen wood stacked around the outhouse was ready to burn. Father Feely's favorite overstuffed leather recliner, thoroughly soaked with gasoline, was perched on the very top of the highly flammable pile.

"The outhouse is filled to the brim with sludge, bacteria, and seepage. The air is going to stink like an open sewer when the flames reach the pile of accumulated waste," Polpetta predicted with an audacious smile.

Deputy Sheriff Bud Light was thirsty and craving a cigarette. He was fed up with the delay in the memorial service and tired of sitting on hard wooden pews. He casually slipped out the back door of the chapel to stretch his legs and satisfy his nicotine withdrawal symptoms. As a friendly gesture of acknowledgment, he tipped his hat in Joey's direction.

Joey presumptuously assumed the deputy was sending him an affirmative signal to light the bonfire.

The fire started slowly and then rapidly gained momentum. Polpetta grabbed a woman's expensive pair of red shoes and a matching leather purse from under the shade of a large oak tree. He casually tossed them into the flames when the adults weren't looking. Raucous laughter ensued from the children who had witnessed the naughty thing that Polpetta had roguishly done with the lady's shoes and purse.

Glowing yellow-orange embers, radiating heat as hot as the fire that created them, rose gently into the sky like a glorious emanation of a flock of lost birds. Bits of burning wood drifted gracefully toward the greenhouse filled with killer bees.

84

MEMORIAL SERVICE

The sober crowd inside the chapel was edgy and bored, impatiently waiting for the memorial service to begin celebrating Father Feely's life. The absence of Father Marcello and Father Adam Baum was upsetting. "A good funeral requires the sensitivity and comfort only a priest can provide," Sister Olivia explained to the audience. "Father Marcello and Father Adam Baum will be here shortly. As soon as they arrive, we'll begin the service."

Lady Vanessa, chief financial officer of Woebegone Dunes Resort and Executor of Jack Daniels's will, wore her hair to one side with a large mass of awesomeness appropriate for a shampoo commercial. She was dressed in a tailored look, reflecting class and sophistication, making it easy to transition to her other world. "I thought growing old would take longer," she bemoaned to her lawyer about her gradually declining physical vitality and idealized feminine appearance. "I always assumed I would be able to spend the rest of my life in front of a gilded mirror reflecting upon my eternal beauty."

British Special Agent Kingsley and Chloe Crouton were tightly engaged in a private conversation. They were clutching hands and sitting tête-à-tête in the back row. A sense of physical closeness and emotional intimacy lingered in Kingsley's imagination. He had a fetish for torrid plus-size, curvy women. Chloe's deep-plunging braless floral cocktail dress enhanced her full figure. Her breasts were magnificently bounteous. His eyes gravitated to her dangerously curvy hips, narrow waist, and hourglass shape. She was beautiful. He fantasized about being squashed while squirming with her under the sheets. Being with a big pale-skinned naked woman in any capacity had always been his ultimate desire and fantasy.

"I love the dimples on your cheeks."

"If you like the dimples on my cheeks, you will love my derrière and thighs," Chloe gushed effusively with a blushing smile, her large brown eyes fixated on Kingsley. She appreciated his virile strength and chivalrous courage befitting a real man.

Lieutenant Dunning stepped to the front of the chapel to break the silence. Speaking in an even tone, making a few statements about life and death, and offering a few sympathetic and kind words about Father Feely calmed the restless assemblage. "The loss of a loved one requires composure, calm, poise, equilibrium, and levelheadedness. The loss of inheritance causes despair, hopelessness, disheartenment, and anguish. We shed tears at funerals for unfinished deeds and words never spoken. Everybody wants to go to heaven, whatever the hell that is, but nobody wants to go now. Death is a devastating event, turning our world upside down and changing our lives forever. Father Feely was a unique man of many talents. People from all over the world relied on him for guidance and financial support. His death will be equal to the loss of a parent for some of you, possibly the worst loss many of you at the Hermitage will ever experience. The death of a dream is the obliteration of hope and the extinction of the soul—rust-belt decrepitude."

Proctologist Seymour Fecal wandered to the front of the congregation to share detailed scientific facts about the ever-present dangers of bowel obstructions. "I have a few things to say about sepsis, bowel perforation, anastomotic leak, bezoars, and renal failure." The audience expressed revulsion and strong disapproval, yet he was unfettered and unrestrained regardless of their feelings. He insisted on floating his medical knowledge. "Most bowel obstructions require hospital admission and surgical consultation. If a strangulated bowel is left untreated, there is a mortality rate of one hundred percent."

An obnoxious young man with scruffy hair wearing a yellow T-shirt emblazoned with bright-green marijuana leaves asked several irreverent questions about how to provide the doctor with a stool sample. "My name is René Malarkey, a local reporter. Can you tell if someone has a bowel obstruction by the smell of their toots? What does an impacted stool look like on an X-ray? Does it look like petrified wood or more like charcoal briquettes? Do you have any laboratory samples to show us?"

Lieutenant Dunning interrupted the reporter to prevent any more discussion. "Please wait patiently. I'm sure things will come to a climax here shortly."

Without warning, a massive *ka-boom*, a terrific explosion accompanied by violent ground shaking, and a thunderous roar originating from the direction of the gas-filled greenhouse filled their ears. The colossal blast blew the roof off a small warehouse building filled with wooden beehives, expelling a fireball hundreds of feet into the air. The heat was so intense that it cracked the windows and bubbled the paint on the red SUV parked by the rock wall. Shards of brittle greenhouse glass with sharp edges and thousands of dead bees began raining down from the sky.

Polpetta was astonished by the way his missing red baseball hat was twirling around like a burning frisbee, leaving a contrail of white smoke behind and setting a tree on fire. Then a laboratory sink tossed high into the air came crashing back down from the sky at the speed of gravity. It landed directly on top of the red Rolls-Royce Cullinan SUV, smashing the windshield, putting a hole in the roof, and knocking the steering wheel off.

The stained-glass windows inside the chapel blew inward with great force. Thousands of brightly colored shards of glass shrapnel rained down on the guests' heads, harshly jarring the entire congregation into a confused state of mass hysteria. A burning ember floating in the air landed on a woman's head, causing her incendiary synthetic wig to burst into flames. A stranger ripped the burning glob of plastic off her head and heaved it blindly into the choir loft. The incident reminded the lieutenant of an ancient battlefield commander tossing a flamethrower into an enemy bunker.

Chloe Crouton stood up so quickly that the pew flipped over behind her, causing the entire row of people to lose their balance and fall backward. She grabbed Kingsley for support, awkwardly twisting him around and pulling him down on top of her as she tumbled over, banging the back of her head on the pew before hitting the floor. Frantically waving her arms and kicking her legs in the air caused her dress to slide up and cover her face.

The Nigerian delegation instinctively assumed a defensive formation. Bo-Bo Bigelow forced everyone out of his way as his team aggressively worked their way toward the back of the chapel. Three black Hummer H2s with blackened windows were parked tightly end to end by the chapel exit. The passenger-side windows were left open with machine guns pointed toward the orphan children as they hastily departed in a cloud of dust. The Hummers left deep tire tread marks in the racing sausage costumes as they disrespectfully drove over them.

The lead Hummer glanced off the burned hulk of a red Rolls-Royce SUV parked by the wall, crushing the passenger door and knocking the rear fender off as it passed.

The force of the explosion caused the fireworks launcher to tilt sideways toward the chapel. A Warhawk missile made a loud whistling sound as it smashed through the passenger window. It exploded with a brilliant bright orange flame that spontaneously lighted the interior of the red Rolls-Royce SUV on fire.

The massive mortar shell containing Father Feely's cremation ashes exploded with a tremendous force directly over the children's heads. A heavy coating of dark gray funerary ashes covered their faces. The children randomly spit in all directions to rid themselves of the ashes tasting like lousy coffee, rotten eggs, and sand. A third skyrocket smashed into the side of the chapel with an ear-piercing scream followed by a blinding flash of light with a brilliant orange hue. Additional explosions randomly continued until all twenty-one rockets loaded with fireworks had exploded.

A full-scale panic ensued. Children were rushed to the bus and sent back to the orphanage. Polpetta opened a window in the bus, smiled indignantly, rubbed black soot away from under his eyes, spit ashes out of his mouth, and blew a kiss to the attractive blond woman from New Jersey. She was standing barefooted beside her luxury Rolls-Royce with a forlorn expression on her face, wondering about the mysterious disappearance of her shoes and purse. Her brand-new car was smoking, ruined beyond repair. The paint blistered. It had broken windows, a collapsed roof, a crushed door, a burned interior. It was dripping with sticky honey. It was a total loss. Polpetta hollered out the window, "I hope you have Farmers Insurance—they've seen a thing or two."

Lieutenant Dunning rushed outside to determine the source of the explosion and assess the damage. Hundreds of busted, fractured, and fragmented sections of white beehives blown to smithereens were everywhere. Each section had a small sliding window with an iPad, identical to those he had observed in Nigeria. He snapped a photo of the debris with his iPhone and texted Colonel James Roberts at the Pentagon. "Case solved—I found definitive proof of the source of the beehives used for biological warfare in northern Nigeria."

"Shall I ask the deputy sheriff to arrest Father Adam Baum?"

The lieutenant was a forceful, energetic dynamo, knowing that a moment of hesitation due to a great uncertainty of mind or fear might cause a lifetime of regret. He carried a firearm at all times, and he never stopped to overthink an urgent situation before taking action. His mind was like a quarterback escaping the pocket under duress to exploit the defense's weakness.

The local fire department capped the broken gas pipeline leading into the greenhouse ruins before treating a few survivors for minor cuts and abrasions. "I'm afraid the gas valve to the greenhouse furnace was carelessly left open," the fire chief reported.

A lone surviving killer bee crawled up the pant leg to the inseam of the owner of the red SUV before angrily stinging him. "It's bound to swell up to epic proportions," Sister Olivia forewarned with her mouth agape with incredulity. "Would you like me to rub it with Vaseline to soothe the pain?"

85

FORTUITOUS DEATH

After the massive explosion, Sister Olivia guided the group to Father Adam Baum's apartment to report the total loss of his beloved greenhouse, warehouse, and extensive honey inventory. His body was lying face down on the hardwood floor, and the corpse was cold, gray, and lifeless.

"Look at that foam coming out of his mouth," Deputy Sheriff Bud Light said, gawking. "I think he died from rabies, choking to death on frothing saliva. Rabies causes brain inflammation resulting in paranoia, hallucinations, and delirium—it's always fatal without a vaccine. I think a rabid raccoon bit him." The deputy rolled up the victim's pant legs to check for animal bite marks.

Lieutenant Dunning was stunned by the deputy's diagnosis. "Father Adam Baum lived a highly eccentric, reclusive lifestyle. He was no longer the healthy, vibrant, intelligent person he used to be. His sense of superior intellectual capacity, physical strength, endurance, rationality, and prowess for problem-solving was an illusion. So, it doesn't surprise me that he died anonymously in an obscure and bizarre way."

Without composure, Emily blurted out, "I'm at wit's end. The mysteries and difficulties we have been facing here in Wisconsin leave me feeling emotionally exhausted. I never sleep anymore. I'm depressed. I'm exhausted and losing the ability to cope. I'm tired of hearing about truly awful, messy, accidental ways to hurtle into oblivion and the gut-wrenching science behind them. If you don't have a strong stomach, abandon hope; you shouldn't strive to be a detective. Nobody even heard his dying words. Does anyone know if he had any friends or family?"

The lieutenant placed a sympathetic hand on Emily's shoulder. She persistently continued sputtering, "This is no place for the meek; there is no place to hide; the end is forever close at hand. I know now why Indigenous people banished the oppressed to this isolated coastal land and buried their dead in this place called Woebegone Dunes. This land is cursed. Door County truly is the 'Door to Hell.' There must be a burning pit of lava around here somewhere. What's going to happen next? Was Father Adam Baum's death another ingenious contrivance by some mysterious force? Was it an unheralded unfortunate accident, a contrived murder mystery, or a natural death? I wonder if his demise is connected in any way to any of the other bizarre deaths at Gravestone Castle this summer. Dusty Rhodes is presumed to have fallen in a septic tank. Why didn't he take a shower? I can't believe a blue ice toilet bomb falling from the sky destroyed Joey's van. A lady's dress caught on fire at the auction. A drunken monkey telephoned the president during the masquerade ball. Now we are faced with the mysterious death of Father Adam Baum and a greenhouse gas explosion."

Lieutenant Dunning was in a cognitive state of empathy, motivated by a conscious drive to accurately diagnose and understand Emily's mental state of mind. She seemed so vulnerable and emotionally agitated. "You appear to be missing the top to your teakettle," he remarked after observing her perplexed facial expression, indicating vexation and emotional distress. "Perhaps the spring in your internal clock running in the background to carry out essential functions and processes has come unwound—again."

"I'm not sure I'm suited to be the next Agatha Christie. I've lost confidence in my abilities as a detective, and I don't seem to have the stomach for it anymore."

Her mind was temporarily devoid of rational thinking, spellbound by illusions and enthralled by superstitions, knowing there were no answers to her questions. Deep breathing produced obnoxious whistling sounds when she exhaled with her mouth open. She catatonically sat speechless for a long moment to the point that she had nothing else to say that she hadn't already expressed in words. Visions of a bewildering black hole with a gravitational field so intense that nothing could escape dominated her thinking the way the riptide carries victims out to sea. She visualized exotic geographic locations where people and money inexplicably disappear without a trace. The Bermuda Triangle, Airport Mesa in Sedona, and the artist enclave in Tubac, Arizona, immediately came to mind, sacred one-of-a-kind places famously known for natural vortexes, where heightened spiritual and metaphysical energy swirls out of the earth.

The lieutenant was feeding off her intense emotions and personal vulnerability, uncertain about what to say next. "If you have a dream, then go for it," he said, desperately wanting to validate her perspective. He reflected on what she was feeling and saying, resisting the urge to judge, before offering his continued assurance. "You're doing just fine. Your self-image determines what you eventually become. Create a positive outlook, and you will modify the personality and human behavior and improve your chances of a better outcome."

The lieutenant poked at the wedge of tobacco stuffed in his pipe, took a long draw, and blew a lingering smoke ring into the air as Coroner Slaughter prepared to remove the body. "You're welcome to use my pipe smoke for a tobacco glyster, if appropriate," he suggested amusedly.

"I can almost assure you that his honey poisoned Father Adam Baum. Poisoning by toxic substances is the number-one cause of unintentional death in this country. Honey has always served as a natural balm for a drooping heart. Still, in this case, the Padre's homegrown honey may have fortuitously caused his death."

The lieutenant removed a rifle from the rack and looked through the scope. "This must be the rifle that Kate saw pointed at her before she stumbled and fell into the bunker."

Emily's mind wandered to another place. She imagined a scenario where she could feel safe and comfortable with a friend who was always ready to have fun. She had visions of slipping away, opening a bottle of Gabbiano Chianti Classico wine, and spending an evening with Jay in the comfort of his chalet. It seemed like her best chance to escape the moment and get her head out of the clouds. She had a strong desire to be positive, to go on an adventure, and to talk in an unrestrained, excited manner about things she and Jay had in common.

86

QUANDARY

The lieutenant summed up the situation. "The good life is over. The fabric of the Hermitage at Gravestone Castle has unraveled and come apart at the seams. Those left behind have no credible religious qualifications or experience and cannot manage their affairs. Charitable contributions have dried up; investment dollars are gone, with nonexistent cash flow. The Hermitage was egregiously founded by faithless and dishonest souls devoid of religious inspiration—demonstrating that it's safer to sleep with a heinous villain in a prison cell than a drunken Christian. Religion is the opiate of the masses; hence the brethren of the Hermitage appear to have done masses of opiates religiously."

"What about Sister Olivia?"

"She may not have lost all of her marbles yet, but there is a small hole in the bag somewhere. Her fallacious lifestyle is a catechism of indigestible vulgarities. She lives in a world of make-believe, pretense, and play-acting. She's an ideal candidate for a retirement home in Quail Creek, Green Valley, Arizona."

"Did you feel the same way about Father Feely, the flatulent emo-tional dwarf with curiously bad habits associated with schizophrenia, repetitive speaking, and auditory hallucinations, singing and hum-ming to himself, sipping Chianti wine, and reading smut magazines all afternoon?"

"Father Feely was a man who knew how to spread the bee's knees and please without fees."

"What about Father Adam Baum?"

"He was a genius when it came to asymmetrical warfare using deceptive scientific methods that average civilians know absolutely nothing. He was a tremendous asset to the espionage community. He was an expert at infiltration, a leader in abstract thinking and devising strategies supporting American foreign policies. He was a member of Mensa International, the High IQ Society. He pioneered methods of asymmetric warfare, implementing ambiguous gray zone tactics using unconventional unattributed force. He participated in numerous covert actions that officially 'never happened.' The majority of his contributions will never be known. A special-ops cleaning crew removed every shred of evidence linking Father Adam Baum to the government. His personnel records were deleted and replaced with a false biography making him appear qualified for the priesthood."

"Are there any research stations similar to Gravestone Castle anywhere else in the world?" Emily was intrigued to know.

"RAF Rudloe Manor in Wiltshire, England, is a prime example, a thirty-five-acre underground subterranean city with an operations center with plotters and controllers, a filter room to determine friend or foe, a large underground weapons cache, and a major military electronics center."

A vivid red color was finally returning to Emily's cheeks. There was more energy in her step and slightly more enthusiasm in her voice. "Is this where the sidewalk ends? Colonel Roberts had a suspicion that Woebegone Dunes Resort and the Hermitage at Gravestone Castle would collapse. That's why he suggested Wayne and Kate Kennedy be on the lookout for a real estate fire sale."

Sister Olivia added another layer of mystery to the plight. "Father Marcello left a note officially resigning from the Heritage. He packaged up some oil paintings, valuables, and antiques. He moved to Lake

Como, Italy, in the middle of the night. Sister Mary Pompino went with him, and they never even said goodbye."

"I also received a note from sisters Lova and Lola Kurvig from Sweden describing their ambitions. This fall, they will be featured on the *Bachelorette* reality television show. As twin bachelorettes, they will have the opportunity to choose a marriage partner from twenty sets of eligible male twins. The uniqueness of their relationship as identical twins is guaranteed to create a tremendous increase in viewership this season."

"Jay Walker would make an ideal interim property manager. Someone needs to assure accountability until the courts determine the rightful heirs," the lieutenant suggested.

"Joey Linguine has already volunteered to manage the property for a fee. His lawyer has had preliminary conversations with Judge Geri Attrick about what might happen next. The judge tipped her hand, acknowledging that Polpetta was the sole heir to the castle. He is the only living relative of Father Cellophane, the last surviving corporate officer and owner of Gravestone Castle LLC. Joey Linguine has volunteered to be Polpetta's legal guardian. Polpetta expects to drop out of the orphanage and be homeschooled by Joey," Sister Olivia informed them. "A brief gala ceremony and distribution of certificates for my pre-nun class are planned for Saturday night, the last formal event scheduled for Gravestone Castle."

The graduation ceremony began with a flourish: brass instruments played with full fanfare, ending with a flamboyant panache as the graduates formally marched into the chapel, badly damaged from the greenhouse gas explosion, including broken windows and crooked pews, a fallen ceiling light, cracked floor tiles, and a dripping water main.

Multiple festive toasts of bubbly champagne with a few rogue shots of tequila followed the award ceremony. The entire entourage shuffled out the door in a celebratory mood with all the commotion and ballyhoo of a high school graduation ceremony. Yet the halls appeared cold, faded, and bare in the dim candlelight. Sister Olivia peered through the gloom, imagining that she could still hear lingering piano notes softly echoing off the walls. Lucid dreams dominated by reticence and insanity vaporized like candle smoke. Old broken hearts, wind chimes, and good times filled her mind. Sister Olivia was unwilling to cast shame aside and expose herself to unpleasant situations outside the bubble of the artificial world she inhabited.

She finally came to an understanding of the meaning of the word *énouement*. It was the bittersweetness and obscure sorrows of having arrived in the future, wishing that you could go back and tell your former self how things eventually turned out. It was the end of an era—a time to reflect on past transgressions, the sins of youth and rebellious ways, regrets, mistakes, and breakups.

She gulped two more shots of Centenario Tequila for courage before stepping outside for the last time. Constantly on edge, she had an anxiety disorder and a claustrophobic fear of the dark. A ghostly image of Gravestone Castle silhouetted in the misty moonlight against slowly passing dark and ominous clouds was a forewarning that a heavy storm was brewing. Opaque ancient trees casting dark shadows on the castle walls triggered flashbacks of nightmares, significant emotional trauma, and unsettling dreams of poison insects, snakes, spiders, and friendships lost.

A sense of doom brewing in the air foretold that something ominous, life-threatening, and tragic was about to occur. Massive life change caused heart palpitations, trembling, and nauseous indigestion. Ingrained primeval feelings of horror and suffering seemed a harbinger of impending predation. Imagining the worst, she tiptoed to the garage with an intense fear of the unknown.

Spirits in the forest shadows came alive, reminding her of deep, dark vulnerabilities and deception. The frightening sounds of a fox and a badger stealthily confronting each other in the shadows startled her and shot chills up her spine. A disturbed seagull guarding the elaborate blackened wrought-iron entrance gate shattered the darkness with a macabre blood-curdling shriek inspiring terror, a dread of anticipation preceding feelings of horror, agony, and imminent danger.

Sister Olivia Seno Grande never looked back as her car stealthily rolled through the massive iron entrance gate. A cloud floating too close to the ground swallowed her. Blurred atmospheric fogginess reduced visibility to ceiling zero, making navigating nearly impossible.

87

FATHER MARCELLO

Father Marcello was highly independent and fearless. He was a popular subject of haughty broadsheets and fawning society magazines, a proud and arrogant man of pompous self-importance. He hastily removed many of the paintings off the castle walls, packed his bags during the middle of the night, and set off for Lake Como, Italy, accompanied by Sister Mary Pompino.

"It's time to move on," he explained. "Lake Como has been a haunt of the wealthy since Roman times. Mountains surround Lake Como. Small picturesque towns with many opulent villas and palaces with beautiful gardens line the wooded shores. There is even an eleventh-century abbey. The mild climate with characteristics similar to the Mediterranean is an ideal draw for tourists. It will be an excellent location to buy and sell expensive art. Switzerland, Venice, and Rome are nearby."

"But where will we live? I've become spoiled living in Gravestone Castle," Sister Mary lamented.

Avoiding disclosure of the full details, Father Marcello seemed neither unfazed nor distraught. "Don't worry. I've got a peaceful, secure place in mind. You're going to love it there. You're never going to miss Gravestone Castle after you see the palace I have picked out. I have an international reputation as a professional art appraiser, and my forgeries are highly esteemed. So I will be able to continue the business of buying, selling, and appraising art for many years to come."

Everything about Father Marcello was a grand gesture of cunning deception. He lived a luxurious life of a European *bon vivant* socialite, unwilling and unable to live within his means. His origins in financial crime led him directly to the world of illegal art sales, where he had become a highly talented and successful art forger. He was unexposed and immersed in deception. Falsely claiming an aristocratic title, knowing the public had a fascination with royalty, he was a monocle-wearing charmer with an outsized ego who seduced everyone he met. Somehow, he had managed to convince dozens of usually savvy investors to fork over tremendous amounts of money. "It's easy to con someone if you give them something of value they want in exchange. The US Justice Department pays out as much as one million dollars a year, plus housing and other expenses, for people in the witness protection program. With this as my backup plan, I have tremendous incentive to continue my lucrative career."

"Will you promise to take me to the seaside resort of Santa Flavia in Sicily next summer? I have some wonderful relatives living on the Gulf of Palermo that I would like to visit. They own the best meat markets. The town is known for many varieties of fresh fish and abundant grapefruit. It is the location of the ancient city of Soluntum, one of the three Phoenician settlements on the island of Sicily."

"I promise to take you there, as long as you faithfully stay by my side. It's time to start over with new identities, experiencing the good life in comfort and luxury that you always dreamed of having, with few problems and worries. Wherever we go, no matter the weather, we'll always be in the sunshine. Being a professional art appraiser and forger is lucrative if you travel in the right circles. It's easy to create a secret persona by fabricating a distorted backstory. How you dress, the distinct way you walk, your accent, hairstyle, and your voice affect how others view you. As long as you are reserved, avoid risks, and remain relatively conservative and cautious, your life will be pleasant."

Six months later, Sister Mary Pompino, with the vibrant auburn hair, abandoned the overrated life of ease Father Marcello had overpromised on Lake Como, Italy. Half-drunk, hollow-eyed, and riding in a car full of designated drinkers, she returned to Wisconsin in the middle of the night looking for a place to fall apart. Hoping for a little more excitement in her life, she accepted a job as the housemother of the Sigma Chi fraternity at the University of Wisconsin in Madison. She acted as hostess and chaperone to provide a smooth transition for incoming first-year students. Referring to the students as "happy enchiladas," she taught etiquette and chivalry to those living in the fraternity house.

She hired the Singing Supremes tribute band for the annual fall party. She invited the organ grinder and his monkey as special guests. The older gray-haired man in the baggy coat was an international celebrity, the second person on the planet hit by a frozen airplane poop bomb. Reporter René Malarkey described the out-of-control college fraternity party as a sensational drunken hazing event. The unmanageable and unruly chapter lost its license and became inactive shortly afterward. She used to play with hula hoops, and now wearing cowboy boots and faded jeans, she told her problems to therapy groups.

Sister Mary never regretted doing anything that made her smile. Every moment was a fresh beginning and a chance to start again. Ignoring the bubbles in her mental barometer, she woke up early, ate a healthy breakfast, and purchased a blue Porsche 718 Cayman GTS with 394 horsepower. She headed for Route 66, venturing off to explore unfamiliar, uncharted places previously unknown. She met a Las Vegas preacher in a cowboy shirt and a big hat on the outskirts of the Mojave Desert, hotter than Italian sausages sizzling on a grill. He held a bottle of Maker's Mark in one hand, a Bible in the other. He lectured about the aesthetic pleasure, entertainment market worth, and inspirational value of gospel singing that feeds the soul. His sermon stimulated an epiphany. With the Grand Canyon in her rearview mirror, Sister Mary Pompino made an abrupt change in direction. She slammed on the brakes, squealing her tires as she made an erratic U-turn.

She reversed direction and headed directly to Nashville, Tennessee, home of the Grand Ole Opry, to chase her dream of becoming a country music star. Traveling down the road with both hands on the wheel, she sang a medley of country songs with gusto: "Blame It on My Roots . . . Okay, I'll Buy Them Damn Cowboy Boots," "You Ain't Fun Anymore Since I Quit Drinking," "You're the Reason Our Kids Are Ugly," "Queen of the Doublewide," and "All My Exes Live in Texas."

She watched as the mirror image of her lively, cheerful, bubbly younger self with her lustrous auburn hair was gradually replaced with wrinkles and silver lace. Acknowledging the bittersweet, sorrowful meaning of the word *énouement*, she dreamed of going back in time to reveal the future to her former self.

88

RIGHTFUL HEIR

The IRS investigation finally reached its peak. Agent Penny Pincher called a meeting to expose her findings. "We have uncovered financial irregularities and misappropriations of funds resulting from deception and fraud that may be criminal in nature," she explained, referring to Gravestone Castle.

"The Patronato is a subculture of wealthy widows that covertly refers to the Hermitage as a 'hunting station' for lonely women seeking companionship. They are all cash donors to the Hermitage. A sexy romantic fling with a priest in a secluded setting has a hint of intrigue and excitement for them. Confidential engagements are scheduled months ahead of time between routine nail and hair appointments. Favorite fantasies include uncensored breakfast chats wearing black Chantilly lace while eating whipped cream and chocolates in bed. Others enjoy discreet hookups known as 'afternoon delights' with perfume, animal furs, and Italian gelato ice cream. Romantic moonlight sonatas are the most popular."

"Where do we go from here? Gravestone Castle is vacant. Who owns it now? What if there is nobody left to prosecute or pay off the debts?" Emily queried.

The slightly upturned corners of the lieutenant's mouth signified amusement and understanding. He unloaded a bundle of repressed thoughts that he had formerly kept in check. "Gravestone Castle is a honeypot for priestly fraudsters engaging in a faux ministry. The priests provide an enticing source of pleasure and reward for a criminally deceptive scandal devised to result in financial and personal gain and perpetuate evil habits, wrongdoings, and an uncompromising lifestyle. Suppose a man of the cloth tells a wealthy woman his hard-luck story about the financial woes afflicting his profession. In that case, she eagerly hands him her purse and credit cards to pay off his bills, buy a new car, a big-screen TV, furniture, plane tickets, and dental bills. Suppose he is willing to fulfill her flight of fancy on a routine basis. In that case, she will willingly pay his expenses and his salary. In a short time, he will be escorting her to Europe and Hawaii."

The lieutenant continued. "We have been witnessing a hypocritical display of virtue. It's time to dispel the notion that this group of frauds, hypocrites, and pretenders believed in the myths they peddled. Charitable contributors have been dutifully loyal to Father Feely, but the priests have responded with sincerity unlikely to be fulfilled. Their pious sentiment is of an exaggerated and affected nature that combines biblical doctrine with an emphasis on individual piety and vigorous spiritual life. Still, it's doubtful they believed in the ideals they peddled. In reality, they love money, guns, walls, fossil fuels, Amazon, meat, private jets and cars, luxury apartments, mansions, and paying low taxes as much as everyone."

"How do people become that way?" Emily wondered.

"The shaping of malleable minds doesn't begin in college; it begins in elementary school and continues in high school. Universities systematically remove religious matters from any objectionable curriculum. The tough questions that expose social hypocrisies and reveal the naked truth are largely unwelcome. The philosophy of ethics and moral duties and obligations are largely lacking in higher education. The basic concepts of good and bad and right and wrong conduct are completely absent from modern classrooms," the lieutenant moralized.

"The debate between those who promote women's rights and those who strive to protect the right of women to be born is an untenable, never-ending battle of wills. Too many people blindly follow the crowd like sheep, lulled into complacency based on false perceptions without thinking or deciding for themselves. As a result, they are unaware of the future dangers, deficiencies, and pitfalls. When the truth is exposed, individuals lacking critical thinking skills and investigative expertise face the cold shock of reality."

Deputy Sheriff Bud Light had something to say. "Those who believe they are entitled to Gravestone Castle will soon learn that standing before Judge Geri Attrick can be an intimidating experience. She doesn't mess around, and she sits up on her high bench while the others stand below. Feelings, emotions, and subjection aren't allowed in her courtroom—only the facts."

"Before anyone can recover money owed to them, there is the matter of discovering the rightful heir to Gravestone Castle," Emily stated matter-of-factly.

"Exactly. Polpetta, Father Cellophane's son, is the legal and rightful heir," Penny Pincher remarked with a wrinkled-up nose, expressing her disapproval.

Deputy Sheriff Bud Light enlightened them. "Joey Linguine came forward volunteering to be Polpetta's legal guardian, the apparent heir to Gravestone Castle. Judge Geri Attrick suggested Joey Linguine get married and legally adopt Polpetta as his son. Several days later, Joey returned to the courtroom. He was linked arm in arm with Sister Olivia Seno Grande to demonstrate to Judge Geri Attrick that they were closely allied. Immediately after the wedding, she threw away the roses and kept the wine. Olivia held up her left hand, proudly displaying her two-carat cubic zirconia engagement ring—the judge was very impressed."

"A man will eventually propose to everyone in the room, if necessary. The ideal marriage would be between a blind wife and a deaf husband," the lieutenant exclaimed.

Penny Pincher agreed. "The die is cast, and there won't be a need to place any liens on Gravestone Castle. Surplus funds in Father Feely's bank accounts can cover all debts owed to the federal government and creditors. I predict Judge Geri Attrick will recognize Polpetta as the lawful heir and owner of Gravestone Castle, provided Joey Linguine and Sister Olivia Seno Grande agree to become his adoptive parents and legal guardians."

Deputy Sheriff Bud Light concurred. "Joey has a lot of big plans for Gravestone Castle. He wants to open an auto salvage yard, turn the historic Woebegone Indian Trail into a motorcycle racetrack, sell guns and ammunition, and build a shooting range. He's planning to fence off a couple of acres for an elk and buffalo pasture and charge his buddies to shoot them. Sister Olivia is in a state of euphoria, knowing that she will be able to continue living in Gravestone Castle as Polpetta's adoptive mother and legal guardian. Polpetta thinks he's gone to heaven. He wants to drop out of school, race a motorcycle, work in the gun store, and help shoot the elk. His ambition is to become a barber specializing in Mohawk haircuts. He has already asked the judge for permission to begin learning the barber trade by giving Mohawk haircuts to the other children at the orphanage."

The loss of his parents plagued Jay's consciousness. A reoccurring dream exposing startling incongruities left him feeling cheated and robbed, unfairly deprived, and taken advantage of with no chance of recovery, like an unfair, one-sided divorce arrangement. It wasn't morally right that someone else was taking possession of his family home and rightful heritage—but what could he do about it?

89

BREAKING AND ENTERING

"*I woke up* in the middle of the night," Jay explained, releasing years and tears of pent-up frustration. "Childhood dreams are hard to get out of your mind. Over the years, I have had a reoccurring dream. My father and I are in a secret underground cavern where he kept valuables, legal papers, architectural plans, guns, money, and liquor. He only took me there once. Hidden in the wall behind a bookshelf in the chapel was a secret door leading to the basement. I forgot about it because, ironically, the government sealed off the secret entrance many years ago for security reasons."

Emily was intrigued. "Are you sure?"

"I need to see for myself if my father's possessions are still there before I'm locked out of my family home forever. I would hate for a stranger to recover and destroy any remaining legal documents. What if I am the rightful heir of Gravestone Castle? Nobody should be allowed access to family heirlooms that belong to me."

"The act of entering a residence through the slightest amount of force, even pushing open a door, without authorization is a criminal act. Even if the door is open, Joey could charge you with criminal trespass. Crimes that are misdemeanors are punishable by a year in jail. Still, if you remove something from the premises, burglary is a serious felony."

"I've made up my mind. Joey and Sister Olivia will be staying in Milwaukee for the weekend. I must take action immediately."

Emily was worried. "I should go with you."

When the opacity of twilight arrived, they acted, stealthily working past the main entrance gate to the chapel without being detected.

"I watched the castle get constructed. Many of the construction details are not readily evident to outsiders, and there are numerous hidden chambers and secret passageways. Even if nobody is here, we still need to be on the lookout for alarms and unexpected booby-traps," Jay warned.

"The earliest settlers constructed a fortified underground bunker when they were building the foundation of the original church for storing food, tools, weapons, and other survival gear. Security is what also inspired my grandfather to continue digging underground. Concealed doors and a warren of underground passageways allowed government scientists and soldiers to transition between rooms without being seen. Incorporated into the architecture were emergency tunnels to escape accidental chemical spills, explosions, fires, or an enemy siege. Secret entrances to the hidden passageways were in unusual places, similar to what you would expect to find in a medieval castle."

Taking Emily by the arm, he escorted her into the chapel. "The chapel was used as a conference room for formal presentations on weekdays and religious services on Sundays. There is a door leading to the vestry on the left side, a place for keeping vestments, furnishings, sacred vessels, religious art, candles, and church records. I doubt if any of the priests ever discovered it," Jay surmised as he pushed and pulled on a large obscure wooden wall panel in the back of the vestment closet. Eventually, a lever released with an elegance and refinement of movement typical of a high-quality Murphy bed hinged on one side. Directly behind the wooden frame was an arched wooden door with iron hardware.

"It's unlocked," Emily announced, peering into a vast, dark void.

Jay grabbed a handful of candles from the sacristy, pulled the cabinet back into the closed position, and mechanically locked the wooden panel behind them. A long set of steps carved out of stone led directly into a large cavernous room with rough stone walls.

"My memories are suddenly coming back to me. My father kept heirlooms, keepsakes, and valuables here. The file drawers contained architectural plans. Property deeds, passports, and important papers are in the old file cabinet. Photographs, memorabilia, and other personal items are in the desk drawers. The safe contains guns, money, heirlooms, and other valuables. The combination for the safe is my grandfather's birthday, my father's birthday, and my birthday." Jay demonstrated by turning the combination lock forward, back, and then back again before opening the door and pulling out several guns and boxes of ammunition. "My mother's antique jewelry and a collection of rare European coins are in this unique wooden box. Everything of value appears safe."

Emily continued sorting through the paper records in the file cabinet until stumbling across a folder labeled "Property Deed" and another labeled "Last Will & Testament of Benedict Walker."

"These documents are more valuable than anything else in this room. The documents filed in court by Father Feely are counterfeit. These documents prove that you are the rightful heir to Gravestone Castle."

"Listen!" The still of the darkness was unexpectedly interrupted by the choppy rotor sounds of a helicopter hovering directly overhead. The sound was so intimidating that the pulsation of Emily's arteries was altered; it dominated the previously passionless phlegmatic mood of the underground chamber.

Emily froze in her tracks. "My heart is pounding. The rhythmic pulsation of the ground shaking is like an announcement of the resurrection of the dead. The military cleaning team Colonel Roberts ordered must be here to obliterate any records or materials left behind by Father Adam Baum. The beehives discovered after the greenhouse explosion triggered the demand for another property investigation to search for additional contraband previously overlooked. Gravestone Castle will quickly become the scene of a whiskey Charlie foxtrot entanglement if anything significant remains. The government will destroy incriminating evidence related to national security, biological weapons, and covert military actions, making retrieval impossible."

When the helicopter blades stopped rotating, a single candle feeling rejection from the darkness around it was the only sign of life, standing motionless in the cold, damp air. The wind from Emily's shallow breathing caused the candle to flicker. Her heart was pumping, and she could feel it in her chest and hear the sound of her irregular heartbeats in her inner ears. Her skin crawled with a childhood dread of darkness, death, and the nightmarish fear of abandonment, isolated and alone in a cold, dark place. Heavy breathing caused an uncontrolled snore-like sound followed by an involuntary whistle.

She confessed, "I have night phobia; a primitive fear of darkness, disorientation, the loss of bearings, and the dread of being lost send me into an anxious primal panic. Please don't let the candle burn out."

90

SECRET UNDERGROUND BUNKER

Jay lit a second candle and placed it on the safe. He poked behind the safe until he could pull a small metal lever forward with the hooked end of his grandfather's walking cane. The lever allowed the safe to rise and move forward freely on the steel wheels. Bracing himself against the wall, using his hips and legs for leverage, he rolled the safe three feet away from the wall.

"Why did you do that?" Emily was eager to learn.

"I'm trying to find the door to the basement."

"But there is no opening."

"There used to be a stairway in this location that led to the basement. It was a cavernous underground bunker carved out of the bedrock. My grandfather kept his sailboat and bootleg whiskey operation hidden from view," Jay said as he leaned his back against the wall and pushed as hard as he could with his legs. A large section of drywall suddenly broke free and slid down the stairway carved out of stone. He grabbed a handful of candles to light the path and squeezed Emily's hand for assurance.

"This is the stairwell to the lower levels I was hoping to find," he whispered. "My father sealed off the entrance with drywall to conceal it. Nobody will find us down here."

"Everything is covered with dust, reminding me of an underground medieval dungeon or unexplored cave. It's as dark as pitch in here, and

I feel like an amateur spelunker. Is there a risk of being trapped without enough oxygen?"

"Walking together side by side in the dark is better than walking alone in the sunshine," Jay reassured her.

Placing their hands on the rock wall for support, they blindly descended into the blackened abyss. A disturbed bat flapping its wings in Emily's face provoked a blood-curdling scream. She tripped and stumbled forward into Jay's loving arms, protecting her from falling. She hugged him tightly to demonstrate her genuine feelings of love, romantic desire, and intimacy.

Jay turned the engraved Victorian antique brass door handle and forced the door open at the bottom of the stairs. The creepy sound of the rusty iron hinges awakened their primal senses into an elevated state of consciousness. Masonic symbols graced the surface of the old wooden door. The silhouette of a large glacial stone appeared in the flickering darkness. "This granite boulder is an erratic rock transported here from Canada thousands of years ago by the Laurentide glacier. My grandfather discovered it in a grove of red oak trees. Carved into the surface are a Knights Templar cross, the all-seeing Eye of Providence, a medieval sword, and several words and symbols that he could not translate. The carvings may offer proof that a small group of Europeans traveled west over eight hundred years ago to explore the Great Lakes region."

"Fascinating—did he ever share this information with anyone else?"

"He extracted the rock from the ground many years ago. He carefully placed it in the underground quarry to protect it from weathering and vandalism. He mailed photographs of the carvings to the Knights Templar. Unfortunately, they never published the amazing discovery. Possibly because they considered it a hoax."

A flash of candlelight reflected off something shiny, causing Emily to squeeze Jay's arm in alarm. "What is that?"

"It's a large brass binnacle compass with a working oil lamp used for sailing," Jay explained as he lifted the canvas cover off his grandfather's boat. He reached out with his hand to feel the soft sloping curve of the hull and the smoothness of the deck boards. "I can't believe it's in such good condition. The boat sits on the original metal frame set on railroad tracks used for launching and retrieval. Using this technique, he could safely load the liquor on his boat underground and conveniently conduct the entire bootlegging operation all by himself. Follow the steel rails, and they will lead you directly into Lake Michigan. Unfortunately, the garage door rusted shut, but there is another way out," Jay said as he forced open the adjacent service entrance. He squeezed through the narrow opening into the heavily forested underbrush with great force. "It's still dark outside. Look at all the stars in the sky."

"The clean-up crew is probably still upstairs investigating," Emily gave as an excuse for remaining alert. "At least we know now that we can escape from this underground dungeon. What is that?" she said, pointing to several large metal containers in the shadows.

"That's my grandfather's vintage potbelly moonshine still, antique copper tubing coils, and other miscellaneous pots and burnt oak barrels used for making moonshine whiskey."

"That's amazing."

"It wasn't illegal to drink alcohol during Prohibition. The Eighteenth Amendment only forbade the manufacture, sale, and transportation of intoxicating liquors—not their consumption."

Emily turned her attention toward a large wooden storage rack with a walnut wood stain. "There are a dozen shelves filled with Gravestone Castle Black Eye Whiskey made by Walker Distillery in 1932."

"Legend has it that my grandfather drank too much whiskey, tripped over a rock, and hit himself in the face with his shovel handle, resulting in a black eye."

"Do you think the whiskey is still drinkable?" Emily asked.

Jay examined one of the bottles in the candlelight. "Whiskey doesn't age once bottled, and all the aging happens in the white oak casks. Unopened whiskey lasts indefinitely. The taste may change slightly over time, but it won't spoil."

"Shall we try it?"

"Sure. We'll know right away if it's any good," Jay said as he poured a generous amount in two tumblers of hand-blown glass with a distinctive tapered shape and commanding heavy base.

An unexpected electric shock of sexuality surged through Emily's body when her breasts accidentally brushed against Jay's arm, causing an irrepressible psychological tug. The curious magnetic pull seemed to be drawing her closer with a ferocious intensity beyond the realm of self-control. The idea of hooking up seemed to be floating in the air. Remarkably, it appeared to be simultaneously entering their collective consciousness at the same time, even though it didn't seem like the ideal situation.

"Grab your glass and follow me," Jay suggested as he pulled the canvas cover off the sailboat cabin. He climbed the ladder and encouraged Emily to follow. The galley smelled of aromatic red cedar and teak wood veneer. The double bed in the captain's stateroom was tempting and suggestive, captivating their senses and promising something heavenly.

"To smell the aroma and taste the layers in the whiskey, swirl, smell, sip, and swallow and then repeat the whole process."

The alcohol had an immediate effect on Jay's brain. A glance directly into Emily's twinkling warm eyes enticed him. Her smile was mysteriously erotic, tempting, and seductive. Feeling erotically excited, he wrapped his arms around her waist and pulled her close. Her hair was silky and smooth with the scent of jasmine. He kissed her neck and caressed her breasts. "I love your beautiful skin and smooth complexion and your smile—you are the loveliest of the lovelies, my dear."

Moving slowly and tenderly, she could feel the heat of seduction radiantly glowing from the gorgeous entity on the other side of the bed, a glorious high unparalleled in the entire universe. The awe-inducing fireworks exploding across the surface of her heart triggered a budding addictive desire to taste Jay's lips, a pinnacle emotion filled with joyous feelings of being blissfully drunk and in love.

Time stood still in the candlelight as their emotions became highly engaged and their hearts started pumping. The alcohol caused their minds to slow down, suppressing psychological inhibitions, increasing sexual arousal and desire. They performed in the most intimate natural way for a lingering time, followed by a joyful altered state of consciousness, one with the other.

91

THE CLEANING CREW

Four hours earlier, a helicopter had hovered briefly over Gravestone Castle before landing in the courtyard. A dozen paratroopers and scientists jumped out. Some wore gas masks and chemical detection gas chromatographs, and others had night-vision goggles. The entire group quickly fell into prearranged formations and dispersed in all directions to begin a formal search of the property. The special-ops cleaning crew had arrived. Former employee and scientist Dr. Whet Faartz remained on high alert in the courtyard, wheezing and coughing and making suggestions on the radio, telling the crews where to search.

A second crew arrived in a rigid-hull, inflatable, high-buoyancy, extreme-weather raiding craft with the stealth of a Mexican jaguar, one of the animal kingdom's stealthiest species. They perched high up in the treetops and hid in thick underbrush, tactics used by predatory big cats with a powerful bite that can crush their prey's skull.

Emily was abruptly awakened from her enchanted sleep as her eyes adjusted to the blackness. Her naked body was silhouetted against the cabin walls, sleek and trim and rakishly curved like a fast-looking racehorse. Jay took great pleasure watching her search for her clothing in the flickering candlelight.

Cautiously tiptoeing to the secret service entrance in the darkness, he forced the old metal door eaten by rust open with his shoulder. The high-pitched, groaning, intimidating creaking sound of the hinges made Emily cringe. Jay placed his arm around her shoulders as they peered into the darkness to observe the stars and gather their bearings. A fragrant lake breeze and light fog mimicked the ebb and flow of lazy waves diagonally rolling onto the shore. Jay listened carefully before whispering.

"We should be able to escape without being caught or seen by now. I assume the commandos are gone," Jay expressed with urgency.

Emily quietly squeezed through the narrow opening leading into the forest. The autumn night air was chilly on her bare arms.

"The exit door is completely overgrown with vegetation. It is invisible and indistinguishable from the outside, reminding me of the sealed entrance to a long-forgotten gold mine—no wonder the government never discovered the entrance. I wish we had a machete to cut our way through the dense, tangled underbrush," she pined.

Jay forged a path through the brambles, tree branches, and thorny bushes, scratching their arms and legs and tearing Emily's blouse as they descended toward the beach. Something moving in the distance startled them. They paused abruptly and ducked behind a large tree as a creepy military silhouette of a soldier with a dark face carrying a gun emerged from the foggy darkness, backlighted by the moon. A surge of adrenaline caused Emily to shake and tremble with fear and excitement, a human reaction mimicking feelings of imminent doom derived from ancestral encounters with meat-eating carnivores with predatory instincts, menacingly close at hand.

Assuming the danger had passed, they held hands tightly to keep from recklessly tripping and falling in the sand. They darted into the water, sheltered behind a large oak tree recently fallen into Lake Michigan, and patiently waited. Holding on to tree branches and treading water in the peaceful darkness of the early morning was tedious and energy-draining.

They were startled by the unexpected appearance of a small group of armed elite light infantry in stealth clothing with darkened faces dropping from tall trees and darting out from seclusion behind dense foliage. The intimidating commando team, employing guerrilla-like shock tactics, gathered on the beach before entering the water. Their boat wavelessly disappeared without a sound into the low hovering lake fog resembling steam rising out of the water.

A cold shiver crawled down Emily's spine as an omen of death and insecurity. Her teeth were chattering uncontrollably. She was unnerved and frightened as the last hit-and-run commando unit trained in guerrilla-like shock tactics, and hand-to-hand combat ran past. "I shouldn't be here. If a special-ops team with guns caught us outside a former top-secret military research center at four o'clock in the morning, imagine what would happen to my career."

"The water is freezing, and it's making your skin crawl. Your heart is racing, and your breathing is labored. Your speech is becoming slurred. I sense a lack of coordination, sleepy behavior, and a weak pulse. Your body is losing heat much too quickly, causing a dangerously low body temperature and hypothermia. I need to get you out of here for medical reasons as soon as possible."

The tactical military formation arrived back in the courtyard and effortlessly flowed back into the helicopter with precision, as quickly and stealthily as they had come. The spinning blade-vortex generated aerodynamic pressures and forces, creating rough acoustic waves that resembled a war zone. The classic sound of the helicopter leaving was insidious and demonic, pounding their hearts into submission.

Emily and Jay waited in fear until everything was quiet and back to normal. The soft lapping of rhythmic waves on the sandy shoreline and gentle forest breezes calmed their senses. The castle was quiet as a mouse, and no creatures were stirring. Jay grabbed Emily by the arm and rushed her back to his chalet. She was hypothermic and trembling uncontrollably. The warm bubbly waters of the hot tub were soothing and therapeutic. Their emotions subsided and became less intense. Relaxing in the spa to rid themselves of the life-threatening effects of severe hypothermia with a small glass of Gabbiano Chianti Classico was sheer bliss. Knowing that Jay had recovered important documents proving that he was the rightful heir of Gravestone Castle brought tremendous joy and comfort to her soul.

The first glimmering rays of the sun reminded Emily of being rudely awakened by her mother as a child. Every morning at six, she flicked on the bedroom light, exposing her messy room and brutally forcing her out of bed.

"I have a major commitment this morning," she stated with urgency. "Colonel James Roberts ordered Lieutenant Baron Dunning and me to attend an important meeting his morning. He will be furious if I don't show up on time. Do you have any clothes I can wear?"

"My sweatsuit is the least objectionable apparel—at least it's dry."

Emily was out of breath and looking unnaturally bedraggled after less than two hours of sleep. Expanding her lungs too quickly caused wheezing followed by an embarrassing whistling sound, an abrupt snort, and a raspberry fart unacceptable to a polite audience. She lacked makeup, and her eyes were dark. Her hair was tousled, windblown, and unkempt. The baggy men's athletic wear she was wearing was rumpled, as if she had spent the night in a cheap motel on a rainy night. She arrived at Woebegone Dunes Resort a few minutes late.

"I was jogging for exercise this morning—guess I overdid it," she offered as a plausible excuse for her disheveled appearance and mild tardiness.

The lieutenant raised one eyebrow as an acute sign of awareness and perception. "I have never seen you intentionally wear a disarranged messy bun hairstyle. Is this your new postapocalyptic fashion brand?"

The lieutenant's brazen observations rattled Emily. His tone of voice disconcerted her composure. She was at a loss, baffled about how to respond. From a positive standpoint, she was glad knowing that the investigation was coming to an end, albeit inconclusively.

"Are you enjoying your luxury golfing vacation?" Colonel Roberts inquired with a superior, self-congratulatory, complacent look on his face, knowing there had been no time for leisure. "Thank you for your participation in Operation Procol Harum. Your efforts have exposed the malfeasants. The majority of eccentrics have already received their just reward. The governor has directed that all of the deaths this summer are the responsibility of local law enforcement. Deputy Sheriff Bud Light will remain in charge of the investigations when we cease our operations."

The lieutenant redirected his attention to Colonel Roberts to ask an important question. "Did you discover anything of value at Gravestone Castle during your midnight search and seizure operation last night?"

"We uncovered a treasure trove of curiosities, a cauldron of dark unexplained science mysteries, so obscure as to arouse curiosity, suspense, and speculation. Father Adam Baum studied microorganisms, viruses, bacteria, fungi, and other toxins produced and released deliberately to cause disease and death in humans, animals, and plants. His warehouse was filled with hundreds of beehives and scientific manuals, proving that he was able to control and direct swarms of killer bees toward specific individuals."

"What you're telling us explains a great deal about the reasons for his ascetic lifestyle, his outlook on life, and his solitary deviant behavior. His lifetime of unrepentant wicked sins caused irrevocable spiritual ruin, condemning him to eternal perdition," the lieutenant philosophized.

Colonel James Roberts summarized his findings. "Father Adam Baum's bioterrorism experiments and intentional release of biological agents in Third World countries caused mass loss of consciousness, convulsions, paralysis, muscle weakness, blindness, and death for thousands of people, food crops, and livestock. Some of his greatest secrets are right out in the open, including his bizarre rogue taxidermy, roadkill specimens portraying an agonizing death. He removed dead animals with broken antlers, crushed ribs, and missing teeth from highways and ditches. Pure awfulness and atrocious hideousness, mind-boggling statues of menacing deformed animals frozen in time with cracked skulls that died in pain, unfortunate victims of hideous car accidents."

The meeting ended without fanfare, flourish, trumpet call, or the fuss of publicity. Emily was exhausted. There was not enough time to change clothes, comb her hair, or brush her teeth before heading directly to the courthouse.

92

CURB YOUR ENTHUSIASM

Jay Walker greeted the lieutenant and Emily at the front door of the courtroom. The lieutenant warmly shook hands while offering his unfettered advice. "Never test the depth of a river with two feet," he warned. "Complaining about the loss of your property with mockery may worsen an already unfavorable situation. The best way to get unstuck from this unrighteous situation is grace and dignity. Show the judge that you live well and authentically and have a big heart. Allow the district attorney to speak for you and present your legal paperwork to Judge Geri Attrick, and cross your fingers."

Joey Linguine's approach to legal matters was the opposite. He was in a self-congratulatory mood, arrogant and overconfident. Sister Olivia Seno Grande was also smug and confident, knowing that Polpetta was the sole heir to Gravestone Castle. She was chewing gum with her mouth wide open, dreaming of a new life of luxury filled with inessentials conducive to unlimited pleasure and comfort. She was counting her chickens before they hatched. Sister Olivia daydreamed about her future as the new owner of a grossly luxurious mansion, marveling at her recent marriage and newly acquired carte blanche wealth. It was an ironic twist of fate that her loveless marriage occurred on Friday the thirteenth during a rainstorm.

"Who cares who you marry if he's rich?" she explained to her family as the grounds for her marriage. "What if my husband is a jerk? Being the heir to Gravestone Castle is like winning the lottery," she rationalized.

Joey's lawyer was as greedy, disrespectful, and as crass as the law would allow. He was a corrupt, double-dealing, underhanded ambulance chaser previously convicted of illegally converting client funds from an escrow account. He had been indicted, charged, and prosecuted several times but only convicted once. He only worked on contingency. "If you don't win, I don't get anything. If you win, you don't get anything. This case is open and shut. Polpetta is the only beneficiary named in Father Cellophane's will. He bequeathed all of his tangible property and worldly goods to his only child, Polpetta."

"All rise for the Honorable Judge Geri Attrick," the bailiff instructed loudly, words heard in courtrooms thousands of times each day throughout the country to show respect for the law.

The attorney for Jay Walker was the first to speak. "The last will and testament of Benedict Walker and the legal property deed for Gravestone Castle currently in possession of the court are false."

The information presented to the court was shockingly unexpected, catching Joey Linguine and his lawyer entirely off guard. Joey's blood ran cold, and his hair stood on end in frustration. He was appalled and paralyzed with outrage at the findings and the potential devastation to his future.

"Objection!" Joey's lawyer hollered. "The rightful heir to Gravestone Castle is Father Cellophane's son, Polpetta."

The lieutenant whispered in Emily's ear. "The greatest inheritance anyone can receive is emotional intelligence; that is the key to both personal and professional success."

Sister Olivia Seno Grande was shocked and sickened because she had recklessly rushed to marry Joey Linguine. She should never have adopted Polpetta as her son. She had foolishly acted out of greed, based solely on the illicit promise of inheriting Gravestone Castle.

"The district attorney is a ninja. She scares the pants off me, and she makes me hurl," Polpetta remarked sarcastically.

The lieutenant summed up his thoughts about children. "There is nothing in the life of a little green caterpillar or a small child that can predict the beauty that lies within; in both cases, they metamorphose into something entirely different. Kids are like golf, and you're always hoping you can do better next time."

The district attorney reinforced Jay's position. "Your honor, I can prove that the existing documents are forgeries fallaciously fabricated to deceive the court and rob Jay Walker of his rightful inheritance."

Deputy Sheriff Bud Light interrupted, exerting his authority and self-importance. "I support the DA's conclusions. Jay Walker is the legal owner of Gravestone Castle, and he is entitled to his rightful inheritance."

"You're so screwed," Joey's lawyer blurted out with a red face, knowing that he would never collect any money from his client now. "Joey Linguine, you've lost your path before you even found it. I quit! Find yourself another lawyer," he protested disgustedly, shit-storming out of the courthouse in a dramatic blaze of glory and fit of anger.

Judge Geri Attrick pounded her gavel to restore order in the court before making a ruling. "Jay Walker, you are the true, rightful, and lawful owner of Gravestone Castle. Therefore, you may occupy the property immediately."

Watery tears of joy filled his eyes. He was hyperexcited, in an emotional state of mental arousal and situational awareness. His heart was racing. Feelings of euphoria overcame him, overjoyed with intense feelings of well-being and happiness. Realizing the immediate changes and new opportunities available in his life, he twirled around. He grabbed Emily, joyously lifting her in the air before kissing her passionately on the lips.

"Will you accept this rose?" he blurted out as a timeless expression of affection in front of the entire courtroom. "Yes, Jay," she gushed unabashedly. She effervesced with tinseled charm and sparkling sentimentality. Today was the happiest day of her life.

93

CANNABIS KITCHEN

Sister Olivia was heartbroken. "My dreams shattered, and I can hardly believe what has happened to me. My newly adopted son, Polpetta, being denied the inheritance of Gravestone Castle by Judge Geri Attrick leaves me dumbfounded and traumatized."

Joey Linguine was a loser, unfazed by her bantering. The loss of one opportunity was always quickly forgotten and replaced with another drunken moneymaking scheme. He was too lively and lighthearted to doubt, too optimistic about being fearful, and too determined to be defeated. "Don't worry, babe—stick with me, and you'll always be farting through silk. Get a big hat in vibrant colors that are flashy and eye-catching to improve your storytelling."

"You promised me that if we got married and adopted Polpetta, we were going to inherit Gravestone Castle. So, what are we going to do now, Joey?"

"Why should I try to fit in when I was born to stand out? Optimism leads to achievement. When I face the sun, my shadow falls behind me. Hope and confidence will ensure that everything eventually falls into place."

Sister Olivia was in a state of confusion. "The brighter the light, the darker the shadow becomes."

"Brain fog is a symptom of anxiety and persistently elevated stress, and it isn't a cause for concern. Don't be a pessimist that always ends up one taco short of a combination plate."

Joey was having difficulty restraining his enthusiasm and was overselling his latest ideas. "Our son's real name isn't Polpetta; I gave him that nickname a long time ago—it means *meatball* in Italian."

"I was unaware of that."

Joey amorously held Sister Olivia's hand and looked her in the eyes while attempting to profess everlasting love for her. "The first thing I noticed about you is the beautiful amber color of your eyes."

Her rebuttal and invalidation were swift. "The first thing I noticed about you is you are an untrustworthy liar."

Disrespecting her gloomy dissenting opinion, Joey optimistically laid out his plan. "Trust me. In Aspen, Colorado, the Food and Wine Classic is the nation's premier culinary event, featuring the world's most accomplished winemakers, celebrity chefs, and cooking experts. Since I attended the event last year, everyone has been raving about my mother's delightful Italian recipes. *Capeesh*—understand?" he exclaimed, using the Italian pointy hand gesture with a rapid up and down movement for emphasis.

Sister Olivia sarcastically pulled the skin down under one eye with a crafty smile. "You clever guy!" Followed by the Italian forearm jerk signifying "up yours, buddy." "The only family recipe I'm aware of is your recipe for disaster. Chaos and confusion surround you. Your middle name should be Mayhem."

Unfazed by her adverse reaction, Joey continued. "Now that marijuana is legal in Colorado, revenues for edibles have skyrocketed. So I'm going to open a classic Italian restaurant in Aspen. I'll call it Linguine Brothers Cannabis Kitchen, using my mother's recipes combined with edible marijuana—food that entire families will enjoy. I'm sure it's going to be a huge success. Featured dishes will include Alcatraz pelican from San Francisco Bay, delivered by Greyhound bus from California; stewed javelina piccata with goat cheese brought to us by poachers in an old tomato truck from Green Valley, Arizona; deranged prune salad with soybeans and brown cuttlefish ink; kale lasagna pigeon pie with goat cheese from Silt, Colorado; and jumping jack catfish stew with blitzed herring, artichokes, and wine-stained meatballs from the Mississippi Delta. I chose Grandpa's Pacific Atoll Radioactive Merlot with explosive cadaverine fruit flavors as the house wine."

He enthusiastically rubbed his hands together. "Our CBD-infused foods will be guaranteed to boost moods, erase anxiety, alleviate arthritis, and combat psychological issues. Aspen residents are naturally uniformly more lighthearted, carefree, and buoyant. Polpetta is eager to learn how to snowboard in Aspen. He will be excellent at recruiting new customers from the local schools for our restaurant. So pack your mittens and snow boots because you're going to love it there."

Polpetta was wearing a *Dumb and Dumber* T-shirt reading "Aspen or Bust." Sister Olivia remained stone-faced as Joey stole a piece of plywood from a construction site. He duct-taped it to the ceiling of the white van to cover the large hole blasted in the roof by the frozen yellow poop bomb.

Her thirteen-year-old son, Polpetta, moved in with his saucy, imprudent junior high school teacher six months later. The restaurant remained a pipe dream. Joey Linguine lived in Woody Creek, Colorado, tending bar at the legendary tavern. "If this doesn't work out, I've been offered a bartending teachers job at Aspen State Teachers College."

Joey exclaimed with glee as he watched the Tournament of Roses Parade on television, "There's my buddy, the flatulent organ grinder, riding on the Salvation Army parade float. He's yawning and talking dirty to himself. His arm is still in a sling. Look at that big scar on his forehead. He still has a black eye."

Sister Olivia Seno Grande paid little attention to anything Joey had to say or do anymore. She spoke dirty in Italian, with creativity and volume. The only way she could get a hickey was if the vacuum cleaner stuck to her neck. The tea leaves had foretold happiness and abundant wealth, while yesterday's lottery ticket lay crumbled on the bed. The marriage eventually turned sour and reduced to hall sex, and no physical contact was necessary. Each time they passed in the hallway, Sister Olivia said, "F... you, Joey!"

With a heavy heart, a messy soul, and a reckless mind, she abandoned her family in the middle of the night. Sister Olivia moved to Quail Creek, a gated Robson community in Green Valley, Arizona. She came alive in those tight-fitting jeans, selling old, used worn-out Navajo rugs out of the trunk of her car on the side of the Old Nogales Highway. Sister Olivia became famous overnight as a trendy party planner, the sensational "Dancing Diva," gyrating her hips in her sexy leotards for everyone's pleasure. She danced like a possum in a cage doing the erotic hoochie-coochie and promiscuous hucklebuck. Her provocative belly dance-like moves made older men jump and shout. She never stopped dreaming. Her senior dating website in Arizona for older adults, called Carbon Dating, was inspiring.

94

THE END OF POMPOSITY

Wayne and Kate Kennedy were patiently sitting in the first row of the courthouse. They were awaiting the arrival of Judge Geri Attrick to determine if the probate court judge would approve their offer to buy Woebegone Dunes Resort.

IRS Agent Penny Pincher explained, "I have found no evidence of cryptic collaboration, conspiracy, or fraud. There is no evidence of a deceitful Ponzi scheme, no remaining debts, and no outstanding liens attached to the property or any external accounts. There are no threats of violence, abusive language, reports of harm, and no arrests or extraditions are anticipated. I present before the court documents that legally transfer the rights of ownership of Woebegone Dunes Resort from the Jack Daniels estate to buyers Wayne and Kate Kennedy in the full amount due, including an amended warranty deed. There is no dispute and no counter complaints. There are no liens or outstanding debts. The affected parties are all in agreement. We are requesting an order to dispose of this case."

Holding hands and temporarily ceasing to breathe, Wayne and Kate were a bundle of nerves. They remained in a suspended state of anticipation, anxiously waiting for the judge to decide their fate. Finally, hearing no standing objections and the lawyers' unanimous consent representing both parties, Judge Geri Attrick addressed the court. "The court recognizes the proposed transition of ownership of Woebegone Dunes Resort to buyers Wayne and Kate Kennedy."

Wayne and Kate hugged with overwhelming sentiments of happiness. Kate's emotional satisfaction was unmanageable. Tears of joy formed in her eyes as a sign of purification and emotional release.

"Vanessa, by order of the court, you are at this moment relieved of your duties as the executor of Jack Daniels's will in return for the compensation offered by this purchase agreement." Furthermore, the judge forewarned, "There is one additional issue before the court."

95

EMBEZZLEMENT

Following a brief recess, the court resumed. The district attorney presented his case. "The next item of interest involves the embezzlement of funds, the misappropriation of money placed in one's trust belonging to the organization for which one works."

IRS Agent Penny Pincher stood before the judge to present her findings. "During my investigation, I discovered a felonious Swiss bank account owned by Lady Vanessa. This secret account was funded wholly by funds stolen from the Royal Enouement Society, Jack Daniels, and Woebegone Dunes Resort."

Lady Vanessa had no legitimate way of defending her actions. Her lawyer, a known builder of shady offshore accounts, had skipped town. Perhaps he had even left the country.

The judge calmly cleared her throat. Then, in a clear voice, she announced her verdict. "Lady Vanessa, you have been defrauding Jack Daniels's estate for more than five years, stealing money by siphoning off funds to line your own pockets. You diverted a portion of every check and wire transfer of funds sent to Woebegone Dunes Resort and the Royal Enouement Society to a fraudulent Swiss bank account in Zurich, solely owned by you. More than a million dollars, embezzled by the diversion of assets using a skimming scheme, were diverted. You purposefully orchestrated an arrangement designed to deceive. Your actions were performed methodically with precautions to conceal the criminal conversion of money from the intended accounts to a fictitious account established by you without anyone else's knowledge or consent."

Lady Vanessa was experiencing a nervous meltdown, a spontaneous episode of intense emotions and extreme fear that set off physical reactions symptomatic of a panic attack. Believing that the threat of doom and destruction was imminent, nausea, heavy breathing, and shaking overcame her as the county clerk read aloud the criminal acts separately and in succession. Knowing that there was no possibility of escape, she filed a blind plea with no bargain in place in exchange for eliminating the trial and the promise of a reduced sentence. With a heavy heart, she pleaded guilty to fraud. She admitted to the crime of manslaughter in the accidental death of Father Cellophane. Her straightforward, muted verbal guilty plea was barely audible. She was convicted and sent off to prison.

Like the tan on her skin, her name in the sand, the tears on her face, and the sun going down, she faded away like sunburned autumn leaves, waving goodbye as the winds of change began to blow. She watched the setting sun and dreamed of all the roads she had been down as her outward appearance faded from fresh flowers to potpourri.

The lieutenant praised IRS agent Penny Pincher's work. "I appreciate your professionalism and calm, unflappable certitude. You're the type of person I would like to have on my team. Sleuthing isn't limited to solving crimes; the real task is the administration of justice through the equitable adjustment of claims and merited punishments," he astutely observed.

Emily's philosophical perception of life was finally falling into perspective. "I'm glad these harrowing events highlighting the dark side of life are coming to an end. I'm finally optimistic about the future, and truth, charity, honesty, and happiness seem just around the corner."

96

ATONEMENT

Emily passively atoned for her transgressions, allowing unique and beautiful perceptions of pleasant reveries of journeys both imminent and serendipitous to fill her heart and mind. Living in holy matrimony with Jay Walker in Gravestone Castle was a blessing and a dream come true.

The wedding took place in the Chapel at Gravestone Castle with all of their friends in attendance, including a busload of ancient high school friends from Dominican High School. Her wedding dress was perfect, and the flowers were fresh and colorful. The wedding ceremony was flawless, and the setting stunning. The classy dinner and reception left her basking in the glow of her wedding. Well-wishers showered her with compliments.

Deputy Sheriff Bud Light was scared to death with the news of Tammy's unplanned pregnancy. He reacted with a mixture of fright and excitement. His face was pale. After taking a few nervous breaths and shots of brandy for courage, he realized there was joy in it. "It's my little boy," he exclaimed in response to her urgent and emotional plea for marriage. "Without guilt, force, or blame, I accept your proposal of marriage."

Tammy was in gleefully high spirits, experiencing great elation and exhilarating joy, rising to the point of light-headedness. She dreamed of honeymooning in an exotic tropical location where she and the Deputy could copulate in a coconut tree.

Lieutenant Dunning was the first to congratulate the newly engaged sheriff and his pregnant fiancée, Tammy. "In metallurgy, 'wedding' is the fusing of two metals with a hot torch. The love you share for each other appears hotter than a Mexican jalapeño pepper. Bud Light, you have found the one you want to pass through life with at your side as your earthly companion. Tammy, you have found the one that you can't wait to talk about gardening and house cleaning with for the rest of your life."

British Agent Kingsley and Chloe Crouton were married at the Brompton Oratory Roman Catholic Church in Knightsbridge, London, an exciting place of winding streets, private buildings, and deadly deceit. With its cloak-and-dagger exploits and dead letter drop boxes, it was a popular haunt of spies and honey traps, an ideal place to engage in the ancient profession of espionage whereby agents light a votive candle, say a prayer, and leave behind highly confidential material of dramatic intrigue.

Lieutenant Baron Dunning secretly conveyed several messages using unique phrases and slang that only a fellow spy would understand. In addition, he provided a mathematical quantity expressing the probability of a particular sequence of symbols, particulars about several brush contacts, digital tradecraft, UNCLE, and an asset validation for a recent false-flag recruit.

Colonel James Roberts called to congratulate them. "Best wishes and commendations to all of you. The Procol Harum investigation is officially over. Terminate all field operations immediately. You've done all you can."

97

DIPLOMATIC IMMUNITY

Lieutenant Dunning detected a sense of remorse and regret in the Colonel's voice. "I'm stunned. The abrupt cancellation of the fact-finding probe without certainty and closure surprises me. I've always known you to be alert, live in the present, and prepare for action twenty-four hours a day. What prompted your change in heart?"

Colonel Roberts kept his emotions in check, preserving his dignity and making sure to get the story straight. He was at ground zero at the Pentagon, with his superiors in a conference room, pondering the ramifications of the order. The colonel expressed gratitude for the work accomplished and hinted at future assignments involving Chinese military aggression, dropping a second bombshell before the lieutenant could respond.

"The United States has awarded Nigerian playboy Bo-Bo Bigelow full diplomatic immunity, a form of legal protection that allows him to avoid the force of the law. He has a safe passage and full freedom of movement. He is immune from arrest or detention, exempt from immigration restrictions, dues, taxes, and criminal, civil, and administrative jurisdiction. No matter the crime, he can still manage to escape prosecution."

Colonel Roberts justified the decision. "Diplomatic immunity is a cornerstone of diplomacy. Bo-Bo Bigelow is one of the most important people globally regarding modern technology components. His actions have the potential to influence the future course of international events. The natural resources Bo-Bo Bigelow provides this country exceed the monetary value for national security. The demand for rare-earth minerals in every industrial sector worldwide is beginning to outstrip supply. The American economy, the computer industry, the space force, the military-industrial complex, and the defense industry depend entirely on rare-earth minerals. We would be in immediate peril if we ever find ourselves on the wrong end of a supply disruption. Bo-Bo Bigelow now has the highest diplomatic immunity from prosecution this nation can offer. He promised to divest himself of all Wisconsin-based assets and property in exchange for this honor and privilege. Of his own accord, he has agreed to continue clandestinely battling terrorists interfering with the export of rare-earth minerals."

The colonel's message was clear as if punctuated with an exclamation point. "This agency is intensely future-oriented. For that reason, my decision to terminate the Procol Harum investigation is irrevocable. Oil embezzlement from Nigeria on a massive scale is only the tip of the iceberg. As a national policy, China has aggressively secured a universal monopoly on the supply of rare-earth minerals deemed critical to our economic success and national security. Assurances of a continuing supply of these materials are of the highest national importance, a burgeoning political crisis, and a potential future catastrophe. As trade tensions rise between the United States and China, rare earth minerals will always be in the political spotlight," Colonel Roberts assured him.

"Bo-Bo Bigelow propagated this entire adventure. He and Father Feely are the common denominators throughout the entire investigation. The millions of dollars in oil and natural resources sold on the black market are incomprehensible. Keeping Muslim terrorists at bay while supplying this country with abundant precious rare-earth minerals is essential for a robust national defense. It's critical to national security that for these compelling reasons, the government has agreed to grant full immunity from prosecution."

The lieutenant paused to absorb the insular, deliberative weight of the rightness and wrongness of US policymakers' value judgments. "Unique circumstances are not always problems to be solved but rather truths to be accepted. The best solutions are the ones that eliminate the problem."

"Exactly."

"Incidentally, Bo-Bo Bigelow sent you a gift-wrapped parcel."

"What's in it?"

"I don't know. I'll send it to you."

The colonel was in a calm state of mind. His posture was straight, and his mind alert, signaling a strong military disposition, strength, and condition of readiness. He had a keen sense of duty, knowing what he had to accomplish. Deliberately and systematically analyzing information, he logically categorized conceptual information. He spoke using precise language with an appropriate tone.

"The risks of China's new Belt and Road Initiative outweigh its benefits. Your next assignment will be to assess the sustainability of Chinese military naval bases in the Atlantic and Indian Oceans and the potential threats to US security they pose. After the next election, a change in political parties is certain to highlight public awareness of the potential threat to American economic prosperity and military security posed by Chinese aggression."

Emily had the last word. "The abrupt end to this investigation reminds me of a newsreel film falling out of the projector."

98

BUD LIGHT

To celebrate their good fortune as the new owners of Woebegone Dunes Resort, Wayne and Kate Kennedy agreed to host a grand opening lunch buffet on the Sol de Terrace overlooking the Holy Fountain sculpture garden. The formal event was a scene of pure relaxation with the guests comfortably seated in the rose garden, with complimentary champagne and a small ensemble providing classical chamber music.

Reporter René Malarkey, reeking of the unpleasant stink of cannabis, directed a question to Lieutenant Baron Dunning. "What about all of the bizarre unorthodox deaths this summer? Were any of the deaths the result of murder, assassination, passion, or suicide? What about the poor guy that died screaming to death clinging to an electric toilet seat? I want to know more about the resolution and disentanglement of the summer-long criminal investigation into all of the unexplained deaths at Woebegone Dunes Resort and Gravestone Castle."

The lieutenant tugged on his earlobes, took a deep draw on his pipe, and blew a thick smoke ring into the air before commencing. "A detective is only as good as the evidence uncovered and the underlying assumptions used to support the facts. When the sources are unreliable, the information is unproven, and the inferences are misguided fallacy or untrue, it is difficult to solve any crime."

By inference, the entire audience turned around to focus on Deputy Sheriff Bud Light standing in the back of the room. He puffed up his chest with pride, knowing he had the attention of everyone in attendance. Motivated by an exaggerated sense of self-importance and a delusion of superior intelligence and authority, Deputy Sheriff Bud Light pompously marched briskly to the front of the room. He had a supercilious swagger and an air of overbearing self-confidence displaying dominance over others as if the audience members were his inferiors.

"I am the official responsible for investigating homicides in this jurisdiction," he stated clearly in plain English. "Please address all of your questions to me."

The deputy was bold and arrogant, but public speaking was not his forte. Formal presentations to large groups caused sweating palms, a shaky voice, a dry throat, difficulty breathing, a lack of volume control, and memory loss, common symptoms of anxiety for the deputy. He was afraid of being judged negatively by the audience and overly timid about being the center of attention. He was startlingly on the verge of freezing onstage. His collar was too tight. Too much time in the sun dehydrated him. His blood pressure was dropping. A failure to breathe appropriately decreased blood flow to the brain, causing a brief loss of consciousness and a decline in posture stability due to a lack of oxygen.

His tongue was hanging out of his mouth. Drool dripped from his chin. Fumbling with his notes and slurring the words of his speech made him appear staggering drunk. Then, feeling lightheaded, dizzy, and nauseous, he fainted. His back stiffened as his eyeballs rolled back, exposing the white part of his eyes. He flailed his arms wildly, trying to retain his balance. Finally, he stumbled backward, accidentally knocking his cowboy hat into the water as he awkwardly and stiffly fell back into the Holy Fountain. An enormous wave splashed several guests. As the deputy lifted his head above the water, the audience saw a remarkable resemblance to the confused brutish-looking neanderthal figure in the background with water dripping from his head. The previously unseen bald spot on the back of the deputy's head reminded Emily of the sun shining brightly through the clouds on a deforestation project.

The sudden full-body emergence into cold water with a high chlorine content made his eyes sting. The pupils in his eyes constricted, leaving his eye sockets looking like two pee holes in the snow. Tammy instinctively grabbed the deputy by the hair to keep him from drowning. Unfortunately, her wet blouse exposed extreme anatomical changes to her protruding stomach due to pregnancy, leading to numerous breathy whispers throughout the crowd.

The crotch in his navy-blue police uniform made a loud ripping sound as it split from the back to the front, leaving a gaping hole in his pants. An enormous cow was sticking its head out of his barn door, and the deputy grabbed a banjo from one of the band members to hide it. Tammy rushed forward with a fresh roll of duct tape to repair the embarrassing tear in his pants and conceal his unsightly baggy white underpants. She attached the duct tape to the back of his pants, reached under his crotch, and raised the animal-print duct tape to the height of his belt buckle. She covered the torn zipper with two extra strips of duct tape and rubbed her hand firmly up and down to make it stick. The final result resembled a crumpled baby diaper.

Tammy held his arm tightly as he regained his balance. She looked into his soul with warm eyes of assurance and encouragement as he bravely rose to his feet and faced the crowd. His waterlogged boots made a squishy sound with each tentative step forward. The deputy ignored the Kleenex she offered and wiped his face on his arm, leaving a long trail of stringy yellow phlegm on his shirt sleeve. He nervously glanced at the audience as if nothing had happened, shook the water off his notebook, and tortuously grasped the podium tightly with both hands before continuing.

The deputy's lack of public speaking ability was appalling. His performance was the worst case of dysarthria Emily had ever witnessed. She was horrified as she watched his mouth and facial muscles move in opposing contorted directions, unmatched by the words he was speaking. He gave the impression he was chewing a wad of sticky toffee with loose dentures. In addition, the deputy couldn't hear properly because his ears were filled with water. His speech was erratically intermittent and losing momentum. His volume control was gone. Some of his sentences were barely audible, while others were uncomfortably loud, causing several audience members to adjust their hearing aids.

News reporter René Malarkey captured the entire event on film. The image of the deputy emerging from the water and tearing the crotch of his police pants was sure to become another sensational national news story. He enthusiastically began sketching a stunning new design for a "Defund the Police" T-shirt.

99

CADDYWAMPUS

The deputy sheriff began in earnest, speaking without predetermination or preparation. "Events that transpired this summer at Woebegone Dunes Resort are like a grossly overweight burlesque performance on *Britain's Got Talent*—nobody was paying attention to the big picture. Everything is caddywampus, askew, diagonally off-center, and not lined up correctly. Circumstances remind me of the way an unpredictable two-year-old erratically moves things around."

Bud Light was emotionally wound up and speaking extemporaneously. The crowd was listening attentively.

"Bo-Bo Bigelow and Father Feely are the root cause of everything that has transpired. Millions of dollars are generated every year from selling stolen Nigerian oil and other natural resources. Father Feely, the lecherous priest who founded the Hermitage at Gravestone Castle, was the henchman, the loyal and trusted subordinate engaged in evil behavior. He was the chief financial officer of Ebony LLC, responsible for currency exchange, international money transfers, and real estate transactions. Gravestone Castle is a valuable niche property, and Father Feely became exceedingly greedy. He had a wild longing to acquire Gravestone Castle for himself. His actions led to multiple moral transgressions and covert actions resulting in the death of Benedict Walker."

"I thought Benedict Walker died from a severe allergic reaction to peanuts," reporter René Malarkey stated inquisitively. "Your report said the onslaught of death was very rapid."

"A handwritten note by Billy Big Ears Bellini requesting a birthday cake made with peanut flour leads us to believe the demise of Benedict Walker was premeditated murder. Father Feely is the leading suspect with the most motivation and gain. He is the most plausible perpetrator and beneficiary. Paying Big Ears to get rid of Benedict Walker allowed him to falsify documents necessary to acquire ownership of Gravestone Castle illegally."

"What about the Mexican laborer run off the cliff by killer bees?"

"Jose Lopez was a federal drug informant. He accidentally fell to his death into Lake Michigan while attempting to escape from a swarm of angry killer bees. We suspect that his death was a planned entomological insect attack perpetrated by Father Adam Baum, paid for by a Mexican drug cartel."

"Who was the pilot of the airplane that crashed?"

"We assumed that a trash hauler from Chicago stole Billy Big Ears's airplane based on fingerprint analysis of a hand found at the crash site. We traced the fingerprints to a one-armed man from Chicago, and he claimed Billy chopped off his hand for not paying his debts. The hand was in the airplane when it crashed. An eyewitness report from two anonymous birdwatchers confirmed what Wayne and Kate Kennedy had already reported that a bomb caused the airplane to crash. Billy survived the crash but with severe head injuries leading to meningitis and death."

"Who buried Father Cellophane in a sand bunker on the golf course?"

"Lady Vanessa informed us that her trusted follower Bruno Greco unscrupulously hit Father Cellophane in the face with a golf ball. He was acting on her behalf, and she admits that it was an act of aggression and intimidation. She suggested Bruno toss the body into Lake Michigan to make the death appear to have been an accidental drowning. However, partygoers engaged in merrymaking at the Hermitage drank heavily and danced topless around a campfire that night. The beach was partially visible in the moonlight, so Bruno dragged the body into the shadows to avoid detection. He stripped off Father Cellophane's clothes and hastily buried the corpse in a sand bunker, exactly where Kate Kennedy discovered the body."

"What about the fiberglass statue of Father Cellophane?"

"Father Adam Baum returned to the cemetery two days after the funeral. He dug up the grave and clandestinely removed the proverbial vicar from the casket. He then wrapped the decaying body in fiberglass using steel rods to stabilize a memorial effigy statue."

"Tell us about Dusty Rhodes, the caddy from Woebegone Dunes Resort."

"We discovered two hundred thousand dollars in cash in his broken-down trailer and a precious historical oil painting worth a fortune. Police investigators assume Dusty shot Johnny Linguine and an art dealer from Atlanta in the head in Estabrook Park. We found the gun he used to kill them in his trailer. He stripped Johnny Linguine of his clothes before dumping his body in the Milwaukee River. The black Audi owned by the art dealer from Atlanta was totaled in a car accident on Capital Avenue in Milwaukee. Dusty removed his clothes and stuffed him in the trunk."

The reporter furiously scribbled notes. "What else?"

"Wrongfully assuming caddy Dusty Rhodes had killed Father Cellophane, Father Adam Baum intentionally shot Dusty in the back with a crossbow as an act of vengeance. A bolt from the crossbow instantly paralyzed him. He lay face down in the ferns for more than a week before succumbing to dehydration. The investigation was closed when Father Adam Baum died from eating poisoned honey."

"Who killed Bruno Greco?"

"Bruno was the victim of a tragic accident when a golf cart belonging to Jack Daniels exploded along with several crates of commercial fireworks. His death may have been an intentional act of aggression and murder directed toward Jack Daniels, but the wrong person died. The cause of ignition is unknown, and it may have resulted from a spark from the electric golf cart."

"What assumptions did you make about the death of Jack Daniels and his malfunctioning electric toilet?"

"We have no assumptions about the reasons for the failure of the electric toilet to function properly. The findings of multiple complex investigations and lawsuits will have to play out first."

"What assumptions have you made about the eccentric, unconventional death of Father Feely, a most out-of-the-ordinary, unorthodox, and queer way to die?"

"According to the autopsy findings, Father Feely died from eating unripe Chinese persimmons. A grotesque indigestible bezoar caused fecal impaction and constipation in his intestine so severe that it killed him."

"What about all the bizarre, wacky things that happened at the masquerade ball? How did the president react when a monkey telephoned him?"

"The president is looking forward to meeting the monkey in person. He is also planning to hire the Singing Supremes tribute band to play at the White House."

"What about the poop bomb that destroyed Joey Linguine's white van?"

"Joey Linguine is suing Ozark Air Lines for damages resulting from a flying blue ice toilet bomb that destroyed his white van. It was not a malicious act of domestic terrorism as we had originally assumed."

"Do you have any leads on the identity of the eighty-year-old woman that shot three people in the Fox and Hounds restaurant parking lot?"

"The FBI wanted all three victims, and I assume the old woman will eventually reveal herself to the authorities to collect the substantial monetary reward."

Emily's left eye uncontrollably twitched as she fidgeted nervously in the background. Constricted breathing caused an embarrassing wheezing followed by a whistling sound.

With a slow shake of his head, reporter René Malarkey responded with utter disbelief. "You remind me of a fisherman with a fishing lure stuck in the back of his ear after the canoe tipped over. The whole situation is a caddywampus debacle, cockeyed and unlevel, fishy and suspicious, out of alignment, skewed, and off-center. This summer, everything that happened seems whacky, off-kilter, and out of balance."

100

THE HOLY FOUNTAIN

Kate raised her hands above her head to quiet the crowd and divert attention from the obnoxious reporter. "Lieutenant Dunning, what do you suppose is the meaning behind the Holy Fountain sculpture here at Woebegone Dunes Resort? It's the most attractive and harmonious architectural feature. So what is the fundamental message the sculptor is attempting to achieve?"

The lieutenant pointed to the enamel pin on the lapel of his jacket, indicating an affiliation with the Royal Enouement Society as an enduring sign of high achievement and elite performance. The lieutenant was a man of letters, full of thought, demonstrating reasoned thinking and careful deliberation. The audience was awakened and energized, leaning forward in their chairs and paying close attention. Crowd engagement was overwhelmingly affirmative and positive.

"The emergence of the entire Western philosophical tradition began with the ancient Greeks. Atlas is the symbol of the Royal Enouement Society. He is an immortal being reminding us to follow through with our worldly duties, commitments, and responsibilities, regardless of the weight of the world on our shoulders. The Holy Fountain conveys an eternal message that is ageless, enduring, and considerably deeper than aesthetics. The message is about integrity and loyalty to rational principles and common sense. It is a reminder never to compromise goodness, righteousness, ethics, and good health. The two figures in the fountain represent opposing philosophies, ways of thinking, and alternative futures of all of humankind. The Greek god wearing the laurel wreath is healthy and wise. He is rational. He is everything good. He has common sense and maintains a high moral ground. He represents truth and reason, as well as morality and ethical values. He encourages us to avoid meekly subjecting ourselves to destructive and malign influences."

The lieutenant pointed to the second figure. "Conversely, the clumsy ogre lacks benevolence, and his ideas are inconsistent and incompatible with justice, goodness, and righteousness. He is simply treading water and not making any progress toward a goal. The Greek god is pouring water on his head to return him to consciousness—to alert him to the reality that his ideas are all wet."

"I see exactly what the lieutenant is saying. The message is a revelation, an awakening of the mind that makes you stop and think about our choices throughout life as individuals and collectively as a society. The sculpture is an ingenious way of disclosing profoundly philosophical ideas of great importance commonly attributed to dramatic works of art," someone in the audience added.

The lieutenant smiled and pressed on with increased intensity. "Behind every successful endeavor, there is an imaginative visionary whose ideas are inherently strategic and resourceful. Jack Daniels was that type of person. The Royal Enouement Society has historical roots that trace back to Plato's philosophy that honors higher learning and wisdom, ethics, and integrity. They encourage individuals to thrive by avoiding compromising morals, ethics, and basic principles of right and wrong. In a nutshell, the choices we make every day reflect the contrasting personalities of the people we emulate—the ogre and the gentleman."

The audience reminded Emily of an enthusiastic flock of parishioners, religious congregation members holding hands, singing, and unanimously coming together in harmonious agreement. Wayne and Kate looked each other in the eyes as a way of demonstrating a fundamental change in their previous points of view and perspectives—a paradigm shift away from one way of thinking to another entirely different way of viewing the world.

101

ROYAL ENOUEMENT SOCIETY

Lieutenant Baron Dunning raised a blue leather-bound book with metal hinges and clamps above his head for everyone to see. Something scarce and unique about the look, smell, and feel of the elaborate and decorative binding with gilt edges, raised ribs, and embroidered cover attracted attention.

"The Royal Enouement Society was founded by Jack Daniels, the owner of Woebegone Dunes Resort. I discovered the handbook in his cabin while investigating his mysterious death by electrocution. The book is a snapshot of the organization's culture that captures values, behaviors, artifacts, and everything you would ever want to know. Jack was a brilliant individual with college degrees in business, finance, and philosophy. He was an intellectual property lawyer, a brilliant tactician, and a successful businessman.

"The philosophy of objectivism enlightens them, invigorates the heart, wires them for success, and gives them a sense of reality. They respect individual rights, view happiness as the moral purpose of life, believe productive achievement is the noblest activity, and hold that reason and logic are the only absolutes. The Library of Congress ranks the philosophy of objectivism higher than the study of any other philosophy, coming in second only to the Bible.

"The naming of the organization is relatively easy to understand.

A *royalty* is a legally binding payment made to an individual or company for ongoing use of their intellectual property, such as copyrights, natural resources, patents, and trademarks. Five percent is the most common and generally fair number.

"In the dictionary of obscure sorrows, *énouement* is the bittersweetness of having arrived in the future, seeing how things turned out but not being able to tell your past self. The art of successful living is to avoid obvious pitfalls resulting in dramatic complications. Imagine if you had volunteered to stay behind at a forgotten outpost somewhere in the past, still eagerly awaiting news from the front. What if you knew where your choices would lead you, which bridges to cross and which ones to burn, priceless intel that you instinctively wanted to know?

"In every profession from business and medicine to the climate, forecasting the future is a complex and critical job. Doctors estimate life expectancy and a patient's likelihood of being cured. Meteorologists use supercomputers to make predictions about future weather patterns. Equity analysts study indicators to predict market movements. Market wizards and motley fools rely on technical analysis to predict stock prices. Analysts identify the intrinsic value of a company to determine future performance and the credibility of its accounts. The more you know, and the better the technical tools you have at your disposal, the greater your probability of success."

The audience was curious with an urgent thirst for knowledge.

"A *society* is an organization that supports the interests of individuals working to serve the public good by facilitating innovation, communication, and connections. The Royal Enouement Society is a preeminent organization of premier professionals dedicated to academic and professional success. They promote the professions they represent by providing a communication network and channel for information. They offer professional development advice as a way of empowering all members to achieve their personal and professional goals."

"Why do they refer to northeast Wisconsin as Arcadia?" someone in the crowd demanded to know.

Lieutenant Dunning responded at full strength with unabated vigor. "The ancient Greeks celebrated Arcadia as an idyllic highlands region isolated from the influences of highly populated urban centers. Worldliness and the material values of ordinary life were less important to them than protecting the environment and preserving their rural way of life for future generations. They believe that when you follow righteousness and goodness and maintain a healthy lifestyle, a cascade of serendipitous experiences and a life of abundance that others seldom achieve are the predictable outcomes."

"Who are these modern Arcadians? Where do they come from?"

"Jack Daniels was a courageous leader and clear thinker who fostered respect globally. He was virtuous. Jack expressed integrity, honesty, and character in all aspects of his life. He encouraged the study of history to understand the world better. Jack viewed philosophy as the ability to think logically, analyze and solve problems, and find the way to a better life. His ideas were attractive to others with similar beliefs. He has friends in many countries.

"In ancient Greece, philosophers contemplated and theorized human nature, ethics, and moral dilemmas. Their ideas are the foundation of Western philosophy. Loyalty, glory, intelligence, and hospitality were vital elements of everyday life. The debasement of moral standards is the greatest threat to civilization. Incremental ethical concessions, corruption, forfeiture, surrender, and depravity are slow processes that lead to a decline in quality of life for everyone. Eventually, the whole nation suffers. Socrates's definition of the good life was to expand the mind to the greatest extent possible, believing that knowledge and meaning blossom when seeking beauty, love, truth, and justice. A rising tide lifts all boats—the idea that a thriving economy benefits everyone. These simple values shaped an entire civilization into a culture that is the most referenced in history."

"But why are they so secretive?"

"Members of the Royal Enouement Society may seem mysterious because they don't reveal much about themselves to outsiders. Their

vision is to empower entrepreneurs by providing legal tools and financial advice to grow businesses safely. Confidentiality in the workplace
is rule number one in the book of business etiquette. The Greek philosopher Hippocrates defined confidentiality as a cornerstone of ethics.
There is a moral value in confidentiality, privacy, and promise keeping
in medicine, banking, legal matters, and national defense. Social Security numbers, credit cards, and bank account numbers are examples of
confidentiality. Intentionally disclosing classified information without
authorization is a federal crime."

The crowd admired how the lieutenant spoke with eloquence and
command of the language. His use of logic and his extraordinary powers of persuasion to finish his statements with a rhetorical flourish to
achieve his goals were exemplary.

"Patent information, copyrights, licenses, royalties, and intellectual
property are held under ethical obligations of confidentiality autho-
rized as required by the *Model Rules of Professional Conduct.* The process of applying for a patent to protect trade secrets, prototypes, and
intellectual property is slow, deliberate, and costly. Without protective
licenses, nondisclosure agreements, provisional patents, and confidentiality statements, there would be no protections for patent holders,
copyrights, and trademarks. The goal of the Royal Enouement Society is to help entrepreneurs and first-time patent holders survive this
tedious and stressful initiation process. The intangible value of patents
and copyrights is priceless. For that reason, limited sharing of confidential information is the best way to ensure legal protection. Witness the
firm, all-American handshake. Trust is the all-powerful lubricant that
keeps the economic wheels turning. Confidentiality greases the right
connections for our collective benefit. Grandma's secret apple pie recipe
is equally as important as the formula for Coca-Cola."

The meeting ended on a high note. People were making introduc-
tions, shaking hands, chatting, taking pictures of the Holy Fountain, and
speaking enthusiastically about membership in the Royal Enouement
Society.

102

EPIPHANY

Wayne and Kate Kennedy spent a sleepless night, tossing and turning, imagining a future together as the new owners of Woebegone Dunes Resort. Wayne wiped the sleep out of his eyes, splashed cold water on his face, picked up the business plan for Woebegone Dunes Resort, and tossed it into the fireplace in a moment of sudden revelation and insight.

"What are you doing? That's an expensive document," Kate demanded to know.

"I now clearly understand the meaning of the Holy Fountain and the worthiness of the Royal Enouement Society. It promotes elastic thinking that lets people unleash their inherent creativity. These are timeless values for the ages essential to having a good character. They are qualities and attributes that are the foundation of being clever, original, and inventive—ways of critical thinking that lead to creativity and increased levels of production."

"You seem outwardly inflamed with enthusiasm and a passion for life that is valuable and worthy. What is your vision?"

"I am awestruck by the profoundly moral fire of Lieutenant Dunning's beliefs and values and his defense of the secret Royal Enouement Society. I love the populist vision of working with local people in charge, individuals who believe in the concept of a modern Arcadia strive to make this part of Wisconsin a place of quiet pleasures and rustic innocence. Preservation of the Royal Enouement Society in its current form should be our highest priority. We need to memorialize Jack Daniels to acknowledge his wisdom, vision, and Herculean efforts to make this a better world. To achieve something great, we need to protect the integrity of the organization and assure the privacy of its members," Wayne explained with passion, determination, and a fire in his belly.

Kate agreed. "I know where you are going with this—the words of Lieutenant Baron Dunning keep ringing in my head. Royal Enouement Society members are exceptionally polite and reliable, inherently pleasant, enthusiastic, healthy, optimistic, and happy. They live with gratitude. They have more positive emotions, self-acceptance, higher life satisfaction, and meaningful relationships with people. I realize now what Jack Daniels was trying to accomplish. He wasn't seeking a high annual rate of return on investment, as we had originally assumed. Jack endeavored to create an out-of-the-way retreat where people feel comfortable—free from discord and strife. Woebegone Dunes Resort should possess highly desirable, nearly perfect qualities for its guests. This region of the State of Wisconsin should be a place where everyone lives in harmony and everything is for the collective benefit of society."

"The peaceful landscape setting of our property and recognition of the entire outlying peninsula as a regional center of excellence is our greatest asset, an ideal setting to create a highly serene and secure environment free of discord, the rush of modern life, and traditional problems. Woebegone Dunes Resort is a spiritual and philosophical place of innocence. It is a secret oasis in the center of a pastoral Arcadian landscape, striving to be a sanctuary for individuals that believe in positive thinking. The Cape Cod of the Midwest possesses timeless values. The picturesque coastal harbor towns, specialty shops, fish boils, cherry and apple orchards, architectural traditions, spectacular waterfront views, and scenic beauty have great emotional appeal. We should make a determined effort to protect those values for perpetuity. We need to be a beacon of light to provide something inspirational and encouraging to individuals that have lost their way, especially those facing the shoals of dangerous waters. The goal is to attract people seeking a healthy lifestyle where everyone is content, and things get done by people who want to do them," Wayne stated.

"Exactly. For that reason, the mission, purpose, and location of Woebegone Dunes Resort should remain secret to protect the integrity and creativity of its members."

"And, so it shall be!"

103

TUSCANY

Crystal was a stunning bride dripping with sophistication and grace. She had a radiance glowing from within lit up with love. Her hair was styled in a classic French twist conveying maturity and poise. Jaws dropped when the bride made her grand entrance into the chapel, knocking Lieutenant Baron Dunning into a frozen dreamlike state. Her wedding gown covered in glittering appliqué and shining white satin was fairytale perfect. The pink-lipped bride wore a long-trained dress frosted with jewels, evoking feelings of luxury and wealth. She had a mesmerizing, almost hypnotic effect on the audience. Her beauty, charisma, and inescapable joy made it impossible to look away from her. She was vivacious and high-spirited, and her sparkling energy was infectious. This enchanting, magical, spellbinding feel put a smile on everyone's face. Her soul, filled to bursting with light and life, was a perfect representation of a joyful bride moment before she says "I do."

Lieutenant Baron Dunning and Crystal honeymooned all over Europe before settling in Tuscany, Italy. They purchased an elegant Roman-style upper-class villa, olive orchard, and vineyard and quietly settled into a life of selling olives and wine, with the local co-op doing most of the work.

The newly married couple was sitting under an umbrella table at a popular outdoor café in Florence overlooking the verdant countryside.

Drinking cappuccinos and savoring a dessert plate of creamy cannolis was one of their favorite traditions.

"I promise to be true to you in good times and in bad, in sickness and in health. I will love you and honor you all the days of my life. You are so relaxed, so happily engaged in the present moment, with the historic Tuscan countryside whizzing by in a kaleidoscope whirl of shapes and colors. There is no pomp or vanity here, just innocent natural beauty warmed by the sun. You are so beautiful. You look radiant, exactly like the type of woman I'd like to run off with if I already hadn't."

"There's music in the air here. Living an extravagant dream in an exclusive exotic location with you as my partner is a lifelong vision of comfort and freedom come true. Living in a state of bliss with the man of my dreams is so delightful. Breathing the air of paradise in romantic Tuscany with you exceeds my wildest expectations," Crystal espoused with open arms and a big smile followed by a passionate kiss.

"I feel the warm hand of serenity when I know you're thinking about me, and when you look at me, I know I'm in love," the lieutenant confessed. "More precious than all the roses in the world is the light in your eyes. Life without love is like a tree without blossoms or fruit."

Crystal smiled. "Lieutenant Baron Dunning, you are a philosopher of the heart with no time for the conventions of ordinary life. You are a legend. You remind me of a scene from a Western movie. Everything has been resolved in a happy, satisfactory fashion after the good guy arrived in a troubled town and solved whatever grave problems it was experiencing. With huge approval ratings, the hero gets on his horse. He rides west in the direction of the picturesque setting sun with his lovely, faithful girlfriend at his side to begin a new happy life."

"Our lives are largely devoid of moral and ethical deliberations, idealized by the slow, dreamy rhythms of the seasons in a world of the imagination. We are the cheerful, lighthearted, carefree owners of the house and farm of our dreams. Chilling on the patio is so delightful. All we have to do now is focus on healthy living. Happiness comes from building relationships, taking regular timeouts, buying things we love, eating tasty Italian food, and drinking wine out of fancy glasses."

The sound of a private courier delivery truck unexpectedly shattered the peaceful romantic mood. The driver parked at the bottom of the hill. The engine was rough idling with inconsistent RPM counts due to dirty fuel injectors, clogged air filter, bad spark plugs, and multiple exhaust system leaks. A deliveryman in a black jacket with purple accents rushed up the driveway with a small package under his arm.

"Signature confirmation is required," he demanded in Italian.

The lieutenant raised his eyebrows and read the attached note before carefully removing the wrapping. "Bo-Bo Bigelow from Nigeria sent me a present."

"What is it?" Crystal inquired curiously.

"It's a lovely bluish-gray bracelet made of the rare-earth mineral tantalum. It's engraved with traditional curvilinear Igbo Uri designs by a famous artist. Bo-Bo says it's a 'get out of jail free token' that will immediately resolve or relieve any undesirable situation with minimal consequences. He promises unconditionally not to steal my identity and burn my clothes in a barrel of oil the next time I visit Africa. As long as I have this rare gift in my possession, I will have diplomatic immunity from prosecution in Nigeria. It's the same reciprocal agreement the United States offered him."

The lieutenant was speechless with an open-eyed look of amazement. He momentarily stared blankly into space, imagining what secrets the future holds. The quietness of the evening was temporarily interrupted by the humming sound of a single-engine airplane silhouetted against the brilliantly backlighted red and orange sunset. The aircraft was unhurriedly traversing the horizon. It was towing a message banner reading "*Carpe diem*—Seize the moment," extolling the virtues of spontaneous behavior as justification for making the most out of today. But, of course, one never knows if everything will eventually fall into place in the end.

Made in the USA
Monee, IL
26 October 2022

16574182R00236